Sweet Surrender
✪ ✪ ✪

A light shone faintly from under his door. She took a deep breath, turned the knob and entered the room.

"Lily? Am I dreaming?" he murmured.

"I'm real," she whispered.

She slipped off her gown, letting it fall to the floor in a swish of silk, and stood before him, waiting. He reached out to touch her. Her legs trembled.

He drew her to him. She sighed, every cell in her body alive. "I've never wanted anything in my life the way I want you, Lily."

"I think I've waited for you all my life," she answered. Bending over him, she sought his mouth in an urgent kiss.

INNISMERE

SUZANNAH O'NEILL

HarperPaperbacks
A Division of HarperCollins*Publishers*

This is a work of fiction. The characters, incidents, and
dialogues are products of the author's imagination and are
not to be construed as real. Any resemblance to actual
events or persons, living or dead, is entirely coincidental.

HarperPaperbacks   *A Division of* HarperCollins*Publishers*
                    10 East 53rd Street, New York, N.Y. 10022

Copyright © 1991 by Suzannah O'Neill
All rights reserved. No part of this book may be used or
reproduced in any manner whatsoever without written
permission of the publisher, except in the case of brief
quotations embodied in critical articles and reviews. For
information address HarperCollins*Publishers*,
10 East 53rd Street, New York, N.Y. 10022.

Cover illustration by John Harris

First printing: July 1991

Printed in the United States of America

HarperPaperbacks and colophon are trademarks of
HarperCollins*Publishers*

10 9 8 7 6 5 4 3 2 1

This book is for my mother
whose beauty, strength, and great joy in life
have so inspired all who know her.

Contents

Lily

✿ ✿ ✿

LILY D'ARCY'S HEELS clicked over the black and white marble floor, echoing eerily through the long gallery. She paused to switch off the downstairs' lights, balancing her dinner tray in her left hand. *No*, she thought. It was frightening being alone in the big, old house; better to let the lights burn all night. She'd given the Kellys—the couple who'd served as cook and butler for the D'Arcy family for over thirty years—the week off. No point in keeping them on when she was the only one to attend. Lily preferred her own cooking to Mary Kelly's heavy Irish fare anyway. More than any of that, she needed to be alone to sort through her feelings and come to some sort of decision about Ian and her marriage.

As she ascended the broad staircase, her shadow passed in a long, distorted swath across the gilt-framed, painted faces of long past D'Arcys. Lily paused on the landing in front of the tall, arched Palladian window looking out on the night-shrouded terrace and gardens. Those painted gallery ghosts with their cold, dark eyes and haughty mien had intimidated her since she'd first come to Kildare to be Ian D'Arcy's bride more than twenty years ago. After all this time, they still seemed to be looking down their long, aristocratic noses at her in patent disapproval. No matter how hard she worked at being a perfect Lady D'Arcy, in their eyes she was still only a common little American dancer, suitable to be a mistress, perhaps, but never mistress of Innismere.

"Damn you all!" she shouted, sending shock waves through the silent house. "You all have your nasty little skeletons, so don't look so superior. I'm just as good as any one of you!" The faces gazed darkly past her in silent contempt.

Fionn and Maeve trotted into the hallway below and looked up at her. Lily felt a twinge of embarrassment at being caught ranting aloud to pictures on the wall, if only by two wolfhounds.

"Here, Fionn," she called. The bigger dog pricked his ears, but made no move to obey. "Come on, there's a good boy," she called again in a more honeyed tone. The dog looked over at his mother who yawned disdainfully.

"Come here this second!" Lily snapped. The dog trotted up the stairs to her, his thin, straggly tail drooping. "Stay!" she commanded the other animal. Maeve padded off to sleep by herself on the drawing room carpet.

They were Ian's dogs. When Lily and Ian had first been married, the forebears of these hounds had had the run of the entire house, leaving their wiry, gray hairs and horrible smell on damask sofas and Aubusson carpets, even sleeping beside the bed at night. Lily's first assertive move as mistress of the house had been to insist that since the dogs were destroying the furniture, they should be kept outside. She'd got quite emotional listing their sins: one had thrown up on a priceless Savonnerie rug, others had chewed antiqué chair legs, and she simply couldn't sleep with them snoring in the bedroom like trains. Ian had smiled patiently at her and said, "You're just not used to animals, my love."

This was true. Lily had grown up in Boston in a narrow, frame house set on a postage stamp yard, elbow to elbow with others almost exactly like it. In such a confinement of space, dogs were looked on, by her mother certainly, as defilers of sidewalks and invaders of private property. "Never touch a strange animal—it might bite you and have rabies" was a cardinal rule.

When Lily grew older, the other big no-no was letting love distract you from using your talent to the fullest. Her mother, a prodigy on the violin, had been forced to give up a brilliant musical career when made pregnant by a handsome soldier on leave from Korea. Though her stepfather had saved her mother from disgrace and raised Lily as if she were his own, her mother had never let them forget that she might have been playing Carnegie Hall instead of keeping house and giving violin lessons. When Lily had phoned her from Ireland to say she was giving up her own dance career to get married at nineteen, it had been the crowning blow in a life rife with disappointment.

"In another year you would have been a soloist in one of the world's great ballet companies, but you give it up to be what. . .an Irish housewife?" her incredulous mother had cried.

"But, Mother, it's a very big house," Lily had protested. Her parent remained unimpressed and unforgiving. Ian's being the ninth Baronet D'Arcy, scion of a wealthy family who'd lived on the estate of Innismere since the fourteenth century, carried no weight either. Lily had thrown her life away and betrayed her God-given talent, not to mention all the time and money wasted by her family on her dance career. For the first few years following her elopement, Lily had communicated only with her stepfather. Her mother stubbornly refused to set foot in Ireland and had only seen her grandchildren, Tristan and Violet, on the few occasions that Lily had brought them to Boston. This estrangement had gone on until recently when there had been something of a death bed reconciliation between mother and daughter at last.

At the top of the stairs, Lily noticed great spiderwebs festooning the enormous Waterford chandelier. Did no one in the country ever look up? After their honeymoon in Paris, she had not been able to rest until she, the housemaid, and a conscriptee stableboy had given Innismere House a thorough cleaning. The corners and elaborate moldings of the fourteen-foot ceilings had been covered with dust and the webs of spiders whose ancestors must have been spinning when the house was built in 1753. Lily still had to constantly get after the present maid, Evileen Mahoney, about looking for dirt above her line of sight. Even if Lily in those days had known nothing about Sèvres or Meissen, Louis XIV furniture, or how to entertain at gay dinner parties, she did, thanks to her fastidious mother, know how to keep a clean house.

Lily switched on her bedroom light and felt the usual lift at the sight of the intensely feminine retreat she'd created for herself. All the furnishings and ornaments had been chosen to please her own taste rather than that of a decorator or previous Lady D'Arcy. Her gaze flicked over the canopied bed swagged with Belgian lace, the flowered chintz chaise longue and chairs plumped with needlepoint pillows done by her own hand. On the *toile de jouy*-covered walls hung rare botanical prints and a portrait of a very young Marie Antoinette; the tall windows were framed with watered silk curtains in a muted rose. Perfect. She'd created an elegant nest for herself in total contrast to her husband's masculine, Spartan, adjoining bedroom. Ian preferred that she not redecorate the rest of the house. He liked things the way he'd always known them, the way his beloved mother had had them.

A longhaired black cat sprang from the cluster of lace pillows on her bed and hissed at Fionn who nervously looked at Lily for support. Lily put down her dinner tray and picked up the cat. "Sorry, Sheba. I know it's against the rules, but he gets to stay in here tonight." She put the cat out of the room and shut and locked her door.

The nearest house, that of the farm overseer, was miles away. Not that there was really anything to be afraid of as crime was rare out in the Irish countryside. Once the Troubles had begun in '69, her mother had pictured Lily daily dodging IRA bombs. Back home in the States, they didn't realize that the strife in Ulster seemed much removed from rural Kildare County southwest of Dublin. In the south, people had become inured to the newspaper accounts of far-off terrorist atrocities. They were an endless part of the Irish scheme, unpleasant, but to be expected like the omnipresent rain. Ian's philosophy was that there was no point in getting worked up over a problem that was insoluble, at least in their lifetimes.

"Lie down, and don't you dare snore," Lily directed the dog. He crouched, eyes rolling, as he took in the unfamiliar territory. This was Fionn's first visit above stairs in the three-story house. That had been the compromise over the animals: they were kept to the ground floor and off the furniture. Fionn was guiltily aware of his unusual privilege and fidgeted nervously as if expecting Sheba to pounce on him any moment. Lily loved the sensuous beauty and cool independence of cats, while Ian hated them, but was putty in the paws of any lumbering, fawning canine. Just one of the multitude of differences between the two of them.

Lily set aside her lukewarm omelet and salad. Her appetite had fallen off the past few weeks, and with it those extra pounds she'd put on as mid-life crept upon her. She should write a book: *The Heartbreak Diet*. It had nothing to do with calorie counting. One only needed to discover that the person one had lived with for twenty-one years, had had two children with, whom one thought she knew best on earth, was really a stranger who had lived a secret life.

She picked up the silver-framed photo of Ian that she kept by her bed and examined his familiar, handsome face. She'd taken the shot herself, catching him in his riding boots and hacking jacket, his hair wind-blown, wearing that typical, dreamy little smile that meant he was lost in thought. Her beautiful, kind, Ian, the most moral person she'd ever known. The image blurred, and she felt as if her heart would crack with the pain of it. How could this terrible thing be true of him? Any other man, but not her Ian! But it was true, she'd seen proof of it in black and white with her own eyes. She lay the picture face down on the table beside her bed and gave in to her grief. There was no one to hear her but Fionn who cocked his head to the side in surprise at the noises emanating from his mistress. What had he done now? Lily sobbed, and the dog whined in accompaniment.

The phone rang. She reached for a Kleenex and took a few deep breaths before picking up the receiver. It was Ian calling from London.

"What's wrong?" he asked at once.

"I'm coming down with a bit of a cold. Did you get your picture?" Ian had gone to Florence for the sale of an art collection. He was a dealer in minor Old Masters, Italian school in particular, which he purchased for small museums, private collectors, and his own shops in London and Dublin.

"It went too high. How are you, Lily—other than the cold?"

"Totally miserable. How do you expect me to be?" There was silence on the line. "So, how's the weather in London?"

"It's raining," he answered, fatigue in his voice.

"That's different."

"I saw Tristan."

"How was he? Does he have enough money? Did he say why he's doing this?" Lily asked in a rush.

"He looked very well. I told him he must keep in touch. He was fairly hostile." Ian cleared his throat. "He's working with a friend from school, an Alistair Amboy, on a photographic venture. Rather vague really. He's staying at Amboy's digs, a houseboat—quite posh, so don't worry that he's in a garret. I tried to give him money, but he wouldn't take it."

"I had so planned on having him home for the summer before he went off to Oxford. He told me he was just going to London for some parties, and then he up and stays there. I've heard him mention this friend Amboy, who I understand is quite wild. Got tossed out of university his first year. I'm terribly worried about Tristan, Ian. This is so unlike him."

"We must let him get this out of his system, Lily. Give him his head a bit."

"He's only seventeen. You must do something, Ian!"

"Now, Lily. Tris has good, common sense, and it's only for a couple of months. I imagine this rebellion is just a bit of overreaction to our difficulties. He'll come round and be ready to knuckle under to the books come fall."

"It's just that he's always been so good, perfect really. Violet was always headstrong, but not Trissy. I worry that he's not worldly enough to be on his own, especially under the influence of this dubious friend."

"Perhaps he'll do some growing up this summer. You know you've always coddled him, Lily. It's time he found out what real life is all about, and just how cushy he's always had it." This was one of Ian's favorite topics: she spoiled her son and tied him to her apron strings, etc.

It was true that her tall, beautiful Tristan with his father's eyes and her own smile was her favorite. As was independent, assertive Violet her father's special weakness.

Angered by Ian's dredging up his old plaint of her spoiling their son, Lily lashed out at him. "I only know we wouldn't all be in this sorry mess if you'd had the decency to destroy those letters instead of saving them all these years!"

"It was you who committed the breach of trust, Lily, when you read my private correspondence. It's you who've made a mountain out of a molehill of a thing that happened before I even met you."

"What kind of fool do you think I am, Ian? It was an important enough affair that you carefully saved those obscene letters for twenty-five years. And you've kept seeing that person, godparent to your only son, all this time! Little, innocent me never suspecting a thing. I feel so damn foolish! The way you've always looked down on your brother—what a hypocrite you are!"

"Surely you know I'm not like Damien. This. . .abberration happened when I was too young and foolish to know better."

"I don't know. Our sex life has just been so. . .perfunctory for years."

"Perhaps I have been neglectful of you lately, Lily, but that's only because I'm so preoccupied with this damned business. My financial responsibilities are always weighing on my mind. You know that I love you, that you are the only person I desire."

"I don't know that. For all I know, you've been carrying on this disgusting affair all along. I feel so betrayed and deceived!"

"You know that isn't the case, because I've told you that I ended that unfortunate business before I met you. We've only been friends since. Nothing at all has been going on behind your back. For God's sake, I'm a more honorable man than that."

"My faith in you is so shaken, Ian. Can't you understand how I feel? I never imagined you capable of such a thing. Perhaps if you had told me from the start, I could have accepted it. You were dishonest not to tell me."

"I was too desperately in love with you to risk it. You'd have run from me if I'd told you."

"I don't know what I'd have done, but at least our relationship would have been an honest one."

"You're being unreasonable about this, Lily. If we're to save our marriage, you must put this aside. For Tristan's sake. That affair happened so long ago, when I was a confused boy. Why must you punish me? Our marriage, our family, are too important for such pettiness. I love you, Lily, and I want to come home." His voice shook with emotion, but she steeled herself not to feel sorry for him.

"I think it's best that you stay on at the London flat for the time being, until I've sorted out what I'm going to do."

"You're not thinking divorce, surely? Have you seen a solicitor, Lily?"

"I haven't ruled that out."

"This is mad. Do all the happy years mean nothing at all? Cancelled out by some ancient indiscretion? How can you be so unforgiving after all we've had together? My God, no one in the family has ever been divorced."

"To hell with your pompous family! They'd rather have affairs or go crazy, but never a tacky divorce!" Lily slammed down the receiver and sat there shaking. How typical of Ian to think of the family name; he fairly worshipped at the shrine of the damned D'Arcys.

Lily lit a cigarette. She'd given them up when pregnant with Violet, but her need for the soothing effect of nicotine was greater than her fear of cancer these days. She caught her reflection in the mirror above the marble mantel. Her cheekbones had come back, as well as purple circles under her eyes. She was becoming a thin, harried, chain-smoking. . .divorcée?

Would it really come to that? Glancing about her perfect bedroom, she thought for the first time about giving it all up. The beautiful house, the privilege, the Lady D'Arcy bit. She had become very used to all of that. If she really had to, Lily thought she had the strength to give it up. The question was, could she give up Ian, the only man she'd ever loved—sweet father and gentlest and most generous of husbands? But how could it ever be the same, now that she knew?

An eerie wail echoed through the house from below, giving Lily a scare before she recognized the sound— Maeve howling for her inseparable son. Something she could understand really. She released a grateful Fionn to go down to his mother. Neurotic animals. The dogs were mad; the whole family was mad!

Damien had told her the truth about the great D'Arcys whom Ian revered above all. Originally descended from William the Conqueror's compatriot Norman d'Areci, the Irish D'Arcys were vassals to the powerful Fitzgeralds who ruled Kildare and figured prominently in Irish history. The family castle, remains of which still stood on the grounds, had been pathetic in comparison to the fortresses of the Geraldines, their wealth and holdings meager. The D'Arcys had only managed to hang on through the centuries because of their constant good fortune and fortuitous marriages. When fortune ran out, shrewd conniving and double-dealing saved the day.

Ian's mother, Siobhan O'Connor D'Arcy, with the even more ancient blood of Celtic kings in her veins, had shot herself in the garden, in a well-remembered local scandal d'amour. Her husband William had been a cold, forbidding man who'd amassed a fortune after the war in somewhat shady stock and land speculation. Damien, as he cheerfully admitted himself, had been booted out of Trinity College after being caught in flagrante with "a very attractive lorry driver from Cork." It was not the buggering, which was hardly unheard of, but that he'd gone "beneath himself," according to Damien.

He was the ostensible black sheep of the family, manager of perpetually unsuccessful rock groups, to add to his off-color panache. Then there was Ian, the flower of the family, loved and admired by all those who were unsuspecting of his true inclinations. A grand lot—the D'Arcys, who had had suicides, mistresses, and sham marriages, but nary a divorce.

Lily washed her flushed face and readied herself for bed. On a whim, she got herself a shot glass of brandy from the decanter in Ian's room. Add alcohol to the list of sins she'd taken up in her great unraveling. She closed the drapes and got in bed with a book she'd been attempting to read. After scanning page twenty-eight three times, she threw it across the room. It was going to be another sleepless night.

She got up, went to a chest in the corner, and found her old scrapbook. Settling back in the bed, she flipped through the pages of clippings, photos, and dance programs religiously saved by her proud mother. Herself at six wearing a pink tutu and a fake smile; Juliette at fifteen; the clipping from the *Boston Globe:* Local Girl in New York Ballet. She could vividly recall that first truly great moment of her life when her ballet school had auditioned for the New York company school, and she had been chosen with a handful of young dancers from across the country for a full scholarship. It all came back to her from over the intervening years as she leafed through the dog-eared pages.

Had her mother been right? Had she made a terrible mistake to give up the dance to marry so impulsively? She recalled the years of sweat, tears, aching muscles, and gut-wrenching competition. Hours and hours of sheer back-breaking, physical labor with feet blistered and bleeding. Lily was self-conscious about her ugly feet which were still deformed by the hours *en pointe*. All the bad had been more than compensated for, however, by the knowledge that she had better extension and could pirouette and jeté more perfectly than any girl in the class, and by the teacher's smiling approval after she'd done well. "Bien, Lily. Brava!" How proud she'd felt when the company director whispered to the teacher as they watched her dance, and she'd known that it was all going to come true as she and her mother had planned. The reward for all their sacrifice: her selection for the corps de ballet at seventeen.

Lily paused at the photo of Alexei, defector from the Bolshoi, star of the company, and one of the world's premier dancers. He'd signed it, "Pour ma petite belle fleur, Lily." What a beautiful, sensual face and incomparably muscled body he'd had then. She saw Alexei every time the company performed in Dublin or London, and he still looked damn good, even if he could no longer do the floating leaps for which he was famous.

Her mind traveled back to the afternoon when Alexei had asked her to dance with him during class. Oh, heart-stopping, adrenalin-pumping moment! She'd brought it off, made not one mistake as she floated effortlessly in his strong arms. He was the perfect partner, made almost any ballerina look good, but she had never danced better. He had kissed her hand and said, "You goot. I keep eye on you." Her knees had turned to jelly then.

Lily closed her eyes and tried to recapture the sublime glow she'd felt on being complimented by her idol. Beautiful Alexei whose aura of sexuality was as powerful as an electric field about him. True to his word, he did keep those sleepy, bluer-than-blue eyes on her from then on. It was whispered that he was sleeping his way through the company. The big question was, would you if he asked? Lily vowed to her best friend Karen that she certainly would not. She didn't fancy being one of such a large crowd. But in her heart of hearts, she knew that Alexei would be the Russian prince for whom she'd saved herself for eighteen years. It would be worth the risk and lack of exclusivity to be able to say that her first lover had been a man whose name would always live in the annals of dance.

It hadn't worked out that way though. Lily closed her scrapbook and lay back on the pillows.

The course of her life had changed because she'd saved up enough to go to a Rubinstein concert, something she knew her mother would want her to do. She'd got to the theater late to find her seat in the middle of an already occupied row. The man sitting next to her seat had legs so long, he'd had to stand up to let her by. She'd apologized, and he'd demurred politely in a deep, musical voice. When he smiled at her as he helped her off with her coat, she'd realized that his looks were as wonderful as his manners.

As soon as the lights went down, and the maestro began to play, she tried to covertly inspect the handsome stranger out of the corner of her eye. He wore a beautiful, European-cut suit that showed an expanse of snowy shirtcuff, reminding her of her martyred hero, President Kennedy. His perfectly groomed, artistic looking hands played on his lanky thighs along with Rubinstein. No wedding ring, but he did wear a gold ring on the little finger of his left hand—a signet ring engraved with a bull; the family crest, he explained later. When he leaned forward to adjust his jacket, she quickly took in his profile. An angular face with prominent cheekbones and a proud, aquiline nose one might find on a Roman coin. Sensing her scrutiny, he turned to smile at her. Face burning, she returned her gaze to the stage.

At that moment her purse chose to fall to the floor with a loud clunk. The stranger retrieved it for her.

"Thanks," she whispered.

"My pleasure," he replied, looking directly at her for a long moment which set her heart to beating wildly.

At the intermission, she stood and quickly moved away from him to show she hadn't been giving him the come on. In the lobby, jostled by the crowd of smoking, laughing, concert goers, she looked up to see the stranger standing before her with two glasses of sherry in hand. He was amazingly tall.

"I'm Ian D'Arcy," he said as he handed her a sherry.

"I'm a dancer," she blurted. A nervous response, but a true, one-word definition of herself. A dancer was literally all that she was at that point in her life.

"Ah, I should have known that," he said beaming down at her from his great height and looking more sophisticated and elegant than any male she'd ever encountered.

"How could you have? I've been so clumsy dropping my purse and everything."

"But that's a dancer for you, isn't it? All grace on stage and barely able to walk, off it."

"You must know a dancer," she said with a giggle. The sherry was so strong. Didn't little old ladies drink that?

"I've known a few," he replied. His eyes were dark, deeply set under straight, black brows. His black hair fell over his forehead in one stray lock and was longer at the collar than that of most men who weren't hippies. His accent was very posh.

"So, does the *danseuse* have a name?" he asked with a twinkle in his black eyes. She told him.

"Lily is a perfect name for you. One would have to be very feminine and beautiful to justify such a name."

That made her blush. Proudly she told him she was with the New York ballet, but he didn't seem as impressed as she'd hoped. The jostling crowd forced them almost on top of each other, and she caught his scent, a wonderful, expensive-smelling cologne she knew didn't come from a drugstore counter.

She asked if he were a musician.

"Why, do I look like one?"

"You were playing your knees rather well during the concert."

He laughed. "I play at the piano a bit. I'm no Rubinstein, but I enjoy it very much." She learned later that he was only being modest, and might well have been a professional had he pursued it.

"You were terribly good on your knees," she remarked, and he laughed as if she were the soul of wit.

Though his accent sounded British to her, he explained that he was actually Irish. He certainly didn't sound like any of the Boston-area Irish that she'd met.

"My family is Anglo-Irish, and I went to school in England," he explained. He'd gone to Eton and Oxford, which impressed her enormously. Her stepfather, a public school English teacher, considered Oxford superior even to hallowed Harvard.

The lobby lights blinked to indicate the concert was resuming, and they returned to their seats, friends now. When his arm accidentally touched hers, she felt the same charge of electricity as with Alexei. They both laughed out loud when, caught up in the music, he began playing along on his thighs again. A woman in the seat in front of them turned around to glare her disapproval, which only made it funnier.

After a standing ovation for the brilliant pianist, Ian helped her on with her coat, letting his hands linger rather longer than was necessary on her arms.

"So, did Artur live up to your expectations?"

"This was easily the most memorable concert I've ever been to," he answered, the warmth in his voice telling her that she was the reason.

"If you're not doing anything, Lily the Dancer, would you like to come have a bite to eat with me? You'd be saving me from a very lonely evening by myself."

She considered for a moment. Her mother's voice whispered in her ear, "He's probably just a very attractive Jack the Ripper."

"I'd simply love to," she replied.

He took her to the Oak Room at the Plaza Hotel, where he was staying while working at the New York branch of Sotheby's for a few months. If he expected her to go up to his room afterward, he had better think again, Lily decided. No matter how exquisite his clothes and manners, nor how darkly romantic his eyes, she was not some little pick-up. She'd never had time for boyfriends and had done little more than kiss a boy good night. "Never let boys distract" had been engraved on her brain. She planned on spurning Ian's offer if he made one, so he would get the message that he'd have to work a great deal harder than this to get her. It would have to be done so as not to discourage him entirely, of course.

She needn't have worried. After dinner, he took her home to her apartment building without making a pass or even asking for her phone number. Sitting on the narrow bed which took up half her room, she felt unbearably let down. He might at least have tried to get somewhere.

He obviously considered her too young and unsophisticated to even bother with trying to seduce.

The next afternoon as the dancers were filing out of the company building after a long day of class and rehearsal, a sleek, green car pulled to the curb. "A Jag," said Karen. "This looks like my kinda guy."

It took Lily a second to recognize the tall, dark-haired man who unfolded from the sportscar. Her heart soared as he waved to her.

"He's for you? Lily, you dog! He's even gorgeous, too," Karen exclaimed in envy.

When Lily went over to speak to him, he said, "My chariot at your disposal for the evening, if you're free?"

"I've never ridden in a Jaguar," she said as he helped her down into its uncomfortable, leather-plush interior.

"It's hired, actually," he said after squeezing behind the wheel. He smiled at her and looked even more handsome than she'd remembered. The other dancers stared after them as they roared away. She wished that Alexei had been there to see what impressive company she was keeping.

"Where are we going?" she asked, though she really didn't care.

"To a showing of Pollock, for a bite to eat, and later to hear some jazz, if you'd like?"

"I'd like!" He grinned at her, and she felt the heat rush up her neck. "I wasn't sure I'd ever see you again."

"Disappointed?"

"Not any longer."

He took her hand, and in his low, musical voice said, "I've a feeling we're going to see a great deal of each other, Lily." Her heart skipped a beat. He was fabulously elegant in a rich-looking topcoat and silk scarf.

"I'm not dressed," she remembered. She'd thrown on jeans over her dance clothes.

"We'll drop by your flat and let you change," he said. Which meant he'd have to see her tacky, little room which she'd left a disaster. And what did she have to wear to such posh-sounding places?

Ian said her room was "charming" as she ran about pulling the covers up over her unmade bed and throwing the scattered leotards and tights in the closet. She apologized, saying that she usually wasn't such a pig—a lie. He apologized for giving such short notice. He said he liked the art posters she'd used to hide the spots on the walls and the way she'd swagged the one window with a cotton India print.

Excusing herself to go down the hall to the bathroom, she raced to Karen's room. The building was full of dancers and run by a motherly old Russian lady who'd been in the ballet herself a million years ago.

Luckily Karen had gotten a ride and was at home.

"Well, aren't you the cute one keeping a secret like him from me," said her friend.

"You've got to loan me your black mini-dress," she gasped.

"Sure. Who's the dude?"

"The guy I was telling you about from the concert. Quick, the dress, your black spikes, and those great, gold hoops of yours!"

"He'll be dating me by proxy. Need to borrow my underwear, or aren't you wearing any?" drawled Karen who was from Texas and had a really dirty mind.

When she was in the dress, Karen frowned. "The hair and makeup need work, babe."

"Help me, I'm a wreck!"

"Here, take a drag off this," said Karen, getting a bulky looking cigarette from an ashtray.

"Please, I already talk stupidly enough. Ian's so sophisticated and older, and I'm a teenage nitwit who can't talk about anything but ballet," she wailed.

Karen put her hands on her shoulders and looked her straight in the eye. "Cool it, Lily. I don't really think he's after brilliant conversation with you, you know." She fixed her long hair in a sleek chignon with wispy curls about her face, and touched up her makeup.

"Don't you dare feel inferior, Lily. You're a brilliant dancer, a future star in the balletic heavens. You're so gorgeous and talented that every girl in the company but me hates you, and come to think of it, you look so much better in my dress than me, I may hate you, too." They hugged each other.

"Have a great time for me tonight, babe, and come and tell me all about it when you get in. If you do get in," instructed Karen, suggestively wiggling her eyebrows.

Lily took three breaths to calm herself down and entered her room serenely. Ian was examining her bulletin board of notes to herself, phone numbers, and pictures of Nureyev, Alexei, JFK, and the Beatles.

"Your pantheon of heroes, eh?" he commented without turning around. "Who's the chap with the hair?"

"Jim Morrison of the Doors," she answered as she waited for him to see her glamorous new incarnation.

"Never heard of him," said Ian. He looked properly stunned when he saw her. "You are a vision! You keep all that in the bathroom?"

"I had to get my dress from the girl I loaned it to."

"It's stunning!" he replied, his eyes traveling down to her legs.

She had no trouble talking to him after all. He explained what Jackson Pollock was trying to do with all the squiggles, then treated her to another delicious, expensive meal. As she talked about herself, the dance, and her family, he held her hand across the table and listened as no one had ever listened before. The entire time he gazed at her with those empathetic black eyes of his—so warm and needy. Beautiful, deep, sad eyes that drew everything out of her soul.

"I admire you a great deal, Lily" he said. You are one of the few people I've come across who know exactly what they want in life. I've not the slightest doubt that you'll achieve every goal you set your cap for."

After dinner, they went to a club in Greenwich Village to hear some cool jazz which he seemed to know a lot about. On the way home, he delighted her by stopping by the park for a buggy ride. Snow was beginning to fall. She shivered in her thin, cloth coat, so he took off his rich, warm one and spread it over both of them. As the horse clopped along the quickly whitening park road, Ian stroked her hand underneath his overcoat. The snow swirled about them like a child's Christmas globe, and it was so unreal and romantic that she felt they were the stars of a film. They didn't get back to her apartment 'til two A.M., the latest she'd ever been out.

"It was wonderful!" she said as they stood outside her room.

"That was only the beginning, Lily the Dancer," he said, looking down into her eyes. She wavered toward him as if pulled by an irresistible magnet. His mouth was softer than anything she'd ever imagined. He stroked her face. "You're the most perfect creature. It's almost as if I dreamt you." He kissed her again, longer this time.

"Good night, Lily," he said with reluctance, then backed off down the hall, still smiling at her. When he'd disappeared down the stairwell, she knocked on Karen's door.

"Shit, I was hoping you'd be out for the night, and I'd get a little vicarious sex through my dress," she said, yawning.

"I think I'm going to get very distracted," she said dreamily.

From that night on, she saw Ian D'Arcy every day. After two weeks of constant togetherness, he had still made no move to take her to bed.

"Maybe he's queer," said Karen. "Sorry, but I've never known any guys that timid. Hasn't he heard we're in the middle of a sexual revolution here?"

"It's just that I'm so young, and he respects me," she said in defense.

"Enough respect already!" said Karen, who always talked as if she were very experienced.

They discussed ways to tempt him into bed.

"Get him in your room, lock the door, and bare your breasts," Karen suggested. "Well, maybe not," she added. Like most dancers, Lily was flat-chested.

"Maybe you don't turn the dude on, Lily."

She knew that wasn't it. When they made out very awkwardly in the Jag, she'd noticed just how aroused he would get. He'd always pull back at a certain point and suggest she needed to get home. She'd tried inviting him in for a cup of cocoa made on her hotplate. He'd drink it, kiss her, and leave. She wanted to scream at him, "Don't respect me. Make love to me!"

Fall passed into winter, and he took her skating at Rockefeller Center, to the zoo, to Staten Island on the ferry—all the cliché, corny romantic places made unique and magical by their enjoyment of each other. Ian was a wonderful teacher as well. He took her to the theater, gallery openings, the opera. At Sotheby's showroom everyone treated him like a VIP. She learned about art from him during long afternoons at the Metropolitan, the Guggenheim, the Frick, and the Museum of Modern Art.

"He's broadened my mind so," she said to Karen. "I know twice as much as I did before I met Ian."

"Yeah, about everything but what you really want to know—S-E-X! Listen, I've finally come up with a fool-proof plan. Tell him you want to see his room at the Plaza—to see his 'etchings' like the old line. He's into art, so he must have some, whatever in the hell etchings are."

"But that's so obvious," she protested.

"Subtle ain't working, right?" Lily had to agree. "Any-way, when you reach the inner sanctum, you whip out this. . .ta-dah!" She brandished a joint. "You toke up, blow his gentlemanly mind, and he reverts to the true, male beast you want him to be. Brilliant, no?"

"No! He'd be grossed out."

"Maybe. Or maybe he'll drop the respect bullshit and screw you senseless. At the very least, he'll see you're not the babe in the woods he thought, but the slut you truly are. Come on, Lily! What have you got to lose but a mil-lionaire hunk?"

The next afternoon after rehearsal, there was a crowd gathered by the bulletin board outside the director's of-fice—the casting for *The Nutcracker.* Just as she and Karen hurried over, Eva shrieked happily. The bad news was there in black and white. Eva would dance Clara for the matinees and understudy for the evening perform-ances. Friends were congratulating Eva while Lily tried to hide her bitter disappointment.

Karen caught her arm. "I'm so sorry, Lily. You de-served that."

"Eva got it because she's more talented," she said, hur-rying off to the dressing rooms.

"Bullshit!" said Karen, keeping pace with her. "Alex-ei's making it with her, I just heard."

"Even if that's true, she deserved the part. She's won-derful."

"Don't be upset," said her friend, seeing straight through her phony graciousness. "Clara—big deal. You'll get better roles than that, Lily."

"Leave me alone!" she said and ran off to nurse her misery in private. She hoped Ian would be late, and she could go home alone instead of having to be charming and sociable.

The green Jag was waiting faithfully by the exit. "Is something wrong?" he asked at once, irritating her with that damned sensitivity of his.

"I feel a bit ill, actually," she said. She was starting to talk like him.

"Perhaps you'd like to go home, forget about tonight?"

She gratefully agreed. All she wanted was to get home without breaking down. They drove by the Plaza on the way downtown to her apartment.

"I hate to be such a poop, Ian. I think I'm just tired rather than sick. Why don't we spend a quiet evening in your rooms? You must have a great view of the park." He smiled and swung the car around.

He suggested ordering some champagne and paté, and she excused herself to go to the bathroom.

She washed her face and used the bidet, a simply wonderful invention she'd only heard of until now. After undressing, she used Ian's toothbrush and deodorant, then donned his heavy, blue, silk robe hanging on the back of the door. She brushed her hair out, pinched her cheeks, and sprayed some L'Air du Temps between her inadequate bosoms. She'd read in *Vogue* or somewhere that that drove men mad. Ready, camera, action!

"The famous view," she said, joining him at the window. Taking in her attire without reaction, he poured them both glasses of champagne which had been delivered while she was in the bathroom.

"It must be wonderful to live in a place like this," she

said, feeling desperate and desperately trying to act cool. The glass of the window was icy to her touch, and the park looked forlorn and desolate in the waning, winter light.

"It's very nice," he said, running his hand along the nape of her neck. "You look quite fetching in that, Lily." She stared at his mouth, willing him toward her. Grasping a handful of her hair, he pulled her to him for a soft, melting kiss.

He jerked away, exclaiming, "Damn, that's cold!" Her champagne had spilled down the front of his pants, and on his shirt as well.

"Take them off," she said, reaching to unloosen his tie. He took it off, then his soaked shirt. "Your pants, too," she said with a giggle.

"I get the feeling our roles are a tad reversed here, Lily," he said, making no move to undress further.

"Oh, excuse me! I really should play my proper part here, be meek and submissive and wait for you to make the first move. Only I'll be an old lady by then," she said, going over to her purse on the table.

"I've realized for some time that you'd like our relationship to progress to a more sexual level, Lily."

She whirled about, marijuana in hand, ready to go for broke. She approached him seductively. "Got a light, mister?" He lit it with his initialed gold lighter, and she inhaled deeply as Karen had taught her to do. Exhaling slowly through her nose, she forced herself not to cough.

"So, what is it, Ian? Don't you want me?"

"You know the answer to that one," he said, black brows furrowing over blacker eyes.

"Then why have we been going together everyday for over a month-and-a-half, and you've never once tried to seduce me? It's not very flattering, you know." Ian took the joint from her, inhaled, and held it for a long, practiced moment, then exhaled. He passed it back to her. "Well?" she inhaled furiously and immediately went into a choking spasm.

He patted her on the back. "Here, have a little sip of champagne and try to relax," he directed as she gasped for air.

"That was cool," she croaked.

"It's not that I don't want you, Lily. I can't think that I've ever been attracted to anyone as I am to you." He touched her hair and brushed it off her shoulder. "Every relationship I've had has been primarily sexual it seems. With you, I want it to be different—to be more. Because you're not like anyone else in my life. You are incredibly special to me, Lily, so I've taken my time with you. I want it to be perfect when we do go to bed at last. Because of your inexperience, it would be very selfish of me to rush you to bed even if I might long to."

"But, I'm ready now," she pleaded.

He smiled gently and caressed her cheek. "There's no hurry. Let's really get to know one another, perhaps even love each other first, as revolutionary as that sounds these days."

"I love you already!"

He took her in his arms. "No, you don't. You're intrigued, infatuated maybe, but it's not love yet."

"How do you know how I feel?" she protested.

"You've never been in love before, or been with a man, have you?" She shook her head. "I knew that. You must be very careful with love, because it's the most important thing in the world. It's not something you use as an excuse for sex."

Her mouth quivered. "I feel like a fool."

"Most men would think I qualify for that honor for turning down such a gift. I may well be one, but I'd rather wait 'til the timing's perfect, Lily." He took the joint from her and stubbed it out, saying, "We don't need this."

Tears filled her eyes. "I'm sorry I tried to force it. I'm sure you're right, it's just that I like it so when we kiss and you touch me. I want to know what it's really like."

"You'll find out soon enough. You can't imagine how I'm looking forward to showing you."

He took her home, and she invited him up for cocoa to postpone the moment of loneliness and defeat over losing the role of Clara. She brought him his mug and joined him on her bed which doubled as sofa in the confined space.

Ian put his arm about her and kissed her ear. "I sensed something very wrong with you tonight. The hashish, the agressiveness, that's just not my sweet Lily."

"Yes, it is. I'm a secret slut driven out in the open by raging, unrequited lust." He laughed. Boys back in Boston would have thought her nuts and definitely not "regular"—a supreme accolade—to talk like that.

"Seriously, did something happen at rehearsal today?" he pressed. She looked away. "That's it, isn't it? Tell me what's upset you."

She explained about Eva.

"I knew it was between the two of us, but she just joined the company, and I thought I deserved it!" She broke down.

He put their mugs of cocoa on the floor and tried to console her.

"I wanted so badly to dance with Alexei," she sobbed. "I've been in Nutcrackers since I was eight. As a soldier, a mouse, a polichinelle, the Sugar Plum. I so wanted to be Clara with Alexei!"

"And you will be, or much bigger parts than this piddling one. It's obvious to anyone with eyes that you are the best by far, of any girl in the corps." He wiped her tears with his crested, linen handkerchief.

"Eva is better; that's the worst part! She's younger and already better. I hate her guts!"

"I loathe the little bitch myself. Perhaps we could put tacks in her toe shoes?"

"She's sleeping with Alexei, too," she hiccuped.

"Damn, does that go on? I thought they were all fairies."

"Not Alexei. He's screwed every girl in the company but me. Mother says he's the fox in the hen house."

"With no other stud foxes to give him competition. What an incredible set-up! I'm just happy he's not got his greedy paws on my precious chick. Thank God you've got some respect for yourself, Lily."

"I didn't fancy being one of a crowd," she said, not mentioning that Alexei had never got around to asking her.

Nor did she tell Ian until many years later, that when she realized she wasn't as talented as Eva, something in her had died. A door had closed. Though she was technically as good as the other dancer, Eva had that indefinable something that made a great ballerina—*La Magie*, magic, Madame Tureyva called it. It was inborn, not a learned thing, and Alexei had seen it in Eva, but not in her. From then on, she mentally gave up on her career. Only recently during the upheaval in their marriage, had she told Ian that she gave up the dance not for love of him, but because she'd realized she could never be as good as Eva. Instead of being a brilliant dancer, she'd decided to be a brilliant Lady D'Arcy. Cruel words to wound him for his great lie.

But back then in her sad, little room, she'd cried in his arms and basked in his concern and boosting words.

"You're the only one I can talk to, the only one who

truly cares," she'd said. "And I do love you. More than ballet, more than anything!"

He covered her wet face with kisses. "I'm afraid I love you, too. It frightens me how strongly I feel about you, my darling."

"Please don't be afraid. Show me how you feel, Ian. I'm ready to love you, I swear it!"

"Lily." He sighed, and his hand touched her breast. She put her hand over his and pressed him into her flesh. He kissed her hungrily. All his qualms vanished in the flashfire of passion between two bodies craving to be one.

In record time, they were out of their clothes and making love on her squeaky, rickety bed.

Afterward, they lay peacefully in each others' arms, amazed at what had happened to them so unexpectedly.

She kissed his sexy nose. "Why on earth did we have to wait so damn long for this?"

He palmed her breast and kissed the nipple. "When I gave my noble, self-denying speech, I said we shouldn't have to wait long for it to be perfect." He checked his watch. "It's been almost an hour. I was correct."

She laughed, kissed him, and excused herself to go to the bathroom, then danced happily back to her room.

"You still here?" she said, looking down at his long nakedness. He smiled lazily up at her and made no move to cover himself. He had dark hair on his body, but none on his chest. His skin was marble-white and so soft and flawless, she simply had to touch him again.

He kissed her. "Were you bleeding very badly?" There was a scarlet spot on the sheet. She felt suddenly embarrassed.

"It's nothing. I'm fine," she said, disrobing and sliding in beside him.

He skimmed his hand over her. "You've got God's own body, and in far better shape than mine."

"I like yours," she said, touching his sinewy thigh. "You're no Alexei, but you'll do nicely."

"I do have more exclusive taste in women than him, if not as defined a musculature."

"You have inches on him, too, and not just in height."

"How the hell do you know that?"

"It's hard to hide in tights. Yours would make a much bigger bulge." He laughed and moved her hand down to himself.

"Care to see something really big, little girl? Just keep doing that, and you soon shall."

She raised up to look. "God, it's huge! No wonder I. . ."

"What? Did I hurt you?"

"It wasn't the worst pain I've ever had, but it was a pretty shocking invasion!"

He pulled her on top of him. "I love the way you talk, Lily!"

"Seriously. Is it normal to be that huge?"

He frowned. "Actually, it's a bit of a condition that runs in my family called 'Priapus Majori'."

"Heavens! What does that mean?"

" 'Big Prick' in the vernacular. It's quite incurable and is the reason the D'Arcys make brilliant marriages and have countless mistresses on the side."

"You're teasing!"

"Never. The family motto is: Speak softly and carry a big prick."

"That's disgusting and highly immodest," she giggled.

"Damien, my brother, coined that one. He's that furious that I got the family weapon as well as the title."

"You're lewd. I always thought you were the perfect gentleman, Ian."

"Secretly I'm a lewd fiend, my little slut."

She hugged him. "We're a perfect, nasty match-up.

Thank goodness we don't have to fake like we're nice anymore."

He kissed her deeply and ran his hands over her bottom. Her body began to hum again.

An annoying banging on the door woke her. Ian's leg was over hers, his arm a dead weight about her waist.

"Lily, it's nine o'clock," yelled Karen.

Lily eased out from under Ian, grabbed her robe, and opened her door a few inches.

"Are you sick, Lily?"

"Just overslept," she whispered groggily. She really wasn't sure if they'd slept at all.

"You look like shit, honey."

"I ought to." Ian called sleepily for her.

"You finally scored!" crowed Karen. She opened the door wider so her friend could see Ian sprawled on his stomach on her bed.

"Fan-tastic! The Great Pot Plot worked?"

"You should write a sex column for the *Village Voice*, Karen." Ian called her name again.

"Your master's voice! I'll tell Madame you were barfing when I left. Congrats! He's got a great tush."

"I can't go to work, I'm totally depleted," Ian moaned when she returned to bed after a quick run to the bathroom.

Patting his cute tush, she said, "So take a holiday. I am."

"A holiday in bed with Lily. But not this one. How can you sleep on this primitive thing?"

"If you'd listened to me in the first place, we'd be in your king-sized bed at the Plaza," she reminded him.

"I'll bow to your wishes from now on, my love. Let's at once repair to my civilized rooms, take a lovely bath together, order up a dozen eggs, a side of bacon, and a vat of coffee. Then we'll christen that great acreage of mattress."

"Please, I'll be in the hospital!"

"I suppose I did get a bit carried away last night, but you're so delicious and such a good pupil. I couldn't contain myself." He pulled her to him and nuzzled her neck.

"Is that usual to do it so much, Ian?"

"Only if you're a sexual athlete. Sorry if I hurt you. I was a bastard to debauch a virgin so piggishly."

"You don't look very contrite."

He laughed and pinched her behind. "It's not like you weren't egging me on the whole time, my little slut." He tickled her and she shrieked.

There was a knock on the door. "Lily, vat you doing in there?"

"Nothing, Zena. I'm sick and I had the radio on."

"Lily, you got a boy in there?"

"Of course not, Zena." Ian tickled her again, and she had to clap a hand over her mouth.

"I sink you have a boy in there. Open now!"

"I'm not dressed. . .and how dare you not believe me!"

"Put on somesink and open the door, so I see there is no boy."

"Quick, get in the closet," she urged Ian. He got out of bed holding the pillow before him and, to her utter shock, opened the door.

"Top o' the mornin' to you, Zena! As you can see, there are no boys in Lily's room."

The landlady gasped in horror. "You are naked!"

"True. However, I'm a grown man."

"Lily, you know the rules. No boys in the rooms all night, and never, never no naked boys. You are immoral girl, and I never sink this. What will your poor mother say?"

Ian crossed his arms, exposing himself. "Madam, you

miss the essential flaw in your argument. I am, I repeat, not a boy, as you can jolly well see for yourself."

"Mon Dieu! Cover yourself!"

"Don't be coy now, Zena. It can't be the first you've seen. You must have been the Czar's tootsie, a great, Junoesque goddess such as you are."

She covered her eyes. "Get out of my house, you extortionist! Lily, you can no longer live here while you are a harlot. Get out of the room today, and take this madman, as naked as a jayberg with you!" She waddled furiously off down the hall.

"Gladly," Ian called after her. "I'm not about to spend another night on a bed you can't get a proper fuck on without rousing the entire building." He slammed the door.

"Extortionist?" said Ian.

She was helpless with laughter. "Exhibitionist, maybe? Who knows. I'll never find another decent place to live this cheap."

"The sensible solution is for you to pack up your gear and move in with me," he said calmly.

She ran to him and flattened him against the door with an exuberant embrace. "I'd live with you any place, even the Plaza. The Czar's tootsie? I love you, Ian D'Arcy!"

They moved her meager belongings into the hotel that day. Zena was swift in reporting her fall from grace, as Lily discovered when she called home.

Her mother raved for five minutes over the line. "Mother, we're engaged!" she yelled at last into the receiver.

"Don't tell me you're naive enough to believe that sorry old line? Who is this boy you've only known a few months? For all you know, he could be Jack the Ripper!"

"He's a lovely man, not a boy, Mother. He's Irish, a

Lord or something. When his father dies, he'll be Sir Ian."

"So he tells you. A man will tell you anything to get you into bed."

"He's an honorable man. Much nicer than me, really. And I'm so happy with him, Mother. Can't you at least be a bit happy for me?"

"Lily, you're so innocent. You don't know how life traps you with the sweet things. All you know is ballet."

"Isn't that all you wanted me to know?"

Her mother sighed heavily. "I suppose there's nothing I can do now. You are on the pill, I hope?"

"Yes," she lied. She did have Karen's prescription filled and ready to begin, but her periods were so scarce, like most dancers, that she hadn't been able to start taking them. She refused to worry about the possibility that she might already be pregnant.

Thus began one of the happiest periods of her life. The two of them spent most of their free time in their cozy nest at the Plaza, only venturing out to Christmas shop. She bought him a cashmere scarf and gloves with her savings from not having to pay rent. On Christmas Eve a beautifully wrapped, large box was delivered to their room. She ripped off the paper and inside found a full-length, fox coat.

"I can't accept this!" she exclaimed. "What did it cost?"

"I'd be very offended if you didn't accept my gift, and a lady never asks what something costs."

"I'm not a lady. This must have cost a thousand dollars!"

"It didn't bankrupt me. Your old coat wasn't warm enough. Here, slip it on." He held it out for her, and she slipped her arms into the satin-lined sleeves.

"It's so fabulous," she said in awe as she ran her fingers

through the rich softness of the pelt. "Ian, does this makes me your real, live mistress?"

"Officially and legally binding." He laughed. "You look smashing in it."

She couldn't stop stroking the fur. "Mother will freak!"

She wore her coat when they jammed into a gallery for an Andy Warhol exhibit. Ian got them glasses of champagne as they were jostled by a crush of media and bizarrely got up art fanciers.

"You'll smother in that," he said, stroking her fox.

"It's worth it," she said sipping the champagne. "I'm never taking it off."

"I believe that's the most rewarding gift I've ever given." She stood on tiptoe and kissed him on the mouth.

"You old sugar daddy, you." He looked sheepish, but pleased. Ian was very uncomfortable at public displays of affection. Zena was dead wrong; he was in no way an "extortionist."

The show had a series of silkscreens of Marilyn Monroe, identical, but in varying color combinations. Lily looked at one of Marilyn with a blue face and orange hair and felt she wasn't getting the joke. Ian went into his teacher mode and explained that Warhol and the Pop artists were debunking the elitist mystique of abstract art. Using commercial advertising techniques, they brought art down to the masses. "Also, Warhol is recording contemporary society in a quite original way. Deifying it and showing its crassness. Who more perfect a symbol of it all than a woman sold to the masses like a packet of crisps?"

"I can't see you liking this. You love beauty," she insisted.

"I bought the series. It's a good investment and good art, I think."

Warhol and his entourage arrived at this point, and the photographers went crazy. He was a tiny, death-pale, bespeckled fellow with an equally tiny sprite of a pretty girl in a micro-mini on his arm.

"Edie Sedgewick," said Ian in her ear. "She's his star of the moment." The girl ran up an open staircase to pose for the cameras. She waved in their direction, and Ian raised his glass in salutation.

"You know her?"

"Not well. Just through Andy. She's very charming, if a trifle spacey."

An extremely beautiful, willowy brunette paused to kiss Ian on the cheek. "Ian, darling, haven't seen you in ages," she said in a British accent.

"I've been busy working, Dorian. Long hours."

"How boring of you. With those silly, old pictures, eh? I've missed you terribly," she pouted, pressing her bosom against his arm. Ian looked embarrassed. The girl took his glass and tossed back the champagne. "You haven't lost my number, have you, darling?"

"I, uh, believe I have it. I'm sure I do," he said, looking nervously at Lily as she did a slow burn.

"So use it!" The brunette kissed him again. "Ciao, baby."

Lily glared at Ian as the woman moved off, waving at someone else. "Am I invisible?"

"Sorry, Lily, but I couldn't recall her last name to introduce you."

"You've slept with her, but you can't remember her name?"

He didn't deny it. "I haven't given her a thought since I met you."

"This party is a drag. I want to leave," she announced. She wouldn't speak to him in the car.

"Lily, what have I done?"

"That bitch treated me like I was the air, and you let her. I was humiliated."

"I think you were jealous."

"I think you didn't want her to know about me," she blurted, her anger escalating by the millisecond.

"This is a foolish conversation," he said, switching on the radio.

"That whole scene was phony and obnoxious!" she shouted over the music. "If those are your friends, I'm not impressed!" He stared ahead at the traffic, jaw clenched.

"Take me to Karen's," she ordered.

"For God's sake, quit being a little bitch, Lily. I haven't done a damn thing." When he braked for a light, she jumped out of the car. A taxi was behind them, and she waved it down.

Ian got out of the Jag and yelled after her, "You're acting like a brat, Lily!" Cars were honking.

"You're a playboy just like my mother warned me. In another month, you probably won't remember my name." She got in the cab, and they pulled out around Ian who stood there staring after her in astonishment.

He was not waiting for her after the performance the following night, nor did she see or hear from him for three days.

Then, there he was at Karen's door, looking distraught, clothes disheveled. Karen excused herself, and Lily waited for his apology.

"Lily, I'm flying back to Dublin tonight," he said, running his hand through his wild hair.

"What?" All her studied coolness fled.

"It's Father. He's had a stroke. It looks like he might not make it."

"I'm so terribly sorry," she said, coming over to him.

He wrapped his arms about her and held her for a minute. "I know you are. Look, I've got two tickets. I want you to come with me."

"But, the company?"

"I *need* you, Lily. I don't think I can make it through this without you." He held her face in his big, gentle hands, and his expressive eyes pled more eloquently than any words.

"If it weren't for my job, I'd come in an instant."

"Lily, if you truly love me as you say you do, you'll do this for me. I need you."

"I'll come," she heard herself say. He held her tightly, his familiar, masculine scent almost making her faint.

"This means everything to me, my darling," he said.

She touched his cheek. "Maybe he'll pull through. We must hope for the best."

"He's in a coma. I wouldn't want him to live if. . .," He sniffed. "I'm making a fool of myself."

"Of course not. Cry if you feel like it. It's just me," she said, smiling through her own sympathetic tears.

"Father's always been so invincible. It was such a shock when Damien called today to tell me."

She held her cheek against his, trying to think of comforting words.

"It's been hell without you the past few days," he groaned.

"For me, too. Can you forgive me for being such a silly, jealous brat?"

"Right now I could forgive you anything on earth," he answered, his face in her hair.

They left that night. Karen was to tell the company director that she had to go home to Boston for a family emergency.

Sir William D'Arcy died the day after their arrival in Ireland, without ever regaining consciousness.

After the funeral, Ian cried in Lily's arms in a great, canopied bed at Innismere House. "I never really loved him," he said. "There was respect, fear even, but he wouldn't let me love him. Nor Mother, nor Damien. If only he'd ever let me know that I wasn't a complete disappointment to him."

Lily's tears mingled with his. How well she knew what he meant.

Two weeks later, they were married in the village church built by his ancestors centuries before. Damien D'Arcy, a small, blond boy near her own age, was best man. None of her friends or family was there.

She never danced on stage again.

Nor did she ever really miss the life she gave up, so absorbed was she through the years in her family and in running the house. It had been a shock, but love at first sight, when Ian first showed her Innismere with its sweeping park and great chimneys, the purple Wicklow hills in the distance. She had had no idea. Ian was obviously well-off, but she'd never expected this.

Lily got out of bed and drew aside the drapes. Dawn light shocked her tired, burning eyes. It had all begun as such a fairy tale, but her prince had turned out to be not quite perfect. Was she making too much of this ancient history of his? Was Ian D'Arcy the man she'd fallen in love with all those years ago, or a stranger living a lie from beginning to end?

She watched a lone, black swan glide through the mist on the lake past the folly-crowned islet. Island in the lake. . . Innismere.

Tristan

✪ ✪ ✪

TRISTAN D'ARCY CHECKED his watch for the fourth time in the past half-hour. Where the hell was the Duke? Tristan had been taking up a table at the bustling bistro, The Cavalier Attitude, far too long to have ordered only a pint and a Scotch egg. There was a queue out the door waiting for tables. Although he'd never been there before, Tristan could see this was a popular spot in Chelsea for upscale young types to take the midday meal. He looked around for the redhaired waitress, caught her eye, and signaled. She came over, looking harried.

"Look, my friend may not turn up, so I'll go ahead and order. Don't want to tie up one of your tables."

The girl blew a vivid strand of hair out of her face. "I don't care if you wait. I'm quite swamped at the moment, if you want to know."

"I'll give you my order anyway, because I don't think he's going to show. Faster table turnover means more tips for you, eh?"

She shrugged. "I'd rather have a little peace. Stay here all afternoon, if you want." They smiled at each other. She had a space between her front teeth, and was possibly the prettiest girl Tristan had ever seen. The waitresses were togged out in braided jackets over white corselets

39

which forced their breasts up, quite fetchingly in this girl's case. Tight knee britches, stockings, and buckled shoes completed the costume. Tristan certainly didn't mind sitting there all afternoon with such a sight as she for entertainment.

"Why don't you bring me an omelet, a bit of green salad, and a Guinness Harp when you have the time. Absolutely no rush."

She jotted this down, then studied him with almond-shaped turquoise eyes. "Are you a vegetarian?"

"Today I am," he said, still queasy from overindulgence the night before. To keep her there he added, "Are you one?"

"Oh, yes. It's disgusting how much meat they eat here. It's a wonder any animals are left, the way they stuff themselves. Makes me want to spew at times."

"We're all a bloody, great tribe of carnivores," he agreed. He was normally a meat-eater himself. "You're not from London?"

"Yorkshire," she said, rolling her eyes. He'd already pinpointed that from her heavy, north-country accent.

"Ah, Yorkshire. One of my favorite parts of Britain."

"You sound posh, but not like the other snobs that come in here," she commented.

"I'm not a snob. I'm an Irishman."

"Go on. My da's from Belfast, and you don't sound like any mick I've ever heard." She had a wonderfully open, unstudied grin set off perfectly by the adorable gap.

"I've gone to school over here since I was twelve," he told her. "So your father's an Ulster man, eh? I'm from the south—County Kildare."

"Out in the country?"

"Very. We have a farm—horses, sheep, a couple cows. That sort of thing."

"Lovely. I've always wanted to live on a farm and have every sort of animal."

"Why are you in London, then?"

"I've come to seek me fortune." Saucy toss of the red locks. "I'll live in the country after I'm rich."

"Excellent plan. One doesn't want to be poor in the country."

The girl looked back over her shoulder. "The manager's getting cross. I'd better get a move on or my tables will be getting testy."

He caught her wrist. "I know your life story, but not your name."

"It's Bella," she said with a smile, then hurried off. How perfectly apt, he thought. He watched her wend her way through the tables on long, shapely legs. The body was every bit as "bella" as the face.

"There you are, you wanker," said The Duke, sliding his bulky frame into the chair across from Tristan.

"You're forty-five minutes late. I was forced to go ahead and order," Tristan groused.

"I was unavoidably and quite forcibly detained by the lovely Ursula."

"That's fucking inconsiderate of you," said Tristan.

"*Tant pis.* So have you seen her?" The Duke gazed about the room.

"On the description you gave me of 'incredible tits and arse,' I've narrowed it down to five girls no doubt hired for those qualifications."

"Ah, there's the beauty!"

"Which?"

"The ginger-haired Venus. God's eyes, she's an Amazon goddess! Wait 'til you see her up close. Got a mole just here on her creamy tit that just begs one to take a mouthful. Legs up to her neck."

Tristan frowned. The Duke had been going on for days

about this waitress who was as dim as she was beautiful. An absolute sure thing for their model photo operation. He hadn't paid that much attention as the Duke was wont to rave on about girls who turned out to be less than goddesses in the flesh. For once he had not been exaggerating.

Bella headed for their table and slid the omelet and salad in front of Tristan. "And your Harp," she said, putting down the bottle and a glass with a flourish and a brilliant smile.

Before he could thank her, the Duke jumped to his feet. "Bella, my dear. I say, you're looking lovely today." She stared blankly at him. "Alistair Cranmont, here." There was no recognition in the girl's candid, blue gaze. "You must recall me coming in here last week? Gave you my card and suggested you come round to my studio for a photo shoot?"

"Oh, yes. Sorry. I'm so silly about faces. You had a very bloody steak, I think."

"You've got me—what a memory!" The Duke let out a high, nasal whinny which passed for a laugh. Tristan cringed. This was a very nice girl, innocent and beautiful, not fodder for the Duke's lecherous schemes. But of course she was exactly the type his friend was always looking for. He preferred the fresh, milkmaid look to tarted-up, been-around girls.

"I see you've met my assistant, Tristan, uh, Desmond here." Tris stood and held out his hand to her, hating every second of this charade.

"Bella Malone," she said, blushing exquisitely. *Why*, he wondered, had he ever thought redheads, so prevalent in Ireland, homely?

"I'd better take your order, Mr. Cranmont. The manager is watching." The Duke ordered cutlets and ale, and Bella Malone hurried off.

"Corker, isn't she?" he said as he leaned out to check her legs.

"Not this one, damn it," said Tristan. His conscience had got a good dulling that summer with Amboy who had undertaken tutoring him in Living on the Edge—and Beyond, but he still had a few die-hard qualms left.

"This is a decent girl. She'd never do what you want, Duke."

"Decent, perhaps, but also ambitious and not really brilliant. She was that impressed when I told her I could get her work as a model. She's just in from the sticks, and if we don't grab her, someone far worse will. She's a sitting pigeon, an exploitation waiting to happen. Procurers all over London are looking for such as she. We will be doing the girl a favor."

"She's not stupid, just innocent and trusting."

"My favorite combination, when paired with a great pair." The Duke grinned.

"Come on, Duke. Leave this one be," Tristan pleaded.

"You fancy her? By all means have her, *après moi.*"

"You're a bastard."

The Duke threw back his head and brayed in delight at the compliment. Tris had to laugh along with him. How could you hate the Duke? He was too ridiculous.

He'd met Marmaduke Alistair Amboy at Eton. Dukeboy, as he was known at school, was two years older and already a legend. Despite being incredibly gawky, poor at games, and ill-favored, he was very popular. This was due to his sense of humor, often self-targeted, his born rebel's way of flaunting all rules and regulations, and his princely allowance with which he was most generous. Dukeboy had been fond of fagging, but never cruelly, and there was nothing even faintly homosexual about him. "Pretty Trissy" had been most grateful for that.

Tristan remembered the time he'd come to Dukeboy's

room and found him and his classmate Simon in bed with a town girl—an amazing rabbit-out-of-a-hat trick considering the cloistered, monastic nature of the school. He'd stood there gape-mouthed at the sight of so much bare flesh, until the Duke had sauntered over, jerked him inside, and shut the door.

"You couldn've knocked, arsehole," growled the older boy.

"I've got the French letters you sent me after," he stammered, handing him the prophylactics he'd spent an agonizing half-hour in a chemist shop to purchase. The shop girl had smiled maliciously at him as she handed the things across the counter. "Here you are, big boy," she'd sneered.

"You're a tad late, me boyo," said the Duke.

"Right. She's already twice preggers," called Simon from the bed. The girl giggled and finally pulled the sheet up over herself.

"Care to join us, D'Arcy?" offered the always charitable Dukeboy.

"Lor, he's just a baby," shrieked the girl.

"But he's got the biggest prick at school. Show her, D'Arcy."

"No thanks," he squeaked. "I've a Latin translation to do."

Dukeboy clapped him on the back and escorted him to the door. "I know I can count on you as a gentleman, D'Arcy, never to mention what you've seen here today?"

"Absolutely—I swear!"

"Good man. You'll go places in this world." From then on, the Duke had been especially friendly and generous with him.

Bella Malone returned with the Duke's dinner.

"I've been expecting to hear from you, my dear. I thought you wanted to be a model?"

"To tell the truth, my friend Edna thought it didn't sound on the up and up. She reads *Tatler* and has never seen any Duke of Putney in it."

"Heavens," said the Duke, waving a dismissive, meaty hand in the air. "My family would be distressed to see the ancestral name in the yellow press. The true aristocracy never get their names in the papers. But titles aren't key here, a mere affectation really. Of course, my partner Tris is a baronet, even if he is only a bog trotter."

"So am I," said Bella with a frown.

"Ha! Forgot your name was a tad Hibernian. Just a figure of speech. Some of my best friends are bog trotters.

"Back to this cynical friend, Edna. Can you believe she thinks we're not legit, Tristan?"

"Edna says you can't be too careful here. She's been in London for two years," said Bella.

"A wise woman. Tell you what. Bring clever Edna and yourself to my studio and see firsthand if we're not on the up and up. When's your next day off?"

"Tomorrow."

"Perfect." He handed her a card. "In case you misplaced the other one. Say around noonish? We'll have lunch as well. Get to know each other."

Bella bit her lip, then looked at Tristan. "You're his assistant?"

Tris nodded unenthusiastically, not wanting to encourage her.

"And a very excellent photographer he is, too. Teaching him everything I know." The Duke winked at him. "I know I have a face not even my mother could love, but would a chap with a sweet angel's face like Desmond here be involved in anything unseemly? I think not."

She smiled slightly at Tristan. "All right. We'll be there tomorrow at noon."

"You'll never regret it."

Bella ran off to another table in her station.

"What hindquarters! You could balance a Guinness on the child's rear end," chortled the Duke. "I may not be able to survive the sight of her naked."

"You'll never see that sight," said Tristan, throwing down his napkin.

"So she has a duenna who wasn't born yesterday. We'll charm the bitch in no time." The Duke lit into his cutlets. He haunted restaurants in the better areas of town on his scouting forays, thereby enabling him to combine his two favorite pastimes, eating and arse watching. Through this method, he had discovered a number of his "models" waiting tables.

This was the deal, as the Duke had explained it to Tristan in the wee hours of a deb party. He would talk attractive, working-class girls into posing for regular fashion shots, ostensibly for a model's portfolio to get them started in the business. A fee of fifty pounds would be charged, though this was definitely negotiable for a candidate with outstanding attributes, such as Bella Malone. From there, the Duke would recruit the most attractive and receptive girls for posing nude for a layout in American *Playboy*'s upcoming feature, "The Girls of London"—a bald lie.

The Duke had something of a deep, spiritual calling for pornographic film, a field of cinematography where lay his ultimate ambitions. According to him, there was a complete dearth of tasteful, intelligent skin flicks with actual plots and post-Neanderthal dialogue. "The business is run by the most unimaginative, uneducated sorts. It cries out for an entrepreneur of artistry and intelligence," he avowed over an almost empty bottle of vodka they'd shared between them. He hoped to make contacts through the still nude photography thing that would be his entrée into the field. Eventually he hoped to produce, write, direct, and maybe even star in his own "really first class" porno films. Tristan had been surprised, as Duke-boy had been regarded at school as having no other ambition in life than spending his father's fortune.

The two of them had been in a photography club at school. Tristan had been fascinated with the subject since he'd got a Nikon on his twelfth birthday. The Duke had gone on to infamy at Oxford where he'd been booted out the spring term of his first year. He'd proudly shown Tris the photo, which, aided by very poor marks, had done the trick—a shot of an amazingly buxom girl clad in the university gown and nothing else, spread-eagled on the steps of St. Mary the Virgin. "Made a hundred quid off prints of this," he boasted. "Took it at night—notice the seductive lighting. Really proud of that shot. Too bad the school hasn't a sense of humor."

The Duke had invited Tris to join him in his commercial endeavor. He'd already printed up handsome cards: Rhinoceros Productions (an allusion to the erotic properties of rhino horn), Alistair Cranmont, Duke of Putney (his nom de porn). "I could really use a guileless, pretty face like yours, D'Arcy, for luring the women. And of course your photographic talents would be an asset as well." Tristan had laughed and said he'd take him up on the offer if he were ever desperate. Little did he know that in a few days he would be.

The Duke left the redhaired waitress a three-pound tip. She gave Tristan a shy, little smile as they left.

"I think she likes you, old boy. That could prove most helpful."

They parted company and Tristan walked on a few blocks to his sister Violet's flat. After ringing a few times, he was about to leave when she opened the door.

"Trissy! What a rare treat! Come in."

"Did I wake you?" he asked, noting her dressing gown and disheveled hair.

"No, no. Yves and I were just lolling about. It *is* Saturday, after all." He tried to keep a straight face. Every time he dropped by, he managed to rout his sister and her painter/lover out of bed. Obviously Frenchmen were all they were cracked up to be.

Violet led him through her small but terribly artistic Chelsea flat to the tiny kitchen. She put on the kettle.

"Nothing's wrong, is it?"

"Does something have to be wrong for me to visit my favorite sister?"

"Your only sister as well. Sit down, love." They both had a seat at a table painted with a Picasso face.

"Daddy tells me he came by to see you on your houseboat, with not very heartwarming results."

"Mmm. Got a fag, Vi? I'm out." She got a packet and a lighter, and took one for herself.

"Makes me ill to see you taking up that nasty habit, Tris."

"Please, no lectures. I enjoy smoking. It relaxes me."

"Of course. We D'Arcys are so high-strung, we're perfect candidates for a hideous nicotine habit."

"Vi, if I wanted a proper nagging, I'd let Mother do it."

"God knows she'd be better at it than I," said his sister with a smile. "About Daddy. I really wish you'd been kinder. Poor darling is so very low these days. I worry about him."

"What did he say about me?"

"That you didn't want his money. That you broke his heart."

"Rather melodramatic of him."

"My diagnosis. I've never seen him so down. It's killing him that you won't even talk to him."

"I've nothing to say to him," said Tristan sharply. The kettle whistled and Violet got up to make the tea.

"Tris, I know you've found out something about Daddy. The same something that's made Mummy throw him out of the house." She turned to him, her thin, handsome face full of concern.

"What is it, Trissy? What could be so unforgivable that you cut yourself off from the most wonderful father? A father you've always admired so. You must tell me. No one will tell me anything, and it's driving me mad."

"I told you before. He's not the man we thought he was. He's a total fraud. I don't blame Mother one whit."

"Did you catch him with a woman? That's got to be it."

Tristan looked away and nervously drew on his cigarette. "I'm not ever going to discuss it."

"If that's it, and it must be the reason Mummy's being such a bitch, surely you can forgive him. Daddy's still very attractive at forty-five, and he travels the world by himself. He gets lonely. It was bound to happen, but that doesn't make him a fraud. Or else almost every other man who can pull it off is as well. He's still a fabulous husband and father, and Mummy should thank God every day that she has him."

They were interrupted by Yves, wearing only jeans, hair down to his shoulders.

"Darling, the tea's almost ready. Tristan's honored us with a visit," said Violet brightly.

"Bonjour, Yves," said Tristan.

The Frenchman grunted without looking at him. He spoke to Violet in rapid French with accompanying vigorous hand gestures. Though Tris wasn't that good at conversational French, he got the message—get back to bed, *tout de suite!* His sister responded sharply, then ran her hand down his bare arm to soften it. Translation:

"Keep your pants on. I'll be there in a minute." Yves made a last gesture that was international and slumped off to his lair.

"Charming seeing you again, too, Yves," Tristan called after him.

Violet fluffed her curly, dark mane and sighed. "He's horrid, I know, but I adore him, so everyone will just have to suffer."

"If he makes you happy, Vi, I'm his number-one fan." She put her arms about his neck. "Trissy, what am I going to do with you? Or Mummy and Daddy? Our whole family has gone to pieces."

He stood up and put his hands on her shoulders. Her hazy, blue eyes were exactly like their mother's. "Don't worry, Vi. What will happen, will happen. It's out of our hands. I'm sure I'll grow out of this awkward phase I'm going through, but meanwhile, could I spot you for a tenner?"

"Look how he slips that in so casually." She laughed.

"I'm a practiced deadbeat by now. Could you manage it, Vi? I'm a trifle short this week."

"Of course." She went to get the money. He felt badly about hitting her again so soon. She probably didn't make that much as assistant fashion editor of a magazine, and she had to support Yves as well. Violet had foregone the debutante bit for living in Paris and studying design at *La Chambre Syndicale de la Couture Parisienne.* She'd brought back with her a great flair in clothes and a French painter who had yet to sell a picture or speak a full English sentence. Yves did have that sullen, feral look often irresistible to women and "other talents," as his sister liked to say.

She returned and handed him some notes.

"Vi, you can't spare this much."

"Yves sold a painting."

"You're kidding!"

She giggled, not being able to pull off that big a fib.

"Wait a minute. Did Dad give you this for me?"

"No. He gave it to me, and I choose to loan it to you. Take it." She closed his hand around the bills and patted his cheek.

"How is your photography studio working out?"

"Not badly. We're expecting more return next month. It takes time to get started."

"But you'll be going off to school, Tris."

"I'm not going this term."

"What!"

"Don't lecture me. I'm not in the mood. It's my life, and I don't feel like going to fucking Oxford! Has anyone ever considered what *I* want to do with my life?"

"I thought you were looking forward to university. You're so bright, Tris; at the top of your class. Mummy and Daddy will have strokes. All D'Arcy first sons go to Oxford."

"Fuck D'Arcy! You get to traipse off to Paris to live the Bohemian life, while I have to bust my chops at Oxford learning crap I have no interest in and will never use. I didn't ask to be the only son."

Violet stepped back and shook her head sadly. "I don't know, Tris. You've changed so this summer. You were always such a sweetie, so eager to do everything right to please Daddy, and now you talk like a guttersnipe. You're in some dubious-sounding venture with a boy everyone says is into low company and drugs. You're worrying our parents to death. What has got into you?"

Tristan threw the bills in the air. "Forget it! I thought there was at least one person who understood me." He brushed off her efforts to stop him and stormed out of the flat.

He exited out onto the sidewalk straight into the path of his friend Julian Neville.

"I say, Tristan, what a superb sight you are, old man. Haven't seen you since when? Arabella Wentworth's party? How the hell are you, lad?" Julian exclaimed, sincere delight all over his pleasant, round face.

"Marvelous," lied Tristan. "It *has* been a while."

"Still seeing Victoria, you lucky dog?"

"This is August, Neville. How long do you expect a relationship to last?"

"Point well taken. I was quite jealous of you, you blighter. Smashing girl, old Vicky."

"Yes, she is—or was. She was too much for me. Has since moved on to someone who's richer, has a greater title, and must be more tolerant of her fickle ways." He sounded flip, but had been deeply hurt when the glorious older girl had dropped him after an affair of only two months.

Julian shook his head and looked more than ever like a genial rabbit. "Women are death. Too bad there's not a viable alternative. So come have a drink with me, Tris. We've got to decide who's to bring the stereo, that sort of business." Tristan was not in the mood to see another horrified reaction to his sudden change of plans, so he postponed telling Julian they wouldn't be sharing rooms at university after all.

"Love to, Julie, but I have an appointment."

"I see. Ring me, won't you? I'm at the Cheyne Walk house. How's life with Dukeboy? As depraved as I imagine?"

"It staggers the imagination. I'll ring you soon, old man." Tristan said good-bye to his goodhearted old friend.

He shivered in spite of the balmy summer air as he headed for the tube station. Julian, of all people to bump into! Julie's father, the Earl of Wycliffe, was his father's oldest friend through public school and university. "Uncle" Tony and his wife Anne were Tris's godparents, and he and Julian had been thrown together all their lives, at Innismere and at the Nevilles' great castle in Surrey where the family was forced to live in the upper floors as the first level was open to the public. Handsome, urbane Uncle Tony made a striking contrast with Ian D'Arcy. A ball of nausea gathered in Tristan's stomach as he pictured the blond head of Uncle Tony against the dark of his father.

Don't think about it, he admonished himself. Think about Bella of the glorious nimbus of Titian tresses sticking in sweaty strands to her flushed cheeks. Her hair was a red-gold he couldn't recall ever seeing before, and her oddly stirring, gap-toothed smile was just the foil to set off her perfection of face. He was willing to place money, which he didn't have, on the Duke's never getting her to do anything dirty. He, Tristan D'Arcy, would not have it! He could only subdue his conscience so far, even if he was very tired of being a dewy-eyed prat and longed to be so hard that his heart could never be broken again. It would take a true monster to take advantage of a girl like Bella Malone. Surely even the Duke couldn't be that much of a sleaze, although he'd never seemed to be burdened by the faintest semblance of a conscience before.

When Tristan reached the Thames houseboat, he found his friend photographing Charlotte, one of his more felicitous discoveries. The ample-breasted shopgirl from Selfridges had taken with robust glee to "naughty" pictures and was now posing coyly in schoolboy short pants with suspenders and nothing else. She was one of the ones Tristan did not feel guilty about. He had told the Duke that he didn't even want to know what became of these photographs, but he was positive there would not be any Playmates chosen from their clientele. Charlotte waved gaily at him, spoiling the shot.

"Taking the afternoon off, are we?" asked the Duke, looking up from his camera.

"Went to see my sister," he muttered.

"I had to do Char's makeup myself. Got rouge the hell over both of us."

"Such liberties he took with his brushes!" Charlotte giggled.

"You seem to have got on very well without me," Tris said, wrinkling his nose at the dense smell of hashish.

"We did rather, eh, Char? You could be expendable, Desmond my man."

"Oh, I missed Trissy! He's such an artiste," crowed the girl.

Tristan shut himself off in his room and flopped down on the bed. What a fuck-up of a day; in fact, what a fuck-up of a life. He had nothing at all to show for seventeen years on earth. He *did* want to be a photographer, but not like this. This made him queasy and ashamed. The truth was, he didn't have the natural talent for debauchery that the Duke thought he had. His conscience wouldn't die. His immersion in liquor, drugs, and sex under his friend's tutelage had left him feeling even more adrift than before. It was an escape for a while, but then his conscience would begin nagging at him, at which point he'd have to dull himself again to escape the guilt feelings. A vicious cycle which was even less enjoyable than the boring, phony life he'd been trying to escape.

But there was at least some solace in being able to forget, if only for a few minutes. Tristan reached under the mattress and retrieved a plastic bag of white powder. Suddenly, without any warning, the scene flashed unbidden into his brain. His father's white face, disheveled black hair, and closed eyes. His hands on the shoulders of someone with blond hair kneeling before him. His father's eyes opening, focusing on him standing there in the hallway. The look of horror in his dark eyes as he realized he'd been found out at last, and by whom. Tristan groaned aloud and dumped the powder into his shaking hand.

✪ ✪ ✪

At precisely 12:05 the next day, Bella and her flatmate Edna appeared at the Duke's floating studio. He showed the girls around his setup. They were impressed by the sumptuously decorated houseboat which belonged to Amboy, Sr., a very successful estate agent. They sighed over the wardrobe of glamorous evening dresses and chic suits which the Duke had acquired from God-knows-where. They might have been stolen for all Tris knew. Bella kept beseeching him with her Mediterranean Sea eyes, but he tried not to give her any encouragement.

After a very genteel lunch of cucumber sandwiches, strawberries, and Piesporter Spätlese on the deck watching the boats go past, the girls had been completely won over as the Duke had predicted. He set up an appointment for Bella's first modeling session. Unfortunately, Edna of the glasses and bad skin would have to be working at that time. As for the fifty pound fee, that could be paid in the future when Bella was making big money as a model.

As soon as the two had left, the Duke collapsed on an overstuffed white sofa and wholeheartedly congratulated himself. "I should try out for the Royal Academy. Olivier couldn't have been more convincing! Damn but that Edna could stop a clock. Is there some unwritten law that beautiful girls must have Medusa for a flatmate?" He lit a joint. "Welcome to my parlor, sweet Bella Malone." He let out a maniacal peel of laughter, but for once, the Duke's black humor failed to score with Tristan.

"Rather a long puss, D'Arcy old bean."

"I always thought you were just out for a harmless laugh, Duke, but lately it's occurring to me that you're a real sonofabitch."

"Bugger you, arsehole. You'll get to shag her, don't fret."

Tristan's job, besides arranging the girls, fitting the clothes to them if need be, and working the big fan for windblown effects, was to do their hair and makeup. "You had a sister. You must know about such," was the Duke's reasoning. So Tristan had studied magazine photos and had gone on a fashion shoot with Violet. What the makeup artist did to the models' faces seemed to him very like painting, which he'd played around with since childhood. His sister assumed he was interested in the girls, but his day among the fashion beauties, who were not that beautiful without the paint, only confirmed his suspicion that the breed was generally vacuous and self-absorbed. After his bruising, first sexual experience with Victoria Fullham-Jones, Tristan had come to the conclusion at the age of seventeen that the girl of his dreams was not to be found in the brittle deb or fashion worlds.

Bella arrived at the appointed time, looking ravishing without even lipstick. Tristan was shamed by her shining-faced eagerness and longed to tell her that this was not going to be her entrée to big-time modeling. He could not do that without incriminating himself, however, and he very much wanted to stay on the good side of the stunning redhead. He appeased his conscience by telling himself that she would come out of it with a professional portfolio of pictures, which was essential if she wanted to be a model. He would make sure that reprobate Duke never took her to Phase II of his operation, and with some luck, might come out of the whole sordid deal a hero in her eyes.

And what eyes she had! It was difficult not going into a trance looking into their extraordinary green-blue-gold depths as he tried to apply mascara to her lashes with a shaky hand. He had only to swish on some translucent powder over her porcelain skin; it seemed a crime to him to cover up the faint dusting of freckles like nutmeg on cream over the bridge of her classic, Greek nose. Her pronounced cheekbones needed only a wash of blush for accent. It was like working on the face of Botticelli's Simonetta after a steady canvas of coarse, Breughel peasant girls.

She was perfectly still while he worked on her. It was a very intimate thing making up a girl's face. His hands stopped shaking after he got into it. He leaned back to study the effect, and she grinned that all-out grin at him. His heart went *zing*. He could actually feel it in his chest!

"Ready for the cover of *Vogue*," he said, his voice light. She looked in the mirror.

"Wow, is that me? I wish I had you to make me look this good everyday, Tristan."

"You're prettier with nothing, I think." Armed with mousse, gel, spray, and curling iron, he transformed her hair into a wild, artfully tousled mane.

"I can't believe that's me," she said in awe as she studied the results in the glass.

"I had an awful lot to work with," he said, feeling very pleased. He had to admit she looked every bit as gorgeous as the finished professional models he'd seen.

She studied him inquiringly.

"What?"

"Tristan, are you, uh, you know, gay?"

He let out a slow sigh of amazement. A prick in the balloon of his ego.

"It's all right if you are. I mean I'll still like you very much. I'd just like to know before. . . .Are you?"

"I think I've just been insulted in the sweetest possible way. Do I seem effeminate?"

"God, no, not in the least! But that doesn't always mean. . .It's that you're so artistic and good-looking."

"Ergo, I must be a faggot."

"Are you?" She was bulldog persistent.

"Would you be disappointed if I were?"

"Awfully!" She had one perfect dimple.

He took her hand. "Haven't you been paying attention to all the electricity that's been passing between us since I first ordered that omelet? I am not now, nor have I ever been, or even thought of being homosexual."

"Thank God!" she said, flushing under her blush.

"Are you always this direct?"

"Well, yeah. I didn't want to waste time finding you attractive if there was no point in it."

He helped her to her feet; she was almost as tall as he was. "Now that we've got that cleared up, shall we get to work?"

Over several hours, they photographed Bella in every dress and a suit and hat. At first she was stiff and posey. Then the Duke put on a rock tape and cracked out a bottle of his father's Moët and Chandon. She began to relax and enjoy herself.

After it was all over, Tristan asked her to have dinner with him. Violet had sent him the fifty pounds along with a letter which said, "Take this, you stubborn idiot! I'm trying my damnedest to understand you and love you no matter what. Your favorite sister."

The Duke gave him a knowing look as they left.

*   *   *

"Am I mad, or are people staring at us?" she asked after the tenth person to walk past their table did a double-take.

"Don't people normally stare at you?"

"Oh, my hair? It *is* a red flag, but it's never been this bad."

Tristan laughed to himself in amazement. Bella had absolutely no conceit. In his experience, very attractive girls always knew it; it was their raison d'etre. Bella seemed to care less that she was spectacular, or else didn't even realize it. He hoped she always stayed that way.

"They're staring because they're sure they've seen you on magazine covers."

"Don't rag me, Tris. Is my hair too wild? I should have brushed it out."

"People look because you are quite stunningly wonderful to look at, Bella."

"Come on. It's your makeup. Do you really think I could ever be on a cover?"

"I haven't the faintest doubt of it." She giggled and shook her head in disbelief.

They had tea with dinner. She didn't need any more alcohol, she said, or she'd never make it home on the tube.

"As soon as we have enough good shots for your portfolio, I'll show them to some people who can help you," he said.

"Like those girls in *Vogue* and *Elle* that got their start with you all?"

Tristan smiled feebly.

She put her hand over his on the table. "You're so sweet. I feel awful that I hurt your feelings about being gay."

"I loved that you asked me that. You wondered, so you asked, and I told you. People should always be that direct.

The people I know never say what they really think. They'll slag you behind your back, but never say anything that straight out to your face. Or they'll couch it as a joke to you, when they really mean it. Please always say what you think to me, Bella."

"Okay. Here's some more. I think you're really cute and nice, and not a snob at all. Alistair gives me the shivers, but I know I can trust you." Tristan swallowed.

Over the remains of their meal, she told him her story. She was the only child of a Catholic Irishman, who, unable to find a job in Protestant Belfast, had gone to England and joined the Royal Navy. He'd married a young, pretty English girl who had Bella, and then, tired of waiting for him to come home from sea, had run off with a door-to-door Hoover salesman. Three-year-old Bella had consequently been raised by an aunt and uncle in a Yorkshire village. Recently her father had retired and settled in Yorkshire as well; shortly thereafter Bella had run off to London.

"It was just so. . .narrow there," she explained. "I didn't want to live my aunt's life, never seeing the world or meeting anyone interesting. Maybe it was Da's fault for always bringing me dolls from Hong Kong and exciting, faraway places. I hated to leave him like that, but I knew it was time to go if I was ever going to get away. I suppose I'm bad like my mother. I could never blame her for leaving, really."

"Never bad. You were very brave to leave the security of home, I think. And dead right to do so."

"Poor Da thinks they'll pump me full of drugs and force me into prostitution in the evil city. I tell him how careful I am, but he worries so."

"It can be a very dangerous city, Bella."

"I've only been flashed once while waiting for the train. I laughed, and I think I hurt his feelings. Can you imagine anything dumber than standing around whipping out your prick all day? It must get so old!"

"Yes, it does. . . and chilly." She laughed.

"Everyone's been generally wonderful to me. And meeting you all—what a stroke of luck! Maybe I'll succeed much faster than I thought." She shook her moussed mane happily.

"But what about you, Tris? Why do you jump when old Alistair tells you to? I'd tell him to bugger off, I would."

"That's my job. It's all his setup. I get a very nice room for nothing."

"I'd think a fellow like you would be going to school."

"I was going to go to university, but I've changed my mind."

"Why?"

"I was enchanted by a pair of faerie blue-green eyes." She dimpled prettily.

"What's the real reason?"

"It's just that suddenly I felt as if I'd been hurtling through my life on a preordained path, not once considering *why?*. Or even if I really wanted to go where everyone is so intent on pushing me. Why should I live the same life as my great-grandfather?"

"Aren't your parents upset?"

"My father can go fuck himself for all I care, and I've only just written my mother. She'll have a collapse, of course."

"Don't you like your father?"

"You should be an investigative journalist."

"Sorry. It's just that you're so interesting."

"He and I have had a falling out of late."

"Over your not wanting to go to university?"

"Prior to that. He and my mother are separated, and I don't want to talk about this."

"Forgive me. I thought you looked sad when you came into the Cavalier."

"I was, but I'm cheering up since I met you, Bella."

"Oh, are you then?" She cocked her head to the side. "I like your eyes and your smile, Tristan."

"Are you attempting to cheer me even further?"

"Yes." She studied him, hand on chin. "I like that you're taller than me. I was the tallest girl in Yorkshire. Your hair is lovely, too. A T-shirt on you looks like it cost a hundred pounds."

He signaled the waiter for their check. "Let's forgo dessert."

He rode with her on the tube to Shepherd's Bush. Bella lived down a narrow, dank street and up five flights of evil-smelling stairs.

"You really shouldn't have come," she said, getting out her key. "I'm ashamed to be living here."

"You'll be moving up to better shortly, I predict," he said, and pulled her to him for a kiss.

"You have such lovely, wide shoulders," she murmured running her hands over them. He kissed her again, more urgently this time, and his hand strayed to her breast. She gently removed it.

"I'd better go in."

"I could use a cup of tea. Isn't Edna still at work?"

"She's home by now, and we're out of tea."

He rubbed the small of her back. "So a cup of anything. . .water. Do you have that?"

She smiled at him and ran her hand down his chest. "Good night, Tris. It was a lovely time. I liked talking to you. I like you."

"I like you, too. Very much." He leaned over for one last, soft kiss. "Good night, bella Bella."

*   *   *

Her next modeling session was the following afternoon. This time when Tristan made her up, there was an easier, more flirtatious undertone. He tried to be businesslike as he made up the canvas of her face, but her eyes kept crinkling up at the corners.

He frowned at her. "Be serious," he said, then smiled.

"Do you have a girl, Tris?"

"I'm in-between at the moment."

"Me, too. A coincidence we both are, isn't it?"

He shrugged. "I suppose. Actually it wouldn't make a hair's difference if we were both engaged to other people. This would still be happening." He tipped her chin up and kissed her on the lips.

"Get that out of the way before I paint the red stuff on." Bella put her arms about his neck and pulled him back for another kiss.

"Dear me, hanky-panky with the makeup man. Very unprofessional, Bella," said the Duke. "I'm waiting, my dears, and my time is valuable. We'll do resort gear today. I've an assortment of shorts and bathing costumes out for you in the dressing room. Show the clients that every part of you is first rate."

"Every part?" she said with a laugh.

"Just a figure of speech, my dove," said the Duke, smirking at Tristan behind her back.

Bella came in to the studio looking embarrassed in a severely cut white maillot. "I think this is a bit small for me," she said, tugging at the leg elastic which was cut up over her hipbones.

"Nonsense," said the Duke. "You look purely edible and the height of fashion. Doesn't she, Tris?"

Tristan gave her a thumbs-up and felt a certain relief, much as he had the night before when she'd turned him away. He'd wanted to have sex with her, but he wanted more for it not to be an easy thing to get. Nothing worthwhile ever was. There had been a nagging little doubt in the back of his mind that perhaps she wasn't as principled as he wanted her to be. More than one sweet-faced, innocent looking girl had been flattered and cajoled by the silver-tongued devil Duke into baring more than her soul to advance her career. Bella was positively cringing in the skimpy suit, so there was no way she would go any further.

Girl's looks could be very deceiving. Bella had a lush ripeness about her and met a man's eye with a frank openness that could be interpreted as easy by some. He'd thought that back at the restaurant before he talked to her. Since he'd gotten to know her a bit, he could see that she was far from a quick make. He could imagine that she could get in trouble for false advertising, though completely unconscious on her part.

To put her at ease, the Duke decided to put on some music. When asked what band she'd like to hear, Bella said U2. "Sorry, I wore my U2 tapes into shreds playing them," said the Duke, making a gagging gesture for Tristan's benefit.

"Edna and I saw U2 at Wembley. Bono is incredible," said Bella earnestly.

"Yeah, it's great to see the micks on top for a change," said Tristan with a grin. "I particularly admire how they don't exploit their female fans, don't you, Du-uh-Alistair?"

"They are an example I try to follow in my own life," intoned the Duke. "I've heard it said that Bono can cure warts with a mere laying on of hands. So, how about Peter Gabriel? He's almost as holy."

Bella was very ill at ease posing, constantly checking to see if too much of her gorgeous figure was popping out of the miniscule maillot. The Duke got a bottle of champagne out of his father's well-stocked liquor cabinet.

"A bit of bubbly to help us all relax," he said, handing her a brimful glass.

"I drank too much of this last time. Had an awful headache later," she said.

"One glass will only warm you up, my pet. Put on the shades and the straw hat. Adorable!" He clicked away. He ordered Tristan to wet her down with a mister for a more sensual look.

"Out of this world! Here, have a jot more champagne, Bella, and I think we'll really get cooking. Tris, put on a Bob Marley tape to set a tropical mood. Drink up, Bella, so you can be nice and mellow like the rastaman."

"I think I could learn to like the old bubbly," she said with a crooked grin.

"Thatagirl. Who cares about tomorrow's headache when you can feel sooo nice today! Tris, my battery is running down, and I don't have a fresh one. Run down to the chemist and get me one."

"Yes, good doggie, Tris," said Bella.

"Go on, I need one. Get me some fags, too."

Bella put her hands on her hips. "Tristan, tell him to stuff the batteries up his bum."

He laughed in surprise. "You tell him for me."

"I will." She did.

Duke snorted with laughter. "You may be the woman of my dreams, Bella Malone. Get a move on, Desmond, you laggard."

Tristan laughed to himself as he headed for the chemist's shop. Bella was very cute when she was squiffed. It had only taken two glasses of bubbly to do the trick, too. Then it hit him—she'd drunk more than that the last time, to less effect.

The Duke didn't hear Tristan enter the houseboat over the loud music. Bella was lying on the floor while he stood over her taking pictures. He was leaning down to touch her when Tristan hit him, knocking him flat.

"What the hell! Are you mad, D'Arcy?"

"You piece of slime!" Tristan helped Bella to her feet, but she was too groggy to stand on her own.

"Tristan, where were you?" she mumbled.

"What did you give her, Duke? She's out of it."

"Nothing. Just two glasses of champagne."

"What did you put in the fucking champagne?"

"Hardly anything. Just a bit of Ecstasy to make her relax."

"She looks a tad over-relaxed to me, you bastard." He picked her up and carried her to the bathroom and sat her on the toilet, then wiped her face with a damp cloth. Her head lolled backward.

"It wasn't enough to hurt a fly. We've taken twice that amount," said the Duke, hanging over his shoulder as Tristan lightly slapped her face.

"Combined with liquor? She's not a drinker. Shit! Should we get her to a doctor, Duke? You're the drug expert."

"No! We could get into trouble. Just let her sleep it off, she'll be all right."

Tristan held her in his arms. "If she comes to any harm, I'll kill you, Amboy!"

"You might have told me you really liked this girl, Tris."

"Couldn't you tell, asshole? Don't you even recognize a good person anymore? Thank God the penny dropped, and I realized what you were up to."

"I never touched her!"

"Only because you didn't have time. Get away from me, Amboy. You make me ill!"

The Duke looked considerably taken down. "I just thought you wanted to screw her."

Tristan picked her up over his shoulder like a limp rag-doll and took her to his room where he laid her carefully on the bed. She was completely out.

"Jesus!" he said, wringing his hands. He turned on the Duke. "You knew she'd never take her clothes off for you, so you had to drug her. How could I ever have liked you, Amboy? You're nothing but a sodding lowlife!"

"Just a bloody minute here," said the Duke. "Don't go so high and moral on me, D'Arcy. Haven't you been enjoying a wallow in the gutter along with me? You're hardly a saint. You've not been above accepting booze, money, and drugs from me all summer. And lots of sex from girls just like this one. Get off this high, moral horse with me, my man!"

Tristan shoved him out of the room, shutting and locking the door. "Get yourself another partner in crime, Duke. I've had all I can stomach!"

"That does it, D'Arcy. Get your gear and that bloody, redheaded cow out of here tonight!" he bellowed.

Tristan sat by the bed and anxiously watched her for a half hour. Bella finally came to, feeling groggy and disoriented. He told her, as he accompanied her home in a taxi, that the heat from the lights and the champagne had caused her to faint.

"Thanks so much, Tris. I'm sure it was because I hadn't eaten today. I'm never having bubbly again, that's for sure."

He took her hand. "There's something I have to tell you, Bella." She nodded and smiled. He closed his eyes.

"My real name is D'Arcy, not Desmond. Alistair Cranmont is Duke Amboy, and Edna was right—there is no Duke of Putney. Rhinoceros Productions is a total fake."

She looked bewildered. He hurried on. "No girls ever got their start in big-time modeling through us. The Duke tries to convince pretty girls like you to pose for risqué shots alledgedly for *Playboy* magazine. I have absolutely no idea what he does with the pictures, and I don't want to know."

She withdrew her hand from his. "You could never be involved in something that shoddy, could you, Tris?"

"I have been. The Duke's been giving me bastard lessons this summer, but they didn't quite take when it came to you, Bella. I never would have let him try any of that with you, I swear!"

"Did anything happen to me while I was out?" she asked in alarm.

"No, I got back in time. But it could have. We are exactly what your father warned you about in the evil city."

She hugged herself and looked at him with wounded eyes. "If this is a joke, it's not at all funny, Tristan."

"I wish it were, but it's all disgustingly true."

"I believed you. God, I'm such a dolt!" She burst into tears.

"I wanted to warn you off, but I couldn't see how to do it without repulsing you, as I'm doing right now."

Bella slid as far away from him as possible on the seat. "I'm so disappointed. I hate you for lying to me."

"I don't blame you. I had to tell you the truth, because I want it all to be straight between us. I want you to know the real me. Believe it or not, I was once considered an honorable person by my friends."

"You tricked and used girls like me. We're too low to even count to snotty boys like you and horrible Alistair or whoever he is. We're just dumb animals to the likes of you." She sobbed with abandon.

He tried to comfort her, and she hit him with her fist.

"Get away from me, you creep! You liar!"

"Everything all right back there, miss?" asked the cabbie.

"No, it isn't. Stop! I want to get out here." The taxi

pulled to the curb, and Bella jumped out and ran down
the street.

"So, what now, lad?"

"Take me back to the boat," said Tristan hollowly.

"Right you are, gov. Got a bit of temper on 'er, but
'at's redheads for you. She'll 'ave a good cry and be right
as rain. Worf every penny a the bover, too, I'd wager."

Tristan leaned back into the hard upholstery and
wished he were dead.

Tristan spied Violet coming through the late afternoon pub crowd dressed in a red suit; her long, black hair
was smoothed back into some sort of a coarse net on her
shoulders—a snood. He'd only seen those in history
books and old films, but leave it to his sister to have one.

Every eye in the place was on her. He waved, and she
came over smiling.

He kissed her cheek, and they sat down at a booth.
"You look fabulous as usual, Vi. On behalf of the women
who are wondering, where did you get that suit?"

"At a jumble sale, of course. Chanel, circa 1952. Divine, isn't it?" Going into a shop and buying a complete
outfit took the sport out of it for Violet. She preferred
to hunt her unique wardrobe to ground at flea markets,
jumble sales, and vintage clothing shops in London and
Paris. Her coats, jackets, and sweaters she found at better
men's stores, always on sale. Her sense of style and imagination was such that she could assemble an outfit from
a pile of cast-off clothes for charity which would have rich
women drooling with envy.

"So, how's it going with Nicky?" she asked, fitting a
Gauloise into a long, ebony holder. She looked like just
the sort of woman one might meet on the Orient Express,
and live to regret.

"Well. I'm learning a lot. He's very good." Violet had got him a job with commercial photographer Nicky Long. "He's letting me a back room in his studio for nothing."

"Good. He's one of the best in the game, Nicky. I feel much better now that you're away from that other boy. I've never heard of anyone who's achieved such a disreputable reputation before he was even twenty."

"The Duke deserves it—he's worked long and hard." He slid a large envelope across the table.

"What's this?"

"Tell me if you think this girl could make it in your world. I'll fetch us a drink. Glass of wine?"

She nodded and opened the packet. When he returned with two glasses of white wine, she was still examining the photos. "Very pretty. Who is she?"

"Her name is Bella Malone—from Yorkshire. I thought perhaps you could use your influence to get her a start in modeling."

"Any experience?"

"None, other than these shots, which as you can see are very nice. Once she relaxes, she's a natural."

Violet took a sip of wine. "I'll show these to Conrad Mailer; you remember him from that shoot. He's one of the top fashion photogs. See what he thinks."

"What do *you* think?"

"I think my little brother has fallen for a terribly pretty girl from Yorkshire."

"You could be right."

"Is she nice, this Bella?"

"She's the nicest person I've met in London. She's . . .*something!*"

Violet smiled. "I can't wait to meet her."

"Well, at the moment she's not speaking to me. I'm not giving up though. The family motto: We shall endure!"

She patted his cheek. "How could any girl resist such a precious child?"

Tristan entered the Cavalier around three, knowing Bella would be off shortly. He had a Guinness at the bar and looked around for her. He soon spotted her moving gracefully through the tables on her long, coltish legs. If she saw him, she gave no indication. She was wearing her hair in a loose, thick braid today. *She's too beautiful,* he thought with a pang. How could people eat when there was this exquisite vision in their midst? Hers was a beauty from another age—not modern. Pre-Raphaelite perhaps, Tristan thought.

At three o'clock the manager put out the sign that said Closed 'til Teatime. Tristan finished the Guinness he'd been nursing and went to wait outside the door for her to exit. She did so shortly without giving him so much as a glance.

Falling in step beside her, he said, "I dunno, I always heard it pays to be honest, but I guess that's just another crock, eh?" She walked on faster, ignoring him. He kept pace.

"My legs are even longer than yours, Bella. You can't lose me."

"Don't you dare say another sexist thing to me!"

"Sexist?"

"I'm just legs and arse to pigs like you. Well, I'm a person. I may not talk fancy like you, but I'm every bit as good. Better!"

"I agree absolutely, but I never thought of you as just a body. I like you because you're warm and nice, and totally honest. Because you don't eat meat, like U2, and have that beautiful, sexy space between your front teeth. Because you are by far the most real person I've ever met, Bella."

"Then why did you do that to me?"

"I would never have let any harm come to you. I wanted to get to know you, to be around you, and that was an excuse."

"You lied to me. You played a game with me. I imagine the two of you had a good laugh at the ignorant country bumpkin."

He caught her arm. "I never laughed at you, ever. Look, my side is starting to hurt. Could we go somewhere and talk? There's so much I need to say to you, Bella."

She jerked her arm free and walked on. "I've heard all from you I ever want to hear."

"Bella!" He spun her around into his arms. "I was totally honest with you when I could have let you go on thinking I was a prince. I took the risk because I want everything to be straight between us."

"Why should you care?" Tears glimmered in her eyes.

"Because I can't not care. I may even be falling in love with you!"

"You don't even know me, and I certainly don't know you."

"True, but I want more than anything to know you. Everything about you. Your favorite color, what you think about a united Ireland, the greenhouse effect, Charles and Di. I want you to know the real me, and the sort of creep who exploits poor shopgirls is not who I am. I swear to you! Just give me another chance, Bella. I know you felt something for me. I think you still do." He took her up in his arms and kissed her. People parted round them on the sidewalk, smiling.

"See, you feel it, too. That magnet thing. I can't think of anything but you, Bella. You've just got to trust me again."

Bella shook her head. "The worst thing about it wasn't that I'd been had about the model thing, but that I'd been had about you, Tris. I told Edna the night we went to dinner that I really thought you were the one. It seemed incredible to meet the one so soon."

"I am the one, at least I want to be. More than anything." He brushed back the hair that had come loose from her braid and held her to him.

Her arms went around him. "Promise me you'll never lie to me again, Tristan."

"I promise. Today is the true beginning of us, Bella," he murmured into her ear.

IAN

♣ ♣ ♣

"SIR IAN, LORD Wycliffe is here to see you," said Miss March over the intercom to his office at the D'Arcy Gallery, Number Six Old Bond Street.

"Damn!" Ian cursed softly to himself. "Send him in, please," he replied into the speaker. He was nervously drumming his fingers on the top of his desk, an early Georgian, mahogany, pedestal library table, when his secretary ushered his oldest friend inside with a slight bow. Miss March was terribly impressed by the Earl of Wycliffe, as were most people, women in particular.

"Have I caught you at an inopportune moment, Ian?" asked Tony, cane in hand as always. He had badly broken his left leg in a polo accident years ago, and though his limp was almost imperceptible now, he'd continued using his handsome collection of antique walking canes.

"No. Just catching up on a bit of paperwork," said Ian, getting to his feet. "What do you want, Tony?" he asked, an icy edge in his voice.

"Actually, I'm in the market for a picture. Anne's birthday as well as our twentieth is coming up, so something rather special is in order, I think." A certain brittle manner betrayed Tony's nervousness.

"What sort of picture did you have in mind?"

"The most beautiful one with the most reasonable

price that you have, of course," said Tony, taking a seat though Ian had not offered him one.

"We're a bit low at the moment, but I'll show you what I have." He returned to his desk and called down to the stockroom. There was a strained silence as the two waited for the pictures to be brought in.

"Damned uncomfortable this summer," said Tony at last. "Wish I'd gone on to Greece earlier. If one is going to be hot, one might at least be in a spectacular place."

Ian stared at him from under his black brows without a reply, and Tony laughed uneasily, the color in his fair-skinned, handsome face stronger than usual.

The tension in the room was broken when two men brought in the pictures and hung them on a blank wall. Ian turned on the spot lighting.

"The very beautiful Madonna on the right is by Bizzelli. The other, a portrait of a Florentine noble, is by Girlandaio and an assistant—tempera on wood."

Tony Neville silently appraised the two paintings. "Which would you advise as an investment?"

"They're both incredible investments. Sixteenth-century Italian old masters are still undervalued despite the craziness of prices lately. The Bizzelli is affordable. I'll let you have it at cost. The other is dearer, a more important picture. It's up to you, Tony."

"Naturally, I prefer the more expensive one, though he is a tad greenish about the gills."

"The green base coat. After several hundred years, the flesh tones begin to evanesce, and the green shows through. It's been cleaned rather harshly I'm afraid. A pity."

"Shall we talk about it over a good lunch at my club? Perhaps we can figure how I can afford the Girlandaio—time payments or something," Tony said jauntily. Money was an ongoing problem for the Earl in his constant struggle to maintain his vast inherited estate devastated by taxes and death duties.

"Perhaps Anne would give you a loan," said Ian with a touch of malice. Tony's wife, heiress to a plastics fortune, was much wealthier than he.

"That would take a bit of the romance out of the gift," replied Tony, refusing to take offense. "Are you free then?"

"I'm not very hungry, and I have a lot of work to do," Ian hedged.

"Please come. I want very much to speak to you, even though I know you'd prefer to continue avoiding me." He fixed Ian with his fine, blue eyes. "We can't shun each other forever, Ian."

"Very well, but I can't spare more than an hour," said Ian, all business.

In the taxi, Ian kept the conversation on the paintings. "I suppose most women, Lily for instance, would rather have jewels for their anniversary. But, for just a bit more, you can give a piece of history, a masterpiece that's stood the test of time, and for less than ten percent of the cost of a minor Impressionist painting. Compare these prices to those a Pollock or Jasper Johns are fetching today. Which would you rather have hanging in your home if only beauty were the criterion?"

"You don't have to sell me. I'm going to get the picture," said Tony quietly. "So how have you been, Ian?"

"Aside from total alienation from my wife and son, I've been simply marvelous, thanks."

"I am so sorry, Ian. I mean that. It's been weighing very heavily on my mind. If there were anything in the world I could do to ease your situation, I would, you know."

"You've done quite enough already, Tony."

"You blame it all on me, don't you?"

"Enough of this boring conversation, please," Ian

snapped. Silence reigned the rest of the way to White's, the private men's club to which Tony was a member.

A liveried attendant greeted them at the door. "Good afternoon, m'Lord," he said with a deferential nod.

"It is indeed, Chesterfield. You remember my friend, D'Arcy of Kildare?"

"Indeed, Sir Ian. How are your horses running this season?"

"Not too badly actually, Chesterfield."

"I'm very pleased to hear that, sir."

"We'd like a bit of privacy for lunch, please," said Tony.

"That isn't necessary," said Ian abruptly. "The dining room is perfectly fine."

"As you wish," said Tony, nodding at the head steward and leading the way into the interior of the comfortably but not ostentatiously furnished club. As the two men made their way to the dining room, Tony nodded and spoke to everyone he encountered. The Earls of Wycliffe had always been members of this club, one of the most exclusive in London. Ian also saw a number of familiar faces, including some clients. Nothing suited the great English houses better than the somber masterpieces he traveled to sales and auctions all over Europe to acquire. D'Arcy's also kept a choice selection of rare sporting prints and paintings, an even more popular genre with the animal-loving English and Irish gentry.

Tony selected a corner table half hidden behind a pot of aspidistra. A waiter appeared at once.

"A glass of sherry for me, Edward. Ian?"

"Just tea for me, please. I've been drinking too much lately."

"So how has Violet's Season been running?" Tony asked, referring to Ian's promising two-year-old filly. When Violet, to her mother's intense disappointment, had declined making her debut in society, she'd said, "Just think, Daddy, you could buy another horse for the cost of dresses, parties, and all that foolishness." She had always known how to reason with her father. So, when Ian had purchased a bay filly at the Goff's September yearling sale, he had christened her "Violet's Season."

"She placed first at Phoenix Park last week, her second win. Been in the money every race we've entered her in so far."

"Wonderful! What a damn shame you've been away for most of it. Do you manage to keep in touch with what's going on in the stable?"

"Thank God I have Connors running things. I ring him several times a week and we discuss strategy."

"But to miss seeing her run, and win, it's damn unfair after all you've put into that filly."

"Lily's been going to the meets in my stead. She quite enjoys being in the winner's enclosure."

"I can picture her," said Tony with a smile. "Next season should be very exciting. Plan on entering her in the 1000 Guineas?"

"We'll see how she comes on. I'd love to, even if the odds are impossible." The top-flight classic Group I flat races were dominated by the most expensive thoroughbreds in the world, many bred and trained in Ireland, but owned by sheiks, foreign millionaires, and syndicates. It was a very long shot for a horse from a small racing stable such as Innismere to compete successfully with such equine royalty.

Their drinks arrived, and Tony recommended the sole. Ian agreed uninterestedly.

Tony took a sip of his sherry. "So, how is Lily, besides being queen of the Irish turf?"

"She's in town, staying at Claridge's. She's come to try and persuade Tristan to go to Oxford."

"I thought that was settled."

"He's changed his mind. Decided he's not going to school this fall. He says he's tired of being railroaded into a life he has no interest in living."

"Damn! What does he intend to do instead?"

"He's working with a commercial photographer who took him on as a favor to Violet. He's living in the back room of the studio—like a pauper, I imagine. Lily's going to be upset about it."

"Julian will be very disappointed. He was looking forward to sharing rooms with Tris at Balliol. Do you think this rebellion is because of?. . ."

"What else?"

"I seem to have wreaked great havoc upon the D'Arcys," said Tony softly. "I still can't believe the deuced luck of Tristan walking in just at that moment. God must have a very cruel sense of humor."

"He was in town for some parties, let himself in with his key. He never told me he was coming," said Ian softly. For a few moments, they each were lost in their own memories of that traumatic scene. "To see his father like that," whispered Ian. "Can you imagine if it had been Julian?"

Tony shook his head. "It's so damned unfair. To have nothing between us for twenty-five years until that day, and then to be caught like that."

"The point is, we were wrong in the first place to have ever let anything happen between us, Tony. It's beside the point to curse our bad luck in getting found out." Ian looked about the room, paranoid that someone might be overhearing their conversation. There was a steady buzz of conversation and clinking glasses; the nearest members were several tables away.

"I don't see our past as wrong. Of course the incident with Tristan is forever tainted, but the times we had in

Morocco and Greece—I'll never think of them as wrong," said Tony.

"Well, I do. I wish to God we'd never let our friendship cross that line. It wouldn't have if it weren't for that damned hashish the first time. And the time at my townhouse, I was out of my mind with worry over Lily's reaction to the letters. You took advantage of the drunken, emotional state I was in." He frowned accusingly at Tony. "Neither of us is that way. We both love our wives and children. We're normal men!"

"Speak for yourself," said Tony, peering into his glass.

"What do you mean?"

"I always knew I was different, Ian. From school age on, I would be attracted to some boy, usually older. Never acted on it. It shamed me in the extreme to have such longings. I recall the first time I saw you at Eton—I was drawn to you at once. Something in your eyes seemed to say, 'I'm like you. I understand!' "

"Well, you misread the message, believe me. I never even had a homosexual thought until that night we were so stoned on Moroccan hashish, with corruption and perversity all about us in that jaded world. All the barriers to behavior were broken down," said Ian agitatedly. He checked nervously again to see if anyone was showing interest in them.

"I remember when you'd play the piano, and we'd sit and listen, all your friends. You were so incomparably beautiful, a shaft of light falling through the window on your hair dark as crow's wings," said Tony, as if thinking aloud.

"Shut up. Don't speak like that. It makes me ill," Ian muttered over his teacup, his hands shaking.

"All the poems I wrote were for you. Oh, I'd disguise it with a reference here and there to a 'maid's ebony eye,' but it was always to you that I wrote," said Tony, smiling at him sadly.

"Jesus!" exclaimed Ian, his face a mask of revulsion.

"You once loved my poems. You were flattered, you said in your letters."

"Those cursed letters. They started all this."

"Ian, I don't understand how you could've forgotten that my letters were in that American lockbox where you'd put them. Something so inflammatory. And to ask Lily to close it out and bring you the contents while she was over there for her mother's illness? It's as if you had a deathwish. Or, subconsciously, you wanted her to find out about us."

"So you and I could be together? God, you're twisted, Tony. I simply forgot I'd put the damn letters in the box. I'm sure I thought I'd destroyed them."

Their luncheon arrived and the waiter poured them each a glass of white Bordeaux while Ian avoided Tony's eyes.

"I can't believe you could have forgotten their existence," continued Tony as soon as they were alone again.

"Perhaps I blotted them out of my memory because I wanted to forget them."

"And me?" There was pain etched in Tony's lined, but still strikingly handsome face.

"Since we've been friends for all these years, you could hardly think I wanted to forget you, Tony. Just the part of our relationship that should never have happened."

"That was the only truly honest period of our friendship, those few weeks when we were all those things to each other that our society forbids us to be."

"I told you when we broke it off, Tony, that I could not live that life. I wasn't going to end up like my poor brother, the object of jokes and scorn. I love women—

I am not homosexual! It's sick and disgusting to me, a weakness!

"If I hadn't been drunk and distraught over Lily kicking me out of the house over the letters, I certainly would never have let down my guard with you again. You took advantage of the state I was in, and now my only son thinks I'm a fraud and a pervert." Ian shoved aside his untouched plate and rested his head heavily in his hands.

"What in God's name am I going to do to put my family right again?"

"Since Lily is in London, why don't I have a chat with her? Tell her it was all a one-sided, youthful infatuation that got out of hand? That absolutely nothing has gone on since."

"That would be a lie, as Tristan knows only too well. If he should say one word to his mother, my marriage is over."

"Would that be the end of the world, Ian? Lily is a bit the bitch, you know. I can promise you that there are any number of younger women, just as attractive or more so, who would love to console you. You married Lily in a great rush, and frankly, she's led you by the nose ever since. She's nowhere near your class, and that has nothing to do with where she comes from."

"I love her! Have you never understood? Lily is the love of my life!"

Tony's expression changed subtly. "Love is blind. How trite but totally true."

"You never liked her because you see her as your rival. If I hadn't met my little ballerina, I might have come back to you. Don't delude yourself. That never would have happened. I see her faults, but her virtues far outweigh them. I can't imagine life without my Lily. She's been a perfect wife and mother, and she's never had any lover in her life but me. You must understand what a shock for her it was to read those very intimate letters. Which of course, honorably, she should not have done, but read them she did, and my marriage is in shreds."

"Ian, I don't mind lying to her. In a sense we've lived a lie the past quarter of a century, so what's one more little falsehood? Except for that once, nothing has gone on. I have no qualms at all about swearing that to her, if it will help you. I can't bear to think that I, of all people, have caused you this anguish. Please let me reason with her. We do respect one another at the very least. It would ease my guilt if you'd only let me try to undo the damage I've done."

"I don't want you to see Lily. If the truth be known, I really don't want to see you again myself, Tony."

"What do you mean, Ian?" Tony's face had lost its usual high color.

"Our friendship is forever marred by what my son saw. It's painful for me to even talk to you now. It's just over, Tony."

"You're overwrought. I'll honor your wishes, of course. I was going to Corfu in September anyway to write my book on Rupert Brook." Tony was the author of several well-received biographies of English poets. "I'm sure that by the time I return, your family crisis will have been resolved, and we can resume our friendship. Just that of course. I understand that."

"No, no! It's better for all of us if we just make a clean break of it, Tony. How could we even continue our friendship, when Lily and Tristan will see our every contact as suspect? For God's sake, just having lunch with you is terribly upsetting to me—I simply cannot handle it. We must cut it completely off." He chopped his hand through the air to illustrate.

"Ian, please. You can't mean that?" said Tony, his voice shaking.

"I do mean it. Believe it. I've got to go now."

"Wait!" Tony caught his arm. There were tears in his blue eyes.

"Don't make a scene, please!" said Ian, trying to pull away. "This isn't easy for me."

Tony held his arm fast. "Easy?" He laughed harshly. "Should it be easy? I've known and loved you for most of my life. Don't think you can brush me off like some bothersome trick you're tired of. You owe me more than this, Ian. What happened with Tristan hurts me as much as it does you, but it's not fair to blame me and punish me for it."

"I'm sorry. I'm just trying to survive, Tony. Let me go, for God's sake. If you care anything for me."

Tony eased his grip.

At this point, two diners took the table next to them, one of them smiling and nodding to Tony. The man seemed on the verge of speaking, but changed his mind when Tony failed to acknowledge him. "I'll never bother you again, Ian—if you really want it that way," he said.

"It's just the way I want it," said Ian, getting to his feet, desperate to be away from this embarrassing, emotional public scene.

"I see," said Tony softly. "So good-bye then, Ian." He drew himself up. "I won't embarrass you any further. I hope that all goes well for you." He turned away as Ian rushed off, almost bumping into the waiter.

"Sorry, sir," said the man in surprise as a wild-eyed Ian hurried past him.

"Would you care for a sweet or coffee, m'Lord?" the waiter asked Tony who was carefully examining a pink rose in a silver bud vase.

"No, thank you. There is absolutely nothing else you can do for me, Edward," said Tony without glancing up at him. The waiter removed the two untouched plates of sole.

"No one can help me now," said Tony aloud to himself.

✪ ✪ ✪

Lily and Karen sat in an alcove of the foyer of Claridge's Hotel sipping their drinks. "I adore this place. It's everything that's wonderful about England," said Karen, looking about the cavernous room, where in a single twelve-hour period, one might see almost everyone important in town, including the royals. This was the spot in London to see and be seen.

"And the music is so?. . ."

"Groovy!" supplied Lily, and they both giggled. They were referring to a chamber music group composed of three very old men and a cellist in his twenties playing most discreetly, nearby.

"The young one's rather cute. What in the world is he doing in a grandfathers' band?" commented Karen.

"One of them died. It was always four grandfathers for years," said Lily. The two of them burst into laughter again.

"Awful, can't help it!" gasped Karen. "Just think, in a few years the others will croak, and they'll hire three more twenty-year-olds to last them another seventy. Life goes on."

"Thank God, I've got you here to make me laugh. It's been mostly tears lately," said Lily, dabbing at her eyes.

"You said you needed me, Lily honey, so here I am. Laughing when you want to cry is the only sane way of getting through it. It's so divine to see you again. It always takes me back to the good old awful days when I didn't even have a Bergdorf's charge. It does take some getting used to, your talking so British, though. I feel like some British alien has taken over my old bud's body."

"It's me, I swear," said Lily. Karen's Texas accent was twangier than ever. "I'm afraid your other prescription for the blues, shopping, may land me in divorce court, if the other business doesn't. Ian is wonderfully generous with presents, but he hits the ceiling if I run the accounts up." She and Karen had enjoyed an exhilarating day on Bond Street updating Lily's wardrobe, which her friend, frank as ever, had told her was dowdy and out of date. Lily was wearing one of their purchases, a black linen retro-sixties chemise which stopped considerably shy of the knee. She'd at first been hurt by her friend's criticism, but had to admit that Karen, still dancer thin, looked fabulously chic and certainly knew the score on what was trendy. She had married a very wealthy Manhattan financier, seventeen years her senior, had no children, and devoted herself to staying young, working for fashionable charities, and lunching with the girls at Mortimer's and Le Cirque.

Under her friend's direction, the two of them had had massages, manicures, and facials. Lily had had her shoulder-length, blond hair highlighted and restyled into a more casual, tousled do which took years off her age, or so Karen said.

"You look fabulous, Lily. I never want to see you dress like an old lady again. You were always much prettier than me. Every man in here looked at you when we walked in."

"I thought they were looking at you," said Lily, highly pleased.

"Well, both of us then," said Karen. "We've still got these, don't we, honey?" she said, swinging a sleek leg across her knee. "One dividend from all the punishment we took."

"I've always done at least a half-hour barre everyday, but lately, I've really been pushing myself."

"It shows, darlin'. I take class four times a week myself." Karen narrowed her eyes at her. "Now all you need is your eyes fixed and a boob job, and you'll be able to pick any young stud your little ol' heart desires."

Lily choked on her drink. "Please! That's really not my thing, neither the silicone nor an affair."

"What do you want then, Lily?"

"I don't know! I suppose I just want it all to be as it was when Ian and I were first together—and for Tony Neville to never have existed! I know you think I've overreacted, but this thing has truly thrown me, Karen. It never entered my mind that Ian had that sort of problem."

"Not even when you couldn't get him into bed?"

"To think how we used to joke about that. It doesn't seem very funny now."

Karen patted her arm. "I'll tell you what I'd do. I'd believe him that it's all been platonic since, because he's a gorgeous, attractive man who loves you. And rich, if a bit stingy with the credit cards. He's a great father, and y'all live a wonderful life at Innismere—well, kinda dull for my tastes, but it suits you. I mean, Lily, there is always some sorta fly in the ointment, and this is just such a long ago, little fly. I love Arnie to death, but I'd trade places with you in a cotton-pickin' minute.

"If you only knew what I have to deal with. To have a man like Ian in your bed—those eyes, no pot belly! I want you to know that if you divorce a sexy guy like that, I'm not picky about who he's been to bed with."

"It just nauseates me to think that he was like Eric and Carlos in the company. I suppose I'm more prejudiced than I ever realized. It's also the deceit—Ian deceived me!"

"He did not. He just omitted telling you about Tony, and why the hell not? It's dumb to tell about past loves. Did you tell Ian that Alexei used to undress you with his eyes—and you loved it?"

"Karen!" They both laughed.

"I don't know. Maybe you're right, Karen. If I could just believe that they haven't been lovers all this time. Maybe I could live with it just being a mistake when Ian was as he says, 'too young and foolish to know better.'"

"Make yourself believe that, honey. Listen, the English ship their little baby boys off to boarding school when they're eight, segregate them off together, so of course it happens, adolescent hormones being what they are. They call it the 'English Vice' even. Ian may be Irish, but he's been raised as an Englishman. It's some sort of rite of passage for upper crust British males. I think they all do it, but they grow out of it, most of them anyway."

"How do I know he's grown out of it forever?"

"You don't really. However, I have very good radar for detecting any gay vibes, and Ian just doesn't give off any. Well, he's not exactly macho, but that's because he's English, and they never are unless they're working class. He's artistic and mild mannered, but still I know he likes women. Or 'woman.' It's the sweetest thing the way he looks at you, Lily. Like he can't believe that he's got this gorgeous creature for his very own. If someone would just look at me once the way Ian looks at you." Karen sighed. "Someone worth looking back at of course."

"He stopped looking at me like that years ago."

"I don't believe that. He's the kind who will gaze starry-eyed at you forever, until you hit him between the eyes with a ball pein hammer or something. Look, you asked my advice, Lily, and I'm telling you, learn to live with what happened and hang onto Ian because he's a prize that a girl doesn't get a shot at very often. Now of course if you should ever catch him in the sack with the stable-boy, you should kill the sonofabitch and take him for everything he's worth!"

Karen's attention turned to something over Lily's shoulder. "Oh, that can't be! Tell me that angelic dream of a young man over there isn't Tristan?" she exclaimed. Lily turned to see her son sauntering toward them.

"Mother," he said, bending to give Lily a kiss.

"Tristan, I can't believe it!" said Karen, standing and holding her hands out to him. He kissed her on both cheeks.

"How are you, Karen?"

"I'm stunned by the sight of you. You were just titty high the last time I saw you, and look at you now—too gorgeous!"

He laughed sheepishly. "Sorry I'm late. Had to work overtime."

"Your mama and I were just passing time waiting for you, darlin', and now I've got to go take a nap before dinner. We've had a killer of a day," said Karen, still clinging to him.

"Now, you've got to promise me that you'll let me take you to dinner before I go, just the two of us. I want to catch up on everything, your love life included."

"That would be great, Karen. I never turn down an invite to dine with a beautiful woman."

"Oh, shit. Just listen to him." She hugged him vigorously, leaving a red smear on his cheek, then went off to her room.

"Phew," said Tristan, sinking into her empty chair. "She must have on an entire bottle of perfume."

"But doesn't she look great?" said Lily.

"You're the one who looks great, Mum. Is your hair different?"

"Everything's different," she said, beaming at him.

"Cool dress, too."

"Karen's been doing me over. It's not too short, is it?"

"It's fantastic. I've never seen you look better, Mum, but don't get to be like Karen, please."

"Why not? She's wonderful!"

"Got that carnivorous look in her eye. I hope you're not going to turn into a man-eater like her."

"Tristan, she loves you like the child she never had. How can you be so unkind?"

"Easily. It's part of my new cynical persona. I've discovered that if you always expect the worst from everyone, you'll be ahead of the game." He took out a cigarette. "Do you mind?"

"I certainly do. When did you start smoking?"

He returned the packet to his T-shirt pocket. "Let's not get into it, Mother."

"And why couldn't you have worn something besides jeans and tennis shoes? This is an elegant place."

"Ahh, I haven't been nagged in so long, it's music to my ears. My hair's too long, too, don't you think?"

"I don't mean to nag, darling."

"I know it's your motherly duty, but why not take the evening off from it?"

"All right. Do you want a drink, a soda or something?" She signaled for the waiter who hurried over.

"Yes, my lady?"

"Nothing for me, thank you, James."

"A Guinness Harp, please," said Tristan crisply.

After the waiter had left, she smiled at him. "See, I'm not nagging about your drinking."

"Come on, Mum. You know you cannot not do it," he said with his perfect smile. Lily drank in the sight of her tall, blond son and thought that Karen had been exactly correct. He was an angelic dream, and so self-possessed. Somehow he had passed indefinably beyond the child he had been only a month before.

"So, how is your work going?" she asked, reaching out to smooth a dark, gold curl just for the physical contact.

"I'm learning a lot about technical aspects, developing and such, but I can't say as I'd enjoy taking pictures of soap powders and dog food all my life."

"Tristan, there's still time for you to change your mind. The fees have been paid, and Julian expects to room with you. How can you forgo an experience like Oxford to photograph dog food?"

"I'm just not ready for it now, Mother. I've been going to school forever, and I'm really enjoying learning about life for a change. I'm not going to alter my decision!" he said with an emphatic hand gesture that was his father exactly.

"All right, I'm not going to make a scene about this. Even if I am unbearably disappointed. If you're not ready for university just now, perhaps you will be later."

He looked at her in surprise. "You mean you've accepted my decision?"

"What else can I do? I understand what it means to be overly pushed by your parents. I was by my mother, although I see it from a different perspective now. I realize that she only wanted what she deemed best for me. At your age, I thought she wanted to live her life over through me. That was unfair to her, I think."

"Please talk to Dad about it. I thought he was going to have apoplexy when I told him."

"Can't you see his side of it, darling? You'll be in his shoes someday, don't you see, and he wants you to be prepared. Innismere is a huge responsibility, and it takes an education to enable you to make the money to maintain it. Unless you're Lord Snowden, you'll never do that taking pictures."

"Christ! That's the crux of it, isn't it? Why do I have to be saddled with this great white elephant? Will Tristan be the first D'Arcy in seven hundred years to blow it all? If only I didn't have this burden hanging over my life and could live normally. It's absurdly anachronistic and obscene. Give Innismere back to the Irish—it was theirs to begin with. It's all so inane, the baronetcy and that. Who cares, really? I'm no better than any other bloke."

"You of all of us have enjoyed Innismere, Tristan. I know you love it. You're always so happy to be home."

"I love it, but I don't deserve it. No one family does. Who needs a house with twenty rooms? And why should one work one's brains out to keep it up as Dad does? It makes no sense to me."

"I've never heard you talk like this in your life. Have you become a Communist?" The waiter appeared with the beer on a silver tray.

When he'd left, Tristan replied, "I've just opened my eyes to what goes on in the real world, Mother. I've always been so protected from anything unpleasant. This summer on my own has opened my eyes to what shitty lives most people lead. And it's worse in Ireland with over 17 percent unemployment while we live like fucking royalty. It's disgusting!"

"Watch your language."

"Sorry, but it's the truth."

"Has this new girlfriend got anything to do with this Bolshevik attitude of yours?"

"Violet's been talking to you, I see. Bella is not a Commie. She's not at all political."

"But she *is* working class, a waitress I understand?"

"You're such a flaming snob, Mother!"

"How could I be? I'm hardly a blue-blood myself. It does make me suspect your newfound sympathy for the downtrodden masses, though, Tristan." He grimaced and shook his head.

"Violet tells me the girl is very pretty and is going into modeling, so at least she wants to improve herself."

"We decided she shouldn't get involved in that artificial world," said Tristan airily.

"Waiting tables is more real?"

"Yes. Mother, can we talk about something else? Such as you and Dad. Are you getting a divorce?"

"We're just taking a bit of time off from each other. It happens at some point in every long marriage, I imagine."

"Is divorce an option?"

"I don't know. I am trying to decide what is best for all of us. It seems to me that just our separation has done a tremendous amount of harm to you in particular, Tristan."

"It has nothing to do with me," he said and took a big gulp of Guinness. "It's between you and Dad alone."

"Whatever we decide, it will affect all of us, Violet and you especially."

"Don't worry about me, Mum. Don't even consider me. Vi and I have our own lives now. We're adults."

Lily frowned. "Tristan, you do want your father and me to stay together, don't you? You were so terribly upset about us before."

"Just do what you think is best for you. If you don't love him anymore, divorce him. If you still do, then stay."

"You're not taking his side any longer?"

"I'm not taking sides, period. I have no right. You have to live and sleep with him, so you decide." He finished off his beer and jumped to his feet.

"Sorry, but I've got to meet someone, Mother."

"But I planned on taking you to dinner. I haven't seen you in so long, darling. I promise, no nagging."

"I'd like to stay, but I really can't. I'm late, and as you pointed out, I'm dressed like a derelict."

Lily stood up and they embraced. "Please come back later for dinner, darling. You're all bones."

"I've always been all bones. I'm a D'Arcy, aren't I?" He smiled down at her. "You look beautiful, Mum. I'll see you before you leave."

"You'd better. I want to see where you live and meet this girl."

"The Commie? My flat's rather basic—don't think you'd like it. I'm just a working class bloke now."

"Oh, Trissy, I love you so much and miss you desperately." Her eyes misted over. When he hugged her again, she noticed that he felt very much like his father in her arms.

"I love you and miss you, too, Mother. Don't worry about me. I'm happier than I've been in ages." He pecked her on the cheek and was away, half loping over the marble floor to the entrance.

He let himself in the rear door of the studio and called her name. No answer, but the light was on in the room that served as their flat. Bella was dancing by herself wearing headphones and her ripped and hideous dressing gown; her hair was freshly washed. She neither saw nor heard him as he came up behind her and shrieked loudly when he grabbed her about the waist.

"Tris, I nearly had a seizure!" she gasped.

"Mmm, you smell clean," he said, nuzzling her neck.

"What?" She pulled off the earphones. He slid his hand inside her robe.

"I said you smell clean, and you feel like heaven."

"I'm as clean as I can get in a wash basin." She turned in his arms to kiss him.

"We'll go to Vi's tomorrow and borrow the shower,"

he said, maneuvering her over to the mattress on the floor. They fell in a heap across it.

"What are you doing?" She giggled.

"I'm famished for you. It's been an eternity since this morning." He opened the robe and rubbed his cheek across her bare breasts. Bella ran her fingers through his hair and closed her eyes.

"How was your visit with your mother?"

"Shh," he said, stripping off his clothes. He lowered himself slowly on top of her. She kissed him and wrapped her long legs about him.

"I love you, Tris."

"I want to fuck you," he said, and kissed her deeply.

"Get your arms out of that damned, ugly thing." He helped her free of the dressing gown and they rolled together across the mattress. He reached under it and pulled out a foil packet.

"You do the honors," he said.

Bella took the condom out of the package, sat up, and put it on him.

He moved on top of her. "Home at last," he sighed. "You're always so ready for me, Bella, and you feel so good, even with this damn plonker on." He moved slowly, eyes closed. Hers were open, a beatific smile on her face. It was such a wonderful thing to watch how he loved it!

"I can't hold it," he groaned. She dug her nails into his buttocks and pressed up against him.

They lay in each others' arms. He kissed her nose. "I can't wait 'til you're on the pill and I can stop using these damn things," he said, removing the condom.

"I should be able to start soon." Bella was very vague about when her next period was due.

"You might already be pregnant," he said.

"But we're so careful every time."

"Except that first one that caught us rather unprepared. It only takes one good shot."

"Surely we couldn't be that unlucky."

"I could be. It's been a trend lately," he said, giving her a kiss and getting up to go to the bathroom.

When he returned, Bella studied him as he walked naked over to get a cigarette from his shirt pocket. He lit it and dropped down beside her.

She skimmed her hand over his pale-skinned body. "You're so pretty, Tris. I didn't know a boy could be so pretty."

He frowned as he exhaled a long stream of smoke. "You make me sound a poufter."

"I meant a compliment. You look like a Grecian statue in the National Gallery, only your skin is soft and warm." She kissed a mole near his nipple. "I thought boys were thick and rough."

"Like Billy Connery?"

She lay back on the rumpled mattress. "I wish I'd never told you about him."

"So do I."

"You never tell me about your old girlfriends."

"Too many to recall."

"Just the very first you made love to."

"I was too drunk to remember."

"Even her name?" She tickled him under his arm.

"Stop that! It is very unwise to kiss and tell. I hate Billy, and I've never even met the poor bloke." Billy was the boy who had loved Bella even when she was a head taller than he. She'd finally given in and rewarded him for his faithfulness the night before she left for London.

She hugged Tristan. "You know you're the first real one, Tris. All poor Billy did was hurt me and come so fast, it was over before it had started. All I could think with him lying heavy as lead on top of me was, 'Is this what everyone's so batty about?' I was never so let down by anything. The first time I ever made love was with you."

"You're the best of the myriad girls I've done it with, bella Bella. The best and the most beautiful, and I love you as well, which makes all the difference."

She cuddled next to him and watched his profile as he smoked. "Let's go dancing tonight. I'm really in the mood, aren't you?"

"I've only got two pounds 'til Monday," he said, putting out his cigarette in an ashtray on the floor.

"I made twenty-five pounds in tips today. We can afford it. Jimmy gave me some salad, so that takes care of dinner." Jimmy was a Jamaican cook at the restaurant who had a crush on Bella. "Come on, Tris. I feel like having fun," she said, sliding a long leg over his thigh.

"The most fun we have is absolutely free, and we don't have to leave the room."

"Please, Tris," she wheedled.

"Oh, all right, if you really want to."

"Brilliant! Let's go back to that place in Soho that had the great band."

"Anything for you, my dove. Only don't get the skinheads worked up this time. Don't wear anything sexy. Your dressing gown is perfect. It will keep the wolves at bay."

"It doesn't keep you at bay."

"Actually, it turns me on. To think that such beauty is underneath such hideousness."

Over their salad, Bella told him the manager was after her to switch to the night shift.

"Has he been behaving himself? No more feeling you up outside the Gents?"

"No, I made it clear that if he ever tried anything again, there'd be no little Joneses in future. He's on me all the time now, though. Just waiting for a chance to give me notice. Too bad that modeling thing didn't work out. I'd adore telling him to stick his bloody job."

"You really wouldn't have liked that world, Bella. It's for the best."

She put on a pair of his jeans and a baggy sweatshirt. Tristan looked at her and shook his head. "It's hopeless. You're even sexy in that getup. The harder you try not to be, the worse it gets." He sighed. "There'll be another riot in Soho tonight."

She slid her hands in his back pockets. "I'll tell them to bugger off. I already have as much man as I can handle."

He smoothed back her vivid hair, fluffy from air drying. "I'm going to marry you, Bella Malone."

Before they left, she let in the huge, ragged-eared tomcat that lived in the alley and gave it a bowl of milk. The problem with sleeping on the floor was the mice that scampered over them in the dark. Tris had set traps about, but they made a horrid racket when they went off, and Bella got hysterical over the little, squashed bodies in the morning. She insisted a cat was more humane.

Tristan locked the studio door behind them. They had to find a real flat before it turned cold, one with a bathtub and a nice, big bed. Arms about each other, Bella and Tristan went off into the damp night.

✢ ✢ ✢

Ian removed the foil from a frozen sole almondine dinner and stuck it in the microwave. The fish reminded him of the upsetting scene at White's with Tony several days ago. He'd been a damn fool to go there with him. He'd thought that by eating in the members' dining room instead of a private room as Tony had planned, Tony would keep himself under control. Which he had done to a point, though he'd spouted all that fag garbage anyway. Ian shuddered at the memory of the love brimming in his friend's blue eyes. It had been Ian himself who had lost control and made something of a scene storming out like that. He'd seen Harry Broughton's startled face when he'd fled past his table. Surely they would figure it out— a lovers' tiff. Ian closed his eyes. As far as he knew, he and Tony had managed to keep their past relationship between themselves. Except for the two most important people in his life, his wife and his son. He groaned aloud in torment.

A buzzer announced that his meal was ready. He poured himself a tall glass of whiskey to accompany it and sat at the kitchen table of his Belgravia flat. He was getting awfully tired of restaurant and packaged dinners. He missed Mary's good, simple, wholesome food, and Lily's more gourmet meals. She'd taken that cordon bleu class and was really quite a cook. He threw down his fork and took a large swallow of whiskey. What was she doing tonight? Having a gay old time with Karen at Claridge's? Picking up tips on how to wear too much makeup, talk and laugh too loudly, and make eyes at other women's husbands? Every time he'd been around her American friend, the woman had all but put her hand down his pants. Couldn't Lily see what she was? Had she told Karen about the letters? An unbearable thought! He speared a limp broccoli stem and put it in his mouth. Lukewarm, tasteless rubber. He ate hungrily anyway.

Afterward, he poured himself another tumbler of Jamesons and went into the drawing room. He was used to being in the flat alone while attending to his London shop, but tonight the empty place seemed almost unbearable. For company, he put on Von Karajan and the Berlin Philharmonic playing Beethoven's Third. Lily had used to come with him to London often, and they'd had good

times here. Once, she'd liked traveling with him on his
forays for pictures, and they'd managed to combine business with pleasure. Then she'd got caught up in the children's activities and her charities and had stayed at home
more and more. Art people were boring, she said. Lily
was right that they'd grown apart over the years. If only
he didn't have to travel so damn much. Perhaps if he
closed one of the shops there would be more time for his
family. But then, it had always been a dream of his to have
Tristan come in the business with him and run the Dublin gallery. Were they too estranged now for that ever to
be a possibility?

He heard the phone ring over the music. Lily? He
turned down the stereo and picked up the receiver hopefully. It was Tony.

"I apologize for embarrassing you at the club," he said,
his voice noticeably slurred.

"What do you want?" Ian asked tersely.

"I can't believe you really meant what you said, Ian.
About not seeing me ever again even as friends."

"Believe it, Tony. I'm sorry it has to be like that, and
that I told you so bluntly, but my family comes first. It's
a matter of survival."

"It's so unneccessary, Ian."

"I'm not going to argue with you, Tony. I either have
to give up you or my wife and son."

"No contest, eh? I'd give up anything on this earth for
you Ian."

"If you talk like that, I'm going to hang up."

"All right, damn it, I'll be like you and button up my
true feelings—hide from reality."

"I'm going to hang up now, Tony. I'm very tired."

"Very well, I'll let you go. Just answer one thing for
me—will you do that, Ian?"

"Yes," he sighed.

"Promise me you'll tell the truth for once, you owe me that at least. Did you save my letters because they were precious to you? Did you love me then, Ian?" Tony's voice cracked with its burden of emotion.

"I told you I forgot about the cursed letters. What we had was youthful curiosity and fondness, of course, but it was wrong. I'm ashamed even to think about those days. You see what has happened with Lily as some sort of subconscious, homosexual wish fulfillment on my part. I see it as divine retribution for my sins. It was the mistake of my life, and I'm paying through the nose for it now."

There was dead silence on the line. "Tony?"

"Good-bye, Ian. I'll never bother you again," he whispered and the line went dead.

"Damn!" said Ian. Why did Tony have to make him feel guilty if he did and guilty if he didn't? "Leave me the hell alone!" he shouted. Suddenly he realized he was sitting on the very couch where he and Tony had been together on that fateful afternoon when his son had unsuspectingly walked in on them. The look of incredulous shock on the boy's face was an image he'd never be able to purge from his memory. He jumped up and turned the stereo on full blast. "I am not like Tony!" he told himself as the music swirled deafeningly about him.

The next morning, Ian was just going out the door when the phone rang. It was George Whitby, an old friend from Oxford days.

"Have you heard the news, Ian?"

"What news?" asked Ian, checking his watch. He was going to be late for an appointment.

"Tony Neville. He's smashed up in a car crash."

"What? How bad was it?"

"He's dead, old boy. Too tragic. I only saw him the other day at the club."

"Tony is dead?" repeated Ian, the full meaning of the words refusing to penetrate his brain.

"Yes. Bunty Montgomery just rang me to tell me. A single vehicle accident quite early this morning. He was going up to the country and seems to have lost it. Ran dead on into a tree. Killed instantly."

Ian caught hold of the door frame to steady himself. "Anyone else hurt?" he managed to ask.

"No, he was alone, luckily. I imagine he must have fallen asleep at the wheel. Not really much of a drinker, old Tony. Can't quite figure out why he was traveling so late."

Ian fought to control his emotions.

"I say, are you all right, old boy? Know the two of you have always been great chums."

"It's a huge shock," he managed to say. "Thank you for calling, George. I must go."

"Yes, surely. We'll all be up for the services. See you there, then. Very sad business. Tony was one of the most charming people I've ever known."

Ian hung up the phone and sat heavily in a chair, his heart racing. It couldn't be. He'd told Tony he never wanted to see him again, and now he never would. Then it hit him—Tony had sounded in bad shape on the phone the night before. Was it an accident? It *had* to have been an accident.

The car park of Wycliffe Castle was already full when Ian arrived. Fitzgivens, the butler, a small man of huge dignity, greeted him somberly. He informed Ian that the countess had been sedated but wished him to come up to see her.

"How is she holding up?" Ian asked as he followed the butler up the broad staircase.

"Remarkably. Her Ladyship has been up since three

this morning, but she made arrangements for the funeral, saw to the menu for the expected guests, and only then did she allow her physician to give her medication," said Fitzgivens, who was more aristocratic in manner than most lords Ian knew.

"And the children?"

"They are in the blue salon with their friends, and are, of course, terribly saddened. The earl was a great family man, as you know, Sir Ian."

Another epitaph, thought Ian with growing queasiness. Tony Neville, charming company and a great father. All true and all obscene to hear.

Anne was lying fully dressed on her bed. She removed a wet cloth from her eyes, almost swollen shut from crying, and held her hand out to Ian. He kissed it. She patted the bed for him to sit. To his great horror, Ian found himself unable to speak; tears filled his eyes embarrassingly.

"So sorry," was all he could manage to say.

"I know you are, Ian," said Anne, rubbing his cold hand between her warm ones. "No one loved Tony like you and I did. Don't be ashamed to cry. I've just done so for a half hour. Had to hold it back 'til then. So much to do." Her voice was slurred, but she seemed in full control.

Ian got out his handkerchief. "I keep thinking perhaps it's a mistake of some sort."

"I know. I had the same mad thoughts, but Fitzgivens identified the body, poor soul. I just couldn't. His face was smashed, his beautiful face." She held a trembling hand to her mouth, and Ian broke down. Anne put her arms about him.

"Poor darling. This may be even harder for you than it is for me. How shall we ever live without him?"

Feeling heartily ashamed of himself for taking more comfort from Anne than he had been able to give her,

Ian washed his face and went down to speak to the children. Julian and his sisters, Ione and Helena, were being very brave—proper, well-trained, upper class English children that they were. Ione, the youngest, burst into tears, and embraced him which set his cursed emotions off again.

A somber crowd of relatives and friends were feeding their long faces at an elegant buffet and bar. There were more glowing tributes for poor, departed Tony.

Anne insisted Ian spend the night in his regular rooms. Lily had called, she said, sounding very bad and suffering from a high fever. Anne would not hear of her ruining her health by trying to come up for the service. There would be plenty of time later for the two friends to get together.

Ian had a difficult time listening to this, as he knew that Lily was perfectly well. Before leaving London, he'd rung to tell her about the accident and had asked her to drive with him to Wycliffe for the burial. Lily had flatly refused to come, saying that she simply could not fake grief that his lover was dead. Ian couldn't recall a time when she'd let him down worse than that.

Tristan was at the funeral, standing beside Julian. Ian appreciated that his son at least had a sense of honor stronger than his personal discomfiture. After the brief, dry, Anglican service and burial, Ian sought the boy out and told him how pleased he was that he'd come.

"I'm here for Julie; he's my friend," said Tristan, looking thin and vulnerable in the bleak October sun. "Mother was ill," he added, defensive of her.

Ian offered him a ride home, hoping for the chance to talk at long last, but Tristan said he had a train ticket and someone waiting for him at the station.

"The pretty, ginger-haired girl I'm hearing about?"

"Yes, Bella. She'd never met any of the family and was afraid she might be intruding, so she rode up with me and waited at the station."

"She must care for you very much, Tris. I'd like to meet her."

The boy shrugged. "I'm sure you shall someday, Dad. I've got to go on now with Julian."

Encouraged by this civil exchange with his son, the first such since the incident, Ian put his hand on Tristan's thin shoulder. Tony's sudden death had brutally brought home to him the whimsicality of fate. He could not bear to go on a moment longer with this terrible breach between himself and his only son. "I love you, Tris," was on his tongue, but the look in the boy's eyes stopped him.

Tristan flinched away as if his father's touch repelled him. "Must go with Julie," the boy repeated.

"Of course. Poor lad. He needs his friends most of all at this terrible point in his life."

Tristan smiled at him disconcertingly. "I think Julian's lucky. Now he'll never have to know what his father really was. . .will he?" His son's black, D'Arcy eyes burned at him, full of reproach; Ian felt the blood rush to his face. Tristan ducked his head and turned away.

People were still at the castle getting their last plate and glassful. Anne went round and spoke to each to thank them. She was amazing, as everyone remarked. She took Ian aside and had him follow her up to her bedroom. Taking a key, she unlocked an exquisitely carved, oriental box.

"I received an envelope in the mail this morning, postmarked the day he died. Inside was a letter to me and a separate, sealed one to you, Ian." She took a letter and a larger folder from the oriental box and handed it to him. He stared dumbly at his name scrawled in Tony's hand on the front of the envelope.

"I haven't read mine, yet, but I know in my heart what it must say. I didn't think I could play the brave widow through the funeral if I did read it. As soon as everyone has left, I shall get a very stout glass of whiskey and open it. The folder contains your letters to him. I found them in his safe when I was going through his papers. Of course I did not read them. I thought you would want them."

Ian stood there in total confusion. He was going to be forced to face what he had known in his heart the instant he had heard of Tony's death. He had hoped against hope that he'd be able to avoid this terrible truth for the rest of his life, but Tony was not going to allow him that. His final revenge.

Anne took his hand. "Tony told me about the two of you before we were married, Ian. There, don't panic, love! This is very brutal what he's done to us, but don't feel guilty. I shan't, because I was never able to make him love me enough to forget you. He warned me from the outset, you know, that he was the sort of person who could only love once, and the once was you. I thought I could change him by my sheer devotion, but of course he knew himself better than I did. I imagine he's put it more kindly in the letter. Tony was always very kind." Ian suddenly felt all his strength sapped from him; he looked about for a chair. Anne took his arm and helped him to a seat, then got them both a brandy.

"I've sometimes thought, Ian, that if your affair had run its course instead of ending abruptly while he was still so consumed by you, that you'd never have become such an obsession with him. No normal passion would have lasted all these years unrequited. I don't know what drove him finally to this, but it certainly was through no fault of ours. You couldn't return his love, just as Tony could never fully return mine. At least I think he did care for me as much as he could any woman."

"He loved and admired you greatly, Anne. Tony always said that," said Ian hollowly.

"Yes, I think he did. We were happier than most couples I know. Our anniversary is in a week." Tears filled her eyes. "We had wonderful years and three fine children. I'm thankful for that, even if he could never feel the passion for me that I felt for him." She sipped her brandy; Ian had finished his.

"Tony was increasingly withdrawn the past month or so. He wouldn't tell me what was bothering him. He kept postponing going to Corfu. I assumed it had to do with the new book; writer's block or something. I only wish I had understood the depths of his despair. If he'd only given me a chance to help him. . .if he'd talked about the pain he was in!" Tears streamed unheeded down her cheeks.

She picked up a silver-framed photo from her bedside. "Tony was so handsome. I'm sure everyone thought he married plain me for the money, but that wasn't entirely true. We honestly liked and respected each other, which is more than most married couples can say."

"He used to say what a lucky man he was to have you, Anne."

As Ian took his leave of her, Anne said, "Promise me you won't feel guilty, Ian. He was a very sane man. He made his decision and did what he wanted to do."

Ian drove like a demon back to London with the letter burning against his chest. He did not let himself look at the scarred oak where Tony had chosen to end his life.

When Ian arrived back at the flat, he found the lights burning. He decided he'd probably forgotten to switch them off before he left so hastily for Wycliffe. Dropping his case on the hall floor, he headed for the liquor cabinet. He poured a tumbler of Jamesons, took a large swallow, and gratefully felt the smooth, burning liquid slide down his throat to sear his empty stomach.

"Ian?" He started in surprise at the sight of Lily in the doorway.

"What the hell are you doing here?"

"I stayed here last night. It was so horribly expensive without Karen to split the room."

"As always, the frugal, considerate wife," he said, pouring himself another glass of whiskey.

"Was it terrible?"

He didn't answer. Carefully he took off his coat and jacket and draped them over a chair. He loosened his tie and sank down on the sofa. "Anne thought it wonderful of you to offer to come when you were at death's door. She hopes you're feeling better."

"I was a rotten coward. The thought of it just panicked me. You know how funerals terrify me."

"I thought you were going back to Ireland."

She came over to the sofa. "I stayed because I felt badly about letting you down. I should have been there beside you at such a terrible moment."

Ian sighed heavily and rubbed his face with his hands. "Tristan was there. I really appreciated that. He was almost friendly to me."

"He's very confused just now. He never would let me come near his flat or this girlfriend, which seemed suspicious."

"She rode up with him to Wycliffe but stayed at the station. Didn't want to intrude on the family grief. Sounds like a sensitive girl."

"Much more sensitive than I. Ian, I've been such a fool to have hysterics over something that happened forever ago. Karen thought I was being very silly. Yes, I did tell her. She's my only real friend, and I needed her advice. Karen said I'd be an idiot to give up on such a man as you. You're not a liar, so I believe you that nothing has gone on between you and Tony since you married me. I understand it's quite common for English boys to have some sort of experience like that in school. Can you forgive me for having doubts about you?" Ian buried his head in his hands.

"I lost it when I read those letters. Tony worshipped you—I've no doubt he did 'til the day he died. For a long time I've felt that your passion for me was cooling, Ian. It was so strong at first, like Tony's passion. I guess those sort of overwhelming feelings just can't last. I wanted to hurt you for ever loving anyone but me like that."

His dark eyes were bloodshot and full of pain. "You are the only one I've ever really loved, Lily. How could you ever have doubted that?" She reached out to him. His arms went about her, his face pressed against her belly.

"Last night here alone without you, I felt so ashamed of myself for not going to the funeral with you, Ian. Such a terrible thing for you to lose him suddenly like that—whatever he was to you. And lying to Anne when she would have been the first to help me had it been you. I had a terrible time sleeping with such a guilty conscience. Anyway, about three this morning, I got up and made myself some weak tea and sat there thinking. Rehashed everything—the letters, the way we seemed to be growing apart even before I read them. I came to the conclusion that our marriage is my life's work, and I'll be damned if I'll give up on it just because a few problems crop up. We've got twenty-one years between us, and the children, and as you said, that's really something important and worth fighting for. So, you're not perfect after all. Well, neither am I, so why should I expect you to be? If our relationship had gone a bit stale, I'm just as guilty as you are. You've been busy with your work, and I've been busy with the house and other silly things while neither of us has been tending to the most important thing—our marriage, you know?

"It was really beautiful with us at first though, wasn't it, Ian?" He tightened his embrace in response. Lily ran her fingers through his hair. "I want it to be again. And I'm going to do everything I can to make it so, because I do love you and I think you truly love me. You must help me though, darling. We must do more things together like we used to, instead of each being caught up in our own world, don't you think?"

"Yes, yes! I'm sorry, so incredibly sorry for ever causing you pain. You and the children are the most important things in my life, and I'll do anything to keep you. I've needed you so, Lily. I've always needed you!" he murmured into the folds of her skirt. She embraced him and kissed the top of his head.

"I've missed you, too, my darling. It's so lonely at home without you!" She bent to kiss him, and he slid his hands under her skirt. His fingers rubbed between her legs, then tugged at her pantyhose. She heard them rip.

"Ian?" she gasped.

"Lie down!" he commanded, standing up to unfasten his belt. She lay back on the sofa and watched him undress. His face was strange and unsmiling as he hovered above her; she felt the same delicious fear as the first time she'd seen him naked. With trembling hands, she unfastened her silk blouse, then her brassiere. His eyes glittered at the sight of her breasts. This was an Ian she'd never seen before, and she wanted him badly.

She held her arms out to him, and he sank down on her with a groan. She kissed him wildly as he roughly shoved up her skirt. She'd never seen him in such a rush, and his fever caught fire in her.

"Yes, hurry!" she cried.

After a few moments of fumbling, he lay still on top of her.

"Ian, what's wrong?"

He sat up, and to her intense disappointment, she saw that his erection was waning. She moved to touch him, but he stopped her.

"Don't. It won't do any good." He covered his face and his arm shook. "That's never happened to me before."

She put her arms around him. "No wonder with all you've been through today." Stroking his temple where silver mingled with black, she said, "I'm sure this would happen to any man under such stress. You've just buried your best friend—had to bear up in front of his family, and I wasn't even there to help you get through it."

"It was the worst day of my life," he said with a shudder.

"I know it must have been, darling. What you really need now is a lovely, hot bath, which I'll go draw for you. Then a massage, and after that, I'll heat up the dinner I've made for us—a cassoulet, your favorite. We'll eat and talk and relax by the fire with a bottle of claret. Just like old times."

"I love you, Lily. Don't ever leave me again," he said in a broken voice. She hugged him to her breast.

Innismere

❂ ❂ ❂

EVEN THOUGH THEY'D spent the past two weeks being pampered at their favorite French and Italian hotels, Lily was excited to see Innismere floating in a silver, November mist on their return. Before they got out of the car, Ian pulled her across the seat for a long kiss. It had been a second honeymoon, and despite their aborted initial reunion, Ian had proved that he hadn't lost all his old fervor. Lily was confident that their problems were all behind them now and felt a guilty relief that her "rival" was no longer in the picture.

Seamus Kelly, the butler who had served Ian's father, crept out to greet them. Ian carried the heaviest bags himself, as Kelly was too old and arthritic to be much more than decoration. He was also quite deaf. Yet when Lily had suggested they retire him, Ian was adamant. "Kelly will buttle 'til he drops," he'd insisted. "It wouldn't be Innismere without him. Besides, a deaf servant has its advantages." They'd turned up the volume on the downstairs' phones and the buzzer in the kitchen; everyone jumped whenever the phone rang, but Kelly could still barely hear it. He did have a hearing aid, but refused to turn it on because it made him hear "noises."

Ian carried on a shouting match with the old man about the condition of things in their absence. Everything was grand, he assured them, and there was a surprise waiting for them in the drawing room. Kelly grinned from ear to ear, but refused to give them a clue as to who or what it might be.

There was a roaring fire in the drawing room fireplace, and standing to greet them were Tristan and a very pretty, tall, red-haired girl. Lily embraced her son. "Darling, we tried calling you a dozen times and finally found out you'd left your job. Violet had no idea where you were. We were terribly worried."

"Sorry, Mum, I didn't know where to reach you. How was your trip?" He held out his hand to his father.

"Splendid! It's wonderful to see you home, son. I see you've brought your friend whom we've heard so much about."

Tristan smiled at the girl who looked ready to faint from nerves. "Mother, Dad, this is Bella." Her hand felt cold as ice despite the blast of heat from the fire.

"Welcome to Innismere, my dear," said Ian, with a warm smile.

"How long are you here for, Tristan?" asked Lily. "It would be wonderful if you could stay over Christmas."

"At least. You see, Bella and I were married last week, and since neither of us has a job or a pot to piss in, you may be saddled with us for a while."

"Married?" said Lily with a nervous laugh. "Tristan, you do love to tease."

"It's not a joke, Mother." He held up his hand to show the gold band. Bella wiggled her fingers and shyly admired her matching one.

Lily looked at Ian who appeared as nonplussed as she. "Son, why would you take such an important step without telling your family?" he asked.

"I knew you would never approve. It's done now, so you'll just have to accept it."

"Tristan, you're underage. This girl must be, too. What did her parents have to say?"

"I met her father and relatives, and he gave her written permission. We went up to Scotland to do it since I didn't have your consent."

"Tristan, I wish you'd given us as much consideration as you did Bella's parents," said Ian.

"You were gallivanting about Europe, and we wanted to get married then. Besides, it would only have caused another family trauma. I knew exactly what you'd say—what you're saying now. You forget you were only two years older, Mother, and had just known each other a few months when you got married."

"The difference being your father was older, graduated from university, and very able to support a family," said Lily.

"It would have been much wiser to have waited a few years, Tris," his father added.

"Well, we haven't waited! I don't believe in waiting when you've found exactly what you're looking for. Bella and I love each other, so we got married. It seems very simple and right to me."

"And foolish!" snapped Lily.

Ian put his hand on her shoulder. "Can we at least sit and calmly discuss this?" Everyone sat, rigid and tense as wire. "Shall I ring Kelly for tea?"

"No, Dad," said Tristan, looking as stubborn and set on having his way as he'd ever done as a little boy. Bella's hand in his showed white knuckles as she looked nervously at their somber faces.

"To hell with tea, I need a drink," said Lily. Ian got up and fixed them both one.

"Bella, I hope you understand we are in no way personally disapproving of you," said Ian. "If Tris loves you, I'm sure you're a very fine person. It's the sudden shock of this, you understand."

"Oh, yes sir, I do. My da was in shock, too, at first. He looks on me as a baby still, you know. But he liked Tristan so much, and he could see how happy I am." She beamed at Tris, and he smiled encouragement. "I was so afraid you'd be upset since you didn't know me from Adam, and the age thing."

Ian smiled at her. She was very appealing in her patent eagerness to smooth over the tense, family scene. "So, Bella, tell us a bit about yourself. You're from Yorkshire, I understand?"

"Yes, sir. There's not that much to tell, really. My father came to Liverpool from Belfast at eighteen and joined the Royal Navy. I went to school and such in Yorkshire, where my mother's family was from, while he was away at sea most of the time. I came to London a few months ago and met Tris, and well, here we are," she said with a nervous giggle.

"What did your mother think about your marrying a boy you hardly knew?" asked Lily.

Bella knit her straight, red brows together. "She doesn't know, actually. She and my father separated when I was small. My aunt raised me."

"They're divorced?"

"Da's Catholic. She's been gone fourteen years. They might as well be."

"Did Tristan meet you through that rather peculiar photography business with Alistair Amboy?" Lily pressed.

"Well, sort of. Tris came in this restaurant where I was working. I served him an omelet and salad, and we liked each other right off. He and his friend, who I didn't like in the least, took some pictures of me, and I tried to get into modeling, but it didn't work out," said Bella.

"Why not? You're a beautiful girl and the proper height for a model," Ian commented. Lily gave him a look.

"This really famous fashion photographer saw my pictures, but he didn't think I could make it because of my hair. Red clashes too much with the clothes or distracts or something. I never thought about it before, but you hardly ever see redheaded models in magazines. And I'd have to get my teeth fixed, too."

"She'd have to turn herself into someone else, and we just didn't think it was worth it," Tristan interjected. "Her hair and her teeth are probably the two things I love best about her." Bella smiled to herself.

"So, you've come home to live off your father. Is that what this all boils down to?" said Lily.

"I assumed you'd be pleased to have me, since you've begged me often enough. Was I wrong, Mother?"

She stood up. "You know I'm always glad to have you home. I just wish it were under different circumstances. If you all will excuse me, I have a splitting headache."

Ian and Tristan stood as she left the room.

"We really are very tired. Traveling about for weeks takes its toll. I think I'll go on up and rest as well." Ian took Tristan's hand. "Congratulations, son, you have excellent taste. Again, welcome to Innismere, Bella. We're more than pleased to have you two stay here indefinitely. I want you to think of Innismere as your home."

"Thank you, Mr. D'Arcy. I'm so excited to be here. Da's always told me about Ireland."

"Kildare's a tad more peaceful than County Antrim. There's not much excitement hereabouts except for the racing."

"Tristan showed me your beautiful horses, Mr. D'Arcy. I can't wait to see them run."

"Please call me Ian, Bella. See you two at dinner, then."

As soon as he was out of the room, Tristan collapsed on the sofa. "Thank God that's over!" He pulled Bella into his lap. "Give us a kiss then, Mrs. D'Arcy."

She did so enthusiastically. "How could you ever be cross with your father, Tris? He's lovely, and his eyes are just like yours."

"He's okay," said Tristan. Since economic necessity had forced him to come home, he was going to have to come to terms with his feelings about his father. Even if he had lost respect, he did still love him. He had no idea if his mother knew about Uncle Tony, but he doubted it. Surely she would have been too disgusted to reconcile with his dad if she did. He for one would never tell her. Tony was dead now and it was best to just forgive and forget, if that was at all possible.

"Your mother thinks I'm common as dirt. I could see that right off," said Bella.

"She's just miffed because she's no longer the most beautiful woman in the family." Tristan palmed her breast.

"Don't! The butler might walk in!"

"He can't see this far."

She giggled. "How old is he?"

"Eighty at least. His wife is a mere girl of seventy-five."

"Poor old things. I hope we're never that old and sad, Tris."

"I plan on it. The question is, will you still love me when I'm deaf and wear a toupee?" Kelly wore an eye-riveting, most unnatural looking jet-black hairpiece which contrasted sharply with his own white fringe sticking out below. It was part of his butlering uniform; he clapped it on whenever the buzzer rang.

"Yes, I'll love you even then. . .I think. But what can I do to make your mother like me?"

"Simply be your adorable self. She won't be able to resist for long."

"I suppose it's because I've stolen away her beautiful baby boy. I've heard mothers-in-law are like that."

"Don't worry about her. Dad's taken a fancy to you, and even Kelly snaps out of his rigor mortis when you're about."

"I want everyone to think I'm the perfect girl for you, Tris."

"As you are, so the rest of the world be damned." He tipped her chin up and kissed her.

Lily was sitting on her bed wiping her eyes with a tissue when Ian came in. "Can you believe it? Just when I thought our problems were over!" she exclaimed.

He sat beside her and rubbed her back. "At least he's come home and seems ready to make amends."

"This is the worst possible thing he could have done. Married at seventeen! Now he'll never go to Oxford with that little. . .tart about his neck!"

"Come now," said Ian. "Bella seems quite fresh and ingenuous, hardly a tart. I liked her very much, and can certainly see why Tristan does."

"Like her, sleep with her, fine. But did he have to marry her? I'm sure her family is pleased as punch that she's snagged a rich boy. They can't possibly make a go of it. How will she fit in with Tris's friends, dressed like a cheap sexpot and talking in an accent you can barely understand?"

"That's hardly important, Lily. It's how well the two of them understand and care for each other that matters. The rest can be dealt with. You and I were from very different backgrounds, but we loved each other, and we've made it. It's not impossible for them to do the same."

"Are you suggesting that I was as tacky as this girl?"

"Of course not. Neither of you are 'tacky' as you call it. Your American background was at least as foreign as Bella's Yorkshire one, however."

"I *was* something! I had a career, could have had quite a career if I hadn't given it up."

"Oh? I thought you gave it up because you realized you'd never be a star like dread Ava—was that her name?"

"Eva. Who got hooked on drugs and never lived up to her promise. I could have been very good, if not the best, and I certainly would never have been so stupid as to blow it all up my nose!"

"I don't doubt that for a second, Lily. You gave up a lot for me." He stroked her hair.

"This girl is so uneducated and unformed. All she knows how to do is wait tables and show off her legs to impressionable fools like Tristan. . .and you!"

"Me?" Ian laughed.

"Telling her how pretty she was, and what a great model she'd make. Really, Ian!"

"It's the truth. Bella is a stunning girl, you can't deny her that. As for her inexperience, she seems very eager and sensitive. I imagine she'll pick up a lot. She's got you as a model for how a perfectly elegant Lady D'Arcy should be. Don't look on the worst side, my love. I have the money to support them while Tris completes his education, so there's no reason this precipitous marriage should prove a hindrance to him—anymore than ours was to me." He brushed her hair aside and kissed the nape of her neck.

"Ian, please, I honestly do have a headache."

"I'll let you rest, then," he said, getting up. "Could use a nap myself."

"Ian?"

He paused at his bedroom door. "Yes?"

"It was a wonderful trip. Thank you for it and all the lovely presents."

"You don't have to thank me. It's my greatest pleasure to give you beautiful things, Lily."

"You're so good to me always. I'm an incredibly lucky woman. I do know that."

He smiled. "Rest well, my love, and don't worry so. It will all work out." He closed the door between their rooms.

Lily got up and opened her crocodile beauty case. She removed a velvet box and opened it. Inside winked the pavé diamond and star sapphire earrings Ian had bought for her at Bulgari in Rome—an early anniversary present. She held one up and examined her reflection in the gilt mirror above her dressing table. "To match your eyes," he'd said when she'd first opened the gift. The cloudy, opaque blue of the stones did match her eyes rather well, she decided. She put them away in her jewel case.

Now the memory of our romantic trip is spoiled by the shock of Tristan's reckless mistake of a marriage, she thought sadly. Surely it couldn't last! From her looks, this girl was obviously of easy morals; the whole attraction had to be based on sex. In a year, maybe less, surely intelligent Tristan would have run through his passion and would realize he was saddled with an empty-headed, common girl. Perhaps it could even be annulled.

This thought cheered Lily immensely. The bishop was a great friend whom she'd often entertained at Innismere. He was well aware of all she had done for St. Anne's, the tiny, beautiful Protestant church in the village, built by the D'Arcys over two hundred years ago. Ian hadn't darkened the door of St. Anne's since his mother had been refused burial in the church cemetery because she was a suicide. Lily, however, never missed a Sunday, was president of the Altar Guild, and opened the grounds of Innismere for a yearly fête to raise funds. She did all this from her sense of duty as Lady D'Arcy rather than for religious reasons. Her parents had been agnostics, and though not particularly religious herself, Lily did enjoy the peace and beauty of the old church, and liked the vicar, a cultured, sociable man who treated her with great deference. So, when her son tired of his child bride, Lily would call in the chits and see if they couldn't get an annulment, easier to come by than a divorce, which was illegal in Ireland.

How could Tristan manage to complicate his life so, when if ever anyone had it all, it was he, she thought with a fresh welling of tears. What was the matter with the boy? It was as if he'd purposely set about ruining himself. But why? To punish his parents for having marital difficulties? It made no sense to her at all.

The next morning, Ian D'Arcy was at the stables by six to check on his horses. He talked briefly with his stable manager and trainer Frank Connors and told him about the new thoroughbred colt he'd lucked into in France. The flat season was over now, and his successful filly was out in her own paddock as were the the dozen other horses he owned.

Ian saddled up his gelding hunter, Rocket, and headed out at a brisk clip. It had been midsummer when he'd last ridden, and it felt marvelous to be back in the saddle on a crisp, November morning at Innismere. Taking Rocket over a fence, he headed for the mountains which protected the estate from blasts off the Irish Sea. Going steadily uphill, they cantered along for a couple of miles, taking fence and wall as they came. He followed a path through the wood, then gave the gelding his head to pick his way at a walk up a steep, grassy, rock-strewn incline.

Reaching the crest, Ian dismounted and led his horse

through the still-standing gateway of what had once been his family's stronghold from the fourteenth century. The square, stone tower, the original keep, still remained intact, but the other rooms built on through the centuries were now reduced to strewn rubble, as though some giant child had grown tired of his game of gargantuan blocks. Ian's ancestor, Richard D'Arcy, had won the hand of an English duke's daughter, and, feeling the need for a more modern house, had used her dowry to build the redbrick mansion in the valley below. The rambling, old Norman castle had been torn down, but for the keep, and the stones used in the foundations of Innismere House and the building of the stables.

Ian tied the reins to a metal ring set in a stone for that purpose and looked out over the D'Arcy domain. It was easy to see why his forefathers had chosen this location to build. From this vantage point they could watch for the roving Celtic bands whose lands they'd taken, and their rear was protected by the Wicklow Mountains. Below him he could see the roof and chimneys of Innismere, the still-green meadows, and the gray-brown, leafless woods of mature trees. The only great trees left in Ireland were on the old estates as the British had stripped the country's forests to make ammunition boxes. In the distance there was a silver thread, the river Liffey wending its way toward Dublin. Though he had seen most of the beautiful spots in the western hemisphere, none, he thought, could match this vista over his own land. Today, however, it failed to give him his usual lift.

Sitting on a mossy stone, Ian took Tony Neville's unopened letter out of his jacket pocket. He had carried the letter, well-hidden, on their trip, but had been neither able to read or destroy it. He'd postponed opening it 'til this moment when he would have the privacy to recover from whatever its contents might hold. He ripped open the envelope; his friend's distinctive handwriting leapt up at him.

Ian,

I know you will resent my doing this to you, but my own pain is greater than my desire to spare you any further on my account. I simply see no point in going on. I might have done had we kept it as you wished, but once the tide was let loose, and I allowed myself to think there was a chance you might love me again, well there's just no putting the genie of my feelings for you back in the bottle. (Pardon that mixed metaphor.)

I've tried substitutions for you—only on my travels; I'd never risk shaming Anne or the children. There are tall, pale boys with raven hair and eyes in Italy and Greece, but none of them were ever you. Sex was always easy to come by; love, only once.

At last I concede to your attachment to Lily, who will never give you up, no matter what she threatens; she's no fool.

You can delude yourself that our affair was just experimentation, searching for sexual identity, or whatever. I am cursed with knowing the truth about myself. Another truth I know: you did love me! Your being ashamed of this is unbelievably painful to me. This "mistake of your life" was the purest, most holy passion of mine.

There no longer seems an excuse for me to take up space. Anne is the best of women, yet I can never give her what she needs and deserves; nor would I ever have the heart to leave her. This way, she can begin her life again with a more suitable man while she's still young. The insurance money will help repay her for all she's invested in Wycliffe, which gives me some final satisfaction.

Julian is very sound like his mother. I know I can count on you to keep an eye on him and his sisters. Ione I especially worry about, as we were very close, and she's a sensitive child. You will see some bastard doesn't marry her for what he mistakenly assumes is a fortune? Ione is the only regret I have in leaving.

By the way, do charge the Girlandaio to my account—I want Anne to have it. Talk about creative financing!

I can't think of a way to bring this to a memorable close. I'm in a very clear state of mind and not in any great emotional distress. Feel quite chipper in fact! More than I have in ages. I'm truly looking forward to not feeling. I hope it all works out for you with Lily, since she is your choice, and I pray that Tristan realizes that he could never have had a better father than you.

                    Tony

Ian sat there staring at the letter for a moment, then took a ring out of his pocket. Tony had bought that ring for him in Greece. It was fashioned out of a gold coin bearing the bust of Alexander, Tony's hero. He slipped it on his finger. It still fit him.

He carefully refolded the letter, returned it to the envelope, and put it in his jacket pocket. Lost in thought, with the wind whistling around the keep, he didn't hear the two young people ride up. When Bella came running around the corner with his son on her heels, Ian was taken by complete surprise.

"Dad," said Tristan, catching Bella about the waist. "Didn't know you were up here."

"I was just leaving," said Ian, hurrying to untie and mount his horse. "Don't be late for lunch," he called, then spurred Rocket off down the hill.

"Goodness," said Bella. "Did you see his face? We came running up on him like a pack of wild Indians."

"Wild Indians with but one thought in mind," said Tristan, pulling her to him.

"And what thought was that?" she said, pressing her hips against his.

"Finding a place where neither Mother, nor Kelly, nor the maid can interrupt us." He unfastened the top button of her sweater.

"There's always our bedroom, if we lock the door."

"Have you no sense of fantasy, woman? We're going to rouse the family ghosts, show them what they've been missing all these years."

Bella rolled her eyes. "Sounds spooky. Are they watching now?"

"Right. And cheering. The D'Arcys were lovers rather than fighters. They gained more territory by marrying than warring."

"The great French lovers of history, eh?"

"Exactly." Tristan opened her sweater and pinned her arms against the stone wall of the keep. He kissed her breasts. "Get those trousers off," he ordered.

"Let me free then." He stepped back, and she unzipped her jeans.

"No panties—good girl!"

"You hid all my underclothes."

"It's more aerodynamic without." She continued undressing while he watched.

"Tris, it's cold," she said, hugging herself. He lifted the

camera strapped over his shoulder. "Tris!" she protested, shivering.

"Come on. Your hair looks so incredible against the moss, your soft skin next to the rough stone. It's a great photo!" He snapped away. "I'll develop it myself, and no one but us will ever see it."

"Stop it! You remind me of Alistair the Creep." She turned her back to him.

"Even better! What a great ass you have, Mrs. D'Arcy! Now look back at me through the hair. Incredible!"

She made a face at him. "Tris, I'm turning blue— enough!"

"Sorry." He took her shaking body in his arms. "It really will make a beautiful picture."

"How is this any different from the dirty pictures you said your friend took?"

"A great deal of difference. Those were inspired by commerce and lust, and these, by art and love. I'll destroy them if you don't like them, Bella."

"It just gave me a funny feeling," she murmured.

He rubbed her arms. "They are for my loving eyes only." He kissed her. "Mmm. Let's go get you properly warmed up. He picked her up and carried her inside the walls of the keep.

"Weather looks like it's turnin', Sir Ian," said Mary Kelly when he came into the kitchen after his return from the castle. "I've put the kettle on. It's a hot cuppa ye'll be wantin' to take the chill off your bones."

"Just what I need, Mary. I'll take it in my room, please."

" 'Twill be a pleasure, Master Ian." She had worked as cook's helper for his father and still slipped back to his youthful title now and again. The distaff side of the Jack Spratish couple who had served the D'Arcys long and faithfully was as plump and loquacious as Seamus Kelly was wispy and taciturn.

"The old man will bring the tea up to you in a jiffy," said Mary. The thought of Seamus doing anything in a jiffy almost made Ian smile.

He headed straight for the drawing room and threw the letter on the roaring fire with a sigh of relief to get rid of it. He knew he'd never get Tony's words out of his brain, but he wanted to make sure Lily never read it. He'd already burned the letters Anne had given him, even if he'd never been as indiscreet in them as Tony had been in his. He'd always been paranoid that someone else might get hold of them.

"Did you go for a ride, Ian?"

He whirled guiltily about to face his wife. "Yes. Wasn't dressed warmly enough, got a bit of a chill."

"Have you seen Tristan? I can't find him."

"Yes. I passed Bella and him out riding."

She joined him by the fire. "I've a feeling we're not going to see much of him, even if he is home."

"They are going to want to be off by themselves. We did as well when we were newlyweds."

"God, don't even say that word," she moaned. "However, I have made up my mind I'm going to try and accept that it's a done thing, and we have to live with it. For the time being anyway."

Ian smiled vaguely and stared off into the fire.

"I just found Evileen trying on the sable."

"What?" he murmured.

"Evileen was trying on my new coat."

"Going to hang her up by the thumbs?" he asked, still fascinated by the flames.

"Not this time. I told her to go look at herself in the full-length bathroom mirror. She was quite giddy with self-admiration." Ian had been totally extravagant and had bought her a knee length, golden sable swing coat at Revillon in Paris because her old fur looked out of date with her new, chic clothes.

Lily ran her hand delicately down his back. "I can remember what life in a thin, cloth coat was like before I met my Irish prince." She leaned against him.

"I'm sorry about yesterday, darling. I was just so overwhelmed."

"I understood."

"Did you? You look so long-faced, I thought you might be harboring a grudge," she teased, playing with his hair.

He didn't respond. "I should have been more considerate."

"I like it that you seem to be interested in making love to me again, Ian." He turned away from her.

"What?" she asked, puzzled by his coolness.

"Nothing. Just in a funk today. The Tristan business catching up with me, I suppose."

She brightened. "Evileen's done the bedrooms, and the children are gone. Why don't we slip off upstairs and cheer each other up? Make up for a wasted night."

"I need a wash," he demurred.

"We could have a bath together. That's always fun."

"Kelly's bringing tea up to my room. I imagine it's ready," he said, moving away from her.

"Ian?"

"Sorry, Lily. We seem to be out of sync," he said and left her standing there, cheeks burning.

Worried, she turned back to the fire. Had he done that to get even for the headache? That was more her style, not his. Something was bothering him deeply. He was obviously much more disturbed about Tristan than he'd let on.

It was then Lily noticed part of an unstamped envelope which had fallen out of the grate. She retrieved it with the fire tongs and shook out the singed contents. Random words which made no sense without the other two thirds of the letter. At the top of the first page was the number "30;" at the bottom of the last page, "ny" was all that remained of the signature. Tony! Ian had been burning an unposted letter from Tony Neville. That's why he'd been so distracted and fascinated by the fire. Hadn't Tony died on the thirtieth of October? Could this have been a last letter to Ian?

Lily threw the scrap back into the fire as if it had burned her hand. The letter had put Ian in his funk, not her headache or Tristan. She covered her ears. Tony was dead; she wanted never to think of him again. He should no longer have the power to come between them, but here he was, haunting them from the grave. She could not let him upset her as he had before with his poison letters. After all, she was alive, and Ian had proven many times over that it was she he loved, hadn't he?

It was a typically rainy November that year in Kildare. Though the country was as far north as Labrador, the Gulf Stream crossed the Atlantic from the States and swept the western and southern coasts of Ireland, keeping the temperatures in the moderate range from forty to seventy degrees year round. It seldom snowed in winter, but the constant precipitation from the great rain-making machine of that warm ocean current could chill one to the bone. The recently installed central heating at Innismere House struggled mightily to keep the damp cold out of the high ceilinged rooms. Even then, fires were kept burning in all the used downstairs rooms and in the bedrooms at night. Everyone wore sweaters as well, but Bella still caught a nasty cold that lasted for weeks.

"And no wonder!" reported Evileen to Sheila who did

the laundry. "Didn't Miss Bella pose in the altogether for Master Tristan's camera? It's a great miracle she doesn't have the pneumonia!" The maid described in detail the photos she'd found in Tristan's drawer when she was putting away his clean socks.

"So how would she be lookin' without her clothes?" tittered Sheila.

"A bloody lot better than the likes of us," Evileen replied.

"Do you think that's what rich people do then? Take naked snaps of each other?"

"What else are they to do, when they're waited on hand and foot by poor skivvies like us? Master Tristan is quite the artiste with his camera," laughed Evileen.

"If they was common folk, ye'd call it smut, not art," sniffed Sheila.

"I dunno. I wouldn't mind doffin' me clothes for art if the young master was doin' the snappin'."

"Go on, you eejit! He'd hardly be askin' ye to with his wife so beautiful," scoffed the laundress.

"I was only teasin'. Wouldn't ye be knowin' when your own leg is bein' pulled? See that you don't scorch his Lordship's shirts this time," said Evileen.

The first week in December, Ian, Connors, and the head groom Paddy flew back to France to pick up the thoroughbred colt Ian had acquired from the Comte de Lazarre, a good friend and client. Ian was very excited about the horse called Charlemagne as he had unbelievable bloodlines and was worth much more than any horse he'd ever owned. Amazingly, the Comte had given Ian the big, black colt for nothing other than his commission on the next two paintings he found for his collection. The rub was that Charlemagne, or Charlie as he was quickly dubbed by Paddy, was a killer. He had a mean temper, and the week before Ian and Lily had visited the Comte at his chateau near Neuilly, had kicked a groom in the head and killed him. Threatened with mutiny from his stablehands unless he put the animal down, and knowing it would be difficult to sell such an ill-tempered, dangerous creature, the Comte had given him to Ian to get him out of the country.

Charlemagne was sedated and flown back to Ireland where he was installed in the largest corner box at the Innismere stable—a shaky, manure-matted, wild-eyed ton of superbly bred racing machine. Which no one could get near even to groom. Connors was of the opinion that, even free, they had got no bargain. Paddy, who had been around horses since he was ten, was more sanguine. Within a week, he was able to brush out Charlie's soiled coat with the aid of a twitch on the muzzle and two very wary stableboys.

It was Paddy's opinion that the colt had been treated harshly, possibly as a yearling before he had been bought by the Comte. "No animal is born that much of a divil, lest some'ats been a divil to him," he said to Ian.

When a spruced up Charlemagne was let free to run in the paddock by himself with tail held high and ears pricked, Ian was deeply moved. No work of any human artist could compare with such living beauty. The colt was sixteen hands of perfect conformation, deep chested, with long, sloping shoulders and powerful hindquarters; his coat was a true, ebony black, rare in horses. Normally Ian subscribed to the old adage that "oil paintings" didn't necessarily make great racehorses, but besides beauty, Charlie had a smooth, effortless stride and a great deal of presence. Paddy said he reminded him of Instigator, Sir William's colt that had won the Irish 2000 Guineas in 1963.

Connors was much more skeptical. Charlemagne had

not raced as a two-year-old because he was a late born colt and immature; in other words, mean. Since every thoroughbred celebrates its birthday January 1, a foal born later in the summer could end up racing horses older by six months, a big disadvantage in training and experience. Ian was determined to have the colt ready to run for its three-year-old season, at least in Ireland. The problem was no one could ride the animal; the exercise jockey had been thrown three times before he refused to get back in the saddle.

The weather worsened and Ian was forced to give up on trying to condition his magnificent, unridable horse until early in the new year. Bella and Tristan had to forgo their daily rides for indoor pursuits, such as exploring the old house from top to bottom. In the attic they discovered a big trunk full of things belonging to Siobhan O'Connor D'Arcy, the grandmother who had scandalously killed herself. There were tiny-waisted dresses and suits from the thirties and forties, pairs of perfect kid gloves, and beautifully tailored riding clothes, including a sidesaddle habit. Siobhan had been a great horsewoman, and a painting of her on her bay hunter, Valkyrie, presided over Ian's study. Bella was very intrigued by the figure in the painting with her graceful carriage, black hair, and luminous blue eyes. Looking through her clothes and a tasseled dance program from a ball of which Siobhan had certainly been the belle, it was especially poignant to think she'd come to such a sad end.

Bella reverently stroked a silk evening dress in the palest apricot. "Does anyone know why she did it, Tris?"

"Father never talks of her, but I somehow seem to have heard, perhaps from eavesdropping on the Kellys, that she was in love with another man. A Ned something, I think. It's not a thing I ever felt comfortable asking Dad or Uncle Damien about. It was a great trauma for every-one."

"I can imagine. She has such a nice face."

"Everyone loved her, I think. The Kellys speak of her as if she were a martyred saint," said Tristan.

In the morning room there was a lovely, impressionistic study of Ian and Damien as children that Siobhan had painted herself. There were several others of her unfinished works in the attic which showed how talented she had been. The piano was another of her interests; she had bequeathed her love of music and art, as well as her raven hair, to her eldest son. As soon as he had inherited the estate, Ian had had a fine marble Venus erected on the spot in the garden where his mother had shot herself. Wild red roses twined about the statue in a riotous profusion that no gardener would go near with pruning shears. She had been an O'Connor, one of the prominent Gaelic clans of ancient times. Her family was wealthier than the D'Arcys, their money coming from dairy shops which sold milk, butter, and eggs all over Dublin and Cork.

A portrait of William, Siobhan's husband, dominated the main drawing room where no one could escape the glare of his piercing black eyes. The picture gave Bella the shivers; there was something frightening in those dark D'Arcy eyes that was thankfully missing in Tristan's and his father's. She was positive that William must have been a hard man, and felt very sympathetic toward his gentle-eyed wife.

The two young people explored the third floor which was kept shut off to save on heating. The furnishings in the dormitory-like nursery were draped with sheets, and their breath froze in the chill air. Tristan opened his toy chest, and the two of them took out his old books and playthings, including a shapeless, moth-eaten, stuffed elephant.

"Ellie!" cried Tristan, holding the bedraggled toy up in the air. "We went many a mile together, Ellie and I."

Bella took the animal and held it to her breast. "You look so sweet in your pictures. I wish I'd known you then."

He flopped down on his narrow, boyhood bed and looked up at her. "I knew you." She sat beside him. "I knew you in my dreams. You'd come to me at night and show me your incomparable breasts."

Bella laughed. "You sound too naughty to have looked so angelic."

"I could never quite see your face, but when I met you, I knew there was something very familiar." Bella lay beside him, still hugging the elephant. He put an arm about her.

"I wonder what our child will look like?"

"We'll find out in a few years," he said, nuzzling her hair.

"It just seems odd that we didn't get pregnant that first time. It was the perfect time for me to conceive."

"I thought it was more like lucky-as-hell than odd, myself. We obviously missed it by a few hours and the grace of God."

"I almost wish I had got pregnant, so I'd know I could. I want a little boy with golden hair and black eyes."

"You already have one of those. You're not serious are you?"

"I think I am. It would be so much fun. He could grow up at Innismere and have a childhood like yours with everything. Two parents who love each other and all the rest of it. Such a golden life, Tris."

He raised up on one elbow, then kissed her cheek. He suspected Bella's childhood had been far from golden. "My love, we're only seventeen, and I haven't a job."

"It's not like we'd be on the dole, Tris. You get all this, don't you?"

"Yes, as unfair as that is to Vi; though I'd rather have a trust than have to shoulder this bloody great lot."

"Have to? Don't you realize how lucky you are—any D'Arcy is?"

He lay back. "It has its drawbacks. Dad is gone half his life to keep Innismere from the taxman."

"I don't care. It's worth it! This is the only place I've ever been where life is really and truly wonderful." He couldn't disagree. "I want us to have heaps of children so they can enjoy all of this paradise."

"We shall, in good time."

"Why not start right away so we can be young parents while they're growing up? One thing I want to do differently though. I refuse to send my babies up here with some stranger to raise them. That's awful! Why do rich people do that?"

"I believe the aim is to see as little of the brats as possible. Have someone else do the hard duty like grotty nappies, then Mummy and Daddy come in looking glamorous for a goodnight kiss and, if they've been very good, a bedtime story."

"I don't like that part of the fairy tale. We'll be different. I want my babies to love me, not some old biddy who's not even kin."

"And has a moustache. Nanny Soames did, but I loved her dearly anyway."

"I'd like to start right away, Tristan. I really would," said Bella.

"You mean you want to get pregnant to prove that you can get pregnant?"

"I mean I want to have a child with you, because I love you more than anything."

He caressed her face. "We shall see, my love, only let's

not jump into this too rashly. In the meantime, how about making a precociously naughty little boy's dream come true?" Smiling, Bella sat up and began removing her jacket and sweater.

With so much time on their hands, Tristan decided to give Bella an "Irish" education. In his opinion, English schools slighted the history of their incompatible neighbor and viewed anything Irish with condescension.

To make the lessons more exciting, they took excursions to nearby sites made famous by Ireland's several waves of invaders: Newgrange, where the ancient Firbolgs had built a Neolithic passage grave; the Hill of Tara where once stood the city of the High King of the Celtic Gaels; Glendalough, in the Wicklow Mountains, center of the Catholic Golden Age in the sixth century; and Clontarf, a suburb of Dublin where Brian Boru defeated the Viking marauders.

For the D'Arcys, history began in the twelfth century with the greedy Irish prince Dermot MacMurrough. Dermot was driven from his Dublin territory by the other tribes because he had taken the wife and lands of O'Rourke of Breffny. Dermot sent to England for help, and Henry II shipped over some rambunctious Welsh-Norman knights, probably to get England rid of them. The Gaels, who dressed in fine linen tunics for battle, were hardly a match for the armor and chain-mail-clad invaders. In reward, Dermot gave the Norman knights' leader, Strongbow, his daughter and succession to the throne of Leinster.

In the fourteenth century, Ormond D'Arcy, a minor Norman knight, vassal to the great Fitzgeralds of Kildare, carved out a small fief just on the edge of The Pale—appropriately, according to Damien. British law and culture prevailed inside the rim of forts and earthworks protecting Dublin; outside, or "beyond the Pale," Brehon (Celtic) law ruled. The Normans built walled cities and stone castle towers, and established a feudal society on lands wrested from the Gaels with whom they were constantly at war. Some were more diplomatic, such as Ormond D'Arcy who married his son to a Gaelic chieftain's daughter.

By the sixteenth century, the D'Arcys had extended their lands to 2,000 acres dominated by their ever expanding stone castle on the hill. All was going well until that great iconoclast Henry the Eighth and his daughter Elizabeth insisted that the devoutly Catholic Celts and Normans convert to Protestantism.

Religious intolerance brought hard times in earnest for Ireland. When Catholic Hugh O'Neill revolted in Ulster, he was defeated by England's James the First who gave O'Neill's lands to Calvinist Scots colonists, thereby setting the scene for the insoluble religious and political schism which still torments Ireland to this day. In the name of God and Protestantism, Cromwell raided and pillaged the country killing half the Catholic Irish and driving the living to Connaught-western Ireland; his Protestant-English soldiers were given confiscated Irish lands. Rather than fleeing to Europe as many did, Desmond D'Arcy converted to save the family's holdings.

When Catholic King James II ascended the English throne, the D'Arcys, always able to adapt to the times, declared themselves secret Catholics. After James was supplanted by William of Orange and defeated at the Battle of the Boyne in 1690, oppression followed under the notorious Penal Laws of the Protestant Ascendancy in Ireland. Catholics were forbidden to practice their religion, inherit land, speak Gaelic, or own a horse worth more than five pounds, among other penalties. Since the D'Arcys were always great horse fanciers, that was the final blow. Edmond D'Arcy, a second son, vowed he'd been Protestant all along and accordingly inherited his elder brother's castle and lands. Tristan explained to Bella that Edmond, from whom they were directly descended, was considered a pragmatic realist rather than an opportunistic traitor. It was very rare for an Irish family to have retained their original lands. The key was adaptability; the D'Arcys had always managed to change with the times. Their motto, "Nous endurerons" was no idle boast.

Tristan used the long portrait gallery at Innismere as he continued with Bella's instruction through the dreary month of December. He pointed to a large painting of a bewigged, benign-looking gentleman dressed in knee britches and frock coat.

"This is Richard D'Arcy, the first baronet. He received the title for his efforts on behalf of Prime Minister Pitt's Act of Union wherein the Irish voted to dissolve their own parliament and send members to Westminster instead. I'm sure Richard was influenced by his English father-in-law, a duke."

They moved on to the portrait of Lady Annabelle, Richard's wife, painted romantically by Gainesborough. "She married beneath herself for love and brought a huge dowry which built Innismere. They liked their women plumpish in those days," he added.

"Richard built this house for her in the 1750s in the latest Georgian style. The German architect Richard Castle, who built many of the great houses of the period, designed it. James Wyatt did this gallery with its neoclassical marble columns as well as the fancy plaster work of birds and garlands on the dining room walls."

Tristan paused before the portrait of a slender, darkhaired woman wearing a rather drab dress with a billowing hoop skirt. "Lady Katherine D'Arcy here was one of the good ones. When the potato crops failed in the 1840s, and a million Irish peasants died of starvation and disease while another million emigrated, Lady Katherine formed a soup kitchen and had her own doctor attend to the sick tenants and villagers. I'm proud to say that the D'Arcys were never absentee landlords, either. Many estate owners would take themselves off to England and more civilized climes, leaving estate agents to run their Irish properties. All D'Arcy eldest sons except me have been educated at Oxford, chiefly for the contacts and marriages they could make there, but we always come back to Innismere. We're really farmers at heart."

"You're not like any farmers I've ever known," said Bella.

"Well, we do love the land and can't bear to be long from it. Back to Lady Katherine's son, Henry. He is a local legend for horsewhipping an unscrupulous agent known for callous evictions. I suspect it was for cheating on the rents, but the people made Henry a hero for it. Later, when rebels burned so many of the great houses, Innismere was never touched but for the stables, and the horses were freed first."

Henry D'Arcy had been painted with his favorite horse and a wolfhound, ancestor to Maeve and Fionn. He had the tall, thin, dark-eyed, haughty look which Bella recognized in Ian and ever so slightly in Tris. "Sir Henry was a backer of Charles Stewart Parnell in his drive for Home Rule for Ireland," Tristan continued. "Home Rule meant the right of the Irish to govern their own domestic affairs. Parnell was named in a divorce suit by the husband of his long-time mistress Kitty O'Shea, and Home Rule and Parnell's political career were ruined. Henry also had quite a collection of rare pornography which Father hid somewhere after he found Violet and I giggling over it. Henry was an interesting man."

In the library, Tristan showed Bella the portrait of his great-grandfather, another Ormond D'Arcy, painted in the uniform of a lieutenant in the Irish Guards, the Victoria Cross and Croix de Guerre on his breast. It was a posthumous portrait as he'd died a hero at the Somme having volunteered to serve in a war during which Ireland remained neutral.

Ireland sat out World War II as well, and William D'Arcy also volunteered, receiving a VC and the rank of major in his father's regiment. In spite of his possible failings as a husband and father, Sir William was a hero and a financial genius as well. The dour Eamon de Valera, survivor of the Easter Rising of 1916, pursued a policy of economic isolation for Ireland, and the country was severely depressed. The more far-sighted Sean Lemass brought the country into the European Economic Community in the sixties, and William D'Arcy took shrewd advantage of the boom that ensued. In the years before his early death, he made a great deal of money in stock and land investments, improved the house, and bought back some of the land lost through the years. He also left his heirs a legacy of holdings to assist them in living as country gentlemen.

The lesson at an end, Bella and Tristan were embracing beneath the drawing room portrait of his grandfather when Lily walked in.

"Didn't you here the bell, Tristan? Luncheon has been kept waiting for the two of you."

"Sorry, Mum. We were deep into a history lesson."

"Is that what you were doing? You know, Tristan, it would be better manners to confine your lovemaking to the bedroom. It's embarrassing to walk in on the two of you. Think of the servants."

"Oh? Should we avoid each other like you and Dad do?" He kissed a pink-faced Bella again. Lily left in a huff.

"She's angry, Tris, and she's probably right," said Bella.

"No, she isn't. I've a perfect right to kiss my wife anywhere in my house. She's only jealous because she and Dad don't have half the passion we have—if they ever did."

"I think we should be more discreet. She already thinks I'm a slut."

"Never let her make you feel inferior, Bella. You are as good as anyone who's ever set foot in this house. We'll go in to lunch, but first give us another kiss."

✛ ✛ ✛

Lily was at her desk in the morning room planning menus for the rapidly approaching Christmas holiday when Kelly announced his arrival with a tactful throat clearing.

"Your Ladyship, there's a lad here to see about a position with the horses," he announced.

"Didn't you tell him Ian is in London? Or just send him down to Connors. He hires the stableboys."

"But it's the race trainer's position he's after applyin' for, me Lady."

"Tell him to come back next weekend when Ian will be home, though I doubt they need him since there's already Frank doing the training," she shouted.

"He's an Aussie from Australia, and a likely lookin' lad he is, too," Kelly persisted.

She threw down her pen in exasperation. "I do not hire the stablehands. Tell him to return on the weekend, Seamus."

He bowed stiffly. "Yes, madam." She watched him shuffle off and felt ashamed for losing patience with him, but damn, she was tired of having to yell. She prayed for the day when Kelly would announce his retirement, though he'd probably keel over into the soup before that happened. Lately he'd been letting the silver go until she had to mention it to him. The only thing he still did well was tend to Ian's clothes, shoes, and boots, which he kept gleaming. Kelly had been Sir William's valet for years until he advanced to butler.

Lily's attention was caught at that moment by the sight of a man on the terrace. She watched him walk to the balustrade, turn, and look back at the house. Had someone left the gate open? It wouldn't be the first time some rude tourist had managed to get past the electronically-controlled gates and wander about the property as if it were a public park. She got up and went to the window for a closer look. No, he was dressed too roughly, more like a workman than a tourist. He wore a cowboy-type hat, and it suddenly dawned on her that he must be the "Aussie from Australia" who had so impressed Kelly. She watched as the man removed the hat and ran a hand through a spiky thatch of blond hair. He scanned the full length of the house, then noticed her standing at the morning room window. He put his hat back on, tipping it slightly in her direction, then turned and sauntered off in the direction of the stables. Fionn noisily bounded at him; the stranger bent to pet him and the dog wagged his stringy tail and trotted off with him as if he were one of the family. So much for the hopeless animal's prowess as watchdog.

She was sure that Connors had given the man the brush-off, since it was his job he was after, but something about the Aussie's insolent nonchalance as he trespassed on the terrace continued to prey on Lily's mind. So much so that when Ian returned from London, she told him about the incident. He assured her that Frank was not about to retire, and the stable wasn't big enough to warrant an assistant trainer.

The man must have figured this out for himself, because he did not come back on the weekend. Lily was relieved and put him out of her mind. Almost. Whenever she looked out the morning room window, she would remember the tanned, roughly dressed intruder staring up at her beautiful house with what seemed to her an expression of contempt. She was a great believer in first reactions to people, and this Aussie had roused in her an instinctive feeling that said "Beware!"

A week before Christmas, Ian's younger brother Damien arrived, followed by Violet, sans Yves who was spending the holidays with his mother in Paris.

Lily was always delighted to see her brother-in-law. "You might have forewarned us," she said on his arrival in a limousine with smoked glass.

He kissed her hand. "Lily my love, I do believe you're more beautiful now than when Ian turned up on the doorstep with you a few Christmases ago."

"You're such a con," Lily teased, enjoying the compliment.

"Would I have had such incredible success if I weren't?" said Damien, joking at his own expense. He'd spent the past twenty years vainly searching for the singing talent he could manage into The Big Time. After being sent down from Trinity, Damien had forged a life unusual for one of the gentry. Brian Epstein, the Beatles' ill-fated manager, had been his inspiration to go into the field of rock management during the late sixties. In the seventies, he'd had a faint whiff of success with an Irish punk band The Daildos, cheekily named after the Dail, the Irish parliament. Then Sid Vicious had put the kiss of death on the entire punk rock scene.

Through dinner, Damien kept them all laughing with

tales of his various doomed bands, such as The Brides of Christ, whose lead singer became a priest; The Raving Maniacs, several of whom went up on drug charges; The Diesel Fops, who only sold records to their mothers; the one-hit wonders known as The Nostril Pluckers; and more recently, the band Up Yours who loathed each other on sight.

Damien, who was well liked in the business because of his charm, cleverness, classy dress, and demeanor, was always just on the verge of discovering the next superstar, while only a trust fund from his mother and frequent loans from his brother kept the wolf from the door.

Damien was great company, however, and the family looked forward to his infrequent visits. Physically he was his brother's diametric opposite: short, with a slight paunch, thinning blond hair, blue eyes, always dressed nattily in double-breasted suits. Bella liked him at once because of the twinkle in his eyes and his self-deprecating humor. He congratulated his nephew on his superb taste in women. Damien was very at ease with his own homosexuality, though he was not at all effeminate. He and Ian had a prickly but fond relationship.

"My brother was always taller, handsomer, better at sports and studies, and more successful than I. It's a tribute to my good nature that I can even stand the bloke," said Damien.

After dinner the first night of his return, Damien shared a glass of brandy and a game of billiards with his brother. "So what is it this time?" asked Ian as he chalked his cue.

"Rather cynical of you to think I've come for any other reason than to be in the bosom of my family on Christ's birthday, brother dear." He broke, and two balls went in.

"I know you, don't I?" said Ian.

"Better than anybody. Actually, now that you ask, I do have a bit of an ulterior motive for my visit."

Ian smiled and missed his shot. "How much?"

"This time I think I've found my singer, Ian. I know you've heard that one before, but it's the truth this time. He's a young lad from Ulster with the most incredible, white soul voice I've ever heard. Has songwriting potential as well. With polishing and seasoning, he could become the next George Michael. Irish acts are hot at the moment, so the timing's right." Damien sank three balls during this speech.

"So, how much do you need to promote this wonder?" Ian banked the six ball off the side into a pocket.

"I need to hire some crack musicians to back him on a demo tape, no damned drum machines. His talent must be showcased perfectly to get him a good contract with a record company. A first rate production, studio time, etc., takes money. He's worth the investment, Ian, I swear. He's a good, clean lad, not like some of the others. Maybe a bit rough about the edges now, had to be to survive, but he's not into drugs and is tremendously ambitious, not just out for a good time. I've had it with ruffian bands who can't get along or stay sober for five minutes. Some woman will always turn them against each other. I want to concentrate all my efforts on this talented lad who will listen to what I have to say. Someone with his talent and my brain can make it to the top for a good long run. The English pop market is absurd these days. No group is a hit for more than fifteen minutes. Where is Frankie Goes to Hollywood these days, along with any number of other flashes in the pan?"

"Who was he?" asked Ian as he tried to body English his ball into the pocket, but failed.

"They. A band which had the mega hit 'Relax' a few years back. I don't want a one-album, U.K. flash. The

U.S. market is the big prize. If you can hit in the States, you're in the money."

"Just tell me how much you need, within reason, and it's yours," said his brother, sipping his brandy as Damien put in five balls in succession.

"Have I ever told you what an incredible brother you are, Ian?"

"I'd have to agree with you," said Ian smiling. They shook hands. "That's what family is for. You'd do the same for me had you been born first."

Damien shook his head. "You've gone way beyond your blood obligation, but I hope to repay you with interest this time round," he said with feeling.

"I'll look forward to that. Shall we deduct the quid you've just won off me from the debt?"

"Right. See what comes from hanging about with the lower classes?" They returned their cues to the rack on the billiard room wall.

"Handsome ring. I've never seen you wear that one before, Ian."

"Got it in Greece years ago. Forgot I had it," said Ian, gently rubbing its gold surface across his palm.

"Terrible about Tony. I was in Belfast and didn't hear 'til after the funeral, or I would have come. Know it must have been rough for you losing such a great friend." Ian nodded. "I don't mean to spread gossip, but I've heard that our Tony was a bit of a switch hitter."

"Who told you that?"

"I don't remember exactly. Someone who saw Neville in Athens with a very pretty male prostitute on his arm. Did you ever suspect he had such inclinations?"

"Never! He was my friend," said Ian, turning away.

"Yes. I remember when he'd visit Innismere on school vacs with you. Handsome fellow. Half had a crush on him then. Sorry, brother dear. I must try to watch my faggish tongue under your roof."

"Tony Neville was a good man. I miss him," said Ian softly, looking at the worn face of Alexander.

Damien clapped him on the shoulder. "I've no doubt you do. The two of you were inseparable in the old days, and he and Anne have been great friends to you through the years. I'm sorry if I've besmirched his character with idle gossip. Homosexuality is not quite the peccadillo for me that it is for you. So. . .I think I'll go on up to bed. See you in the morning and thanks again for your belief in me, brother."

"Goodnight, Damien." Ian stared out the window into the black, Irish night.

✪ ✪ ✪

Christmas at Innismere that year was especially festive with the entire D'Arcy family together for the holiday. Ian, Tristan, and Damien took a farm lorry into the wood to find a tree, while Lily directed the ladies baking cookies, cakes, and other goodies.

Bella and Violet went up to the attic for the tree ornaments, and while they were there, Bella showed her sister-in-law Siobhan's trunk.

"Look at this one," said Bella, removing the tissue from the apricot charmeuse gown. Violet examined the beautiful dress and looked at the label.

"Yes, I thought so. It's a Vionnet!" she exclaimed. "Madeleine Vionnet was a French couturière from the twenties and thirties. She invented the bias cut so that her dresses mold to the body and move like no one else's. This is in perfect condition. I bet it would look gorgeous on you, Bella, with your figure."

Bella held it up to herself. "It wouldn't be right to try it on, would it?"

"Of course it would. But let's go down where it's not freezing." They took the gown to Violet's room and Bella slipped into it. It fit as if it had been made for her in Vionnet's salon.

"Incredible!" said Violet. "I never understood why you didn't at least go to that appointment I set up for you with Conrad. You'd have made a brilliant model."

Bella frowned. "I thought he said I could never make it with my red hair and funny teeth?"

"No. How did you get that impression? I told Tris that Conrad was very much taken with your portfolio. Tristan told me that you'd decided you weren't interested after all. I was embarrassed after taking up Conrad's time. Ginger hair is very fashionable now, and your teeth are charming, probably even an asset in that they add personality and individuality to stand out from all the other perfect faces." Bella bit her lip and looked down. "Oh, dear, don't tell me we've caught Trissy in a bit of a fib?"

"Why would he tell me the photographer didn't like me? It was all his idea."

"Must have been the old green-eyed monster. When I told him Conrad raved about you, he must have had second thoughts. Don't worry about it, Bella. I have contacts in Dublin if you still want to get into it. And you must wear this dress. It's made for you!" Violet embraced her.

"I'm so glad to get this chance to know you, Bella. Tristan seems happier than I've ever seen him. You must not worry yourself over this misunderstanding over the modeling gig. You've a better life than any model I know."

On Christmas Eve they decorated the great fir tree which had been set up in the hall so that the top could be trimmed from the stairs with the beautiful lights and ornaments collected by the family for generations. The mantels, banisters, and chandeliers were festooned with holly and evergreen boughs which filled the rooms with the very scent of Christmas.

Tristan and Bella drove into Kildare town for Midnight Mass. Bella was very quiet on the drive home afterward, prompting him to ask her if she were missing her family.

"I do, but I'd rather be here with you," she said quietly.

He took her hand on the car seat. "You looked very beautiful, very holy when you took communion. It's a side of you I've never seen before."

"I never missed Mass 'til I went to London."

"What did you pray for tonight?"

"I thanked God that we're so happy together, and I asked him to please help you not to lie to me again, Tris." Her eyes were filled with sad reproach.

"I haven't since that business with the Duke."

"Why did you lie to me about the modeling thing? Violet told me that photographer liked my pictures. That ginger hair is in now."

"Good old Vi let the cat out of the bag, did she?"

"Why, Tris? You sent my photos to him. It was all your idea."

"Was being a bloody model so important to you?"

"No, but your being straight with me is. You promised me you'd never lie to me again!"

"I was afraid. I've seen Conrad Mailer in action, and he's a devilishly smooth character, has affairs with his girls and the like. I was afraid I might lose you, Bella. I didn't want you to become one of those empty headed, self-absorbed creatures. I wanted you to stay just the way you are, always." He looked over at her anxiously. "You can understand why I did it, can't you? Tell me you're not cross with me."

She slid across the seat and leaned her head against

his shoulder. "How could I ever be angry with you, Tris? I just wish you'd told me the truth."

"You mean if I'd said, 'You have a great chance of being a model, but I don't want you to because I'm too insecure,' you'd have understood?"

"I'd have never left you for some lecherous old man. I'm not that brainless and easy, you know. Besides, I already knew you were my future then. I'd a thousand times rather be your wife than on the cover of *Vogue.*"

He hugged her to him and kissed her cheek quickly. "I swear to you, Bella, that I shall never lie to you again."

When Lily returned from the midnight Christmas service at St. Anne's, she saw the light coming from Ian's room. She put on her dressing gown and rapped on their connecting door. He was in bed, a book on his lap.

"How was the service?"

"As usual. There were only ten other people there. It's such a pity to waste that beautiful, old church." He removed his glasses as she perched on the edge of the bed.

"Everyone in the area is Catholic. The Protestant Church is on the decline in the Republic as you well know."

"I suppose. Did you and Damien have a good chat?"

"Mmm. He's very excited over this new singer of his from Derry."

"Probably the latest in a long line of losers. Poor Damien." She smoothed the silk of the gown she'd got at Montenapoleone in Rome. "What are you reading?"

"It's that old one about Communist moles in the British government. Rather good."

She sighed and played with the sash of her dressing gown. "Wish I had a good book. I'm too keyed up to sleep, don't know why." Ian looked very handsome in his dark blue pajamas, his hair ruffled instead of perfectly groomed as usual.

"Darling, would you mind if I slept in here tonight? I feel so. . .lonely."

"Of course not." He made room for her, and she doffed her robe and slid under the covers.

"Go on reading. It won't bother me."

"I'm at a good stopping point." He closed his book and turned off the light. They lay in the dark not touching each other.

"Ian, can you remember when we couldn't get enough of each other, like Tristan and Bella?"

"Yes, of course I do."

"Were we as passionate as they seem, or have I just romanticized it?"

"We were very much in love. We are still in love."

"I miss our passion," she blurted, tears burning her eyelids.

"I know you do. You've been very understanding, Lily," he said hoarsely. "I'm sorry. . ."

"Do stop apologizing! I know it's beyond your control. Did you see that specialist in London?"

"Yes. It's nothing physical. It's just some temporary thing that will go away if we're patient."

"I'm being very patient," she said.

"I know you are, my darling, and I appreciate that. This is very humiliating for me, for any man."

"It's not just the sex I miss, Ian. It's holding each other, the tender kisses." He put his arm about her, and she turned to him.

"I've been so absorbed in my problem that I haven't thought how lonely you must feel, my love." He kissed her forehead, and she clung to him.

"I miss feeling your body, your heat." She sniffed. "I don't care that much about the sex, really, I swear."

He rubbed the small of her back. "I love you very much, Lily. Never think this is in any way a lack of desire. Whatever is causing this, it's not you."

"Darling, don't you think it might help to see a psychiatrist? If it's not physical, it must be mental."

He stiffened. "I hardly think I need to go to that extreme. It will probably cure itself shortly, as Dr. O'Neill said."

"Ian, could it possibly be tied up with Tony? With his death?"

He turned on his back.

"Please, you must talk about it. When you keep things within you, they fester. You need to air out your feelings—catharsis!"

"I'm not in a mental crisis, and this has nothing to do with Tony. I'm sure it's just overwork and the emotional cataclysm our marriage just went through."

"Everything was wonderful on our trip. Why did this problem crop up again as soon as we got home?"

"I don't know, Lily," he said, turning his back to her. "Let's get some sleep. I'm not in the mood for an argument."

"I'm not arguing. I want to help you, and I know you well enough to sense you're holding something back from me. You're always so close with your real feelings. I'm your wife, darling. You can tell me anything." He was silent. She slid her hand under his pajama top. Ian had the softest skin, almost softer than her own. She pressed her mouth to the back of his neck.

"I love you, Ian. Please let me help you."

He turned to her and pulled her against him. "If you want to help me, Lily, just leave me be. I'll work this out by myself." She nestled under his arm, and eventually fell asleep.

Charlie

❖ ❖ ❖

IT WAS THE first week in January, and Ian was beginning to worry that Connors might have been right about Charlemagne. He'd had a go at riding the black colt himself and had been tossed into the mud for his efforts. Time was running out. If Charlie was to be raced as a three-year-old, he had to start conditioning at once for the flat season which began in March.

Ian called Frank into the stable office to help him decide what to do. "I'll never have another chance to run a horse with this one's potential and bloodlines. It would be an incredible crime not to race him, Frank."

The race trainer looked across the desk and sucked on the unlit pipe he always had ready between his thin lips. "Aye, 'tis a crime, but the bloody bastard can't be ridden. As I see it, we can work on him and possibly race him as a four-year-old, or we can put him to stud. That's his real value even if he never runs on a track."

"If we could just find a work jockey to get him into shape. He'll be at his peak this season, and I don't want to give up without really trying. Young Rafferty says his brother Thomas could ride Charlie. He's a work jockey at the Curragh. Thomas can ride the 'divil himself' according to his brother Billy."

"This would certainly be his chance," said Frank. "The

153

horse needs to be ridden every day though, to get him into condition, and Rafferty is already employed at the Curragh."

"I'm going to get him out here anyway and see what the lad thinks of Charlie. Maybe we can arrange something."

The two walked out of the office together to find a man waiting, hat in hand.

"G'day, Mr. D'Arcy. Mr. Connors." He held his hand out to Ian. "Brett Fallon's my name. I spoke to Mr. Connors a few weeks ago about a job here." He had a firm grip and a hand not shy of hard work from the rough feel of it.

"You must be the Australian," said Ian.

"I've told Mr. Fallon we were over-employed if anything, Sir Ian," said Frank. He excused himself with an air of patent disapproval.

"He did tell me that, sir, but I thought I'd like to hear that from the boss's mouth first," said the Aussie with a confident grin, showing even, white teeth in his sunburned face.

"I'm afraid it's true. I only have one racehorse in contention this year, so I'd hardly need another trainer."

"That would be your filly Violet's Season. Hear she had a great year as a two-year-old. But what about your new French colt? I understand he's somethin'."

"You've been doing your homework, Fallon."

"Horse gossip seems to be as big over here as it is at home. They say the colt's got a mean temper on him."

Ian smiled. "The word's out, is it? They didn't lie. No one's been able to ride the bastard, so it looks like we won't be running him this season."

"I've yet to meet the horse I couldn't ride, sir. I'm not quite jockey size, but I could condition and train him for you."

Ian was enjoying the accent and the cool confidence of the man who looked to be in his mid- to late twenties. "So, you're good, are you?"

"Yes, sir. I am."

"What is your experience, Mr. Fallon?"

"My father bred and trained flat racers at our station south of Sydney. He had the Melbourne Cup winner in '70. I've worked horses all my life. Racing is all I know really."

"Why did you leave, and why come to Ireland?"

"My mother was from Wexford. Fallon, my stepdad, died last year, and since I had no real ties there anymore, I thought I'd check out the country of my roots. See a bit of the world as well."

Their attention was attracted by a ruckus down at the other end of the long stable corridor. Two boys were trying to bathe Charlemagne much to his displeasure. "So that's your rogue colt then?" asked Fallon.

"That's the rascal himself. Great bloodlines, conformation, and speed, but he's a decided bastard."

The horse kicked the stableboy trying to rinse the soap off him. The boy fell to the ground and rolled out of the way with a howl. Charlemagne reared, and the other boy holding the twitch let go and ran for his life. The powerful animal snapped the rope holding him and galloped wildly down the stable corridor toward Ian and the Aussie. Ian waved his arms to keep him from bolting out the open stable door, so the horse thundered past to the other end of the corridor. Finding his way blocked, Charlemagne turned to face the approaching stablehands, eyes rolling and ears laid back, ready to fight for his newfound freedom.

"Easy does it, lads," cautioned Connors. "Don't rush him."

To everyone's surprise, the Aussie began moving

slowly toward the nervous colt. Charlie pawed the saw-dust and snorted, eyes on the approaching man. Fallon paused, but continued, speaking in what sounded like French to Ian. They all watched in amazement as the Aussie reached out very slowly and caught the colt's head collar, then calmly stroked the great, gleaming, black neck.

"I'll be damned," said Billy Rafferty.

Fallon led Charlemagne back to where he was being washed and retied him. "Were you using cold water?" he asked the stableboy.

"It was neither hot nor cold," Rafferty hedged, though the hose he'd been using was in clear sight.

"Try using the same temp you'd want in your own bath. This gentleman is a king, and should be treated like one."

"Do as he says," Ian ordered, and Billy ran off to fetch some heated water.

Ian walked outside with Fallon, who lit a cigarette after first offering him one.

"You're a bold bastard," Ian said.

"I've a way with animals, always have had," said the Aussie matter-of-factly.

"How'd a chap from the outback learn fluent French?"

"My mother was a teacher. She met my stepfather when she was governess to his four sons. I'm not ignorant, Mr. D'Arcy."

"Of course not. The French was just a bit unexpected. Certainly seemed to do the trick though."

"It's his language, eh? So, Mr. D'Arcy, I'll make you a deal. I think I can have your horse fit to race by midsummer at least. I'll work a month for you for room and board only. After the month is up, you decide whether or not you want to keep me on. I'm not picky about salary. If you think I'm not as good as I say I am, you can send me packing."

Ian shook his head. There was something irresistible about this persistent young man. "Come on up to the house, Fallon, and we'll discuss it over a cup of tea."

"Thanks. I could use a cuppa."

As they walked to the house, Ian asked what had made him pick Innismere out of all the stables in County Kildare.

"Since I arrived in Ireland, I've been staying with my mother's family in Wexford. I came up to Kildare since it's the center of racing in the country, and asked about. I heard of Innismere as a likely up-and-coming small outfit. They say you run a first class operation and are a fair man. I wanted to get my start in a small place where I could expect to run things in a few years. Then the talk about your new horse intrigued me."

Fallon was nothing if not confident, yet Ian somehow did not find his attitude offensive.

Lily was making chocolate mousse for dinner when they came into the kitchen. She stared in undisguised dismay at the intruder from the terrace as he stood hat in hand in her house.

"Put on the tea, please, Mary," said Ian, taking off his jacket. "Lily, I'd like you to meet Brett Fallon. He's going to attempt to train Charlie for us. Fallon, my wife, Lily."

"G'day, ma'am," said the Aussie, extending his hand. Lily wiped hers carefully on her apron before taking his hand, rather limply.

"I thought you were overstaffed already, Ian."

"We are, but Mr. Fallon is very difficult to say no to. He's already proven he has a rapport with Charlie, so I'm giving him a month to see what he can do." The two men sat down at the table, and Mrs. Kelly placed a pot of tea and some fresh baked brown bread before them. Ian introduced her to Fallon.

"Wouldn't Australia be a long way off from Kildare,

then?" commented Mary who was consumed with curiosity.

"Ireland's the country to be in for racehorses, and Kildare is the center of it all, ma'am," Fallon replied.

"Where exactly would ye be comin' from?" asked the cook as she handed him some butter and gooseberry jam for the bread he was hungrily consuming.

"Fallon's Station. It's southeast of Sydney, between Katoomba and Woolongong." The exotic names fairly quivered in the air of the old-fashioned kitchen.

"Goodness, sounds as if there'd be cannibals there," exclaimed Mrs. Kelly.

"I've heard it said that the Aboriginals had a taste for the odd Chinaman, but I think they've given that up lately," said Fallon with a grin.

"Them with the boomerangs and such?"

"That's chiefly for the tourists nowadays, along with the stuffed koala bears."

Lily, who'd been avidly listening to all this, put the finished mousse in the refrigerator, and left the room to prove she couldn't be less interested in koalas and Aborigines.

Ian sat at the table over his tea and studied the young man across from him as he finished off the last piece of crusty, brown bread slathered with butter and jam. It had obviously been a while since Fallon had eaten. In spite of his rough appearance and brutal accent, there was something about him that suggested good breeding. Fallon had good looks, seemed intelligent, and there was the French. He had an air about him that had immediately commanded the respect of the stablehands. Ian decided that Brett Fallon might be a valuable find. Frank was getting on in years and was very rigid in his ways.

"How soon can you start, Fallon?"

"This minute, sir. I've got my gear with me."

"Sure I'd take you on, eh?"

"Hoping. I travel light." He had a very appealing smile.

"I'll have to put you up in the house until we can arrange quarters for you. Get your things, and I'll show you to your room. You'll take your meals with Mr. and Mrs. Kelly."

"I'm looking forward to that," he said, turning to Mary. "I haven't had such grand brown bread since my mother passed on."

"Go on with ye!" said Mrs. Kelly, highly pleased. "We eat at six for breakfast, noon for dinner, and six for tea, and I don't like me cookin' to go cold."

"No chance of that with me about," said Fallon. "If you'll excuse me, Mr. D'Arcy, I'll go get my gear."

"Well, Mary?" asked Ian as soon as Fallon had gone out the back door.

Mary drew herself up and delivered her considered opinion. "A likely lad. Well spoken—has a way about him. I've always heard that the Aussies were divilish charmers."

"Perhaps I'd better warn Seamus that the chap's already made a conquest," said Ian with a twinkle in his eye.

Lily was on her way up the stairs when she met the Australian coming down. "What are you doing?" she asked in astonishment.

"Going downstairs, ma'am."

"What were you doing above stairs is the question. What are you up to? I saw you checking out the house the first time you came here."

"I know. I saw you checking me out," replied Fallon, not bothering to hide a smile.

Lily flushed. "You are impertinent! You have absolutely no business anywhere in this house but the kitchen."

"What is the problem?" asked Ian, coming up behind her.

"This stable man has been roaming through the house, Ian. I just caught him sneaking down from upstairs."

"Lily, he's staying in the far wing bedroom until I can arrange something else. I told him to put his things away."

She looked at Fallon whose face was infuriatingly innocent. "Well, you might have told me," she said, feeling foolish.

"Sorry, ma'am. Didn't have the opportunity. Excuse me, I'll be getting on to work now." He trotted down the stairs.

"Why in God's name, Ian, are you hiring that man, much less putting him in a guest bedroom? Have you lost your senses?"

"Now Lily, the chap's made an excellent impression on everyone but you and Connors. Frank's antipathy is understandable since Fallon is a potential rival for his position, but why have you taken such a dislike?"

"I'm a very good judge of character, and this man is up to no good, I can just feel it, Ian."

"You've met him only once, and he was very polite, although you were not. Your hostility seems uncalled for, Lily."

"The first day he came here I saw him looking at the house when he was unaware that he was being observed. His expression was. . . I don't know how to describe it. As if he wanted to tear Innismere down brick by brick. He's trouble, Ian, I know it. In fact, it even crossed my mind the way he made up to Fionn that he could be a thief, or even IRA!"

Ian laughed. "My God, you've an imagination! An

Aussie IRA? They are clever, aren't they! And at Innismere—for heaven's sake why?"

"Don't forget Shergar," she said. The Irish Revolutionary Army was allegedly responsible for the theft of the great stallion from nearby Ballymany Stud, and the Irish Derby winner worth millions had never been seen again.

"Ah, I see now. Fallon's here to horsenap Charlie. It all falls into place."

"Ian, I'm serious. Maybe IRA is too farfetched, but the man is dangerous. I can feel it even if it doesn't make sense."

Ian smoothed her hair and looked down into her eyes. "My darling, until you have more substantive reasons than mere women's intuition, you'll have to trust me to be a decent judge of men. You've misread the fellow. He seems quite open and unmysterious to me. The only thing he's after is a start in the Irish racing business. I believe you've been reading too many novels of late."

"What else am I supposed to do with my nights?" she retorted—and instantly regretted.

Ian dropped his hands away. "I'll go have a shower. I smell of horse."

"Darling, I'm sorry," she called after him, but he kept on going up the stairs as if he didn't hear.

As Ian had feared, Frank Connors, who had been his father's trainer before him, was not pleased by the hiring of Brett Fallon. Frank offered to resign if his work with the horses was unsatisfactory. Ian assured the trainer that he had valued his services through the years and hoped to have them for many more to come. Diplomatically, Ian asked Connors to train Fallon and teach him all he knew. "I know that you've forgotten more about racing than this lad will ever know, Frank, but he shows potential.

When that very sad day comes that you decide to retire, perhaps, with your help, he'll be able to step into your boots if not fill them. We do want the great work you've done to go on into the future. I know that you want what's best for Innismere."

The trainer was somewhat mollified by the flattery, but made one last jab at his rival. "This Fallon does not have a work permit, sir. I asked him. The government's not keen on foreigners taking jobs when good Irish lads are going without."

When Ian asked Brett Fallon about the permit, he replied, "I thought it would be easier for you to get me one with your connections, Mr. D'Arcy. I'm not getting paid for a month, so there's time."

"I suppose I can pull some strings. If we're mutually satisfied, of course. You did say your mother was Irish?"

"Yes sir, my father as well. I'm one hundred percent mick."

"There shouldn't be a problem, then. I'll need your passport and birth certificate to get the papers, however."

"I'll have to send home for my birth certificate."

"Do that right away. How old are you, Fallon?"

"I'll be thirty on May thirteenth, sir."

"How's a good-looking chap like you avoided marriage all this time?"

"Let me say, I do like women, Mr. D'Arcy. Best clear that up. I suppose I've just never run into the right one. I like to stay unencumbered."

"Didn't mean to pry into your personal life. Been married twenty-one years myself, so it's difficult to imagine your state of unencumbrance."

Fallon shook his head. "Twenty-one years of lookin' across the table at the same sheila—now that's hard to imagine! Mrs. D'Arcy is easy to look at though, even if she can't stand the sight of me."

Ian chuckled. "She's taken it into her head that you're a bit of a dangerous chap, possibly even IRA, Fallon."

"I am flattered! I fancy myself a rebel, but hardly that serious."

"Just work your charms on her the way you do Mary, and she'll come round."

"I've a feeling it would take more than a bit o' blarney to get round your wife, sir."

"Speaking of flattery, kowtow to Frank a bit. He's sensitive about your taking his position."

"I understand. Are you satisfied with what I'm doing with Charlie?" Ian replied that he was indeed. Fallon spent hours everyday working with the black colt on a lunge line, brushing, stroking, and talking to the animal as if he were an unbroken yearling. In return, Charlemagne would allow him to enter his box without challenge as he only did Paddy before.

"Charlie's really not a killer at heart. I go along with Paddy that he's been mistreated at a young age. Someone's tried to break his spirit, and I don't believe in that. I expect to ride him this week, now that I've got his trust."

"I'm looking forward to seeing that," said Ian.

"Frank's looking forward to seeing me land on my backside," said Fallon with a grin. Ian clapped him on the shoulder; the Aussie felt hard as a rock.

Although she'd managed to avoid the new trainer for the week he lived in the house, Lily felt relieved when the intruder had moved to a refurbished room above the stable. As the stable was minus a shower, Fallon still had to use the downstairs' bathroom, and now and then she would run into him coming out of it, hair wet, towel over his shoulder. He always greeted her with a friendly smile, and a "G'day, Missus," and went on his way. Something about the man annoyed Lily no end. She was sure that beneath the pleasant, polite exterior, beat a heart full of contempt for his betters. The way he called Ian "Mr. D'Arcy," infuriated her. Her mild-mannered husband merely said, "I imagine he's not had to deal with titles where he comes from." Ian rarely thought ill of anyone, which was one reason Lily always felt she had to be more suspicious in compensation.

The thing she disliked most of all about the race trainer was the way he had all the females in the household in a dither. She found Fallon averagely decent looking, but in no way someone she'd give a second glance to on the street were she in the habit of doing that sort of thing. Evileen, however, was so busy checking herself in the mirrors and hanging about the kitchen when the Aussie was there, that she barely had time to clean.

Of course, the man fancied himself a lady-killer with that cheeky, too-familiar smile of his. Lily had been on her knees looking for a tart pan in the scullery cupboard, when she'd witnessed him in action. She'd heard Mary gasp out loud, and looking round the corner, had seen Fallon nuzzling the old woman's jowly cheek, his arms about her ample waist.

"So when are we going to tell the old man about us, Mary?"

Mrs. Kelly cackled loudly. "Go on with ye! You'll not get any extra portions out of me with such carryings on," she tittered, pleased as punch at his absurd flirtation.

"It's not food I'm after, Mary. You know I'm smitten."

"Stop it! You'll give me a seizure, and me old enough to be your mother. Such a playboy ye are, Brett!"

"You're breakin' me heart, Mary! Any more cake left from lunch?"

"Just sit yourself down, and I'll cut you a slice, and some tea to wash it down."

Far more worrisome to Lily was the friendship which had sprung up between Fallon and her son and Bella. They often took the Aussie with them to Dublin and elsewhere on his time off. Lily was not at all sure it was camaraderie Fallon was after, either. She'd caught him checking out Bella's legs when the dim girl bent over in one of her too-short skirts. If her son's marriage had to break up, she did not want that sort of thing to be the cause.

The more Lily distrusted Fallon, the more Ian seemed to be pleased with his new man. He told her how Fallon had improved efficiency at the stable; the hands worked harder for him because they admired him. He was easy and joking with them, unlike stiff, old Connors for whom they did as little as they could get away with. The Aussie was now riding the killer horse who was gentle as a lamb in his hands. "He talks to him in French, Lily. It's the damnedest thing," said Ian. Even Frank was coming round to grudgingly respect Fallon's horsemanship and hard work.

Ian had her come down to the half-mile track beyond the stables to watch the trainer give Charlie a workout. In spite of herself, Lily had to admit that the man looked as if he knew what he was about on a horse. Ian clocked them as they galloped twice round the track, the Aussie's blond-streaked hair a bright banner in the March sun.

"A second off his best time!" Ian yelled as Fallon slowed the horse to a trot. He took him round once more at a slow trot, then reined to a halt in front of them.

"He can do much better than that," said the trainer when he heard the time. He patted Charlie's lathered, black neck. "He purely loves to run!" Fallon looked quite attractive in a dark blue sweater, the sleeves pushed up to show strong looking, bronzed forearms, Lily noticed.

He walked the colt round the track a few more times to cool him down.

"What good is he if only Mr. Fallon can ride him?" Lily asked.

"Tommy Rafferty's been up on Charlie as well. He's just got his jockey's license and is very impressed with the horse. He's agreed to be our jockey if Brett can get him ready. So what do you think of him, my love?"

"He's beautiful, fast, and dangerous," she answered, her eyes on Fallon's blond head in the distance.

✪ ✪ ✪

Ian had to go mind the London store for a week, and Lily found herself increasingly nervous and irritable. When Tristan greeted her one morning with, "G'day, Mum," she lost her temper with him.

"Not you, too. I am so sick of Australian!"

"It's Strine, Mum. You know Brett's a fair dinkum laddie," said her son.

"He's a con man, and I seem to be the only one who knows it."

"Give the bloke a break. He's really very nice if you'd get to know him. He just gets your ruff up for some reason I can't fathom."

"If I were you, I wouldn't be so taken with him. I've seen how he looks at Bella." Tristan's grin vanished.

"He's just such a flatterer. He makes me feel very uncomfortable."

"Brett likes Bella. Who doesn't like her—only you, Mother."

"I'm very fond of Bella."

"Bugger that. You're not very nice to her. In fact, you've been a bear to everyone since you and Dad got back together. It's too bad the world can't live up to your standards, Mother."

"Don't talk to me like that. You see yourself the big, married man, but you're still the child whose dirty nappies I changed."

"Once? Or was it twice?"

To her dismay, she burst into tears. Tristan was contrite at once.

"I'm sorry, Mum." He put his arms about her. "Please, Mother, I shouldn't have talked like that." He gave her his handkerchief. "I know how hard it's been on you," he said, patting her back.

"You were right, Tristan. I don't even like myself much these days."

"You should have gone with Dad to London. You never get out of the house. I think you're bored from not having enough to do. You used to get involved in those charities, Mum."

"It all seemed so pointless, and I was tired of dealing with groups of women."

"You could get a job. You're very intelligent and capable, yet you waste yourself."

"I have plenty to do just running this house properly. Do you really think I was a bad mother?"

"I didn't mean that. You were great. It's not your fault all D'Arcys have to have nannies."

"Maybe I didn't change many of your diapers, but I did read you stories and spend time with you. I loved you to distraction, Tristan." Her voice broke, and he kissed her on the cheek.

"I haven't forgotten those times, Mother. They're dear to me."

"Your father thought I'd make a sissy of you the way you'd sit on my lap. I'd only have to think, 'I want my Trissy,' and here you'd come as though you could read my thoughts. Until you went away to school, and then you'd have no more to do with me."

He kissed her hands. "I still love you, Mother, very much! I hope that Bella will be as good a mother someday as you were to me."

Lily embraced him tearfully. "I'm sorry I've not been nicer to Bella. She really is very sweet and tries so hard. I'll try to be better to her, I promise."

"That would mean the world to me. And at least try going out for a ride sometime. The air clears your head of all the cobwebs."

On the next pleasant day, Lily decided to take her son's advice. Dressed warmly in riding clothes, she appeared at the stable and asked the thin, little cross-eyed boy whose brother was a jockey to fetch her mare.

"Yes, ma'am, your Ladyship," he stammered, looking shocked at the sight of her in the stable. He scurried off to get her horse.

While she waited, she strolled down the corridor looking into the stalls. Things did seem cleaner than her last visit. Turning the corner, she saw a blacksmith working on Charlemagne. She paused, afraid to get too close to the dangerous horse who stood docilely enough while the smith filed a hoof. The man stood up, and she saw that it was Brett Fallon.

"My goodness, you do everything!"

"Couldn't get a farrier brave enough to work on him," said Fallon who wore a leather apron over his jeans and undershirt, and had a black streak on his ruddy cheek.

"You're the bravest man about, are you?"

"He's used to me. We've a truce."

"How did you learn to do that?" she asked.

"I watched the farriers at the station. It interested me, so I learned how. It's a great way to work out your frustrations. Should try it sometime." He smiled slightly and began hammering a glowing, red-hot shoe.

Lily flushed. What did he mean by that? "I suppose we could all use a go at it," she yelled over the racket.

Fallon held the hot shoe to the hoof to check the fit, then thrust it hissing into a bucket of water. He wiped the sweat off his face with the back of his hand, adding another streak of grime to his chiseled cheekbone. "Some of us more than others," he said, looking up at her with what she interpreted as a mocking smile.

The stableboy appeared with her gray mare before she could think of a comeback.

"Enjoy your ride, Missus," said Fallon without looking up to see the anger in her face. She mounted Lady Jane and coaxed her into a brisk trot out the stable door.

How rude he was, she thought. Was it that obvious to everyone? Was there a sign on her forehead which said, "This woman's husband has not touched her in three months"? How humiliating! Ian had at last gone to a psychiatrist, but his problem was still there. What if it were permanent? Sex wasn't everything, but when it was absent—well it was getting to be a pretty damn big thing! It was so obviously to do with Tony, yet that was a verboten topic with Ian. She hoped he was being totally honest with the doctor.

Lily slowed the mare and took deep breaths. It was nice to have fresh air in one's lungs; Tristan was right. It was lovely out. The moisture-laden Irish air seemed to make everything clearer, the colors more intense. But neither riding nor a job would cure what was ailing her.

The image of Brett Fallon at the forge flashed unbidden into her mind, his muscles bulging as he pounded the horseshoe. Although not as tall as Ian, Fallon was heavier through the chest and shoulders. A fleece of gold curls spilled over the top of his sweat- and soot-stained undershirt, and his ruddy tan turned to cream on the skin that never saw the sun.

"Damn!" she said aloud, and Lady Jane flicked her ears back. Lily petted her dappled neck. There was something so disturbing about that man!

❂ ❂ ❂

At tea, Tristan announced he had tickets for all to see that evening's performance of Sean O'Casey's play *The Plough and the Stars* at Dublin's Abbey Theatre.

"That's sweet of you, darling, but I'm sure the two of you would have a better time by yourselves," said Lily.

"Mother, I already have the tickets. Center orchestra seats. We want you to come."

"Please do come," said Bella as if she really meant it.

So she agreed even though she suspected they were only feeling sorry for her. Lily had always liked that play and enjoyed going to the Abbey, the famed Irish National Theatre formed in 1904 by the poet Yeats and Lady Gregory as part of the movement to promote the country's arts and language.

"We'll eat dinner after at the Shelbourne. I've already told Mary," said Tristan.

Lily dressed carefully and put her hair up for the occasion. Tris was a darling to arrange this to cheer her up. She tried on the new sable—a bit much for Dublin, but why not?

Downstairs she presented Bella with a pair of pearl earrings. "These are part of the D'Arcy jewels, and I never wear them. They should look marvelous on you with your complexion."

Looking very pleased, Bella tried them on. They did look very well on her. Lily thought she really must take the girl shopping and get her some nicer things.

"Looks like I'll be with the two best-looking women in Dublin tonight," said Tristan.

To Lily's surprise, he turned the Mercedes down the stable drive. "Where are you going?" she asked.

"I forgot to mention that Brett's coming, too. He's never been to a play before. Can you imagine?"

"You forgot on purpose. You knew I'd never come with that man along."

"Come on, Mother. Brett's a damn jolly chap. You're going to be forced to discover that tonight. I'd already asked him a week ago, so I can hardly uninvite him. Please be a sport, Mum. This can be an excellent evening if you'll just relax and enjoy it." He honked the horn below Brett's stable room.

"It's just that it doesn't look right with your father away."

"Who cares how it looks? Don't be such a stick, Mum. Dad's his biggest fan. I know he would approve. Here he comes. Please be decent, Mother."

Fallon got in the back seat beside her. He greeted everyone, looking at Lily last.

"Hello," she said, drawing her fur about her.

"Evening, Mrs. D'Arcy," he said with that infuriating, cocky grin.

Bella pulled back her hair to show him the earrings.

"Beautiful, Bella. You're all looking flash tonight. Don't know if I'm up to the company," said the trainer.

"Aye, but it's grand-looking you are yourself tonight, Brett. Isn't he, Mother?" said Tristan, glancing at her in the rearview mirror. Lily let her gaze travel over Fallon who, dressed in a black turtleneck, cords, and tweed jacket, did look nice, even if he weren't in suit and tie.

"Mr. Fallon cleans up very well," she said.

"At least I've no horseshit on my shoes," he said, looking her straight in the eye. Lily turned away. This was going to be some evening!

When they reached the city, Tristan drove along the

quays on the south bank of the river. The Liffey divides Dublin in two halves. In general, the "haves" live on the south side of the river where there are beautiful Georgian townhouses, the fashionable Grafton Street/St. Stephen's Green area, and Trinity College. North of the Liffey, except for a few magnificent buildings fronting the river, lies flashy O'Connell Street, and the slums and lower class neighborhoods of the "have-nots." Tristan pointed out the Guinness Brewery, largest in Europe, Christ Church Cathedral, built by Strongbow in the twelfth century, and Dublin Castle, former seat of British rule. Across the river they could see the lighted facades of The Four Courts and the Custom House, splendid reminders of the eighteenth century when Dublin was the second city in the British empire. They crossed the Liffey on the broad O'Connell Street Bridge to get to the Abbey, no longer in its original location. So many historic buildings had been burned or damaged during the fighting for independence in the twenties.

Brett Fallon laughed and seemed to enjoy O'Casey's play, a realistic account of life in Dublin's teeming slums at the turn of the century. Afterward, Tristan told of the play's first production in 1926 when the audience had pelted the actors with vegetables, fought in the stalls, and stormed the stage. All because O'Casey had portrayed Dubliners realistically, warts and all, instead of making them saintly patriots. One character was even a prostitute. Critics deemed it "Sewage School Drama" and a lewd insult to Irish womanhood, even though only blocks away the red-light district of the Monto had long flourished.

"We're one of the most hypocritical countries in the world," Tristan asserted. "We drove away our great men of letters like Joyce, O'Casey, and Beckett with our stupid, two-faced intolerance."

They drove up and down the city's main artery, O'Connell Street, past the statues honoring Parnell and Daniel O'Connell and the columned front of the General Post Office, site of the Easter Rising in 1916. To Lily's surprise, Fallon was knowledgeable about Irish history. He explained that his mother had been a schoolteacher from Wexford. Since she had left Ireland, many of the fine old buildings which once lined O'Connell Street, the broadest street in Europe, had been razed by urban developers. Young people thronged the sidewalks, probably hoping to banish the boredom of unemployment in the dance halls, pool rooms, and fast food places that now fronted the street.

They drove back across the river to the more genteel side of town to the Shelbourne, the city's most famous hotel, on St. Stephen's Green. At the coat check for the dining room, Fallon helped Lily off with her fur. He did seem to have manners, she noticed. She quickly scanned the restaurant, hoping not to see a familiar face.

Lily asked the maitre d' for a table in the rear. He said nothing about Fallon's lack of a tie.

"They really suck up to you when they know you have a few quid," the trainer commented.

"Disgusting, but helpful at times," said Tristan.

"Ian and I have been dining here for twenty years. Henry is a friend, not a toady," she told Fallon.

"Oh? I thought it had to do with the big tip he expects, didn't know he was a close, personal friend," he replied.

"Enough of a friend that he didn't embarrass you about your lack of a tie, Mr. Fallon."

"Well, I think what we need here are shots of whiskey all around to warm us up," said Tristan, giving Lily a warning look from under his brows that made her suddenly miss his father.

"Just a glass of white Bordeaux for me," she said.

"I'll have her whiskey and mine. I feel a chill," said Fallon.

After they'd ordered dinner, Tristan asked Brett how he'd liked the play.

"Interesting, considering it's over sixty years old, though the lingo was hard for me to follow at times."

"Look who's talking about lingo," said Lily. She smiled at him; she was not going to be a bitch.

"I talk fine. It's the rest of you that have the problem," said Fallon.

"Mum's a big fan of Strine, Brett," said Tristan, grinning at her. "Little words like 'tucker' and 'bonzer' are cropping up in her vocabulary."

She had to smile. "It *is* very colorful, but it almost seems like you turn it on for our benefit."

"It's the only way I know how to talk," said Fallon with a shrug. "I'm not trying to be Crocodile Dundee."

"Who?"

"A movie about this Australian character, Mum. They never go to films," he explained to Fallon.

Their drinks arrived—the trainer had actually ordered two shots of whiskey and water, to Lily's embarrassment. To show her son she was trying, Lily asked about life on Fallon's Station. Brett explained how his Irish mother had immigrated to Sydney and had been hired by Mr. Fallon, a widower, to teach his four sons.

"He married her after a year, could get her services cheaper that way," said Fallon.

"So this station owner was your father?" said Lily.

"I'm a bastard. I never knew my real father," he said. That silenced the conversation for a second or two.

"How big is Fallon's Station?" Bella asked brightly.

"Three thousand acres. They have cattle as well as horses."

"Goodness, he must have been rich!" exclaimed the girl. "Was it very exciting growing up there?"

"If my stepdad was rich, he never let on to us, and if you enjoy ten hours hard work a day with dust down your throat, it was exciting. It was rugged, but a good life. One could have had a lot worse."

"I've never understood why you didn't stay there if you had such a racing stable as you say," said Lily.

"When my stepdad died, he left the operation divided equally between his four sons and me. He was a hard man and tight with a dollar, but very fair. Never treated his own sons any better than he treated me. Anyway, one of my stepbrothers and I never got on from day one, and he talked the others into buying me out. Nothing I could do about it. I thought I'd check out the other end of the world, and here I am."

"Did you get a fair price for your share?" asked Tristan.

"Enough for a one-way ticket to Dublin and living expenses for a bit."

"That's not right!" said Bella.

Fallon shrugged. "The way I look at it, dolly, I never expected to get anything in the first place, so what does it matter?"

Over an excellent dinner and a bottle of wine, Tristan kept Fallon talking about Australia. Lily studied the race trainer's face. There was something familiar about him, but she couldn't place what. Did he look like some film actor? He had a strong profile and a good nose with a slight scar across the bridge. He really was better than average looking after all, she decided, especially his eyes, which were a clear blue with a dark-ringed iris and very deeply set under his blond brows. They made one uncomfortable when they zeroed in on you.

There was a nervous energy about the man as he talked, about Aborigines now; a feeling of a coiled-up spring. Lily imagined that he had quite a temper, and that he was probably very good in bed. She chastised herself for this unworthy thought. What did that mean anyway? All she knew was her husband, and at the moment, almost any man would be good compared to poor Ian. Fallon gestured a lot with his hands as he talked about the Dreamtime, the Aboriginal idea of the creation. Lily liked to think that a man's hands were clues to his character; but his, despite nicks and scratches, were long-fingered and artistic looking. That certainly didn't jibe with anything she knew about him.

"The Abos get a bad rap. There's prejudice against them just like American blacks, but they are a very spiritual people," he was saying with earnest intensity. "They believe it's a man's sacred duty to care for the land and the animals—that we are in fact all one. Who are the wisest, the Abos who've maintained the land for thousands of years, or the whites who are managing to rape and pollute it in a mere two hundred?"

"How do you know so much about them?" asked Bella.

"We had some of them working seasonally on the station. I was friendly with one of them named Jim when I was young, and he took me to visit his relatives. His father was one of the elders still in touch with the old ways, and he'd tell stories about the Dreamtime. Now and then he'd go 'walkabout,' the ritual journey where they trace the path of their Dreamtime ancestor. It was damn fascinating. They're a much nobler people than they're given credit for."

After dinner, Tristan suggested they stop by the Horseshoe Bar across the hotel lobby for a nightcap. When he took Bella off to chat with some school friends, Lily was left stranded at the bar with Fallon. She ordered a Ballygowan water, the Irish answer to Perrier, and he demanded a "pig's ear," Aussie rhyming slang for a beer, which he, of course, drank straight from the bottle. Lily fervently prayed that no one she'd ever known would see them together.

"So, Mrs. D., looks like we may be forced to speak to each other," said Fallon, smiling at her and leaning an elbow on the bar.

"Don't strain yourself," she said, returning his smiling challenge.

"It's not the problem for me that it seems to be for you."

"Actually, I thought I was being perfectly charming to you all evening, Mr. Fallon."

"Were you?" He raised his heavy eyebrows. "I understand you suspect me of being IRA?"

Lily felt a flush of anger. How embarrassing for Ian to tell him that! "Let's just say I don't think we've seen the real Brett Fallon yet. Except possibly when I caught you looking at the house the first time you came to Innismere."

"Afraid I was planning on nicking the silver, were you?"

"That thought did occur to me. You had the most amazing look on your face when you thought no one was watching."

"I was properly impressed by the size of the place."

"It was more like you hated the thought of anyone living so grandly." Fallon took a swig of his beer and looked away. He was much too robust and outdoorsy looking to be in such a place—some working class pub was a more likely habitat.

"You misread me entirely. But why were you studying me so hard, my Lady?" He used her title for the first time as if he were making fun of it and her.

"I was wondering what a strange man was doing walking about my terrace and gaping at my house."

Fallon turned his dead-level, blue gaze on her with a force that almost made Lily flinch. "Tell me, are you as frustrated a bitch as you seem?"

"How dare you!" she gasped.

"It's the way you come across. You've got a good husband, a palace to live in, a terrific lad in Tris, furs and jewels on your fingers, but you are as unhappy a woman as I've ever met."

Her natural dread of making a scene helped Lily repress an urge to toss her drink in his rude face. She carefully placed her glass on the bar, turned her back on him, and left.

She told her surprised son that she wanted to leave at once and hurried out of the bar to the coat check.

Before she could object, Fallon took her sable from the checker and held it out for her. The insufferable prick was even smiling! Lily jammed her arms in the sleeves. "Nice animal," he said, stroking the fur. She whirled away from him. Bella and Tristan exchanged puzzled glances.

Conversation was strained on the ride home to Innismere. Lily huddled away from Fallon on the back seat.

"Did you and Brett have words?" Tristan asked as soon as they'd dropped him off at the stable.

"I do not like that man. If you and your father want to associate with him, fine, but leave me out of it!"

When she was at last alone in her bedroom, Lily vented her anger by punching her lace pillow with all her strength, "I hate you, you rude, common, son of a bitch!"

The next morning, Lily was doing her daily ballet workout in the empty ballroom Ian had had rigged with mirrors and a barre. She was trying to remember the steps to Giselle's first act solo. Though she'd danced in the company production of the ballet as one of the Wilis, she'd longed to do the lead role. Suddenly, reflected in the glass, she saw a figure standing in the doorway watching. She stopped at once, turned off the tape deck, and grabbed a towel.

"Is something wrong at the stable, Mr. Fallon?" she asked as she blotted the perspiration off her face and neck.

"No, ma'am. Something is wrong, but not with the horses. I wanted to apologize to you for my behavior last night. I had no right to say what I did and have been feelin' badly about it ever since."

Slinging the towel around her neck to cover her bra-lessness in the leotard, Lily walked over to him. Fallon was not wearing his trademark mocking smile today and in fact looked nervous.

"I believe you're a bit worried I might tell my husband you insulted me, and you'd be out on your ear."

"I don't think you'd do that, but I wouldn't blame you. When I've had a few, I revert to the old Aussie custom of 'bagging'—that's this sarcastic sort of put-down. I forgot I was in polite company last night—it just leapt out of my mouth. You should have tossed your drink in my face like you thought of doing."

"A mind reader, are you?" she said with a smile.

"Mmm. I could see only iron self-control saved me a dousing. I really enjoyed the play and the meal and that, but it brought out the worst in me being out with the poms. Insecurity I suppose."

"You insecure? That *is* an admission!"

"Yes ma'am. I'm not used to socializing with the likes of the D'Arcys. Tends to make me feel all thumbs and clubfooted, and prone to sticking my clubfoot in mouth. It did get my Irish up as well to see how desperate you were not to be seen with the likes of me." The truth of that made Lily flush.

"Anyway, I thought maybe you and I could call a truce. I know you took an instant dislike to me because I looked at your house wrong, but I swear I'm not IRA, and the silver is safe. Tris was wrong to try and force you and me into socializing, but I would like to end this war we seem to be having. I like this job, and you're the boss's wife. I could go about my work easier if we were, if not friends, at least not enemies. So I've said my piece then."

"I don't care for rudeness, but I do like straightforwardness, Mr. Fallon. Ian likes what you do with Charlie, and I wouldn't want to interfere with that, so I accept your apology."

"Thank you, ma'am." He held his hand out to her. Again she noticed the warmth and roughness of his grip.

"So, you were a real ballerina then? You still look damn good at it."

"Don't try to flatter me like you do Mrs. Kelly."

He laughed. "I would never be so stupid. I've seen your picture in the tutu in Mr. D'Arcy's office. You were professional, eh?"

"A very long time ago in another life."

"From what I saw, you haven't lost the knack." His eyes traveled down her figure. "Looks like ballet must be the thing for keepin' a body first rate through the years."

Lily inhaled.

"I'll let you get on with it; not good to cool off in the middle of a workout. I'm pleased we've called off the fencing match, Mrs. D'Arcy, and I promise to try and not be such a rude bastard in future."

"Does that call for me to promise not to be such a bitch?"

Fallon grinned broadly at her. "I'd best get on to work. G'day, Missus."

Lily stood there amazed at the shock of his apology—the one thing she'd never expected. She certainly had intended to report his rudeness to Ian, but if the man had the balls—or the cleverness—to apologize. . . . She could still feel the touch of his callused palm on her hand. A tremendous warmth in his grip, almost an electric charge. How cheeky of him to compliment her body. She certainly was not going to be taken in by him, though. Even if he was rather charming in spite of the roughness, was definitely intelligent, possibly even sensitive, as his speech about the Aborigines had shown, there was still something wrong about the man. Her first instinct had been correct, she was sure.

On the other hand, Fallon's appearance on the Innismere scene had stirred things up a bit, given her something to think about besides Tristan and her awful marital problem. "You're really very intriguing, Brett Fallon," she said aloud to her mirrored reflection. "Definitely a worthy adversary!"

That afternoon, one of the women Lily had worked with in the Dublin Ballet Guild rang her to ask for assistance with a fund-raising ball.

"I'd love to, but I'm afraid I'm involved in a new project that takes all my time," said Lily.

"How exciting! What is it?"

"I'm writing a book about ballet, as a matter of fact," Lily lied.

"Fascinating! You will send me a copy when it's out?"

"I promise. You'll be first on my list," said Lily, rolling her eyes.

"By the way, darling, Laetitia Butler told me she saw you last night at the Shelbourne with a terribly attractive young man. Not keeping secrets from me, are you, pet?"

"That was Ian's new race trainer, and my son and daughter-in-law were along as well. Surely you didn't think I was running around on my husband?"

"As attractive as Ian is, don't be silly. But what are people to think when they see two people not married to each other having an intimate tête-à-tête?"

"They'll think nothing at all if they're my friends. Good-bye, Evelyn!" Lily slammed down the receiver.

Bitch! That was exactly what she had been afraid of. Dublin was just a small town really; by evening it would be all about that she was doing a Lady Chatterly with the horse trainer. People loved to jump to the worst possible conclusion.

When Ian arrived that evening from London, Lily ran to embrace him at the front door. "I'm so glad to have you home," she said and meant it.

"I'm pleased to be home if this is the kind of welcome I get," he replied. He lifted her off her feet in a passionate kiss. "I think I need your help in unpacking, my darling."

In his bedroom they undressed quickly and moved to his bed. Lily trembled with excitement as he stroked her body.

"You're a sight for sore eyes," he said.

She gently stroked his erection, thinking, "So is this."

"I could eat you up, you're so delicious," she said, and bent to take him in her mouth. His hand gripped her head, forcing her down on him. For a long moment she fought the old panic that she might choke—then he let her go. She realized with profound disappointment that he had climaxed.

"Damn, I'm sorry. I didn't mean to do that," he said.

She wiped her mouth. "It's a beginning anyway." Premature ejaculation was a step up from no ejaculation, she supposed.

Ian pulled her up into his arms, and kissed her brow. "You've been a real brick through all this, Lily. I know it's almost as hard for you as it is for me."

"That doctor must be helping. Ian, do you have problems with other women, or is it just me?" She held her breath, flabbergasted that she'd actually asked.

"Do you really want to know?"

Her heart sank. Part of the question was already answered. "Yes."

"It's only with you." She closed her eyes.

"Did you, on your trip?" she whispered.

"With a prostitute."

"What?" She sat up, horrified.

"A very expensive one, with excellent references. Not some street girl, Lily. She was a very fastidious woman and wore St. Laurent, for God's sake."

"A couture whore can have diseases, too. My God, AIDS!" She clapped her hand over her mouth.

"I protected myself. She'd just had a test."

"Ian, that makes me ill! You don't want me, but you pay Lord knows what for a hooker. How do you think that makes me feel?"

He gripped her arms. "I did it for us, Lily. The doctor suggested I do so to see if the problem was universal."

"A doctor prescribing a hooker?"

"A sex therapist. I'd be damned if I'd do that."

"This wasn't the first time, was it, Ian?"

"I'm away from you often, and I have needs, Lily. It's not being disloyal to you, it's just satisfying an appetite like having a good meal. It's just a business transaction. I love you."

"I have needs, too, Ian. What am I supposed to do about them? Hire a gigolo to do what you can't? It looks as if I'm going to have to, if I'm ever going to have a nice 'meal' for myself!" She got out of bed and ran to her room.

Ian pounded on the locked door. "Please, Lily! I was just trying to get through this without going mad. You tell me you want the truth, and when I'm fool enough to believe you, you run from me. That's not fair!" There was only silence from her room.

He pressed his forehead against the wood. "Damn you, Lily!" he groaned.

Ian was in his study the next morning going over his mail when Brett Fallon knocked on the door.

"Brett, come in. Haven't had a chance to get down to the stable. How's Charlie coming on?"

"You should be able to race him by May. He's doing better than I expected."

"Excellent! Have a seat."

Fallon handed him an envelope. "My passport, trainer's license, and birth certificate, sir."

"Well, I'll get to work on this, and you should have the permit shortly."

"Actually, there may be a problem. You'd better take a look at those papers. You may not want to keep me on."

Ian frowned as he opened the envelope. "Don't tell me you have a police record?"

"Nothing like that. It's the birth record you need to look at." Brett fidgeted nervously with the rim of his hat while Ian scanned the document. He looked up quickly.

"See what I'm getting at, sir?"

"Your mother was Cathleen Culhane?" Ian's face was dead white.

"Yes, sir. The same Cathleen Culhane that worked as governess here at Innismere over thirty years ago. My father's name look familiar?"

Ian passed his hand over his eyes. "This is not possible."

"I'm standing here, living proof that it is. I wasn't sure how to break this to you, and in fact, if I didn't like and respect you, I never would have. But I do, and since I want to stay on here and have a go with Charlie, I thought I'd best get the truth out and let the chips fall where they may."

Ian shook his head as if trying to clear it. "I always understood she had an abortion."

"Thank God she didn't. My mother took the money your father gave her to get rid of me, and instead she immigrated to Australia. In those days they paid the passage of immigrants. She used your blood money to survive on 'til I came. Later, she went to work for Fallon."

"What do you want from me?" Ian's face had a stricken look.

"Not a thing. No more than you've given to me as a stranger turning up on your doorstep, sir."

"Why did she never tell me? I would have helped her—and you. I thought the child was dead all these years."

"My mother didn't tell me about you until she lay on her deathbed. She said you were only a boy, and she didn't want to make problems for you. She blamed herself, not you, for getting in the jam."

Ian covered his eyes; his hands trembled. "How did Cathy die?"

"Cancer. It wasn't an easy death. She got a rotten deal in life all the way round. Was more cook and housekeeper for Fallon than anything else."

"I'm sorry. She was a kind and lovely woman."

"Yes, she was. It's partly for her that I came here. Her life seemed so pointless somehow." Fallon went over to the window and gazed out. "I thought meeting my father might make some sense out of it, for me at least. When you were away the first time I came here, I thought to hell with it, but then, I couldn't go back home without at least seeing what sort of man you were."

"I don't suppose she told you that my father was involved with her, too. You could be his son rather than mine."

"That's a bloody lie! She said your dad came creepin' round her room at night, but she never let him in. She hated him, but she loved you, even if you were only sixteen. 'I loved only Ian D'Arcy my whole life,' she told me when the pain was so bad even the morphine couldn't help. Who do you believe? Her or that hard-eyed, bloody bugger of a father of yours?"

Ian shook his head. "I always thought he might be lying. I couldn't imagine her doing that, but at sixteen, what did I know of women?"

"Well, he lied about her. You are my father, like it or not. She said you offered to marry her, that was the main reason she went so far away. She didn't want to ruin your life, and she couldn't take mine, so she forfeited her own. And here I am, for what it's worth. I would understand if you felt it too awkward for me to hang around, but I had to tell you the truth."

Ian stood up and came around to him. "I'm glad you told me. Of course I want you to stay on. It's just such a shock to find out at forty-six that I have a son I never dreamed I had. It's going to take some getting used to the idea."

"Yes, for me, too. I'm pleased you want me to stay on. This can be our secret as far as I'm concerned, sir."

"No. It's your right to be acknowledged. I'll tell everyone in due time, but not at once. My wife does not like surprises."

"She particularly won't like this one," said Fallon with a smile.

"You two still at odds?"

"We're walkin' about sniffin' each other like two dingos before a fight. I don't think she'll relish the thought of bein' my stepmum."

Ian smiled ruefully. "This is a very odd situation we find ourselves in. The last I heard of your mother, she'd gone to Paris to get an abortion. I wanted to go after her, but it seemed so hopeless, as young and powerless as I was then."

"I understand. Ma never blamed you for anything— nor do I. It was an unfortunate situation. I hope you know I don't want anything from you. I just wanted to know my blood father."

Ian went over to the drinks cabinet and poured two shots. He handed one to Fallon.

"To a father and son getting to know each other."

Long after Brett had left, Ian sat at his desk sipping a whiskey and water and considering the latest threat to his marriage. It seemed all his old ghosts were returning to haunt him. Cathleen Culhane with her warm, blue eyes and sympathetic face. . .how long had it been since he'd even thought of her? It was simply too incredible to have her—*their*—son turn up after all these years. He should have seen the resemblance in the eyes and Brett's smile. Although Cathy wasn't the beauty Lily was, she'd had those lovely eyes and a miraculous bosom which had haunted a virgin boy's nights.

He'd been in a tailspin that long ago summer; his mother dead by her own hand that spring, and his father even more remote and austere than usual. Miss Culhane, well-educated and from a respectable, middle class family, had been hired as governess to get Damien ready for public school. She talked to Ian as if he were an adult, had a ready, throaty laugh and a smile which made one feel gifted to receive it. They talked about his mother, and he showed Miss Culhane the portrait of her on horseback which his father had banished to the attic along with the paintings she'd done herself. His father had given all her clothes to charity except for one trunk which Kelly had managed to save. It was as if he were trying to get rid of every trace of her, and Ian wanted to remember, to never forget the person he had loved most in the world. He and Miss Culhane examined the box containing his mother's scent bottles and heavy, silver brushes, and he was moved to tears.

"How could she leave me?" he cried, holding her hand mirror.

Sympathetic Miss Culhane held him to her bosom. "Poor darling. It's always so hard for those left behind." He wept in her arms and found himself with such an obvious erection that in desperation he cried, "Please leave me. I want to be alone."

Later that night when the house was dark and quiet, he tiptoed to her room and knocked timidly on the door. "Who is it?" she asked.

"Ian," he whispered. "I need to talk to you." He was shaking from head to toe. Miss Culhane had on a demure white gown, nothing over it.

"I wanted to apologize for acting like a baby this afternoon, and to thank you. . ." he began. She pulled him inside and shut the door behind them before he could complete his rehearsed speech. She stood there staring at him, her blond hair tumbling about her shoulders, her majestic bosom rising and falling with her breathing. The hairs on the back of his neck stood up, and all the earth stood still for that never-to-be-forgotten moment when he had known a miracle was about to happen.

"I know exactly what you want and what you need," she said. She opened her arms to him, and that was the beginning of the greatest night of his life to date. Such a relief to pour out all his frustrated, adolescent lust into her soft, responsive body, and afterward to lie in her arms and think, *I am a man!* It banished all those doubts aroused by his friend Tony's gazing at him with such obvious and disturbing admiration. *I am a man. I can satisfy a grown woman!* he had thought to himself that blissful night in the arms of Cathleen Culhane.

Instead of being a dismal summer, it became the summer of his life. Sneaking to her room every night as soon as the house was asleep; riding out separately, then trysting at the castle ruin. One warm night when his father was away, they swam out to the island naked. She shivered, but he warmed her up all right! All in all, it was a damn glorious summer, fulfilling all his sixteen-year-old fantasies.

The idyllic dream had ended in late August when she told him she was pregnant. What a crash of Nirvana on the shoals of reality! Contraceptives were of course illegal, so they'd tried to use the rhythm method. He'd got a few French letters off a stableboy who went regularly to Ulster to get them; a lot of good they did.

"I'll marry you," he said.

"Don't be ridiculous." she said, making him feel still the child in her eyes. "That's very sweet to offer, but you must finish your schooling. I'll simply go away and have it." Arguments and tears followed—he was due to go off to England to school soon. As he always did when he had problems, he rode up to the castle to think what to do. When he returned, Cathy was gone—he never saw her again.

"You damn, young fool! Did you think you were the only stud who'd had the mare?" his father had said. That had crushed him. He couldn't believe it, but then she'd taken him straight to her bed and had been more than willing to try any sexual thing his perfervid brain dreamt up. Emotionally drained, he had been more than a little glad that the thing had been decided for him. Yes, he'd missed her and had nightmares about her suffering an abortion alone in Paris, but after returning to school, he'd soon put her out of his mind. Only when he came home and visited their old trysting places, had he realized how lonely he was without her. In time, he'd relegated Cathleen Culhane to a distant warm and guilty memory—until now when Brett Fallon had brought it all back.

Ian's biggest concern was Lily's reaction to the news that there was yet another skeleton in the closet of his past. Would there be a trauma like the one caused by Tony? How in the world could he break the news to her that the person she so disliked was in reality his son? How very prescient of Lily to distrust Fallon on sight. There really was something to that woman's intuition business.

He remembered the time he'd been sitting for his mother when she'd suddenly dropped her paintbrush. "Something terrible has happened!" she'd exclaimed, looking wild-eyed at him. A half hour later, a phone call had told of the death of their neighbor and his mother's great hunting friend Ned O'Sullivan in a fall from his horse. Siobhan D'Arcy had gone dead pale and retired to her room for the rest of the day. A week later, when he was back at school, she'd gone out into the garden and put a bullet through her heart. There had been a storm, so no one knew of her death until the morning when the gardener found her body. His father had never forgiven her for so obviously killing herself over her lover, making him look the cuckold. Up to then, he hadn't minded her adultery; after all, he had his mistresses in London and Paris.

But why had his father sullied Cathy's name? Ian was sure now that he'd lied about the governess. How could he have ever believed such a thing of a woman who never lied to him? Had his father branded her a whore out of spite for her spurning his attentions? Out of sheer meanness of spirit? Or to keep him from running after her and mooning his life away over a thwarted first love? He would never know.

Ian held up his glass. "Here's to you, Cathy Culhane. I swear that I shall do right by your. . .our son, as I never did by you!"

Brett

⊕ ⊕ ⊕

THE FOLLOWING WEEK, Violet arrived unexpectedly at Innismere saying she'd decided to take some time off from work. Lily helped her daughter unpack.

"You know Yves is perfectly welcome to come with you, Violet. I can't pretend that I like him or think he's near good enough for you, but we will be gracious, darling. Of course you'd have to have separate bedrooms out of respect for your father's feelings," said Lily.

"I can just picture you and Daddy being ever so insincerely polite to him," said Violet.

"Well, since I'm not very good at French and Yves refuses to learn English, I shall only have to be insincere in pantomime. Ian is fluent so he'd have to carry the burden, which he'd do gladly for you, darling. We'd both do anything to get to see you more often."

"You won't have to be burdened with any visits from Yves, Mummy. You see, it's all over between us," said Violet with false brightness.

"You mean you've broken it off?"

"Right. Kaput, fini, whatever. Kicked him out on his derrière." Violet picked up a brush and began nervously fussing with her hair.

"I'm so sorry, darling."

192

"Sorry? Please, Mummy! I know you and Daddy are both ecstatic since you've always disliked him so."

"I'm delighted you've come to your senses, but I hate for you to have to suffer the heartbreak of ending such a long affair." Lily sat beside her on the dressing table bench. "Do you want to tell me about it, baby?"

"No, I never want to speak of that son of a bitch again," she replied, slamming down the silver brush on the table. She buried her face in her hands.

"Right," said Lily, smoothing the girl's tangled, black curls. "What's his name is a non-person as far as I'm concerned—always was." Violet's shoulders shook. Lily put her arm about her.

"I caught him in bed with the char lady who does my flat," Violet sobbed. "I went berserk and squirted an entire tube of cadmium red on them."

"I'm proud of you, darling," said Lily, giving her a squeeze.

"She wasn't even attractive, Mummy. I'd never have taken on a pretty char. The *cochon* had such horrid taste that he's been screwing this fat, stupid.. . ."

"Shh, love. Don't waste any more tears on him. We all cast our pearl before at least one swine—well I was lucky enough to run into your father from the first. You must dry your eyes and not give him another moment of your time. It was for the best you found out what a jerk he was, because he's been using you to avoid facing that he'll never make it as an artist. His manners were beyond frightful, and he surely had a deodorant phobia."

Violet began laughing through her tears. "God, why did I waste three years of my life on that fool?"

"Just be thankful it wasn't a whole lifetime, darling."

"Really." Violet reached for a tissue and blew her nose. "So, I suppose I just get on with my life. The next fellow I get involved with will be like a rose, I swear, Mummy."

Lily laughed and patted her flushed cheek. This was the closest she'd felt to her daughter in years. The girl had always been so strong in herself, never seeming to need even in adolescence the motherly advice for which Lily longed to be asked. This had been in part due to her daughter's native independence, and to Lily's careful avoidance of dominating Violet's life as her mother had done hers. As a young child, the girl had done ballet along with her, and though she'd shown a decided talent for it and had a long-limbed, graceful body perfect for the dance, Lily had never tried to sway her into choosing that for her career. The leotards had been discarded in favor of boots and jodhpurs, which in turn had given way to a fascination with clothes in general. Lily wanted Violet to choose her own life's interest, and she had done so with great energy. Lily had certainly not tried to direct and shelter her daughter as her own mother had done, and she thought the results of her parenting showed she'd taken the right approach. On the other hand, she wondered if she'd overdone it in giving her daughter so much growing room, because she seemed so much more attached to Ian. Perhaps now that Violet was an adult, they would become closer and have other moments such as this together.

The morning after her arrival, Violet entered the kitchen in her dressing gown and found Brett Fallon having his breakfast.

She sat across from him at the kitchen table. "Tea and toast, please, Mary, love. And who in the hell might you be?" she inquired of Brett with a friendly smile.

"He's Mr. Fallon, your father's new race trainer," supplied the cook with a disapproving glance at the girl's state of undress.

"The Aussie? Tris wrote me about you."

"You must be Violet. I've seen the picture of you on a pony in Mr. D'Arcy's study."

"I went through rather a horsey period, but I quite grew out of it," said Violet, inspecting him with frank interest. Mrs. Kelly set a plate of buttered toast in front of her.

"You should eat in the dining room as is proper, Miss Violet."

"Oh pooh, I always eat in the kitchen in London. Don't have a dining room, actually. Besides, I want to hear more of Mr. Fallon's gorgeous accent. Tell me about yourself, Brett, is it? Tris thinks you're the last of the heroes."

"He's been having you on I'm afraid, Miss D'Arcy."

"He usually has very good taste in people, so I'm sure we shall get on brilliantly. Do please call me Vi."

"Mr. Fallon has to get on with his work. He's not got all morning to chatter," grumbled Mary.

"Don't be such a grouch, Mary. When do you finish work, Brett?" Mrs. Kelly harrumphed and banged the pots in the sink.

Lily picked up Sheba and stroked the heavy cat's thick, black fur. Before closing the drapes for the night, she parted the lace sheer and peered out into the dark. There it was again—the light coming from the stables. At first she'd thought someone had forgot to turn the lights off down there; then she'd realized it was coming from the second floor room of Brett Fallon. Was he also an insomniac? Lately, when she'd get up at two or three A.M. unable to sleep, the stable light was always on, a sight which Lily found oddly comforting.

A movement on the lawn caught her attention. She watched intently as a figure ran from the direction of the stables across the grass to the terrace entrance of the house. In the moonlight she recognized her daughter. Why on earth would Violet be down at the stables at such a late hour? The obvious answer hit her, followed by a hot wave of emotion. Violet was sleeping with Fallon!

Anger rose in Lily's throat at the thought of that grinning, cocky bastard taking advantage of a hot-blooded young girl. She should have known something was up, because Violet was suddenly much cheerier and had taken a renewed interest in riding. Mary Kelly had told her that the girl was giving Mr. Fallon "the wrong idea," so she'd talked to her daughter about the race trainer.

"He's your father's employee, not a friend for you and Tristan," she'd said to her only that morning. "It's unfair to him, really. He might misinterpret your friendliness, putting the both of you in a very awkward situation. You don't want the man to get ideas."

"I certainly hope he does," Violet had said with a throaty laugh.

"For heaven's sake, please don't make another mistake so soon after the other one," Lily had said to her in alarm.

"But Mummy, Brett's terribly sexy, or haven't you noticed?"

"Fallon is a ladies man and a flatterer. I wouldn't trust him for a second. Worst of all, he doesn't know his place."

"I know. He's dreadfully uppity—one reason he's so irresistible, but he's hardly a lecher. Tris says he hasn't been near a woman since he's been here, that he knows of, anyway."

"I'm sure he's got women in the village or somewhere. Men like that have always got women."

"Mummy, you're all excited just talking about him. I believe you must fancy Brett yourself."

"Don't be disgusting," she'd said. Violet always knew how to make her lose her temper.

Now it was too late; her daughter was already involved with Fallon. She was simply going to have to tell Ian. Maybe that would open his eyes to what a snake in the grass the Aussie really was. Lily was so disturbed, she didn't fall asleep until almost daylight.

She overslept the next morning, throwing off her daily routine which normally began at seven. Ian had already breakfasted and was reading the *London Times* in the drawing room.

"Good morning. Sleep well?" he asked without looking up from the paper.

"No I did not. I was up 'til after four."

"Dreadful. Should have taken a sleeping tablet."

"It wouldn't have helped. Ian, I saw Violet coming back from the stable very late last night. Sneaking back, I should say."

He frowned. "What are you suggesting?"

"Discounting a midnight ride, I would suggest she had a rendezvous with your Mr. Fallon. I told you before that Mary said she was spending too much time with the man, and you pooh-poohed the idea. Well, now she's got herself sexually involved with him."

"I don't believe that," said Ian, putting down his paper.

"Don't tell me you're going to bury your head on this one!" she exploded. "I knew Fallon was up to no good, and Violet is senseless when it comes to men. You've got to fire him before your daughter gets used again by another unscrupulous man."

"Brett is an honorable man, and he wouldn't touch Violet. I know that absolutely."

"I saw her coming back from him—the light was on in his room. Please face this one head-on, Ian. Violet's got a wild streak in her, and this Fallon is just the sort to exploit it."

"I'm telling you, Lily, that Brett has not touched her. You're misreading the situation. Perhaps Violet was attracted to him, but rest assured that he has not taken advantage."

"Why are you so sure? You've only known Fallon a few months, and Violet has thrown herself at him. If you don't do something about this, I give up!"

"Calm yourself. I will take care of it. Should have done before it ever came to this."

"Really! Now Violet will be hurt and angry with us for interfering, and you'll have to let Fallon go."

"It won't come to that," said Ian, getting to his feet.

"You can't keep him on after this."

"Lily, you jump to conclusions. Let's at least find out the truth of the matter before we punish anyone."

Brett Fallon was watching the jockey Tommy Rafferty take Charlemagne round the track when Ian joined him.

"G'day, boss."

"Morning, Brett. How's Rafferty doing?"

"He and Charlie get on fine. Rafferty's not heavy on the whip which only gets Charlie's temper up. I think we've got ourselves a jockey, sir."

Rafferty slowed the colt down to a walk and came over to the fence.

"What's the verdict, then?" asked Ian.

"He can fairly run, that's certain. He's a fast sprinter, but has staying power as well. There's not a horse I've been up on at the Curragh that can beat his spirit and talent." Rafferty patted Charlie's sweaty neck. "I'd ride him just for the crack, Sir Ian."

"I believe we can manage a decent pay packet for you as well," said Ian.

"Well now, sir, I wouldn't be turning your money down."

"Take him for a cool-down now, lad," Fallon directed.

Turning to Ian he said, "Never thought I'd have a chance to work with a horse with royal blood like that one. Allez France and Native Dancer on the dam's side, Never Bend on his sire's for size and strength. He's a dream horse."

"An impossible dream 'til you got him under control, Brett. That bad temper he must have inherited from Tourbillon in his pedigree is rarely in evidence these days."

"As long as he's treated with respect, and you never forget that he's dangerous, Charlie should be fine."

"Right. Brett, I need to ask you something rather personal." Ian looked back at the house and put his hands in his pockets. "Has Violet been. . .how shall I put this?"

"Yes sir, she has. I made it clear to her as nicely as I could, that it was no go, but I'm afraid her feelings were hurt. I'm thinking it's not a good idea to keep them in the dark about who I am."

Ian sighed heavily. "You're so right. I should have realized something like this could happen—Violet's a bit impetuous like her mother used to be. Naturally you'd be the sort of man she'd be drawn to. I'll explain it all to her at once."

"I felt very bad about it. It's damn weird being in my shoes," said Fallon, shaking his head. "She's a nice girl. I hope this won't queer our friendship."

As he walked back to the house, Ian thought how ironic it was that Brett was the first man his daughter had been drawn to that he found worthy of her.

Violet was still in her rooms though it was late morning. He found her in her dressing gown, packing her bag.

"I've got to go back to London if I want to keep my job at the magazine," she explained. "They were very tolerant to give me time off, could tell I'd have a nervous breakdown if they didn't." She threw a sweater in her case.

"This visit home hasn't helped your peace of mind, either, has it?"

"Actually, it's helped me decide that I shan't ever let my happiness depend on a man again, Daddy." Her mouth quivered, and she turned away from him. Ian put his arms around her.

"Why am I such a fool, Daddy?"

"Of course you're not. It was my fault about Fallon, not yours," he said stroking her hair.

She looked up at him in alarm. "You know?" He nodded. "God, spare me the humiliation that he's asked you to talk to me," she moaned.

"Sit down with me for a moment, Violet. I've something to tell you—something you should never have been kept in the dark about." They sat on the bed, and Ian explained about Cathleen Culhane and Brett.

"I feel ill," she said weakly. "Do you know how awful that makes me feel to think that I've been lusting after my own half brother."

"You must not reproach yourself! Of course you were attracted. Brett is very appealing to women, I can imagine. This is all my fault for not telling everyone as soon as I found out about him myself. It's just that your mother is not very good at adjusting to rude shocks, and as you're no doubt aware of, our marriage has had its ups and downs of late."

She leaned against him affectionately. "Poor Daddy—what will Mummy think? She loathes Brett, thinks him so beneath us, and here he is of the blood royal after all. She'll absolutely die!"

Ian looked fondly at his daughter. An objective eye might find Violet's face too thin and angular, her nose too pronounced for accepted standards of conventional feminine beauty. She'd got the D'Arcy black Irish looks which someone once said looked marvelous on the men of the family but less so on the females. To Ian's eye, or that of any admirer of the bold and unique, Violet D'Arcy was quite beautiful. She leaned her head on his shoulder.

"It's not been going very well for me lately, Daddy. I seem to be having a rotten run of luck."

"It's sure to change, my love. Brett felt very badly about your being hurt so unnecessarily. I hope you'll be able to put this aside and be friends with him."

"I will. He was really very sweet when he put me off. Said that he couldn't get involved with me since he was your employee. Still, it was not exactly a moment I ever want to remember."

"I hope that eventually everyone will think of Brett as a member of the family. He is a D'Arcy, and I've got a great deal of making up to do with him."

"Don't worry about me, Daddy. I quite like Brett, aside from the misguided passion. I'll have a chat with him before I leave. Poor thing must have felt so awkward."

"Good girl." He kissed her forehead. "I never worry about you, my little flower. You're much too sound. Don't trouble yourself about men—someone so fantastic even I might approve is probably just around the corner."

"Never anyone as perfect as my darling daddy. I hope Mummy's not being too hard on you. She must know that you're the best, most wonderful man in the world."

"Don't blame your mother. Our problems are really all my fault," said Ian darkly.

"I don't care. She should be able to forgive you anything. Any woman would."

"I don't know about that," he said, stroking her arm. She smiled up at him. "This reminds me of sitting in

your lap and listening to your stories, Daddy. Do you remember 'The Flower Garden?' "

"How could I forget. You had me tell that one a million
times."

"Yes—how did it go? There once was a handsome Irish
prince who searched the entire world for the most beauti-
ful flower for his garden. Then at last he found a perfect
Lily growing between the cracks in the pavement of New
York City, and he brought her home to the garden at
Innismere."

"And the perfect Lily and the handsome prince had
a daughter, an exquisite Violet. A not-so-shrinking one,
however," said Ian, taking up the story.

She laughed. "That part was always a bit confusing to
me—how a man and a flower could procreate. A tad
kinky that."

"Poetic license, my love."

"Yes. Remember how when Mummy was pregnant, I
looked everywhere for flower names?"

"Daisy for a girl and Valerian for a boy."

"Uncle Damien came up with Valerian. I quite fancied
Hyacanthos. I was terribly disappointed when Mummy
named him Tristan."

"Perhaps you'll have your own Hyacanthos someday,
my darling."

"I don't think so. I have this feeling that children
aren't in the cards for me." She embraced him again. "I
do love you, Daddy."

Ian told his son about Brett that same day. Tristan was
at first amazed, then delighted. "No wonder I liked him
straight off," he said.

"I'm pleased you're happy about this, son, but don't
tell your mother. I'm waiting for the perfect time to break
the news to her."

"Good luck, Dad. Those two will never like each other."

That night, Ian and Lily made love successfully for the first time since their return to Innismere.

"Thank God!" said Ian as they lay in each other's arms afterward.

Lily kissed his throat. "I'll second that."

"I hope I've laid that monster to rest," he said. In no time he was asleep, leaving Lily to stare wide-eyed at the ceiling. She could not get comfortable and didn't feel even faintly sleepy, so she got up and went to her own bedroom.

She lit a cigarette. Maybe this would be the breakthrough that would end Tony's tyranny over their marriage. What if it hadn't been satisfying for her—Ian had had an ego-boosting time of it, and that was the important thing.

Pulling back the curtain, she saw a pinpoint of light winking back at her through the rainy night. She climbed in bed and finished her cigarette. Too bad Violet had to be humiliated over the race trainer. Ian had said the two had just been playing cards 'til late, and that Fallon swore nothing sexual had occurred. He must have put her off, poor child. That was the obvious reason for her sudden departure for London. If it was true, Lily had to admit that it made her think more highly of Fallon. How many men would turn down a proffered gift like that?

She snubbed out her cigarette and turned off the light. Lying rigid in her bed, she faced the night, an interminable passing of hours that must be got through somehow. "Please God, let me sleep," she prayed fervently. Lily had a distrust of pills in general and sleeping tablets in particular; they made her feel as if she were wrapped in cotton wool all the next day.

She hated the nights when it was impossible to switch off her brain. No matter how she tried not to think, random thoughts slipped through her mind like an unstoppable ticker tape.

What *was* Fallon doing with that light on to all hours? Was he as wide-eyed and desperate as she? Violet had said, "I think you fancy him yourself, Mummy." Was that possible? She had certainly revised her opinion about his attractiveness. The image of him hammering the horseshoe on the anvil, biceps swelling, veins distended, the Stanley Kowalski undershirt, still haunted her. There was something Brandoesque about Brett Fallon. Not the way he looked; more the way he looked at you. The mocking smile—his air of mysterious aloneness. Sort of an earthy, no-bullshit quality about him, as well. She imagined Fallon would bring an intensity to lovemaking that would be like nothing she'd ever experienced. What was he doing with that light on over there?

Lily closed her eyes and pictured the horse trainer lying on his bed above the tack room. The image reminded her of one her favorite childhood stories—Cupid and Psyche. She'd had a beautiful picture book of Greek and Roman myths; the stylish old-fashioned picture that accompanied that particular story came to her now quite clearly. A winged, athletic, handsome god of love (not some chubby cherub), his golden arrow poised to strike the side of the sleeping mortal princess Psyche. Something about the story had entranced her, and she'd returned to it again and again. Venus's son Cupid had fallen in love with Psyche and had whisked her away to his mountaintop palace where he visited her only at night. He never let her see him in the light, because he wanted her to love him as a man, not a god. Prompted by fears that her mystery lover might be a monster or dragon—he had wings; she could feel them in the dark—

Psyche lit a lamp and looked at him while he slept. Instead of a dragon, she found him the most beautiful young man with golden hair and shimmering, pearly wings. A drop of burning oil fell from the lamp and woke him. He flew away from her saying, "Love cannot dwell with suspicion." The story had ended happily with Psyche becoming his immortal bride on Olympus despite her penchant for wanting to know what was really going on. It was only later when Lily had learned that in the Greek version of the myth, Cupid was Eros, that she'd at last understood her fascination with this most erotic and romantic of tales.

Lily imagined getting out of her bed and moving through the darkened house out into the chill April rain to the outside stairs up to Fallon's stable apartment.

The door is unlocked. She slips inside, out of breath, her nightgown wet from the rain. She sees Fallon lying asleep on his narrow, iron cot, his naked body half out of the covers. She turns off the light and crosses to the bed. Runs her hand down the muscular hardness of him until she finds something soft.

His hands in her hair. "Who are you?" he whispers.

"Your dream lover. You know me."

"Yes. I leave the light on for you every night." He pulls her down to meet his mouth. Then she explores every inch of his body with her hands and lips. She lifts her damp gown and settles astride him. Ride, ride, his hands moving over her with the perfect touch. Until everything is obliterated, and her screams are heard by the horses asleep in their boxes below.

Lily curled into a fetal position in her bed, her heart pounding. That fantasy had been so real, she was afraid Ian had heard her imagined screams of passion in his bedroom. She felt guilty yet relieved. At last she might get some sleep, she thought closing her eyes.

*   *   *

Lily sat on her gray mare and watched the horse racing across the field below, Fallon's blond hair mingling with the colt's flying black mane; her excitement grew with Charlie's increasing speed. They reached the top of the uphill gallop where the horses were conditioned every day, and the Aussie slowed the black horse to a trot, then a walk. She kicked Lady Jane's dappled flanks and cantered over to meet him.

"Looks like he's really coming on," she said as she pulled alongside.

"Should be able to enter his first race in a month," said Fallon.

"It will be so exciting having two good horses with Innismere colors. Are you through with your workout?"

"He's had enough for today." The two horses fell in together on the path back to the stable. Charlie pranced and pulled at the bit.

"Did you have a pleasant ride then, Mrs. D'Arcy?" he asked, giving her his dangerous smile.

"Lovely. I rode up to the castle. Have you been up yet to see it?"

"No, but I've heard about it. I don't have much time for pleasure jaunts."

"You really should. The view is spectacular, and the ruins are so mysterious and romantic."

"The original D'Arcy digs, eh?"

"Right. There's only the keep and the gateway left standing, but you can imagine how wonderful it must have been once. They owned the land past the village in those days."

"A great, landed, aristocratic family, the D'Arcys," said Brett Fallon. Lily thought she detected a hint of sarcasm.

"Nothing like some of the other Norman lords, but

a great deal more aristocratic and landed than any of my ancestors," she replied. Charlemagne tossed his head and skittered sideways; Fallon easily controlled him.

"By the way, I want to thank you for the way you handled the problem with Violet. I appreciated your sense of honor in that sticky situation."

He glanced over at her. "I'm not sure what situation you're speaking of, Mrs. D'Arcy."

"It was obvious to me that she had an interest in you, and you were a gentleman not to take advantage of her." He was silent. "Violet has been hotheaded since she was a child. It was probably good for her to find out she can't have everything she wants."

"I could see it coming, did everything I could to avoid it, but. . .She's a great gal. I like people who are direct."

"She'll get over it. I tried to warn her, but she wouldn't listen, as usual."

"I wish to hell it had never come to that," said Fallon. Charlie bumped Lady Jane and started bucking and plunging, as the Aussie fought to restrain him.

"What's the matter with him?" Lily asked in alarm. Fallon halted the colt and fell behind her mare.

"From the look of her tail, she's coming in season."

"Oh, my God! What should we do?"

"Go on ahead," Fallon ordered. She kicked Lady Jane into a brisk trot. She heard the colt squeal, and looking back over her shoulder, saw Fallon reining the horse in a tight circle. She dug her heels in the mare's flanks.

When she reached the stable, she dismounted and handed Lady Jane over to the stableboy. "Cool her off for me, please." It was very bad form to ride a horse in heat like that. "You should have told me she was coming in season. Charlie got terribly excited."

"Didn't know you'd be comin' near Charlie," said the boy.

"I ran into Mr. Fallon, and it almost caused a problem." Muttering something under his breath, the boy slunk off with her mare.

Lily waited for Fallon to ride in, the big horse now walking meek as a lamb. He dismounted, replaced the bridle with a head collar, and fastened Charlie with a rope.

"I'm sorry. No one told me the mare was in that condition," she apologized.

"No problem," he said. He removed the saddle and took it into the tack room.

"I was frightened there for a moment," she said when he emerged.

"I had him in hand. You weren't in any danger." He began vigorously grooming Charlie with a dandy brush, roughing the hair against the grain.

"He's so powerful. I wondered if even you could control him when he was so excited."

He grinned at her over the horse's back. "Have to feel for the bugger getting teased like that. Never been laid, and a beautiful bitch in season switches her tail at him." He was slicking down the coat with a body brush now, moving efficiently head to tail while Charlie stood there quietly letting him do it. "Not fair is it, lad, coming so close and having it snatched away?"

"I see it more from Lady Jane's viewpoint as something of a narrow escape," she couldn't resist saying.

"Ho now! She might have enjoyed a bit of sport herself," he said, really grinning now.

"It doesn't look like much fun for the mare," she said and at once regretted sounding so priggish and frigid. If Fallon had a snide retort, he bit it back.

Taking a wet cloth from a bucket, he began to wipe the colt's genitals. Lily felt her face redden. Was that part of the grooming procedure, or was he doing his best to embarrass her?

"Why are you doing the grooming?" she asked, her cheeks still burning. "Isn't that Paddy's job?"

"I like to do it. Part of gaining his trust. I've brushed a few coats and mucked out my share of boxes in my time." He ran his hand down the gleaming satin coat. "Time for some tucker and afternoon in the paddock. Not a bad life, eh?"

"I can't get over how gentle he seems now," she said.

"He's just a big baby, aren't you, Charles? *Le grand bébé, n'est ce pas?*" Lily shivered involuntarily as Fallon stroked and cooed at the big horse.

He untied the rope, the grooming at an end. "Nice talkin' to ya, Missus. I'm glad you've eased up on your vision of me as a terrorist," he remarked with a sly smile.

"I'm not totally convinced, yet," she teased.

"I can sense that," he said with a wink, then led Charlie off to his box.

Lily grinned to herself all the way back to the house. Fallon could be very pleasant really—when he wanted to be. He'd almost been flirting with her there at the end. She laughed aloud to think of her wild imaginings about him the night before. That would really put a grin on his face if he had an inkling he'd starred in her erotic fantasy.

What of turning fantasy into reality? It would never even have occurred to her to think of the possibility if it weren't for Ian's problem—and that was getting better. But hers wasn't. Something wasn't right in the marital bed, even if Ian could do the deed at last. Perhaps she'd caught it from him. She was impotent now. His hands no longer stirred her. Was it the thought of his affair with Tony or his confession about the prostitutes? Or both. Even if he didn't consider that adultery, she certainly did. It was revolting to even think about. Besides, she didn't really believe that was the extent of his infidelity. She'd seen any number of ladies, emboldened by a few drinks at parties, make sultry eyes at her tall, handsome husband. He fascinated women with his courtly manners, brooding eyes, and air of aloofness. She imagined Ian had had a countess or two in his dealings with the very rich European world of art patrons.

She might have had affairs herself; there was certainly the opportunity with him away so often. Lily loved her husband and prided herself on being a virtuous woman with an immaculate reputation—unless it was getting about that she was dallying with their race trainer. How infuriating to get the blame, but none of the pleasure. Besides, didn't Ian's philandering relieve her of the obligation to be faithful to him? What was the point in being such a goody-goody? Why not have an affair with Fallon?

To be honest, the Aussie had in no way given her any indication of interest, other than that bit about her having a good body, and that was suspect since he'd been trying to get in her good graces to hold on to his position. That cheeky wink, the smiles, were no more than he bestowed on every female including Evileen and Mary Kelly. Those blue eyes did have a way of traveling up and down that made her feel warm to remember, but did it mean anything? Besides, the thought of some messy affair under her family's nose was distasteful to her. She had enough problems without adding another potentially fatal one to the list.

No, a love affair was not what she wanted—just the sex and passion that she and her husband seemed incapable of recapturing. It occurred to her that what she really desired was one good night's lovemaking with no emotions or strings involved. To be like Ian and very matter of factly offer to buy Brett Fallon's services for one evening. Offer him say fifty pounds to relieve those frustrations he had so astutely noted in her. The thought made her laugh. How furious the man would be—insulted to the core. Or would he? What a power trip to march up to his room above the stable, slap the money down on the table, and tell him to take his clothes off.

What would Fallon do? Laugh? Or would he take his clothes off, throw the money in the toilet, and fuck her mercilessly? The beauty of it would be that she would only be doing what Ian had done, no doubt many times, and didn't even consider wrong. What could he say about her doing the same thing? She imagined the look on Ian's face when she told him, "But, darling, I was ever so hungry, and there was this tasty morsel down at the stable—but it has absolutely nothing to do with us." The only flaw in her little plot of sex and revenge was the enigmatic Mr. Fallon. No way could she picture him playing the part of some docile gigolo.

✪ ✪ ✪

It was May at last, time for the first classic races of the Irish flat racing season: the 1000 and 2000 Guineas held on consecutive Saturdays at the Curragh track in Kildare. Ian had decided to enter Violet's Season in the first race which was for the cream of three-year-old fillies, a Group I rated event. It was doubtful she could win, given the competition from top stables, but they hoped she would make a decent showing to enhance her viability as a brood mare.

The Curragh, Ireland's most famous racecourse, is situated on a 6000-acre plain of the same name in the middle of County Kildare. The ancient Celts raced their horses here centuries ago, and it has always been the heart of the Irish racing and breeding industry. The limestone beneath the Curragh Plain is said to give the animals that graze on its grasses the strong bones which make Irish bred and raised horses the best in the world.

Though Charlie was not ready to run with the best

three-year-old colts in the 2000 Guineas, Brett brought him up to board at the track stables and work out daily with Violet's Season on the exercise gallops on the Curragh Plain. He would be running his maiden race at the Curragh later in the month, so it would do him good to get accustomed to the area. Ian and Brett commuted to the track daily, and Lily found life at Innismere exceedingly dull. She was also disappointed that Ian had to go to Geneva on business the weekend of the race, forcing them to decline a number of parties. She was not the sort of woman who enjoyed socializing without her husband.

"Why not have Brett escort you?" Ian suggested.

"How would that look?"

"As if you had an attractive young escort for a change," he replied.

"People would talk, Ian. They would jump at the chance."

"Don't be so preoccupied with appearances, Lily. If you were having an affair with him, you'd hardly be bold enough to take him to a party with all our friends. I was only trying to save you from missing out on the festivities. No one would think a damn thing of you and Fallon. You are 'Lily White,' after all."

"It would cause gossip, Ian. People aren't as charitable as you. Wouldn't that bother you at all?"

"I trust both of you, and I don't give a damn what people say, as long as I know it's untrue. When you've been through the fire as we were over Mother, you learn to ignore gossip."

"But why do you trust Fallon so? Is it so impossible for him to be attracted to me?"

"He's already proved that he's an honorable man, hasn't he?"

"Oh, now I see what you're getting at. If he turned Violet down, he's not going to be interested in a middle-aged frump like me."

"For God's sake don't go to the damn party then," Ian said in exasperation.

Lily took Bella into Dublin to buy dresses for the parties given by the young racing crowd. They both enjoyed themselves. Bella, who was much more agreeable than Violet had ever been, took Lily's suggestions as gospel. After their shopping spree, they had coffee at Bewley's Oriental Café. Bella confided that Tristan was seriously considering going to Trinity in the fall, and that certainly raised Lily's spirits. She longed for her son to get his life back on track as soon as possible. To her delight, she saw that Bella was very keen on the idea as well.

Over their sticky buns and second cup of coffee, Lily steered the conversation on to Brett Fallon. Did he have a girl in the village? No, Bella didn't think that he did, nor had he ever mentioned one. "It is a bit odd that he doesn't, as nice as he is," she said. "When he comes out with us, women are always staring at him, but he pays them no attention. I think he must have a girlfriend back in Australia."

Lily enjoyed helping Bella get dressed for the party, and let her take her pick of D'Arcy jewels for the occasion. She couldn't seem to make up her mind, or else was overwhelmed by the sight of the sparkling stones, so Lily decided for her. Bella stared at herself in the glass as Lily fastened the four-strand pearl choker with a cabochon emerald clasp which had once graced the neck of an Edwardian Lady D'Arcy.

"There. Oh, that looks wonderful! It shows off what a lovely, long neck you've got, Bella. You must wear your hair up for the full effect. The earrings I gave you will be perfect with it."

Bella looked at herself and fingered the smooth coolness of the pearls. "I never imagined that I would wear such a thing," she said in awe.

"Well, that's where you and I differ, darling," said Lily with a laugh. "All of this will be yours when Tristan inherits, so get used to them."

"Heavens, that's scary," said Bella with a look of real alarm on her face.

"I can think of better adjectives. I want you to wear the pearls in the collection. They suit you. I'm really not a pearl person somehow, and they need to be worn. They say if you don't wear pearls, they die, turn gray or something. The oils from your skin help them keep their luster."

When Tristan and Bella came down to leave for the party, they looked so splendid it brought tears to Lily's eyes. *Maybe they'll make it,* she thought as the two of them got in Tristan's new sportscar. She'd lost her original antipathy to the girl as she'd got to know her, and was enjoying her Pygmalion role. Bella was a delight to be around, always pleasant, and there wasn't a bone of conceit in her body, as pretty as she was. It was really a pleasure to teach such a grateful, receptive pupil all Lily had taught herself about being Lady D'Arcy. She almost wished she could have gone along with them to the party to see the grand entrance her son would make with his stunning, red-haired wife, properly got up by her to look every bit as elegant as any aristocratic woman there. Of course the image would be shattered the minute she opened her mouth, à la Eliza Doolittle. Perhaps she could somehow tactfully suggest Bella work on losing her Yorkshire accent, not to mention the shocking bits of coarse language which popped out of the girl's mouth now and again, however innocently.

The night before the 1000 Guineas, a great ball was being given by Muhammed Abdullah, the immensely wealthy Mr. Big of Thoroughbred racing. At the last minute, Lily decided she didn't want to miss the party of the season—Tristan would be there to keep an eye out for her anyway. It would be an excuse to show off her sapphires and the glorious slink of a St. Laurent she'd got in Paris.

The Abdullah estate was the largest in the county, his stud and racing stables second to none. It was said the Arab owned equally magnificent homes in France and his own country. The sheik and his wife, both attired in elegant European dress, greeted the guests in the drawing room of their Gothic castle.

"St. Laurent, number sixty-four," said the handsome, Arab woman admiring Lily's gown. "I almost bought that one myself, but I'm so glad I did not. I should hate to have to compete with you in it, Lady D'Arcy." Lily didn't tell her that it was a model's dress which she'd got considerably reduced. The sheik bowed to her and admired her jewels. Feeling enormously pleased with herself, Lily followed the other guests out to a huge marquee pitched on the lawn for dining and dancing. There was no sight of Tristan and Bella who had already disappeared into the crush. Lily joined the hungry revelers thronging about a banquet table laden with a mountain of Beluga, and silver tubs of iced vodka. She had just bitten into a slice of toast decorated with a healthy mound of caviar and accouterments when a voice behind her said, "If they called it fish eggs, no one would touch the stuff." She nearly choked.

"Surprise! They let the riffraff in with the nobs," said
Brett Fallon, grinning from ear to ear.

"Did you crash?" she couldn't resist asking.

"As a matter of fact, his majesty asked me himself. Ian
introduced us at the track, and the bloke insisted I come
tonight, so how could I refuse?"

"Absolutely not. Anyone in the race game should cul-
tivate Abdullah," she said, hoping there were no little
black fish eggs between her teeth.

"Seems a nice man. He remembers Charlie from the
Deauville sale where that French count bought him. Said
he was interested in him himself, but was leery of his tem-
perament."

"Wise of him. Had he heard that Charlie's killed a
man?"

"No. It appears the count kept that nasty secret under
wraps. I mean, after all, it was only a groom, right?"

"But a good groom is so hard to come by these days,"
she said, playing along.

"True. Why aren't you washing that foul stuff down
with some vodka? It's the real thing." He drank off a shot.
"Phew! Fair takes the enamel off your teeth."

"I'd love some champagne. There must be some somewhere—Abdullah usually has fountains of it."

"I shall find you some, my Lady," said Fallon. She
watched him shouldering his way through the crowd, his
gleaming hair curling down over the back of his collar.
He really looked marvelous in a dinner jacket; she wondered where he'd got one. Evening attire could make
even a plain man look distinguished, and it transformed
the horse trainer into the equal of any man at the party.
Lily smiled to herself. The evening was definitely looking
up. Normally, once she'd made her entrance in a beautiful dress and jewels, the rest of the evening was an anticli-
max and generally a drag talking to bores and people who

were interested only in one thing—horses. Now, she was very glad she'd decided to come.

Fallon returned with two glasses of champagne. "I'd like to make a toast to you and me putting the knives away, Mrs. D'Arcy. May we both find out that neither of us is as bad as we thought." They clicked glasses.

"Have you decided that I'm not a cold, frustrated bitch after all, Mr. Fallon?"

He considered this for a moment. "I never said you were cold, and I don't really believe you're a bitch, though I've seen you act one."

"I imagine that's been said behind my back, but you're the first who's ever called me that to my face."

"I've already apologized for that faux pas, Mrs. D'Arcy."

"Please, if you and my husband are on a first name basis, we might as well be, too—it will make me feel less bitchy. Do you know my name, Brett?"

"Lily, then. That's a beautiful name. You look one tonight."

"The liquor must be getting to you. That was a compliment."

"I always tell the truth, Lily, and you're the most beautiful woman here."

She flushed violently. "Don't overdo it, please. I'm not Mary. That sort of line may get you a special pudding, but it won't get you anywhere with me."

He frowned. "I'm not trying to get anything from you—it's just what I think. There's not a woman here can hold a candle to you but Bella. Don't pretend you don't know that, Lily." His piercing, blue eyes were relentless.

"You are very good at making me feel uncomfortable, Mr. Fallon."

The blue eyes softened. "I wouldn't want to make you

uncomfortable. I'm sure there are more important people here that you'd rather be spending your time with. I wouldn't want to ruin your evening again." He half bowed and left her with her mouth hanging open.

The man was incredible! He never failed to stir her up into a hornet's nest of emotion whenever they were together for more than five minutes. It was as if he were laughing at her, mocking everything she represented. Well he was only too right; there were many more attractive and important people there, and it was time she found them.

For dinner, Lily was seated at a table with their good friends Marian and Morris Ross. Morris, sweet but dull, was on her right, and a major whose last name she immediately forgot was on her left. The tables were lovely, set with linen cloths, heavy sterling, crystal, and china, a Sèvres pattern Lily knew to be priceless. The wealth of the Arabs was staggering. The heated marquee was illuminated by crystal chandeliers, lavishly decorated with flowers, the ground covered with Oriental carpets—a pasha's palace transported to Kildare.

For the first course, waiters in native dress appeared bearing platters of exotic-looking Middle Eastern dishes called "mazza." The major who'd lived in Saudi Arabia explained. Lily passed on the "kibbi," raw lamb tartare, and nibbled instead on olives and the wonderful flat bread served with it. They cleansed their hands afterward in fingerbowls of scented water adorned with rose petals, before the next course, a chilled yogurt soup sprinkled with raisins and fresh mint arrived. Then followed fish in mussel sauce, a salad of lettuces and pomegranate seeds, and the main course of rack of lamb with herbed rice, grilled tomatoes, and stuffed, baby aubergines—each course served with a different wine. Although the host was a strict Moslem, he was unstinting in the liquor service. The thick, sweet, Turkish coffee served after the dessert, fresh figs and a flaky pastry with pistachios in a rose-sugar syrup, did not dim the high felt by most guests by the end of the banquet.

Lily, though a bit lightheaded from the wine and champagne, was in better shape than most who had trouble standing when the orchestra began to play. Trapped into dancing with the major, she was treated to ten minutes of trodden feet and bumping from a paunchy belly, while he denounced the Arabs for driving the small stables out of business by running the prices up at the yearling sales and buying all the best horses.

"But they do know how to throw a party," Lily had to say. She wanted to add that the major had done his best to get even on the food and liquor. Morris Ross thankfully broke in, and after one dance, she excused herself to go to the ladies' room. Actually, she longed to leave if she could but find Tristan to take her home. If only Ian had been there, it might have been an enjoyable party. On her way to the loo, Lily discovered that the young people had their own adjoining marquee with a much livelier rock band. She saw Bella's red hair on the dance floor; she and Tristan were cutting a handsome figure—Bella was a very good dancer she saw, somewhat to her surprise. Of course Tristan was—it was in his genes. They really did look good together, the two of them. Not for the first time Lily realized how much in love her son was with his wife. It frightened her somehow for him. She couldn't tear them away when they were having so much fun, so she turned to go back and suffer with the old, dull crowd when she saw Brett Fallon sitting at a table by himself, staring at her.

He stood up as she approached. "Why aren't you dancing? The music's much better in here," she said.

"Bella forced me into one go-round, but that was all

she could take. I'm not much of a dancer, especially to this rock stuff."

"Are you any good at the slow stuff?"

"I can fake my way at that a bit."

"Good." She held her hand out to him. "You can't be any worse than my last partner. Come with me into the adult tent where you belong."

"I thought you didn't like to be seen with your stable-hand, Lady D'Arcy."

"Would you stop being so prickly and difficult? Do I have to order you as your employer?"

"I'm off duty, ma'am," he said, smiling at her.

"All right then, I'll pay you to dance with me. What would you charge to be my escort, Mr. Fallon?"

"It depends on how difficult you plan on being, my Lady."

"I plan on being an absolute angel, Mr. Fallon."

"In that case, I can be had very reasonably." He offered her his arm, and they returned to the other tent.

"Now this is more like it," he said, taking her in his arms, one callused hand about hers, the other firmly at her waist.

"I get the feeling I should let you lead," he quipped.

"I can."

"I'm sure of that," he said, smiling down at her. After a few minutes, they both relaxed and grew attuned to each other.

"Look Ma, I'm dancing," he said in her ear.

"Not badly at all," she said. Her forehead was even with Fallon's mouth, whereas she fitted easily under Ian's chin. His shoulder felt massive under her left hand.

"That was some dinner," he commented. "Don't know what I ate, but it was fantastic."

"Especially the sheeps' eyeballs—the round things in the first course."

"You're mucking about with me?"

"If that means teasing, yes. They do eat those I've heard, but not on tonight's menu."

"Had me goin' there for a bit. I've had caterpillars, but don't think I could go an eyeball."

"Caterpillars?"

"Yes, ma'am. Witchetty grubs—an Abo dish. Very tasty."

"Let's change the subject."

"Do you know all these people, uh, Lily?"

"I know who most of them are through racing, but I can't say I really know many of them well."

"A well-heeled bunch, I'd guess."

"Rather. See that plump, darkish man over there? The Aga Khan."

"No kidding? I *am* in a swell crowd."

Lily caught sight of the woman who'd accused her of running around on Ian; she waved vivaciously, but Lily pretended not to see her.

"Someone was trying to get your attention," said Fallon.

"I know. I'm ignoring her. She saw you and me at the Shelbourne and spread it around that we're, you know, having an affair. Now she'll really be convinced."

"So that was why you were so nervous being with me?"

"Yes. It's just a small, gossipy town, really. Ian doesn't care what people say, but I do."

"Insulting to your rep to be slumming with the help, eh?"

Lily stopped still in his arms. "That's not the point. I don't have affairs, period."

"Sorry, I didn't mean to insult you."

"You have a very quick lip, Brett!"

"And you have a very quick temper. . .Lily."

"And that is why we're into it five minutes after we've said hello," she retorted.

He put his hands on her shoulders. "Calm down and unruffle those pretty feathers. I can see you're a virtuous woman. Ian is a very lucky man."

"Even if he isn't very virtuous himself."

"Eh?"

"Nothing. Look, Brett. Would you do me an immense favor? I'd really like to leave this party, but I've had too much to drink to trust driving alone back to Innismere. Would you mind terribly driving me?"

"Sure. You're paying me for the evening, right?" He smiled like a pussycat.

Brett left to get the farm lorry he'd come in while Lily went to tell Tristan and thank the hosts for a lovely evening.

It was interesting getting in the high cab of the truck in the form fitting gown; Brett helped her, again showing that someone had taught him nice manners somewhere along the line. *To hell with it if anyone sees us leaving together,* she thought. She felt a sort of recklessness building that wasn't entirely due to drink. It was a combination of everything she'd been through the past winter and spring, Ian's not being there with her, and the heady, physical effect of Brett Fallon's stimulating company in her husband's stead. As they took the road to Innismere, Lily felt a little thrill of excitement at what the evening might bring. How wonderfully exciting not to know exactly what lay ahead! Maybe nothing; maybe everything!

Fallon offered her a cigarette and managed to light it for her without losing control of the lorry. He appeared to have assumed an air of suave urbanity along with the rented or borrowed dinner jacket—without losing a dot of the rough virility which made him so "irresistible" as

Violet had put it. *Watch yourself, Lily,* said a voice in her ear, but she pretended not to hear.

"I really do appreciate this, Brett. I hope I haven't spoiled your evening?"

"Not at all. I don't care much for parties myself, especially with a bunch of rich poms I don't know. I get attacks of that foot in mouth disease like I had at the Shelbourne."

"I think you're just a tiny bit shy, Brett. I hadn't guessed that about you."

He shrugged. "Maybe. I'm used to being the outsider. The truth is, it's more that I'm a snob, as bloody ridiculous as that sounds."

"Are you?" she laughed. "I know I'm one."

"Yeah, I don't see that many people that I want to waste my time on. I'd rather be alone."

"I can understand that perfectly," she said, leaning her head back. She'd had decidedly too much wine at dinner on top of the champagne. It felt very nice.

"So maybe you and I have something in common after all, Lily. Can't get used to calling you that."

She smiled at him, admiring his strong profile. "I'm glad I can call you Brett now. I quite like you, when I'm not hating your guts, Brett."

"Ha! My sentiments exactly. I'll try to control my quick lip, and you hold on to your famous temper, and maybe we'll be mates, eh? I like you, too, Lily. I did from the start."

"How could you? I've been horrid to you."

"True, but at least you're straight. If you don't like or trust someone, you say it right out. I admire that in people, even if it's me they don't like."

"Let's don't be too nice to each other, Brett. I quite enjoy our little fencing matches." He smiled over at her.

When they reached the house, Lily, reluctant to let him

go, invited Fallon in for a nightcap. He declined, saying he wouldn't be able to get up at five if he had anymore to drink.

"I'll make you some tea then," she insisted. She put the billy on as he called it and set about finding the teapot, while he sat at the kitchen table and had another cigarette.

"Tell me, Brett, why has an attractive man like you not got a girl?"

"We *are* being blunt tonight."

"Now that we're mates, I thought I'd ask what's been puzzling me about you. You admire honesty, remember?"

"Why would you care, Lily?"

"I don't. It would just seem normal for you to have one. I hear women are very attracted to you."

"Do you?" He seemed to be laughing at her.

"Are you engaged to a girl back home in Woolly Bully or wherever it was?"

"Wollongong. No. Why are you so interested?"

She poured them both a cup of tea and sat down at the table across from him.

"Do you really think I'm attractive, Brett, or was that just your usual, flattering bullshit?"

"It's obvious to anyone with eyes, including yourself, that you are a beautiful lady."

"Am I? I used to be pretty I think, but when you get older, you wonder if you've lost it. Ian would think me beautiful if I were a hag."

"You are not a hag, and you haven't lost it."

She smiled at him. "Thank you. There, did I accept that compliment better this time?"

"Yeah. You damn well fished for it, too." She gave him a look over the top of her teacup. "Sorry. Pardon my Aussie lip."

"So, here we are," she said. "In spite of my bitchy temper, you find me attractive for my advanced age, which isn't that much more than yours by the way, and I think you're very attractive."

"But dangerous, insulting, and a bullshit artist?"

"Absolutely. All qualities which add to your attraction, I hate to admit." They smiled at each other.

She took a deep breath and leapt ahead. "It's been a very long time since I've done this sort of thing, so I'll just say it straight out the way you like it. Would you like to spend tonight with me, Brett?"

He knocked his cup over and the tea spread across the wooden table. "Jesus!" he swore.

"That wasn't very subtle, and I've put you off terribly, I can see by your face. It's just that when we were dancing, I fancied you might be interested. I knew you were!"

"What was all that patter about your never having affairs? Just to throw me off guard?" he said as he got to his feet. The tea was running off onto the floor now. Lily tried to staunch the flow with the quilted cozy.

"I don't have affairs, and I'm not interested in one with you," she said, wishing that she'd never begun this. "Ian and I are having sexual problems. We love each other, but it's not so good in bed lately. He's been getting his satisfaction elsewhere, so it occurred to me that it's only fair for me to do that, too. I don't want some messy affair that will threaten my marriage. All I want is, well, sex, and God, you must, too. Am I horrifying you?"

Fallon shook his head. "Lady, you're the damnedest female I've ever met. There's no way I could do that. I'm sorry about the two of you, but I'm not the cure."

"I know you're not the cure—don't flatter yourself. I was only looking for a little temporary relief. You're obviously not interested, so forget I even suggested such a thing. I wish to hell I hadn't! I've had too much to drink!" She struggled to keep the tears back.

Fallon ran his hand nervously through his bright hair and looked undone. "This has nothing to do with my being interested, Lily. It's just that I can't."

"Of course. Please leave," she managed to say.

He paused at the door and looked back at her. "I'm very sorry. I mean that," he said softly. She turned away from him to hide her tears of humiliation.

As soon as she heard the door close, she said aloud, "Congratulations, Lily. You've just reached the nadir of your life!"

The next afternoon before the race, Lily D'Arcy sat in the reserved enclosure of the Curragh, the picture of cool elegance in her black wide-brimmed hat. Inside however, she was seething with unsettling emotions. Her hangover was compounded by the wave of nausea which threatened every time she remembered the mortification of Fallon's rebuff. Moreover, she was furious with herself for getting in such a spot. She'd avoided Fallon so far today, but he couldn't be shunned forever. Now he had this awful thing over her; it was unbearable! What had got into her, besides too much liquor, to make her forget that blunt aggressiveness never worked? Men had to control sex, or think they did, just as they had to control everything else, the pricks!

Just then the horses were off—the crowd hushed in anticipation and everyone craned their necks to the right. Lily focused her glasses on the field as the horses galloped down the grassy turf of the right-handed Curragh track which was horseshoe-shaped rather than oval like American tracks. It had taken her years to get used to horses running clockwise instead of the reverse as they did on left-handed American tracks. Quickly she spotted the lavender and chartreuse silks of Innismere Racing Stables. To her delight, Violet's Season had come out of the gate brilliantly and was in the front pack. By the half mark in the mile race the filly was in front. Lily screamed in excitement as they came down the finishing straight to the wire, a photo finish between their horse and one of Abdullah's. It was terribly disappointing when the Arab's horse was declared the winner by a nose on the nod—the forward stride—but it was still a great coup for Innismere to be second. Violet's Season had done better than anyone ever expected, considering the competition. Lily and Bella embraced, and Tristan threw his cap in the air.

In the unsaddling enclosure Lily hugged a startled Frank Connors. She received the check for second place, a nice sum even if the prize money didn't compare to that of French and American races. Ian would be so pleased. So far it had been a lot of money going out and not much coming back in—a very expensive hobby really, until this marvelous filly.

"That'll help pay for her oats," said a voice over her shoulder. Lily stiffened.

"Yes, indeed," she said, putting the check in her purse without looking at Fallon.

Tristan, Bella, Brett and the others went off to a pub to celebrate, but Lily drove straight home.

She was desperately glad to see her husband when he returned from Geneva that night. He was ecstatic over the win and went straight off to the stable.

When he returned quite late, she could see from his face that something was wrong. The filly had come up lame on her right foreleg, and the vet and Connors had her packed in ice, hoping for the best. It was a bowed tendon, a strained tendon behind the cannon bone, the lower part of the leg. The vet thought it was caused by stress; the filly had given her all in the race, and the full weight coming down on the one leg as it does at a gallop had pushed the limb beyond endurance. Ian was very depressed because not only would the horse miss all the important Oaks, she might be out for the season.

Lily put her arms about him as he poured himself a drink. "I can't believe that you didn't get to see her win. It's not fair."

"There'll be other races, other horses," he said, sounding tired and dejected. "Brett says Charlie took to the Curragh like a duck to water."

She kissed him. "I missed you awfully. I went to the Abdullah party, but it was no fun at all without you."

"Sorry I missed it. Did you wear the St. Laurent?"

"And the sapphires. Men fainted at the sight of me."

"I can imagine. Did the sheik fancy adding you to his harem?"

"Possibly. He definitely admired your taste in jewelry though."

He tipped her chin up. "I don't know if I like the thought of you running about without me, Lily."

"You told me to go."

"Yes, but I didn't really mean it. Don't know if I like the thought of Abdullah and any number of other men lusting after my beautiful, unescorted wife."

"I had Tristan, and Mr. Fallon danced once with me. You needn't have worried. No one wanted me."

"I know someone who wants you. Wants you very much indeed." She laid her cheek against his chest and thanked God and Mr. Fallon that she hadn't betrayed him.

Lily slept late the next morning. When she went down for breakfast, Ian had already eaten and gone to the stable to check on the filly. Taking a cup of tea to her desk in the morning room, she was checking through some bills to be paid when she noticed Ian and Fallon walking up from the stable. They were deep in conversation—about Violet's Season she imagined from the solemn expression on their faces. They stopped on the terrace; she could just hear their voices through the open window.

For the hundredth time she felt a flush of shame over her behavior after the party. How could she have almost done that to Ian! *Please God, never let him find out,* she prayed. What power the horse trainer had over her now should he choose to exercise it! Of course it would only be his word against hers, and she was sure her husband would believe her.

As she watched the two of them, Ian put his arm around Brett's shoulder. She clearly heard him say, "Don't worry. I'll tell her—I promise you." Ian went in the terrace door, while Fallon headed for the rear entrance to the kitchen.

Lily sat there for a minute digesting what she had just seen and heard. The intimacy of his gesture with Fallon struck her as odd. Ian was not the sort of man who physically engaged people, except for his son, and lately not even him. The only other man she could remember him being demonstratively affectionate with was Tony Neville.

She felt a sudden hollowness in the pit of her stomach. Why had she been so blind? No wonder Ian had hired the Aussie on when he didn't need him. Of course he knew Fallon hadn't touched Violet. "I can't," Brett had said. He meant that literally. Brett Fallon didn't need women at all. Her mind raced. She should have recognized it from the first. The blond hair and blue eyes—he was a younger, sexier replacement for Tony.

Lily gasped aloud in horror at the thought of her throwing herself at Brett Fallon. What was it Ian had promised to tell her? Leave Fallon alone; he's not interested? The light on in his stable room to all hours of the night was a signal for Ian. Come to me and share the kind of sex that really turns you on. She jumped to her feet. They weren't going to get away with it. Ian would not make a fool of her twice.

When she found him in his study, Ian was looking at the portrait of his mother. She forced herself to talk normally. "How is the filly?"

"It's bad, I'm afraid. She's out for the season. It's up to Charlie now to fly our colors."

"I'm sorry."

"The whole race game is a gamble. We lost this time," he said wearily.

"I saw you talking to Brett on the terrace. He looked upset—about the horse, I suppose?"

"He feels badly as any horseman would. It hurts him to see a fine animal like that wasted."

"Exactly what did you promise to tell me, Ian?"

"Oh, that." He looked evasive.

"I know what it is, in case you've not got the nerve to tell me." She held herself in check though she wanted to scream and rage at him for his deceit.

"You know? How could you?"

"I watched you two together through the window, and at last it came to me why your relationship with Fallon is so much closer seeming than with your other employees. Suddenly, I just knew."

"Your intuition amazes me, Lily. I suppose there is some slight resemblance through the eyes and the nose."

"You're not even going to deny it this time? How could you lie to me all these months?"

"To be fair, Brett wanted me to tell you long ago, but I didn't think you could take another shock coming so soon on the heels of the other one."

She reached out for a chair to steady herself. How incredibly cool he was! "I hope that no one else knows about this. That you've been discreet," she said.

"I've told the children. I had to tell Violet after that unfortunate misunderstanding with Brett."

"My God! How could you have told them? What a terrible shock for the poor things."

"It was a shock, but they had to learn sooner or later since he is a member of the family now. Both of them were very pleased, by the way. They like Brett enormously."

Lily feeling her legs buckle beneath her, sat heavily in the chair. Had she entered the twilight zone? Violet and Tristan were thrilled with their father's new lover who was now to be a member of the family?

"My dear, are you all right?" said Ian looking alarmed. She shook her head, but words failed her. He went to a decanter and poured her a drink.

"Here, sip this. I suppose the shock of having your feelings confirmed about Brett are affecting you."

"The children are happy?" she whispered.

"Yes. They're delighted to learn that Brett is their brother, thank God."

"Brother?"

"Yes—just as you thought. I suppose you want to know about his mother. She was Damien's governess when I was sixteen. We became involved, and she got pregnant. Father gave her money to get an abortion, but she went to Australia and had the child instead. I had no idea of Brett's existence until he turned up here."

"Brett Fallon is your son," she said.

"I swear I would have told you I had a son if I'd known about him. I was going to, but I was afraid of your reaction. Brett was very insistent that I must tell you the truth." Lily began laughing; Ian looked bewildered.

"Brett is your son," she said, laughing with tears running down her face. "I knew I'd seen him before. It was you in him that I saw. I'm such an incredible fool!"

He knelt beside her and took her hands. "Are you all right?" This was not the reaction he had expected from her. Was she hysterical? "Lily, please say you forgive me, that you aren't furious with me again."

She sniffed and gripped his hand. "How could I have doubted you, Ian? I'm such an idiot!"

"Never. I want you to know that Miss Culhane was never to me what you are. I don't know if I was really in love with her or if it was just gratitude and relief. You are my only love, the only Lily in my garden." She put her arms around him and began crying afresh.

Later when she'd regained her composure, her anger with Brett Fallon began to grow. As usual, her first instinct had been the right one. He did want something—Innismere. It had been greed and envy that had so distorted his face with emotion that first day on the terrace. He coveted all that life had cheated him of.

Worried, she asked her husband if his bastard son had any claims to the house and title as his oldest male heir. Ian told her that though Brett had no legal claims since he was illegitimate, he certainly planned on providing for his son's future. She couldn't understand that—why any of Tristan and Violet's share should go to Fallon.

"He can take care of himself. He has a profession," she insisted.

"Lily, I owe him something. To make up for the hardship he and his mother had to suffer. I would have provided for them all along, if I'd only known."

"I think Fallon exaggerates this almost Dickensian childhood with the cruel stepfather and greedy brothers. He wants you to feel guilty."

Ian naturally refused to see any ulterior motive in Fallon's appearance on the scene and would not be drawn into an argument. "Lily, Brett is in no way a threat to you or the children. Please let's just get on with life and try and be as pleasant as possible about this." His attitude to life in a nutshell.

So she dropped the subject, but she certainly didn't forget it. It wasn't fair for Brett to have any of her children's portion. One thing was dead certain—she'd never trust Fallon again. He'd allowed her to make a fool of herself when he should have told her right out who he really was, even if Ian was too cowardly. He had flirted with her at the party, led her on with his compliments. It was not her imagination that she'd felt desire in him when they were dancing. A man's body didn't lie. He had let her assume it was leading some place, and then had a good laugh at her expense.

Her humiliation was nothing, however, to what Fallon had done to Violet. The poor child! And coming right off that other unhappy experience with a cad. For the pain and embarrassment he'd caused her daughter, the man would have to pay.

Lily spent the next morning in the garden setting out new plants and dividing crowded perennials—her own prescription for forgetting the blues. Timothy the gardener took care of the fruit trees and vegetable garden, but the flowers were hers. She'd changed the flower beds a great deal since Ian's father's time. Although Lily had known nothing about plants to begin with, she soon became an expert with the help of books and Timothy, a goldmine of horticultural knowledge. She'd not been able to rearrange the house much, because Ian disliked change, but she had been ruthless in renovating the gardens. Out went the harsh oranges, yellows, reds, and fuchsias. Other than the thousands of naturalized daffodils in the front park, only the softest, pale, yellow daylilies were allowed in her garden which bloomed from April to October, an Impressionist painting of blues, lavenders, soft roses and pinks with accents of purple and white. She eliminated any plant too stiff in form, like the ramrods of delphiniums so beloved of English gardeners. In the center of the great circle of flower beds, she had erected a cast-iron pergola planted with old roses with romantic names like Gloire de Dijon and Reine des Violettes.

The only part of the garden which she hadn't made her own was the side garden where Ian's mother had killed herself. Here, a great unruly ramble of red roses all but covered a statue of Venus Ian had had placed there. She'd tried to prune and clean it up a bit, but it was useless the way the thorny vines took over. The Irish being famously superstitious, Timothy refused to even enter that part of the garden. Bella was the only one who ventured into this wild memorial and often kept a bowl of the blood-red flowers in her bedroom. There was something a little bit fey about her daughter-in-law, Lily thought.

Lily was on her knees firming the earth about a newly set clump of pinks, when a shadow fell over her.

"So the lady doesn't mind getting her own hands dirty?"

"Your habit of sneaking up on one's backside is very tiresome," she said without turning around.

"So, I imagine I'm back on your shit list, eh?"

"You were never really off it."

"I wish to hell I'd told everyone who I was the day I came here. It would have saved a lot of grief."

"I think you very much enjoy causing grief. It's your revenge."

"Revenge for not being legit? For not being born to all this crap you're so involved with? That's not true. I don't give a damn about any of it. And I never wanted to hurt you or Violet, believe me."

"Didn't you just! I imagine you've been having a jolly good laugh up your sleeve at us. Really getting off on our guilt and embarrassment when we found out who you were. I will never forgive you for doing that to Violet." She worked her weeder furiously.

"Look, it was Ian's place to tell you all. He didn't want to, so what could I do?" Lily flung a clump of weeds over her shoulder and heard it hit him.

"I know you hate me now, and I don't blame you," he continued. "I don't want to cause problems for anyone, I swear, Lily."

"Mrs. D'Arcy to you. What did you come here for?"

"I wanted to feel that I belong somewhere on this earth."

"You do not belong at Innismere," she said as cruelly as she could.

"You're probably right. I just want to say to you that I wish to hell that hadn't happened between us the other night." She tensed, waiting for him to rub salt in the wound. "If you had been any other person than his wife, you'd never have had to ask me."

"Never mention that to me again," she said.

"I understand. I don't want to be your enemy, and I apologize for the pain I've caused you and Violet. Please don't hold this against me."

She heard him leave and clenched her teeth to keep from yelling curses after him.

That evening there were five places set at the dinner table. Lily looked at Ian.

"I told the Kelly's. Brett will be taking his meals with us from now on," he said.

"It's your house," she said coolly.

Tristan, Bella, and Brett came into the dining room talking and laughing together and took their places. Lily rang the bell for the first course without looking at Fallon. Kelly came in and began serving the soup from the tureen on the sideboard. He put Brett's bowl down with a clatter and a scowl so noticeable that Tristan commented on the butler's ill humor as soon as he'd gone back to the kitchen.

"He's pissed at me. He and Mary both. I'm damned if I know what to do about it," said Brett.

"They'll get over it," said Ian. "From what I've seen, Mary dotes on you."

"Not anymore, she doesn't."

"Some people don't like being lied to and made fools of," said Lily.

"Please!" said Ian sharply.

"Oh, sorry. I forgot I was supposed to be pleasant no matter what." Turning to Fallon with a faked smile she said, "Brett, it's just heaven having you here with us, darling. I've always wanted a son almost my own age."

There was a moment of shocked silence, then Fallon stood up. "I appreciate your asking me to eat with you, Ian, but Lily and the Kellys are right. I don't belong here—excuse me." He left the room.

"Jesus, Mother!" said Tristan in disgust.

Ian threw down his napkin. "I will not have him treated rudely by the servants or you, Lily. He has every right to be at this table. I'm going to have a word with Seamus right now." He got up and went to the kitchen.

Needless to say, dinner was a shambles.

Tristan stroked Bella's stomach. "I think I scored a bullseye that time—certainly felt like it." He lay his cheek against her flat belly. "Are you in there, already dividing?"

Bella let his silky hair slide through her fingers. "We've been trying for three months now. You'd think I'd be pregnant."

"They say it can take time after you've been on the pill."

"Tris, what if something is wrong with me?"

"Absurd. No one as perfect as you on the outside could have anything wrong with her insides. We're in no great rush, bella Bella. We've a few breeding years left yet."

"I keep worrying why I didn't get pregnant the first time, and why I still haven't. Perhaps I should see a doctor about it?"

"Bollocks! I think you're already pregnant as we speak. The timing is perfect. What do you think of the name Valerian? Valerian D'Arcy?"

"Sounds posh. Would he be Val then?"

"Or Erian, whichever you prefer," he said with a smile. "What if it's a girl?"

"I think this is bad luck to think of names before it's sure."

"What about Siobhan?" She smiled. "I thought you'd like that one," he said.

"Tris, if it doesn't work this time, I want to see a doctor to make sure everything is okay."

"All right, so you'll stop worrying about it. In the meantime. . ."

From Ian's cold silence that night and at breakfast the next day, Lily realized she'd gone too far; he was determined to have Brett Fallon treated as a member of the family. It was a sunny day in the sixties, so Lily put on a cashmere sweater, riding britches, tied her hair back with a ribbon, and set out for the stables to undo the damage she'd done at Fallon's debut dinner. He was sitting in the sun on the steps to his apartment.

"Gorgeous day, isn't it?" she called gaily. He looked back over his shoulder as if she were speaking to someone else. "What are your plans for the rest of this rare afternoon, Brett?" she asked.

"Why do you ask?" he said, crossing his arms and regarding her with justified suspicion.

"You never give a straight answer, do you?"

"You ask loaded questions, Mrs. D'Arcy."

"This is simple enough. I'm riding up to the castle— if you're free, why not come with me? Your ancestors did live there, after all. The view will be lovely on a clear day like today."

"Why should you want to ride with me, when you can't stand to sit at the same table with me. . .Mrs. D'Arcy?"

"You once very graciously apologized to me for your atrocious behavior. I'm trying to do the same. Ian is cross with me for being rude to you, and I want to make amends. You will be as forgiving as I was, won't you. . .Mr. Fallon?"

He considered her for such a long moment that her dazzling smile began to tire. Then he stood up and ambled over to her. "If you put it that way, I suppose I would be a lout to refuse."

"Yes, you would." As the two of them entered the stable, she said, "If we're going to be one jolly, big family, you and I will have to forget all the silliness we've been through and start over."

"Too right. I'll go along with that one. . .Lily. Or do I overstep myself?"

"You may resume calling me by my first name, Brett."

He bowed to her, and she had to laugh. Oh, she did like sparring with him. Even if he was totally not to be trusted.

Lily waited while he saddled Lady Jane and Virago, a big chestnut mare Ian used for hunting.

"Since I won't be riding alone, I would love to ride a horse with a bit more spirit. Could I try Virago?"

He switched saddles and gave her a hand up on the tall mare. She flopped ungracefully in the seat.

"All right?"

"Of course," she said, scrabbling to get her feet in the stirrups.

"You forgot your cap."

"You don't wear one," she replied.

"I know how to fall, and I have a very hard head."

"I'm sure of that," she said, giving Virago's flanks a good kick. The mare lurched into a trot, almost leaving her behind. They burst out of the stable door and clattered across the cobbled stableyard before she had the reins in hand well enough to slow the horse down. Fallon caught up with her, looking oversized on Lady Jane.

"Virago's very responsive. You don't have to urge her on as strongly as this one," he said.

"I am well aware of that," she replied, moving the chestnut into a trot again, a bit more smoothly this time.

He dismounted when they reached the paddock gate. "Can't we just jump the fence?" she asked.

"Virago can," he replied with a twitch at the corner of his mouth.

She wheeled the mare around, got a galloping start, and taking a surreptitious handful of mane, sailed over the three-foot fence with a foot to spare. Reining in her mount on the other side, she felt very proud of herself for having jumped something so high.

Fallon took the gray mare over and cantered past. Lily followed, trying not to feel too vulnerable so high off the ground with her life dependent on her ability to control a thousand pounds of flighty, dumb beast beneath her.

They galloped along, taking a wall and another fence without stopping. Lily led the way through the forest and up the trail to the old ruin. She slowed Virago down to a walk and let her have her head to pick her way up the stony incline as Ian had taught her. Reaching the summit of the hill, they rode once around the crumbling castle, then dismounted and tied their horses to the ring in the stone.

"Aren't you impressed? I don't believe they have anything as old as this back in Australia."

"There are Aboriginal rock paintings that make these Norman blokes look Johnny come lately, but you're right, we don't have any buildings this old." They examined the keep and climbed the winding stone stair that remained, though the wooden floors and roof had long since rotted away. Fallon noted the thick stone walls pierced by narrow window slits for firing down at the enemy.

"It must have been something in its day," said Lily. "I try to imagine what it was like whole, bustling with people always on the alert for the wild Celts bursting down on them from the mountains. It reminds me of the western forts built against the American Indians."

"They must have felt invincible up here behind their strong walls," said Fallon. " 'Gaze on my works ye mighty and despair.' No matter how thick your walls, it means naught to the turn of the centuries."

"My, a philosopher and a poet. Shelley, isn't it? You are full of surprises, one has to give you that, Brett Fallon. Or is it D'Arcy now?"

He took out a pack of cigarettes, lit one protecting it from the wind, and offered it to her. She accepted it, the filter damp from his lips. "I'm Fallon. Too late to change now," he said, and lit one for himself.

She pointed out the various landmarks across the valley and the misty, mauve shapes of Lugnaquilla and Table Mountains. In the distance, low, scudding clouds drug their black bellies over the trees. It wouldn't be nice for long.

"If you think I covet all this, that I've got onto a good wicket here, Lily, you're dead wrong." He regarded her with those disturbing eyes.

"It would be very normal for you to want it," she said. "Who wouldn't?"

"I wouldn't." He gestured broadly with his hand. "All this would be a two-ton anchor to me. I never like to own more than I can carry off in my duffel—wouldn't want the responsibility. If you've got it into your head that I somehow want to horn in on Tris's birthright, forget it. I'm delighted it's all his. He'll make a bonzer Sir Tristan some day."

"Since I know you have no legal claim to Innismere, that doesn't bother me, Brett." She smiled sweetly at him.

"Tell me, does the responsibility of a woman, a family, scare you, too?" she asked.

"You could be right about that."

"You know, it once occurred to me, before I knew who you were, that you might be homosexual, Brett. It salved my pride a bit." He laughed. "Let me add that you're the least likely candidate for that I've ever seen, but to be turned down like I was, what other conclusion could I come to? Certainly not that you were my husband's son."

"Would you rather I'd have been a faggot?"

She considered. "That is a truly hard choice. Let me think about that for a bit." A gust of wind ruffled Fallon's hair and made her shiver. Those distant storm clouds were gathering upon them with furious speed.

"Bit of weather coming our way," said Fallon. "We'd better get back." He flicked his cigarette off the tower and took her arm as they headed down the narrow stone steps. They reached the horses, skittish now with the approaching storm. He helped her on Virago and was trying to mount a prancing Lady Jane, when a fork of lightening rent the darkening sky followed instantly by a deafening clap of thunder. Virago reared in terror, tossing Lily off backward. Fallon hurried to help her; she'd only had the wind knocked out of her, but Virago had bolted off down the hill.

Huge drops of rain were coming down now, so he helped her up, and they headed for cover under the gateway, the only part of the ruin left with a roof over it. By the time they crowded under it's protecting canopy with Lady Jane, they were drenched.

It was a wild storm on the exposed hillside. Another crash of thunder from an immediate lightning strike caused Lily to cringe back against Fallon, who was struggling to hang onto the frightened mare. A wall of water fell in front and behind them. Another clap sounded right on top of them, and Lily instinctively turned to him.

He put his arm about her. "Steady on. It won't get us."

"I'm terrified of lightning," she said, burying her face against his chest. Lady Jane whinnied and jerked her head, but he held her bridle tightly.

"Easy does it, ladies. Nothing's going to get you while I'm here." His hand reassuringly stroked her back, and she could feel his voice rumble in his chest as he spoke. Brett Fallon smelled of tobacco, horses and soap; he felt very solid and safe. She looked up at him.

"It's passing—just hang on," he whispered. She nestled against him, not wanting to leave the snug harbor of his strong arms.

"Are you cold?" She nodded. He rubbed her arm briskly, and her forehead touched his cheek.

He cleared his throat. "Yeah, the worst is over. We'll live to duel another day, Lil."

Lady Jane, no doubt jealous, took this moment to butt him with her head, and Fallon moved away to attend to the mare. "I hope you had extra oats, my little beauty, because you're going to have to carry both of us home," he said, rubbing her charcoal muzzle. He removed the saddle and stacked it against the wall to be retrieved later.

"You much of a bareback rider, Lily?"

"I have trouble staying on with a saddle, as you well know."

"Time for a lesson, then." He leapt lightly on the gray mare like an Indian, then held his hand down to her and swung her up behind him.

As they walked the horse back home in a light rain, Lily had to hold onto his belt with both hands. The heat coming off his body and the steady rhythm of the mare's hooves had almost an hypnotic effect on her. The two of them rarely spoke, but she was acutely aware of Brett's every movement—the flexing muscles of his back, her thighs alongside his, their bodies supply swaying to-gether in time to the animal's stride. She longed to give in to the intensely sexual feeling of it and lean her weight against his back, but she kept her body carefully apart from his as if resisting a magnet. The memories of her humiliation at his hands strengthened her resolve. It had been only the night before that she'd sworn undying en-mity towards him.

The sun was out by the time they reached the stable. Fallon threw his leg over the front of the horse and hopped down, then helped her off. Lily pushed back her straggly, wet hair and hoped she didn't look like the drowned rat she felt.

"You'd best get out of those wet clothes and have a

hot bath," he suggested, looking down at her with eyes as blue as the sky behind him.

"You really should, too." She smiled back at him and tried unsuccessfully to suppress the image of them taking that nice, hot bath together. She turned to leave, then called back to him.

"Don't forget that tea is at 4:30, Brett."

"Is that a command?"

"It is. I promise to be sweet as pie to you—as long as you don't call me 'Mum'."

The azure eyes narrowed. "No way could I ever picture you as me mum, Lily."

In her bathroom, Lily stripped off her damp clothes and examined her body in the mirror. What a shame she'd spent her youth fretting that she wasn't voluptuous enough to be really desirable to men. Why hadn't she appreciated her lithe figure while she'd had it! Now, though still firm from a lifetime of dance, her buttocks were much lower than before she'd carried two babies and marred by faint stretch marks and even some of that horrid, puckery flesh they wrote of in books about shedding. Her belly was no longer perfectly flat, but her breasts at least were decent and unsagging. At last some reward for being small-busted. She was far from perfect, but she wasn't sloppy, fat, and out of tone like so many women nearing forty, Jane Fonda excepted.

Lily climbed in the steaming bath and let her body float while her mind reflected in careful detail over the ride with Brett Fallon. He had looked wonderful even wet, with his blond hair darkened and sticking up in ridges where he'd run his hand through it. She'd certainly never forget taking shelter from the storm with him. It had felt absolutely safe with his arm about her, curled up against his chest. He had called her 'Lil'—such an intimate ring to the way he said it in his husky voice. No one had ever called her that in her life.

She sat up in the bath and began vigorously soaping herself. What was she doing? Hadn't making a total fool of herself once been enough? Of all men off limits to her, Brett Fallon was the farthest. Things were looking up with Ian, and she shouldn't even be having these traitorous thoughts. It was all the fault of that cursed wild imagination of hers. Erotic fantasies intruded themselves in her brain, no matter how she sought to shut them out. Brett was extremely attractive, but she must never forget who he was, and what he might be up to. He had to want to be more than just the horse trainer. It was money or revenge he was really after. The man was a potential threat to everything and everyone she loved, and she must be on constant guard against him. She could almost hear her mother warning her about him. Brett Fallon was a living, breathing example of everything her mother had taught her to be wary of in life.

But still. . . . Lily could not diminish the pleasure of those moments in the storm with him—the ride back together, no matter how many warning gongs went off in her brain. Those half-innocent memories were more sensually exciting to contemplate than the complete act of love with her husband. She had forgotten what it was like to feel excitement, mystery, even a bit of fear in the presence of a man. To have all her senses, every cell in her body alive at the touch of his hand. Perhaps replaced by more solid, lasting values, but God, how she missed what a mere look from those blue eyes could stir in her breast!

Lily regularly made a checklist of linens and small valuables about the house to prevent them from disappear-

ing. About a week after the ride to the castle, she came
up short on the towels.

"I expect they're down at Mr. Fallon's," said Evileen.
"I'll go have a look and take him some fresh ones as well."

"I'll do it," said Lily.

"Don't bother yourself, madam. That would be my job
after all."

"I said I'll do it," Lily insisted. "I've been meaning to
see if his rooms are comfortable enough."

"Yes, madam," said the girl with a glint of suspicion,
or so it looked to Lily's paranoid eye.

She went down to the stable flat straightaway, counting
on Fallon's still being out at the gallops with Charlie.
Running quickly up the outside fire stairs, she found the
door unlocked as in her fantasy. The single room was a
mess, obviously a bachelor's digs; muddy boots strewn
on the floor beside a pair of jeans that looked as if Brett
had just stepped out of them. On the tiny table was a
dirty plate and an empty Fosters lager bottle filled with
cigarette butts. The single bed was unmade, and beside
it on the floor lay a pair of briefs and a book, an equine
veterinary guide—not Kafka or something to add to his
intrigue. She felt a twinge of guilt at invading Fallon's privacy like this, but not enough to make her forsake her
mission.

The tiny bathroom contained a toilet, sink, medicine
chest, and a pile of soiled towels in the corner. Lily put
the fresh linens on the back of the loo and opened the
wall cabinet. Inside were Band-aids, razor cartridges, and
a box of condoms. She smiled—he did not plan on re-
maining celibate forever.

Guiltily she closed the door; this was making her
queasy. It didn't bear thinking about what Fallon would
do if he ever discovered she'd been snooping.

Grabbing up the used towels, she returned to the bedroom, knowing she should get out of there quickly before she got caught. An antique dresser looming too fine and oversized for the tiny, basic room caught her eye. Lily put the laundry on the floor and went over to examine it. On top of the dresser were a billfold, a pile of coins, a hairbrush, and nail clippers. Holding her breath, she pulled out the top drawer. Neatly arranged socks and a cheaply framed photograph stared up at her. Aha! She picked up the picture and studied the image of a dark-haired young woman holding a blond toddler in her arms. His girl from home? Could that be his child? So engrossed was she in the photograph, that she didn't hear Fallon enter the room behind her.

"What the hell do you think you're doing?"

Hiding the picture behind her skirt, Lily turned to face him, her heart pounding. "My goodness, you startled me."

"You've been going through my things," he said, grim-faced as he shut the dresser drawer.

"Of course not. I brought you some clean socks and towels," she said edging away.

He caught her arm. "You're not the maid. Evie brings the laundry."

"Normally, but I was doing the laundry inventory and came up short on the towels. I thought you might have the missing ones, and you did. I'll get them back now for Sheila to wash." He held on to her arm.

"You're hurting me!"

Fallon caught her hand and pulled it from behind her back. "This is not your fucking laundry." They both stared at the incriminating picture.

"I'm sorry," she sputtered, her face crimson.

"You should be. You may own this place, but it doesn't give you the right to snoop through my things." He took the photo from her and returned it to its hiding place in the drawer.

"What were you bloody looking for? Proof that I'm really a criminal?"

Lily rubbed her arm where she could still feel the imprint of his strong fingers. "I did come about the linens, but curiosity got the better of me."

"Stone the crows! She finally admits it since she's caught red-handed with the goods! Look, lady, if you want to know anything about me, just ask me." His eyes flashed blue fury at her.

"So, I apologize. It's just that you're so mysterious," she said, trying to charm him into a lighter mood with a smile. He wasn't having it.

"What the fuck's so mysterious about me, Lily? I've told you everything you have a right to know. I have no nasty secrets or hidden motives, damn it!"

"Who is she?" she blurted.

"That was my mother and me."

"I thought so. That's really what I was after. I want to know about her—about Ian's first lover. I thought you might have a picture," she said, running with the idea.

"That, Lady D'Arcy, is a bloody, bald lie," he sneered.

"It's the truth."

"Don't try and bluff me. I don't get you, Lily. One day you're cutting my balls off, the next you're coming on to me, and the minute after that you're ransacking my room. What the hell do you want from me?"

Lily held her head high. "I came about the laundry, and Ian wanted me to see if your room was nice enough. I did err in letting my curiosity about you and your mother get the better of me, and I have apologized to you. Now, if you'll excuse me." She picked up the towels from the floor and headed for the door with as much dignity as an apprehended sneak thief could muster.

He nimbly moved to block her escape. "Not yet. I want some straight answers here, Lily. I've had it with the hot and cold bit. If you're trying to drive me mad, you're doing a damn good job of it. Are you trying to get me the boot or get into my bed?"

"How dare you speak to me like that!" She tried to get by him, but he knocked the towels out of her hand and shoved her against the wall.

"Get away from me, or I'll scream," she gasped.

"Scream away. I imagine everyone, including your husband, will be interested that you were rifling my drawers. I know I certainly am." She swung at him, but he pinned her wrists behind her.

"Tell me what you were looking for, damn it!" His eyes were murderous, not even kin to their usual bemused twinkle. Fallon's temper was every bit as awesome as she'd imagined.

"I was looking for something to explain you. I want to understand you," she said, telling the truth at last.

"Maybe you thought I had drugs, jewels I nicked at the Arab's party—a list of women I've raped. Some evidence to use against me with Ian, right?"

"I've answered you honestly, now let me go or I will tell Ian about this, and he won't think you're so damn wonderful anymore."

"I don't think you'll tell him you were in my room, Lily."

"I will—you're frightening me!"

He let her go. "I wonder what he would think about his lovely wife propositioning me, eh?"

"It would be my word against yours, and he loved me long before he ever heard of you. You can guess which one he'd believe."

"I'd never tell him anyway, wouldn't want to hurt the poor bastard like that. It's a damn shame Ian can't give you that all-night fucking you're begging for. That's still what you're really after, right, my Lady?" His smile was intolerable. She lashed out at him, catching him hard across the face.

He crushed her against the wall and forced his mouth on hers in a brutal kiss. "You want it so bad, you don't even care that I'm his son," he snarled. "If that's the kind of whore you are, let's quit playing footsy and get the deed done. Come on!" He shoved her toward the bed. "No more cat and mouse bullshit, Lily. You want me— I want you. It's high time we both got rid of our frustrations." He unfastened his belt.

"I wouldn't go to bed with you if you were the last man on earth," she cried in rage at his seeing through her pretenses. "Ian is a million times the man you are, and besides, you smell like a horse."

He laughed at her. "Good. It would have only been a mercy fuck. I don't really care to bed a spoiled, sneaking, bored bitch willing to cheat on a good man."

"You prick!" she screamed and ran past him to the door. His laughter taunted her as she stumbled down the stairs past a gape-mouthed Billy Rafferty pushing a barrow of manure.

"What are you staring at? Get back to work, you idiot!" she snapped.

Ian asked Lily to plan a special surprise family party for Brett's thirtieth birthday coming up on the thirteenth of May.

"Of course, darling. I can't think of anything I'd rather do," she replied.

He kissed her forehead. "I know you're really been making an effort with Brett, and I'm very grateful. I can't think of many wives who'd behave as well in such an awkward situation."

"Neither can I. I'm doing my damnedest because you asked me to."

"I love you even more for that, my darling. But, you must admit, it's not that difficult to like Brett. He's really very pleasant, don't you think?"

"He's a real charmer," she said without looking at him. "You seem to enjoy Brett's company more than that of your own son these days."

Ian frowned. "I have to deal with Brett on racing matters everyday, and, yes, I do enjoy his company. Tristan is busy with his pictures and Bella, of course."

Lily didn't comment further, but the coolness between Ian and their son since the separation was a continuing worry to her. It wasn't just that Tristan was busy, either. Things between the two were noticeably changed from the days when the boy had openly hero-worshipped his father. The growing intimacy between Ian and Brett made Lily jealous for her son.

Putting aside her feelings of loathing for the horse trainer, Lily went about planning his birthday party with the same energy and dedication she put to any task she undertook. In a Dublin bookstore, she found a handsome, leather-bound copy of Shelley containing the poem "Ozymandias," and at Brown Thomas, a cashmere turtleneck that would match Brett's striking, blue eyes exactly. The sweater would be Tristan's present, since it seemed too personal to come from her. With Mary Kelly, she planned a special meal of all Fallon's favorite dishes, and she herself made him a cake.

On the evening of the thirteenth, the family assembled early at table. When Brett came in the dining room, he found them already seated and sporting various hats Lily had selected.

"Is it some Irish holiday I don't know about?" Brett

asked with a laugh as he looked at Ian's crown and Tristan's tiny, black derby.

"Put yours on," said Bella in her golden halo, handing him a small, felt, cowboy hat. Everyone broke up at the sight of it perched on his blond cockscomb.

"Is it silly night at Innismere, or what?" he laughed.

"This is a very special night," said Ian, signaling for Kelly to pour the champagne. When the butler had retired to the kitchen, Ian lifted his glass in Brett's direction. "Although this is birthday number thirty for you, this is your first birthday with us, and that makes it very special and symbolic of all the ones we so unfortunately missed out on." Lily glanced at Fallon's face; it was naked and vulnerable.

"So let's all drink a toast to Brett's thirtieth," Ian continued. "In the years to come, we shall gather here to fête him, but this will always be his first birthday as a D'Arcy and as my son."

Fallon's mouth twisted and he looked ruddier than usual.

"Speech!" said Tristan.

Brett cleared his throat. "I didn't even think what day it was today. I can't believe that you remembered," he said, looking at Ian who was emotional as well. "This means more to me than I can say. I'm rotten with words, really. I'm more than proud to have a brother like Tris and to have a man like you for a father."

"Well said!" Tristan exclaimed. "I feel exactly the same." Bella leaned over and kissed Brett on the cheek. He looked down at his plate, the first time anyone had seen him at a loss for words and minus his usual smooth assurance.

To give him time to recover, Lily rang the bell to start serving. "Silly night is over. I'm dethroning myself," she said, removing her tacky, rhinestone tiara.

"Leave yours on, please, Brett. I love it!" said Bella.

"I'll wear it from now on. It's me, don't you think?" said Brett. They all agreed.

After dinner, Mrs. Kelly brought in the chocolate cake with one fizzing sparkler in the center and set it in front of Brett.

"You made this for me, Mary?"

"Oh, no sir. Didn't my lady make it for you with her own two hands."

"You may wish Mary had baked it, but I do cook better than I ride horses," said Lily.

"Thanks," he said, looking at her with obvious puzzlement. "It's bloody gorgeous!" He sliced into it. "Grand, it's chocolate inside, as well. Haven't had a cake since I was about six, I think. Devil's food is my favorite."

"I knew it would have to be," said Lily with a little smile.

"Fallons weren't big on celebrations, eh?" asked Tristan.

"They weren't big on anything that took you away from work. My mother always did something for me though."

"Fallon should have been Fagin," commented Lily. Ian gave her a warning look from under his brows.

"Well, you're a D'Arcy now. We celebrate every opportunity," said Tristan.

Champagne flowed, and by the time they adjourned to the drawing room, everyone felt quite jolly. Tristan took pictures while Brett opened his gifts, exclaiming over each one. There were riding gloves from Bella, and a framed black and white photo of him up on Charlie from Tristan.

Brett opened the sweater and held it up. "I may look a D'Arcy, yet."

"Try it on," said Bella, and Brett unabashedly pulled

off the sweater he was wearing, treating everyone to the sight of his creamy, muscled chest. He put on the cashmere. "Jesus, the feel of it," he said, running his hands over himself.

"It's just the color of your eyes," said Bella. Lily had to agree, and silently complimented herself for her excellent choice.

"Who's this from?" he asked, looking for the card.

"Actually, I bought it for Tristan and Bella to give you," she explained.

"Mother, I am an adult," her son protested.

"Sorry, darling. I still see you as my little boy."

"Well, thank you, Lily. This is really something. Feels like sin itself," said Brett.

"Have to lock up Evileen and Mary when he wears that," said Ian.

"Please, too much woman for me," Brett protested.

"But you'd eat very well," Ian laughed.

Next opened was the book of poems. Brett looked up at her as soon as he saw what it was. "Thanks again, Lily. This is fantastic." He scanned the table of contents and smiled to himself.

"You fancy Shelley?" asked Ian in surprise.

"Yeah, and Blake, and Yeats of course. We Irish are all poets at heart, eh?"

"How'd you know he would like that, Lily?"

"How could your son not love Shelley, darling?" Ian beamed at her, and she felt a bit ashamed of her genius in coming up with inspired lies at the drop of a hat.

The last present was very small and contained a set of keys. "Shall we step out front and see what those operate?" said Ian looking pleased with himself.

They all went outside, and parked in the drive was a classic Jaguar XKE in a burnished dark green with pigskin upholstery, the top down.

"Say something," said Tristan giving a transfixed Brett a nudge.

"Shit! Excuse me, but this is too much."

"Nonsense. It's high time you had a car," said an exhilarated Ian.

"But a bloody Jag. I can't take this!"

"No. You couldn't get it in your duffel," said Lily.

"I could handle two cars if you don't want it," said Tristan who had gotten a Mercedes 450 SL sportscar for his eighteenth birthday in February.

"Go take her for a spin, and then tell me you don't want it," said Ian.

Brett climbed inside and ran his hands over the steering wheel. "Who's brave enough to ride with me?" Lily opened the door and sat beside him. "Hold on to your wig, Mum!" They took off in a spray of gravel.

At the end of the long drive, he turned out of the gate toward the village. His hair was whipped back by the wind, his teeth clenched in concentration. *He loves speed and danger,* thought Lily; something inside her softened toward him.

He glanced over at her. "Too windy?"

"Yes, but I love it," she yelled over the roar of the motor. She could see that pleased him. Cornering at high speed on the narrow, rural road, he seemed to know just how to work the gears. "You drive very well," she told him.

He threw her a quick grin. "I like fast horses and fast cars."

"But not fast women," she had to quip. He slowed down and turned onto a dirt lane to turn around, she assumed. Instead, he braked to a stop and cut the motor. Her heart lurched.

"All right, you win. You are hands down the most confusing, contradictory woman I've ever met, Lily. What in hell are you up to now?"

"What do you mean?"

"You know what I mean, damn it. A few days ago, unless it was just a bad dream, we had that big row in my flat. I go crazy and half expect the wallopers to come haul my arse off to gaol. But, no! Instead of getting even with me for bein' such a brute to you, though you damn well deserved it, you bake me a cake, and give me the Shelley. Aside from your little barbs about the duffel and that, you're all sweetness and light. So I give up trying to figure you, Lily. It's impossible."

"After I had calmed down the other day, I realized you had every reason to treat me as brutally as you did. I probably would have been just as hideous to you had the shoe been on the other foot. Ian asked me to give you a good birthday, so I did, in a way as apology for my being so wrong invading your privacy. He wants more than anything for us to get along, so I'm putting aside my personal misgivings about you. If it had been totally up to me, I might have put arsenic in your cake." She smiled at him to show she might be kidding.

He shook his head. "You really are something, Lil. There'd never be a dull moment with you about. I'm confused as to whether it's hate or love you feel for me," he said, staring intently at her.

"I really don't know myself. Perhaps it's both. You say I confuse you. Well, you confuse me, Brett."

He took her hand. "You know it can't be, Lily. You and I are damned attracted to each other, but it can never, ever be. It would fuck everything. For the first time in my life, I've stumbled onto something really good here, and it's got nothing to do with money. It's beginning to feel like family with love and caring and closeness. That's something I've never had before, and I don't want to jeopardize it. In almost any other situation, I'd let myself get involved with you, Lil. That would be so easy for me to do. But the reality is, we can't without hurting him and mucking it all up. Do you understand me?" She managed a nod.

"I'm tired of fucking up. I've had a lot of experience in that department. So, please help me by not tempting me like you've been doing."

"I was only trying to be nice to you," she protested.

"I know—for Ian's sake. So be nice, but quit tempting me to cross that line we'll both regret. I'm not made of iron, damn it."

"You have misread my intentions, Brett. My marital problems have improved lately. It was just drink and the weakness of the moment the other time, and I'll be eternally grateful to you that nothing happened. I love my husband. I don't want anything from you, damn it!" He just smiled at her and she was glad it was too dark for him to see how red her face had got. He put his hand on the key.

"That woman in the picture wasn't your mother, was she? I imagine she must have been very blond."

"That was Josie."

"Is she your lover at home?"

"She is my stepbrother's wife."

"Ah, I see—the experience from which you speak?"

"We had a thing for each other. My stepbrother was fifteen years older than her. Always been a bastard. Always hated me."

"Is this the real reason you left?"

"Yeah. When I say it can fuck everything, I know what I'm talking about."

"Look, Brett, I was attracted to you before I knew who you were, but now that I know, it's horrible to even contemplate. As I said, thank God you weren't as tight as

I was the night of that party. I do love Ian, and I want our marriage to last."

"Right. And sleeping round won't help that."

"I never have, and don't intend to start now. You can rest assured that I won't assault you. Had you been kind enough to tell me the truth in the first place, I never would have made such an error in judgment."

"It wasn't easy to turn down a fine offer like that, even knowing the truth, Lil."

"Thanks for being gentleman enough to say that."

"You know I'm no damn gentlemen. It's the truth. So, are we friends again, now, or should I continue to watch my back?"

She smiled at him. "Friends. . .for now."

✚ ✚ ✚

The following week, Ian and Brett were off to Kildare every day to work Charlie at the Curragh for the upcoming Gallinule Stakes. Ian mentioned to Lily that they'd run into their neighbor Hubert Pynchon and his daughter Daphne at the track stable. Daphne and Brett had hit it off very well, he added.

"Daphne? The old maid with the overbite?" she asked, putting down her needlepoint.

"She had her teeth fixed years ago. A jolly, attractive girl, Daphne. Wouldn't be surprised at all if Brett rang her up."

"Surely he can do better than that," she sniffed.

"He hasn't so far. I know you think he's a lothario, but I disagree. Brett could certainly do worse than a pretty, intelligent girl who's well off and mad for horses."

"Who resembles one as well."

"If I didn't know better, I'd say you sound jealous of the girl," said Ian.

"Jealous? Please!"

"All the trouble you went to over his birthday."

"You asked me to do that, so I did. It appears I've done too good a job of trying to please my husband," she huffed indignantly.

"I'm sorry. That was uncalled for. I do appreciate how hard you've been trying with Brett."

Lily busied herself with her handiwork in offended silence, her mind on Brett and Daphne. Surely he wouldn't be interested in that plain little thing? Daphne was now in her late twenties, but in her teens had taught Violet jumping and dressage. She'd been one of those rather pathetic, boyish girls who cared more for horses than for dates. Lily hadn't seen her for years, but she couldn't imagine that she'd somehow become attractive.

The D'Arcys gathered in excited anticipation to cheer their new colt on race day. Brett was very nervous before Charlie's maiden race at the Curragh. Dressed in his blue birthday sweater, and the britches, jacket, and boots Ian had outfitted him in from his Dublin tailor and bootmaker, Brett Fallon could hold his own with any blueblood, thought Lily. Without any clothes, he'd no doubt be far superior. His good breeding, even from the wrong side of the blanket, showed in his chiseled bone structure and proud bearing. It had been the shaggy hair and cheap clothing that had prevented her before from noticing his natural aristocracy.

When she took her seat with Bella and Tristan in the reserved enclosure, Lily noticed a blond girl a few rows lower waving at them. She recognized the gentleman next to her as Mr. Pynchon, and so deduced that the blond was Daphne. She *had* got prettier. Lily smiled and returned the greeting. Hubert Pynchon was a prominent Dublin barrister who spent most of his time now raising steeplechasers which his daughter trained. His wife, who'd been a casual friend of Lily's, had died a few years previous. From the square set of Daphne's shoulders, Lily decided that the girl was still a jock, albeit a more feminine looking one.

The horses walked across the Sheep Graze in the track infield to get to the start of the mile-and-a-half race on the horseshoe-shaped course. The Curragh presented a beautiful pastoral setting on a nice day as this was with the green, Irish countryside rolling into the distance. The race announcer's voice over the PA hushed the crowd, and binoculars trained on the starting gate. They were off! Lily followed the lavender and chartreuse of Tommy Rafferty up on Charlie who was stuck in the middle of the bunched field for the first part of the race. The favorite broke ahead by a length. Lily saw Rafferty raise his stick, and Charlie surged forward, making his move. She and Tristan screamed their encouragement. As if urged on by their collective will, Charlie moved into second place behind the favorite who looked as if he could be starting to fade. As the horses swept to the uphill finish, Charlie passed on the outside and won by a good length.

Bella and Lily hugged each other in excitement. "I can't believe he won!" cried the girl in tears.

They hurried off to the winner's enclosure and found a jubilant Ian and Brett. Tommy Rafferty rode in the winner and dismounted, as they all crowded around a sweaty, prancing Charlie, still ready to run. Photographers took pictures of them standing all together smiling happily. Lily was acutely aware of Brett's hand on her back during the posing. While Ian congratulated Rafferty, she quickly turned to Fallon and kissed him beside the mouth.

"All that hard work and loving care you've put into that horse has paid off, Brett. We owe this to you for believing in Charlie when everyone thought it was impossible."

"He gets all the credit. He's a bloody hell of a horse," he said, beaming down at her. She started to say more, but the Pynchons were coming in to congratulate them.

"Hubert, isn't it exciting!" she said, holding out her hand to the portly, florid-faced gentleman.

"It appears Innismere has found a winning combination in your colt and trainer here, Lily."

"Absolutely! Aren't we lucky," she replied, keeping tabs out of the corner of her eye on Brett and Daphne who were engaged in an animated conversation. She tried to make coherent, appropriate responses to her kindly neighbor's remarks, all the while straining to eavesdrop on the much more fascinating dialogue nearby. Ian joined them and suggested they all go into a pub in Kildare to celebrate. Naturally, he invited the Pynchons along.

In the pub, they crowded into a snug, a glass-walled booth, relic of the days when women weren't allowed into the pub proper. Brett had stayed behind to see that Charlie was cooled down and taken care of as he wished.

"There's nothing like winning," said Daphne, seated next to her.

"Really. One can hardly get enough of it," replied Lily, studying the girl from a closer vantage. She was much improved from her days as a bucktoothed teen, even if she was the sort who never wore a jot of makeup. Her wan appearance might have benefited greatly from some lipstick and a coat of mascara on her pale, blond lashes, Lily thought.

"You may have a chance to get used to winning this season," said Daphne. "He really is quite something."

"You mean Mr. Fallon?" said Lily innocently.

"I was referring to your colt, but that goes for Brett as well. He must be a very good trainer. Local gossip had your Charlie unmanageable."

"Mr. Fallon is very good with horses and women,

wouldn't you agree? His secret is a firm hand and lots of French sweet talk. It works equally well on both."

"He seems very pleasant," said Daphne, smiling nervously.

"Very good looking, too, don't you think? Everywhere we take him, the girls come flocking."

Daphne's smile faded. "I hadn't really thought of Brett as such a ladies' man."

"Consider this a gentle warning from one who was a good friend of your dear mother's. The man is a professional charmer."

"I'm surprised to hear you say that. He almost seems shy, and he's very respectful."

"Surely at your age you aren't taken in by the old 'shy' gambit? I know this is none of my business, but I'd feel so guilty if I didn't warn you, and you were hurt by him."

Daphne shrugged. "I appreciate your concern, Lady D'Arcy, but we've only just met. There's no need to warn me off him. If it should ever get to that point, as you said, at my age, I should be able to handle myself."

A din of congratulations drowned them out as Brett Fallon joined them. He squeezed into the booth beside Daphne, and was stood to a double shot of Black Bush by Ian who was as elated as Lily had ever seen him.

Daphne, not looking in the least apprehensive about her proximity to such a dangerous man, kept up a merry-sounding conversation with Brett while the rest of them rehashed the race stride for stride. After a half hour of watching the two of them with their blond heads together, Lily persuaded Ian to take her home.

"You're very quiet," he commented as they drove back to Innismere.

"A bit of a headache with all the smoke and din in there. It was very exciting though, darling. I'm so glad you were here for a win."

"It was grand—what a horse! I knew he was the first moment I laid eyes on him at de Lazarre's. Brett deserves tremendous credit for bringing him along so brilliantly. Not a single tantrum the entire event. He's worked a bloody miracle with the colt. He's been training him on the uphill gallop so that uphill finish at the Curragh is nothing for Charlie."

"You were right about them both—Charlie and Brett."

He picked her hand up off the seat and kissed it. "You look very beautiful, my dear. A winning horse and the best looking wife in Kildare—I am a damn lucky man."

She patted his hand and tried to smile.

"I think Brett's definitely interested in Daphne. Did you notice how they were getting on? They make a striking couple—the blond outdoorsyness of the both of them," he said.

"I just hope Brett doesn't hurt her."

"Lily, why do you persist in seeing him as a Don Juan?"

"I know for a fact that he can be ruthless with the ladies, Ian. He told me himself that he'd had an affair with his brother's wife that ended very badly. That was the real reason he left Australia."

"He told you that—you of all people? How did the topic ever come up?"

"I, uh, happened to see a picture of her, and he told me about the affair. The night of his birthday party—he was a bit tight. I can't imagine why he did tell me. It's hardly something to brag about. But the point is, don't you think we should warn Hubert? I would hate for this poor, motherless girl to bite off more than she can chew with Brett. Think how responsible we'd feel if it turned out badly."

"Just because he's had one unfortunate affair doesn't mean he's a bounder, Lily. Brett gives every indication of being a very decent person, and it's high time he met a suitable girl. Daphne is perfect. Be good for both of them."

Lily rubbed her forehead, realizing that she really did have a headache.

Unbeknownst to Lily, Ian had invited Daphne Pynchon to tea at Innismere the following afternoon. Lily had to suffer while Brett, again looking natty in good, new clothes, chatted away with Daphne as if they were old friends.

It was a gloriously warm day, and after the tea had been cleared away, Tristan suggested they row out to the island and go for a swim. Of course the young people were all up for it. Lily took Daphne to find her a bathing costume. She selected a severe, black maillot that she knew would be unflattering to Daphne's pale, flat-chested body. She was right.

"I don't know," said the girl, looking at herself skeptically in the glass. "One really needs a super figure to carry off a suit like this."

"You have a perfectly fine figure. It's charming on you, Daphne."

"If you think so," said the girl, sounding unconvinced.

"By the way, I want to apologize to you for running poor Brett down. I do like him, and as Ian says, just because he's had a dubious past, one shouldn't judge him. It was just a mother's concern for you, Daphne. Silly of me to even think you would be seriously interested in a man of. . .well his background."

"Why wouldn't I?" said Daphne fixing her with her round, blue eyes.

"Well, you know. Your father wouldn't possibly welcome him as a serious suitor. As charming as Brett may be, what sort of prospects does he have?"

"He could be one of the top trainers in the country. Daddy is very impressed with him. He isn't a snob, nor am I," she added.

"Very broadminded. I don't suppose your friends are snobs either."

"If they are, they're not my friends, Thank you for the costume, Lady D'Arcy." She put her dress on over the bathing suit and went down to join the others.

Taking the binoculars up to the third floor window facing the lake, Lily watched the four young people row out to the island. Ian had taken her there their first summer, and they'd made love in the folly, a copy of a marble Greek temple to Poseidon—very romantic with the willows trailing in the water.

Brett lifted Daphne from the boat, and they all stripped down to their costumes. His was very brief. Lily held her breath to steady her hands with the glasses. He was splendid! His legs were long with muscular calves, and he had that marvelously fit torso. A shapely curve of behind, too, in his little, black suit Lily noticed. She had to smile when she moved the glasses on to Daphne. The girl looked anemic, anorexic even, in the black maillot. Really awful. How wicked of her to do that to the poor child. Lily laughed aloud.

Unaware that they were being spied on, Tristan carried Bella, bursting out of her suit like a ripe peach, to the end of the little island pier and tossed her in the water. He dove after her. Brett, acting the perfect gentleman, held skeletal Daphne's hand as she waded ever so slowly into the chilly water. The lake was spring fed and never warmed up. Giving up on her, Brett dove under and came up several yards away. With long, graceful strokes, he swam to the middle of the lake and floated on his back spouting water like a whale. Lily wasn't surprised that he was a good swimmer; Brett Fallon was one of those perfect physical specimens who was good at everything.

She lowered her glasses and leaned her forehead against the glass. What was happening to her? Here she was spying, sneaking, lying—all because of her fascination with this man. Tears burned the lids of her eyes. With all her heart, she longed to be one of them—young, perfectly bodied, and free to love this glorious god of a man. "I don't want to be Lily D'Arcy any longer," she cried aloud.

Eros

✿ ✿ ✿

IAN ASKED LILY to accompany him on a week-long trip to Bonn, Munich, and Vienna, but she made excuses. The afternoon following his departure found her pacing her bedroom like a caged lioness. The hideous truth was that she could not tear herself away from Innismere while Brett Fallon might be getting involved with Daphne Pynchon.

"I'm obsessed," she thought in desperation. How had she managed to go from active dislike of the man to the point where she had to see him every day or go mad? It was frightening, losing control over herself like this. Indeed she was as dependent on Brett for her happiness as a junkie was on drugs. She could almost despise him for doing this to her. So enraged was she by her dependence, that she was barely civil to Fallon when she was around him, and unable to think of anything else when she wasn't.

It didn't help that he'd admitted his own attraction to her, that only his past bad experience and respect for Ian kept him out of her bed. It was too frustrating imagining him lying awake nights thinking of her, just as she did longing for him.

"I cannot take this another minute," she said, stubbing out her umpteenth cigarette of the day. She dressed in jeans and went down to the stables to find him. Brett had been busy getting Charlie ready for his debut on Dublin's Phoenix Park course, but he would be finished by this time of the afternoon. Lily found him in the tack room, cleaning a saddle with Paddy and the stableboy. They all stood when she entered.

"Afternoon, Missus," said Brett with that infernally arousing, lazy blue-eyed smile of his.

"I thought you'd be finished by now. You do like to do everything yourself," she said, eyeing the saddle.

"I'm showing them how to do a proper Aussie job of it," he said with a wink at Paddy.

"Go on with ye. Micks were cleanin' tack before the convicts ever got to that rock," retorted the groom.

"Don't forget that a good number of those jailbirds were micks, old man."

Billy laughed. "There'd be Raffertys over there, it's certain." Lily leaned against the door frame, enjoying the male banter.

"Did you want me for somethin', Mrs. D'Arcy?" Brett asked. Why did every word out of his mouth seem to have a double meaning?

"Yes, I do need to speak to you about something." She turned and walked out into the corridor to show it was to be a private conversation.

"Surely, your Ladyship," said Brett, arching a brow for the benefit of the stablehands. He set aside the saddle and followed after her.

Billy Rafferty grinned at Paddy. "Shut yer gob and get on with that bridle, lad," said Paddy, blinking his rheumy eyes.

"So, what is it, Lily?" Brett asked as soon as they were out of earshot.

"Why do you call me 'Mrs. D'Arcy' around them?"

"For appearances. I do the same with Ian. They don't know who I am."

"Of course they do—the Irish grapevine is incredible. I expect everyone in the village knows you're Ian's son by now.

"Look, Brett, I'm going absolutely stir crazy. I wonder if you'd mind taking me out to dinner and a movie tonight?"

"I thought I detected a bit of tension in you lately, Lil."

"Yes. Things have been preying on my mind, and with Tristan and Bella away at the beach for the weekend, this empty house is getting on my nerves. I would truly enjoy going into town for a pub meal and a movie. That 'Crocodile Dundee II' is showing in Naas."

He stroked his chin. "I would really like to, but I've got plans tonight. What about tomorrow?"

"I may be stark raving mad by then. Couldn't you change your plans? It would mean a lot to me."

"You see, I promised I'd take Daphne to a flick, but I'm sure she wouldn't mind if you joined us."

"She'd be horrified."

"Daphne's a good gal. She'd understand your not wanting to be alone here. We were going into Dublin to see some French film she's heard about. Crocodile's a crock. You wouldn't like it, Lil."

"No matter—I'll be fine. I have a book to read," she said, backing away. "You two are having a date, and I would be intruding. Daphne would certainly think so."

"Well, I feel badly now. Come along with us. You could be chaperone." The blue eyes twinkled at her.

"No thank you. Are you seriously interested in Daphne?"

"She's good company. We have fun together."

"Are you sleeping with her?"

"Damn, you always go straight for the jugular, don't you, Lil?"

"I don't see how you could possibly desire her unless you're very hard up. The girl is barely attractive. I can only think you're using her."

He laughed in disbelief. "Jesus, is stepmum giving me a moral lecture now?"

"I don't give a damn about your morals or about stupid Daphne. It's you I care about, and it's driving me crazy!" Lily knew she'd lost control and felt a reckless disregard in doing so.

"I think about you day and night, Brett, and I know you're in the same fix—I can *feel* it! In your touch, in the way you look at me. So just stop pretending you don't!" He was no longer smiling. Lily couldn't read his expression, but she knew she had his full, undivided attention.

"I don't care if it would fuck everything up, I just don't care anymore," she cried.

He held his hands up as if to stop her flood of emotion. "Watch what you say, Lily. I know you'll regret it. I thought we settled this between us."

"I don't care if I regret it—it's better than this living hell of denying my real feelings. I can't hold them inside another minute. I'm doing things that horrify me because of you. I just can't stop wanting you even if you are the last person on earth I should ever want." Tears were coming now.

"Lily," he said gently, putting his hands on her shoulders. "Don't talk like this. Don't let it out in the open, because if there's one thing I cannot do, it's want you. You know that," he pleaded.

"You can't, but you do. At least admit that to me."

"I don't ever let myself think of you in that way, Lily. We've been over this territory before."

"You're a liar and a bloody coward! You want me just

as badly as I want you!" Blindly she turned and ran from him down the stable corridor.

Reaching Charlie's box at the corner, she impulsively opened the door and stepped inside. Wiping away her tears, she faced the big colt who stood at the far end of his large box regarding her with pricked ears, wisps of hay hanging from his mouth. Holding her hand out, she moved cautiously toward him.

"*Beau garçon,*" she crooned, straining to recall any of her high school French. Charlie pawed the straw and made a snuffling noise. "*Vous êtes si beau!*" Every inch of his shining, black body quivered with suspicion.

"*Tu es si magnifique,*" she said, trying the familiar form in a faltering voice. Suddenly the colt bolted around the box, halting between her and the door, blocking her exit. He faced her, ears laid back menacingly. Terrified, Lily backed into the corner by his water bucket.

"What the hell are you doing?" called Brett from the doorway. She was unable to speak.

"Be very still," he said, stepping inside the box and reaching for Charlie's head collar. The horse whirled away from him, and Lily screamed.

"Shut up!" he said. "You're spooking him." Slowly he edged toward the colt.

"*Viens ici. Tout va bien.*" Charlie backed away from him, ears flat against his skull.

"Move along the wall slowly toward the door," he ordered. She took a tentative step, but froze in fear when Charlie wheeled in a tight circle, squealing. Brett reached her, took her arm, and they started for the door. "Damn fool," he muttered.

Suddenly the colt charged. Brett shoved her toward the door, but was caught himself by a flailing front hoof. Lily screamed in horror as the enraged animal trampled him into the straw.

Grabbing a bucket, she hit Charlie on the back, and the horse bolted out the open door of the box. Lily was kneeling beside Brett's crumpled, bleeding body wailing, "What have I done!" when someone pulled her away.

Frank Connors felt for Brett's pulse. "Is he dead?" she pleaded.

"Alive, just unconscious," said Connors. "The head wound isn't as bad as it looks, but his arm's broken." She noticed the unnatural bulge in the center of his forearm. "Medical kit," barked Frank, and someone ran to fetch it.

Brett's eyes fluttered open, and he moaned. "Lie still, lad. You're messed up, but it will all mend," said Frank, sounding calm and in command of the situation. The medical kit arrived, and the trainer searched through the contents.

"I'm so sorry, Brett," said Lily, wringing her hands.

"What the hell happened here?" asked Connors, unraveling a length of gauze.

"Charlie went mad. Brett was trying to save me."

"You mean you went in his box? You knew he was a bloody murderer," the trainer growled.

"He seemed so tame around Brett. I thought he was safe to go near now."

Brett tried to move and cried aloud in pain. "Jesus, how bad am I?" he gasped.

"Simple fracture of the arm, lad. I'll splint that up now so the bone won't come through. Anything else hurt you?"

"Left leg," he groaned. Frank took out a pocket knife and slit Brett's pants leg. The lower limb was swelling and bruised, a curving, hoof-shaped cut on the shin oozing blood.

"You're lucky. It's fractured, but the break could have been much nastier. Lady D'Arcy, would you bring my sta-

tion wagon round. He must be got to hospital at once."
He tossed her the keys. "Lads, I need a board big enough
to carry him on. Rip one off the wall if you have to."

Lily ran to do as she was told. Her fingers were blood-
stained and shook so badly she had trouble getting the
key in the ignition. She backed the long vehicle into the
open door of the stable, let down the seat back, and
opened the rear door so they could load him easily.

When they carried Brett out, his eyes were closed, a
blood-stained bandage around his head. Lily stood by
helplessly as they tried to get him in the station wagon
without hurting him.

"Up front with me, Paddy," said Connors, getting behind the wheel. "Rafferty, in the back to keep him from
sliding about."

"I want to do it," said Lily, scrambling in beside Brett
before anyone could object.

Connors did his best to avoid bumps, but it was not
a smooth ride in the back. Brett groaned with every lurch
and bounce. Lily held his good hand and braced herself
to keep the board he was strapped to from moving.

She wasn't sure if he was really aware of what was happening; she hoped he wasn't. "I'm so very sorry, Brett,"
she whispered in his ear, just in case.

"Should be," he said through gritted teeth. She
sobbed aloud. "Just mucking about with you," he said,
trying to smile.

"I didn't realize he was still so dangerous."

"He didn't know you, and you invaded his territory.
God, I hurt!" His teeth were chattering now, though
they'd covered him with a clean horse blanket. "F-fuckin'
f-freezin'," he stuttered.

"It won't be long," she lied. It was twenty minutes at
least to the nearest hospital.

"Turn up the heat," she yelled. Connors put it on full

blast. She took off her cardigan and spread it over his chest.

"Better?"

"Cozy as hell," he chattered, trying to smile. He licked his lips. "I'd die for a pint about now." A tire hit a pothole, and he cried out.

"Sorry," said Connors. "These bloody roads!"

Brett was shaking violently, tears on his thick, dark-blond lashes. "You were right, Lily. I am a coward," he whispered.

"You're hurting—it's allowed. Squeeze my hand if it helps." He was already gripping it painfully, but she barely noticed the discomfort. A spasm racked him, painfully jarring his injured limbs. She tried to get as close as possible without hurting him, to share her body heat.

"Mmm, you feel good," he murmured. "I'd have a hard-on, if I weren't dying." She laughed. If he could joke, surely he would make it.

She stroked his springy, gold hair. Paddy and Frank were concentrating on the traffic. "I'll never forgive myself for making you hurt like this, but I'll make it up to you, I swear," she whispered.

They rode like that, close together, until Connors pulled the station wagon up in front of the entrance to the casualty department of the hospital in Naas.

"Tell Ian it wasn't Charlie's fault," said Brett before they loaded him onto a stretcher.

While Brett underwent two hours of surgery, Lily tried several times to reach Ian at his Munich hotel. There was no answer in his room. Where was he that late at night—with some German hooker? She almost didn't care, she was so worried about Brett.

At last the surgeon came out of OR and asked if she was the patient's wife. She explained that she was his stepmother. Brett had sustained a concussion, and fractures of the right ulna, in the forearm, and his left tibia, the shinbone which had been repaired with a metal plate. He would need to be in hospital for a week. When she asked if she could see him, the doctor suggested she wait 'til morning to give him a night's recuperation from the operation.

Lily was back at the hospital by 8:30 the next morning, knocking on the door of the private room she'd arranged for Brett to have. She found him dozing, his left leg in a mid-thigh cast, elevated on some pillows, his right arm in plaster as well, an IV drip in his good arm.

He opened his eyes and smiled wanly at her. "Lily, I'd get up, but. . ."

"You look like a war casualty," she said, trying not to sound too shocked by his appearance.

"Feel like one." His voice was weak, eyes sunken.

She touched his good hand, blinking back her tears. "It should have been me!"

"Were you there, Lil?"

"You don't remember?"

"I recall you and me getting into it because I couldn't take you to the flick, but how that ended up with Charlie doing a tapdance on me, I don't know. The doc says it's the blow to my head. How did it happen?"

Lily considered revising the story to show herself in a more favorable light, but decided against telling any more lies. "It was all my fault. I was furious with you, so I went in Charlie's box—don't ask me why, because I don't know. Charlie got between me and the door—acting very aggressively. I was terrified. You saved my life and were hurt yourself. I can't believe I've caused you to be hurt so terribly, Brett!"

"You knew how dangerous he is, Lil. Why?"

"He's like a lamb around you. I thought he was all right

now. I wasn't thinking clearly after the row we'd just had. You don't remember that at all?"

"You asked me to take you to a movie, but I'd already promised Daphne. You got dead angry when I suggested you come with us—then it all goes fuzzy. Did I say something to make you want to do yourself in?"

"No, you were very nice. I was just in this desperate mood. I'm glad actually that you don't remember how silly I acted."

"Next time I'll change my plans, Lil. It seems it doesn't pay to turn you down."

"Are you in dreadful pain?"

"Not too bad. High as a kite, actually. See this little gizmo—I can add more painkiller to the IV just by pushing a button. Clever, eh?"

Lily reached out to touch the purple row of sutures on his forehead. "I thought I'd killed you."

"I told you I had a very hard head, Lil."

She bent down to kiss his temple. "Frank and the others are waiting to see you, Brett. Frank was magnificent—like Field Marshall Montgomery in action."

"Was he? Yeah, he told me he was a medical orderly in the war, met Sir Willy when the bugger was wounded. I'll have to thank him."

She touched his hair, the only part of him still vigorous looking; even his eyes had faded to a washed denim. "I'll leave you now so that you can have fun with the lads. Mary sent you some brown bread and gooseberry jam. She's terribly worried about you; Seamus as well. Oh, I rang Daphne to explain to her why you stood her up."

"Thanks, Lily. Look, don't let them do anything to Charlie—promise me that. It was just an accident. We didn't play by his rules."

"I was wrong, not Charlie." She rested her hand on

his shoulder. "Rest and take care, Brett. We'll treat you like a king when you come home to Innismere."

"Home?"

"Yes, home."

His physician let Brett Fallon leave the hospital after only three days. Lily had had the Mandarin bedroom, the nicest in the house, prepared for him. The invalid was ensconced in an ornately carved, eighteenth-century Chinese bed, and the household fluttered about him, anxious to help in any way.

The first thing he wanted to know about was Charlie. She told him that she'd persuaded Tommy Rafferty to resign at the Curragh, and he would be exercising the colt daily to keep him in condition. They had pulled him from the Phoenix Park race, however. Brett was much relieved.

"I hated to see all the progress he's made go for naught. Frank wasn't keen on keeping him running."

"I overruled him, insisted he get Rafferty to work him for you," said Lily.

"Thanks, Lily. That means a hell of a lot to me." The warmth in his eyes, which were again back to full-force, cobalt wattage, showed how much he meant that statement.

Mary Kelly brought him his first luncheon tray herself, her special barley soup guaranteed to cure any ailment.

"One bowl of this, and I'll be able to dance about the room, eh, Mary?"

"Sure, and it may take a bowl or two," beamed the old cook. Brett seemed to have redeemed himself in her eyes, Lily noted. "You just lie back there and heal yourself, Brett, and I'm going to feed you better than anyone ever has."

"Good on ya, Mary. I'll be a great fat bloke by the time I'm up."

"If I have anything to do with it," said Mrs. Kelly, patting his hand and looking teary-eyed to see him such an invalid.

Lily stopped by his room to check on him the first evening of his return. There was a light under the door, so she knocked. No answer; she peeked inside. Brett appeared to have fallen asleep with the bedside lamp still burning. She tiptoed over to turn it off. There were two pill bottles beside the lamp—one, an antibiotic, and the other labeled "codeine" to be taken every three hours for pain. She'd taken that before, and almost preferred pain to the doped feeling the drug induced.

Before switching off the light, she took one last look at Brett's sleeping face. A wave of guilt washed over her; he looked so hurt and vulnerable. The blond lashes fluttered.

"Lily." He smiled sleepily up at her. "Come to tuck me in?"

She smoothed the covers across his chest and tried to smile. "I was just checking to see if you needed anything before going to bed."

"There is one thing I need badly, but I haven't the strength to do anything about it." His words were slurred—she realized he was half-buzzed from the codeine.

"Are you comfortable?"

"Feel fuckin' fantastic. S'cuse my language. I've tried to clean it up now that I'm in the bosom of the great D'Arcys, but I just can't give up that one word, ya know? *Fuck* says it all, don't you think, Lil?"

"I think you need a night's rest."

"Right. Give me a goodnight kiss, then, like me Mum used to." She kissed him chastely on the brow.

"Mmm. You wear beautiful perfume. I always remember the smell of you, Lil."

She smiled and drew her dressing gown about her. "Goodnight then, Brett. I'm so very sorry."

"He's a dangerous bugger. At least I'm not dead like the Frenchie. He probably would have hurt someone sooner or later, so don't blame yourself."

"After all you've done to gain his trust, it should never have been you that he hurt. I shall always blame myself for going in that box."

"It wasn't a brilliant move, but I don't blame you or Charlie. It was a freak accident. Let's get on with life and forget about assigning blame."

"You're just being nice about it."

"Bugger that. I'm not nice, Lil."

"Bugger that! You can be very nice. If the truth be known, you're probably very tender and poetic at heart, Brett."

"Please, don't make me laugh. It hurts. How the hell do you figure that?"

"From the way you are with Charlie. I just know that you are, even if you try to hide it."

"Are we going to argue over whether I'm nice or not, Lil?"

"Yes." She laughed. "Why do we get into it so?"

"Maybe because we're both alike. Tough on the outside, and hurtin' on the inside." He took her hand and squeezed it. "Forget about the guilt trip over this, eh?"

She nodded. "I'm sorry I woke you. Go on back to sleep now." Reluctantly, she pulled her hand out of his.

"G'night, Lil," he whispered, eyes half-mast. She switched off the lamp.

"Lil?" Her heart skipped a beat. "Would you mind puttin' on the bathroom light? It's an old habit."

Smiling, she went to do as he asked. The mystery of

the midnight light at the stable was solved. Brett Fallon was afraid of the dark.

When Ian arrived from Germany, he had the first ever television at Innismere installed in Brett's room and ordered a half-dozen pima cotton nightshirts for him to wear. He also had his first misgivings about acquiring the French colt. Brett was Charlie's biggest defender.

The routine of the family adapted itself readily to caring for and entertaining the invalid. Every morning, Lily and Evileen gave Brett a sponge bath as he was to remain flat on his back for two weeks. He was right-handed and nicked himself badly with the razor in his left, so they shaved him as well. Lily enjoyed this last as an excuse to admire his face. Brett had very good bone structure: a stronger chin than Ian's, the high D'Arcy cheekbones, as well as their famous aquiline nose. The architecture of a face did more to determine beauty than mere pretty features, she thought. Of course, Brett also had those stunning eyes, a sensual mouth, and good teeth. How had she ever thought him average looking? He'd lost most of his Aussie tan but still had high color and such very nice skin, soft to her touch as she went about caring for him. It seemed to her that he was studying her just as closely as she carefully wielded the razor.

"I feel like an emperor in this bed with you ladies working on me," he said as Evileen sponged him with great concentration. "What is this thing I'm lying on?"

"An opium bed," said Lily, wiping the bits of shaving soap off his chin. "You're supposed to smoke an opium pipe and loll about in it."

"I have my painkillers."

"How many of those do you take a day?"

"I dunno—whenever I need one."

"You should be more careful, seriously. You wouldn't want to develop a dependency on them, Brett."

"This bed is a bad influence on me. Don't be such a spoilsport, Lil." Evileen looked at her quickly, then away. That was the first time he'd called her by the more intimate name in front of anyone else.

The girl was washing his torso now, getting closer to the lower part of his body under the blanket. Brett put his hand over his groin.

"I can do that on my own, thanks."

"They washed you there in hospital, I imagine," said Evileen.

"They were nurses, and I was out of it. I prefer to do it myself, thanks, Evie."

"Well, if you have any difficulty, I'm more than willin'," said the maid with a grin.

"Evileen!" said Lily.

"Pardon, ma'am. He knows I was only havin' him on, right, Brett?"

"Sure you were. Just leave the soap and water, and I'll wash later. In private."

They put a fresh nightshirt on him, and Evileen held a mirror for him to see the results. "Hair's bog dirty," he said, running a hand through it so that it stuck up in tufts.

Evileen giggled. "You look like a Grafton Street punk."

"We'll wash it tomorrow," said Lily. "Evileen, get on about your work now, thank you." She left reluctantly.

Brett sighed heavily. "It's damn humiliating to be a helpless burden to everyone like this."

"We don't mind. I'm sure Evileen would rather wash you than the floors."

"And you, Lily?"

She smiled. "Are you comfortable in this bed, in this room?"

"It's something. What is all this oriental gear about?"

"Different D'Arcys have collected these things through the years. I think it's the handsomest room in the house. The Prince of Wales Edward VII slept in this bed on a trip to Ireland for the races."

"Did he have his wenches with him? Lillie Langtry, wasn't she his mistress?" He grinned at her.

The room did look fitting quarters for a prince. The walls were covered in a twining pattern of vines and birds on a peacock blue silk ground, and a ceremonial kimono embroidered in gold thread hung above the fireplace which was guarded by grimacing carved dogs. Next to the bed, a Chinese Chippendale table held a collection of boxes and fans.

She adjusted his pillows. "I've been having the most incredible dreams in this bed, Lil."

"Sloe-eyed geishas catering to your every whim?"

"Something like that."

She went to the window. "I chose this room for you, because you can see the track. As soon as you feel better, we'll move a chaise over here, and you can watch Charlie work out."

"Great! I appreciate all you've done for me, Lily."

"I only wish I could do more," she said, looking back at him.

Lily and Bella managed to wash Brett's hair the next day. Bella styled it for him with a brush and her blow-dryer. She held up a hand mirror. "There, you look like a film star."

"Not bad, darlin'. Do you give haircuts, too?"

"Sure. I trimmed Tris's hair all the time we were in London, when we didn't have any money."

"You might have been a hairdresser, Bella," said Lily.

"I thought about it for five minutes. It's fun making people look nice, but I think it would get old awfully quick, doing it all day long."

When Bella left to go riding with Tristan, Brett said to Lily, "You look down on Bella, don't you?"

"I'm terribly fond of Bella. Who wouldn't be?"

"You don't think she's good enough for Tris. It's obvious the way you give her the subtle knife."

"Maybe I am a bit resentful of her—can you blame me? Tristan should not be married at his age. It was a heartbreak for Ian and me that he married her instead of going off to Oxford as he should have done. But you're wrong in thinking I look down on her. It's not her fault she's so young and naive."

"Pure is the word. Bella may be the only pure female I've ever run across."

"Pure?" said Lily, who couldn't quite see that adjective applying to her sexy daughter-in-law.

"Yeah. No ulterior motives. Bella's like the sunlight. What you see, is what you get. Nothing false or cloudy in her—no dark corners. Tristan is a very lucky lad."

"I do see what you mean, but sometimes I think he would be better off with a girl who would push him a little, so he won't waste his whole life taking pictures. A bit of deviousness isn't so bad, if it's well-directed."

"You would think that," said Brett dryly.

"Now that you bring up the subject, it also worries me that she has no sense of propriety. She'll bend over and show off her legs up to her neck—unconsciously of course. She has no sense of her effect on men. Like wearing that too little bathing suit to go swimming with you all at the lake. I'm always afraid that some unscrupulous man might take advantage of her innocence."

"Bella acts that way because she hasn't a dirty mind,

isn't wrapped up in herself like most beautiful girls. She's just natural—she does what comes to her, without worrying about what the effect will be." His eyes narrowed. "How did you know what suit she had on? We stripped down to our bathing togs on the island."

"She has only the one that I know of, and there's not enough of it," Lily retorted.

"Looked damn good on her to me. By the way, I got a letter from Daphne. She says she's called several times, and you keep saying I can't have visitors yet."

"You've just got home from the hospital, Brett, after a traumatic accident. I didn't think you were up to seeing anyone outside the family 'til you can at least be fully dressed."

"I'd damn well like to see visitors. Lying here hour after hour, I can use as much distraction as I can get."

"In that case, I'll immediately ring the girl and ask her for tea. Are you happy now?"

"It's just like Bella. You're so damn insecure, you can't bear to have any attractive, younger female about."

Lily went over to the vase of salmon peonies on the table and fussed with the blooms, her mouth a grim line. The fragrance of the flowers was almost suffocating.

"You're a bit of a bastard today, Brett."

"I'm a bastard every day of my life, Lily," he returned.

She turned back to him. "I object to Daphne, because you can't possibly have serious intentions toward the girl, and the Pynchons are our good friends and neighbors. It isn't fair to string her along."

"Who are you, my fuckin' mother?" he shouted.

"Your fuckin' stepmother. I have a right to voice my disapproval."

"The hell you do. What if I don't have 'serious intentions' toward Daphne? Who knows yet? She's of legal age, and it won't ruin her life if we go to bed. Might help the hell out of her, and I know it would me. It's been a long time, and I am not a monk. Anyway, it's a moot point as long as I'm trussed up like this. So, yeah, I would like to see Daphne, but most of all, I'd like you to butt out of my affairs, my sex life in particular!"

Lily did call Daphne that day, and she visited Brett regularly from then on. Lily herself boycotted the sick room, and let Evileen handle his care alone, much to the maid's pleasure.

$$\maltese \ \maltese \ \maltese$$

The third day after their falling out, as Lily was passing by Brett's room, he called out to her through the open door. She went in to see what he wanted.

"When are you going to be over this snit you're in, Lil?"

"I don't know what you're speaking of."

"Over Daphne. You know what the hell I mean."

"Still testy, are we? I don't give a tinker's damn about Daphne. Do whatever you like with her." She turned to leave.

"Wait!"

She felt a second of triumph. "Yes?" Brett raised himself almost to a sitting position, groaned, and fell back. Lily hurried over to him.

"Shit!" he said, looking ashen.

Worried, she asked if he needed a pill. He informed her he'd taken the last of the codeine tablets. Little beads of sweat stood out on his brow. He felt warm to the touch, as if he had a fever. She put the thermometer in his mouth.

"Don't be pissed," he mumbled. "You haven't been near me for days."

"Keep your mouth closed. I've been busy." She took out the thermometer and held it up to the light.

"Daphne's coming over again today. Don't be cross with me because of that, Lil."

"One hundred and three degrees! I'm calling the doctor. . .and Daphne. You are too sick for visitors—really."

"I can do without her. It's you I miss. Life's too dull and pleasant without you." He caught her hand. "I'm not kidding. Don't punish me for Daphne. I've got to find some sort of legal outlet for these feelings of mine, or I'll go mad lying up here day after day, thinking. . .She takes my mind off what it shouldn't be on. Do you understand me?"

"Why do you think I work so hard in my garden everyday? Now lie quietly. I'll get a cool cloth and some aspirin for you, and then I'm going to call the doctor."

He grabbed her wrist. "I had this dream in hospital, Lily. You were lying beside me—I could smell your perfume. I could feel your body against mine. I can't get it out of my mind, it seemed so real."

"It wasn't a dream, Brett. I rode with you to the hospital. It must be coming back to you. I have to call the doctor. Your fever worries me." She smoothed his sweaty hair. "If it's any comfort to you, I punished myself much more than I did you by staying away."

He looked back at her with burning eyes. "Why the hell are we torturing ourselves like this?"

"Because this is the way you wanted it."

Brett's leg had developed a staph infection which had to be cleaned out, requiring a three-day stay in hospital. When he was home again, Lily gave his new prescription for pain pills to Evileen to dole out—he'd taken the others far too frequently.

Lily affected nonchalance about Daphne Pynchon's

continued visits. She tried to limit her own visits, and then only in the company of others.

Brett was soon much improved, and a comfortable chaise was placed by the window looking out over the track so he could watch Charlie through field glasses. He timed the colt and kept a daily record. The jockey and Connors came up to see him often to discuss the training and progress. The Irish Derby, a classic race for three-year-old colts with the richest purse in European racing was in June. Fallon decided against entering Charlie against the best in the world so early in his career. Instead, they would prep him for a less competitive race at the Leopardstown track near Dublin.

On her way out to work in the garden one morning, Lily heard the sound of the gong stationed by Brett's bed to summon help in emergencies. Racing back up the stairs to his room, she burst in, afraid of what might have happened.

"My toes!" he said, looking agitated.

"My God, what's wrong with them?" she gasped. Did he have gangrene from a too-tight plaster?

"They're itching like a bugger, and I can't reach them."

"Lord, I thought you were dying."

"You look damn disappointed I'm not."

"It is a bit of a let down." She scratched his protruding toes.

He closed his eyes. "Ecstasy!" She scratched harder. "I think I'm coming," he said with a beatific smile.

She slapped his cast. "Behave yourself."

"Sorry. Little things get me off these days. Got on your grotty jeans, must be going out for another stimulating day of digging in the dirt."

"Right. Nothing like a good wallow to take the mind off. Can I get you anything else before I go?"

"Yeah. I'd like a six pack of Fosters lager and a nubile lady to warm me cockles."

"My, we are full of it today. I believe you're getting better, Brett."

"I'm getting crazy and damn sick of this crawly wallpaper. There are exactly twenty pheasants, thirty finches, thirty-seven butterflies, and eighteen salamanders in this room, in case you've ever wondered."

"Times must be bad when you're counting the wallpaper. Would you prefer to move to another room? We have several."

"It would get old twenty-four hours a day in any bloody room. At least I can see the track and the garden from this one. Looks very pretty, your garden. Could you help me into the wheelchair, Lil, so I can go over by the window? The walls are closing in today." When he was settled in the chair, she opened the window so he could get the fresh breeze.

He inhaled deeply. "I'm beginning to appreciate what it must be like to be in prison. I haven't been inside this long since I was sick with the measles when I was six."

"It must be awful for you. If they'd only had the sense to put in a lift."

"You never appreciate things 'til they're gone. I've been thinking of my mother lately. I always liked bein' ill as a boy. I'd have her all to myself then. Those were the best times."

"What was she like?"

"She was very beautiful—or she was 'til she got so she didn't care. She was quiet and had a voice like music. Never fought back though, just took what life dealt out to her without complaint—with a smile."

"I've a feeling we're two very different women."

"Yeah, but there's something similar. I can't put my finger on it, but I can see how Ian would love both of you." She touched his shoulder to thank him for that. He put his hand over hers.

"Why don't you come with Evileen anymore, Lil?"

"It's just too damn hard," she said, letting her feelings show more than she intended.

"I know what you mean." He stroked her hand. "I wash and shave myself now, anyway. That girl makes me nervous."

"Still trying to wash where she shouldn't?"

"Mmm. I'm not that desperate. . . yet."

She pulled away from him. "If you don't need any other scratches itched, I'll be getting on to my garden."

"Hand me the glasses, please, before you go."

"They're not using the track now."

"Bird watching—my latest form of excitement."

"Don't get overly excited now." She left him and continued on her way out to the garden.

It was beautiful, she thought as she pulled on her gloves. Bleeding heart, poppies, foxglove, and late tulips were all in bloom. If she only knew how to paint, now would be the morning to capture it. Putting on her straw hat, she went about dead-heading spent blossoms and filling her basket with flowers for the lavish bouquets she liked to keep about the house.

She knew he was watching her. Bird watching—he did have a cute sense of humor. Glancing up at his window, she saw him wave, glasses trained full on her. She felt a little surge of triumph. Before, it had been she possessed to the point of spying; now the tables were turning.

"Why are we torturing each other like this?" he'd said. Let him suffer a bit as she had for months! She'd tried her damnedest to cure herself of this obsession—praying for strength, refusing to let herself think of him sexually any longer. It had worked to a certain extent. All because Brett had said that was the way he wanted it. Now it seemed he was weakening, but she must not. The minute they crossed over that line, her marriage would be doomed. That she knew in her heart. Other women might play and get away with it, but not she. She'd given up much to be Lady D'Arcy and would not forfeit everything for mere sexual gratification. That would be a mistake she would regret the rest of her life.

Lily looked back at the house, but Brett was no longer at the window. She felt a sharp twinge of disappointment.

Finished with her gardening, Lily was seasoning the cut flowers in a deep bucket of water in the scullery, when Evileen came to her with a woebegone face. It seemed she'd sent Brett's codeine tablets through the laundry in her apron pocket, and now he was in pain and had nothing to take for relief. Lily contacted his doctor for a refill and determined to hand them out to the patient herself this time.

✠ ✠ ✠

Tristan came out of the Dublin specialist's office grayfaced. He wouldn't speak to Bella until they were in the car.

"It's me. I knew it couldn't be you," he said, starting the engine.

"Oh, Tris, it's not?. . ."

"Permanent? It looks that way." He drove fast out the Kildare motorway, not volunteering anything else.

"Were you born that way?" Bella asked softly at last.

"No. Give me a few moments, will you. It's not the cheeriest bit of news to find out you're sterile." His jaw clenched tightly, the muscles working.

"I'm so sorry, but you know, it doesn't matter that much, as long as we have each other," said Bella earnestly.

"Doesn't matter? You've talked of nothing for months

but how badly you want a child; how we should have five or six at least, so we'd better get going right away. Don't give me any it doesn't matter shit. It matters more than anything to both of us."

"We can just adopt them."

"Drop the subject, dammit. Nothing you can say will help me now." He turned the radio up loudly, and Bella looked out the side window to hide her misery. No baby. . .ever?

When they got home, Tristan quickly changed into his riding clothes and went out by himself until dark. She was lying on their bed when he returned. His face showed the ride had not raised his spirits. While she fretted over what to do or say to cheer him, he went in the bath and turned on the taps.

He was in the tub staring stony-faced at the ceiling when she came in. "Tris, this hurts me, too, but it's hurting even worse the way you're shutting me out," she said in a trembling voice. He closed his eyes, his lashes wet.

She knelt on the floor beside the bathtub and touched his hair. "I love you, Tristan," she said tearfully. He turned to her, and she embraced him tightly.

"I'm only eighteen—it's not fair!" he gasped.

She kissed him, the sleeves of her dressing gown trailing in the water. "It's hard, but we can take it, Tris. The only thing I couldn't take would be losing you. We love each other. That's what matters!"

The tears ran down his cheeks into the bath. "I can't believe that after almost seven hundred years, I'm the first to come up with blanks. This will destroy Dad."

"At least you're not impotent. Think of it like that."

He gave a painful laugh. "I suppose it could always be worse."

Bella slipped off her robe and stepped in the bath with him. They embraced. "No," he said when she touched him. "I'm feeling impotent as hell right now. That would be all I need."

She caressed his face tenderly. "Do you know what caused it?"

"An infection I had over a year ago before I met you. An 'asymtomatic chlamydial' infection, courtesy of a former girlfriend. There were no symptoms, so I didn't know anything was wrong 'til I woke up one day with my testicles in a vise. A course of medicine cleared it up right away. The doctor says those two weeks it went untreated really fucked up my epididymis, the sperm-storing place in my balls."

"Can't they operate or something?"

"It's not fixable. It was a fluke it ruined both testicles. If one is operating, you can still have children. My usual luck."

"I think it would be wonderful to adopt a baby. Just think of giving some child with nothing all our love and Innismere, too. How wonderful!"

He shook his head. "Don't want to think of that now. You would have made the most incredible mother, Bella."

"I have everything I need to make me happy right here in my arms, Tris. I don't need anything else but you."

Before retiring, Lily stopped by Brett's room. She found him sitting up in the wheelchair, wearing one of Ian's dressing gowns. He thanked her for getting him more pain pills.

"That's absolutely it on refills. You shouldn't need them much longer."

"It's only when I jar my leg, or I can't sleep for the ache in my arm. I hear you're the warden of the pills now?"

"Yes. I'll be more careful than Evileen."

"You don't really trust me, still, do you?" He grinned

up at her like a bad little boy who knows he can charm his way out of trouble.

"You haven't been cautious enough about the codeine, Brett. Those are serious pills, not aspirin."

"Yeah, they make me not give a damn. I like that feeling, Lil."

"You worry me. I shall be a lot harder to get around than Evileen. So, if you don't need anything, I'm going on to bed."

"Mind helping me back in my opium den? I half killed myself earlier in the day doing it." She pushed the chair over to the bed and held up his plastered leg while he stood on his good one, doffed the dressing gown, and transferred himself to the bed.

"It's absurd for you to hurt yourself getting in and out, Brett. Please call for someone. We're all anxious to help you."

"It's too damn embarrassing banging the gong every time I need to go to the toilet."

"Don't be silly." She arranged the covers over him. "There. Sleep tight and don't be shy with the gong."

"Thanks, Mum. I enjoyed watching you in the garden. I'd like to have a snap of you in your straw hat and grotty jeans midst the flowers."

"Poor boy. You really are hard up for entertainment."

"You were very beautiful. Had dirt on your nose—I could see it through the glasses."

She smiled and smoothed the linen sheet over his chest.

"How's about another g'night kiss, Mum?" She bent to kiss him on the brow, but he caught her and kissed her full on the mouth. A very unfilial kiss.

She drew back, flustered. "Ever tell you about my Oedipal feelings, Lil?"

"That is not funny," she protested. He grinned his bad

boy grin up at her, his heavy-lidded eyes studying her in a way that was unmistakable.

"You're right, it isn't funny," he said, catching hold of the sash of her dressing gown and pulling it open. She had on a thin, décolleté, silk gown underneath. He reached up to brush her breast lightly with the back of his hand, his touch going through her nipple like an electric shock.

"No!" She jerked her dressing gown together.

"Why the hell not? It was you who put the idea in my head in the first place, Lily." His eyes shone furiously blue at her.

She stepped back away from the bed. "And it was you who called me a whore for even thinking of such a thing! How dare you make me feel guilty, torture me for months, then change your mind because you're stuck in here and bored to tears!"

Brett threw up his hands. "All right, let's argue about this, too. We are permanently at cross purposes, aren't we? You're the coward now, eh, Lil? Yeah, I remembered what you said before you tried to get me killed."

She was shaking with emotion. "Do you remember what you said? I have tried my best not to think of you sexually, Brett, because you were right. We can't do such a terrible thing to Ian. 'It will fuck everything,' you said, and you were dead right. I was the one in the wrong."

He lay back on the pillows, groaning. "Fuck all! Get the hell out of here and leave me alone, damn you!" Lily ran from the room.

✪ ✪ ✪

Lily stayed away from Brett after that, giving Evileen two pain pills a day for him. By the time of the Leopardstown race, he was feeling strong enough to attend. They carried him down to the car. He was trackside in his wheelchair when Charlie came in second—disappointing, since he'd defeated much tougher competition at the Curragh.

It had been a warm day, and Lily ended up carrying Brett's tweed jacket for him. While hanging the jacket in the cupboard at home, she discovered a bottle of pills in the pocket—the prescription supposedly destroyed in the wash. Four tablets remained.

Ian was laying out clothes for a trip to Paris when she entered his bedroom. "Are you packed, my love?" he asked. She had planned on going with him this time, to get as far away as possible from Brett and temptation.

"Something's come up," she said, holding out the pill bottle.

He examined it. "Brett's pills—so?"

"This is the prescription Evileen said she destroyed in the wash." He looked puzzled.

"Don't you get it? He talked her into lying so he could get another bottle full. Brett's got an obvious problem with them, Ian."

"Couldn't there be another explanation?"

"I know I'm right. Brett's had a very casual attitude about them all along."

"Do you want me to speak to him about them?"

"No, that would embarrass him. You may be his father, but you two don't have a father-son relationship like you and Tristan."

"Do I with Tris either?"

She took the bottle from him. "Let me deal with him. He's used to me nagging. It would save face for him, don't you think?"

Ian shrugged. "I suppose."

"Darling, I really don't think I should leave now with this crisis at hand. Brett's got to be cut off these drugs, and I don't trust anyone else to stand up to him."

"Lily, I was terribly looking forward to your coming with me this time. I've got the suite at the Ritz, and the weather will be fine."

"I know, and I'm disappointed, but family comes first, as you always say."

"I don't see how it could be that serious, Lily. Surely he couldn't become an addict that quickly."

"He's certainly abusing them, Ian. The doctor says he shouldn't be in pain any longer. If I went with you, I should spend the entire trip worrying." Smiling at him, she said, "I'll come next time, I promise."

He kissed her. "I do appreciate the care you've given Brett, Lily. You've a kind heart."

"I feel obligated since the accident was my fault," she said, hiding her shamed face against his chest.

"I was quite looking forward to our third honeymoon in Paris. Will you stay with me tonight then? To give me something to think about for a lonely week?"

"Of course, love." *I doubt that you'll be lonely for long,* she thought to herself.

Ian left the next morning before Lily had awakened. In her bath, she thought about the night before. For the first time in ages, she'd really been satisfied. She'd managed it by thinking of Brett Fallon—his mouth and hands on her body, not Ian's. How much worse could it be to actually commit adultery?

On her way down for breakfast, she met Evileen coming up with Brett's tray. "I'll take that, and I have something very serious to discuss with you later," she told the startled girl.

"Evileen ill?" Brett asked as she entered his room with the tray.

"No, but she may very well be later."

"Cryptic answer from the unfathomable Lady D'Arcy," he sneered, crossing his arms and looking surly.

Lily arranged the lap tray over him on the bed without comment.

"You mean I get to have your company for breakfast? I am honored," he said when she made no move to leave. "Won't you join me for tea? There's a dirty cup over there on the table. You can have the clean one. Does the enigmatic lady take milk and sugar?"

"The lady takes it straight," she snapped.

"I shouldda known that." He handed her the cup. "Thought you and Ian were going to Paris this morning?"

"He went. I decided not to."

"Couldn't bear to leave me, eh?"

"I couldn't bear to leave while you're pulling stunts like this." She took the pill bottle out of her pocket. "Can you explain this, Brett?"

He took it from her. "My dope. Don't tell me you're going to let me have four at once?"

"This is the prescription that allegedly went down the drain in Evileen's apron. It looks in very good condition to me for having been washed and dried."

"Where'd you find it?"

"In your jacket pocket, as you very well know."

"Ah, wondered where I left that. Thanks." He nonchalantly set the bottle on the bedside table.

She grabbed it back. "How could you be so stupid, Brett?"

He bit into a piece of toast. "Care for some brekky, Lil? I've got plenty. Mary's serious about fattening me up."

"Stop it! Are you still in that much pain, or did you just take them for the high?"

"It's obvious that I'm a liar and a junkie," he said, popping a fat strawberry in his mouth.

"You are obviously a fool, and I'm very upset with you."

"You should be. I'll be mainlining heroin any day now, and it's all your fault."

"You said you didn't blame me for Charlie."

Brett lifted the tray of food aside. "Look, I don't like to be yelled at while I'm eating. Gives me indigestion."

"Stop being so damn flip! I want to know how bad a problem you have with these codeine pills?"

"Not too bad a one. If I rob chemist's shops now and then, I should be able to satisfy my craving."

"This is not a joke. I want a straight answer from you, or I shall have to ring the doctor."

Brett lay back on the pillows and regarded her languidly. "I don't have a problem, Lily. You've been watching too much telly and are obsessive on the whole f'n subject."

"Don't try and gloss over this, Brett Fallon. Something is terribly wrong when you concoct an elaborate lie to make sure you have enough drugs. Now, do you still need the codeine for pain?"

"Yes."

She put down her untouched teacup. "I'm calling the doctor then, because something must be wrong. You are no longer supposed to be feeling such discomfort."

"I don't need them for any physical pain. I need them for the pain of existence in this house with a man I admire and like, and with a woman. . .You know what the hell I need them for, Lily." They stared at each other in emotional silence.

"Were you high on them the other night, Brett?"

"Damn right. You made the mistake of walking in on me when I was just at the blissful point of not giving a shit. And there you were, looking so beautiful in your silks and nothing else. I didn't care any more about silly qualms, or that you are, what did you say, 'the last person on earth' I should ever want? I just wanted you, Lil, and I knew that you wanted me."

"Stop it!" she cried, backing away in fear.

"Right. Let's just both keep fucking each other in our minds, Lil. I'll lie here every night going crazy wanting you and feeling you down the hall wanting me. Smelling your perfume under the door. If I weren't so busted up, I'd leave this bloody place and get as far away from you as I could! I should never have come here—should have known it would end up in some twisted friggin' situation again. Shoulda run the second I saw you staring at me through the window. So, do you understand why I need those pills now, Lil? I can't get through the night without them!" He turned his face to the wall, chest heaving.

"I'm sorry, Brett. I never meant. . ."

"I know, all you wanted was a good screw since he couldn't give it to you. I wish to hell I'd obliged you then, instead of being a righteous asshole. It would probably have been over by now between us, and I could get a night's rest."

"Brett, it's not that easy for me making love with him and seeing your face."

"So, we're both up a gum tree, right?"

"I can't sleep with you, Brett, no matter how much I want it, because it would betray my marriage."

"Don't want to get even with him anymore for fooling around, eh?"

"It's past that point now, don't you see? I truly care about you now. It began as lust and frustration and revenge a bit, yes. Now it's more than sex. I would truly be betraying him if I sleep with you now."

Brett began laughing. "Are you saying that you can't make love with me because you love me?"

"Something like that. I'm sorry my love is so amusing."

Brett grabbed the teapot off the tray and hurled it against the wall. The dark liquid ran down the priceless wallpaper in rivulets. "That did it! I'm completely bonkers now. Would you leave me forever the fuck alone, damn you, Lily!"

Lily looked at her clock—2:30 A.M. by the illuminated hands. It was an unusually muggy night for Ireland, and the heat, in addition to her fevered brain, was putting sleep out of the question. The curtains were open, allowing in the moonlight but nary a breath of cool air. She sat up and lit a cigarette. There was no way she was going to get the scene with Brett off her mind. Evileen had gone up to clean the mess and had returned with his uneaten tray of breakfast and the shards of the teapot.

"Sure and he's in an evil mood today," the girl had said. "His hand slipped with the teapot, he says. All the way across the room it slipped. He even cursed me, madam."

"He had good reason to. If you ever pull another stunt like you did with his pain pills, I'll give you notice, Evileen," she'd told her.

Lily puffed nervously at her cigarette. Don't think about it, she admonished herself for the hundredth time that night.

Stubbing out the half-finished fag, she got up and went into Ian's room for a shot of brandy. Maybe that would do the trick. She sloshed some in a glass and took a sip. It burnt like fire down her throat. How did people drink it? Unless they were desperate, as she was.

Ian's room was simple and masculine in its decor. It smelled of him. That was one of the first things about him that had attracted her—his male odor of money and class. She gulped the rest of the brandy.

Brett's words suddenly came to her. "Your perfume

coming under the door," he'd said. He had laughed at her for saying it was impossible now that she really cared about him. Couldn't he understand that? It made perfect sense to her. No longer would it be simply slaking an appetite, like Ian with his whores. Was she in love with Brett Fallon? All she knew was that nothing in her life meant more to her than he did.

Lily wiped her mouth with a trembling hand, then put down the empty glass.

✪ ✪ ✪

A light shone faintly from under his door. She took a deep breath, turned the knob, and entered the room. The bathroom door was ajar, letting a wedge of light into the dark. She couldn't see the bed, but moved silently across the floor in its direction.

"Lily?" She held her hand out blindly, and he took it.

"Am I dreaming?" Brett murmured.

"I'm real," she whispered.

The bed creaked with his weight. "I had this feeling you were coming—I was almost sure of it." She could just make him out now, lying nude on top of the covers in the heat.

She slipped off her gown, letting it fall to the floor in a swish of silk, and stood before him, waiting. He reached out to touch her breast—she inhaled sharply. Slowly he circled her nipple. Her legs trembled.

"Put on the light. I can't see you clearly."

"No," she whispered, putting her hand over his. His callused palm rasped the soft flesh of her breast. He drew her to him, his plastered arm rough on the small of her back, his mouth wet on her belly. She sighed aloud, every molecule in her body alive at this moment. Her hands were in his thick hair and down his back.

She moved beside him on the bed. "I've never wanted anything in my life like I want you, Lily."

"You couldn't possibly want me the way I want you."

"Let's don't argue about it," he said, covering her mouth with an urgent kiss. He grazed her skin roughly with his cast.

"Sorry. Damn, I wish I were whole!"

"I've never met a man more whole than you," she murmured, running her fingers down his muscular thigh, then back up the inside of his leg where he was silky-skinned and warm.

"Look what you do to me, Lil," he said, moving her hand to him. "You've already got me on the brink."

"Don't you dare!"

"Well, we'd best get to it then. How the hell shall we do this?"

Lily pushed him over on his back and threw her leg over him. "This is how we'll do it," she said, smiling down at him.

He closed his eyes and sighed as their bodies joined. "I wasn't the only one ready," he said, stroking her breasts with his good hand.

"I think I've been ready for you all my life, Brett Fallon," she whispered and began to move. He curled up to take her nipple in his mouth. Her nails raked his back. Gripping his shoulders, she rose and fell on him faster and faster.

"God!" he cried out and lay back on the pillows. Bending over him, she sought his mouth, her cries drowning down his throat.

She lay on top of him feeling light, weightless, as his hands skimmed her body with an infinitely sure and gentle touch.

"That was a long time coming," he said. Lily kissed his cheek, his eyelids.

"It was forever coming," she agreed.

"Disappointed?"

She kissed his mouth. "What do you think?"

He grinned and embraced her, his arm cast chafing her skin again. "I think that I'm finally going to be able to sleep."

"*Sleep?*"

"Yeah, sleep. I'm out of sexual shape and an invalid besides. I'm not ready for an insatiable wench like you, Lily."

"You made false promises to me then," she said sliding beside him.

"Hmm, that all-night business coming back to haunt me. Just let me catch a quick nap, Lil, and then I'll really give it to you." Smiling, Lily nestled under his arm and closed her eyes.

When she opened them again, bright sunlight had filled the room. She sat up and gazed in shock at Brett snoring softly beside her. It was 9:00 A.M. by the clock. Evileen was due any moment with his breakfast tray. Lily carefully got out of the bed without disturbing him and threw on her gown. One last look at him lying sweetly asleep on the bed, penis drooping innocently in its nest of dark-gold curls—nothing hidden but the blue of his eyes. She had to give him one last kiss, then hurried out, checking the hallway first. Luckily no one was in sight all the way back to her bedroom on the other end of the second story.

She shut her door and leaned against it, breathing heavily, safe at last. Going to her bath, she sat on the edge of the tub and turned on the taps. Her elation at having seemingly got away with it began to be dampened by pangs of guilt. Had they done a terrible thing? By almost any standard, yes. She pulled her gown off and stepped into the burning water.

"I don't care," she said aloud. "I couldn't bear to never have him—at least once."

That afternoon, Tristan and the stableboy carried Brett down to the car to take him into Naas to the doctor. Lily was very nervous as she got behind the wheel of the Mercedes. She needn't have worried. Brett greeted her with his usual, "G'day," as if nothing had transpired between them in the night. Indeed, listening to the banter between Tristan and Brett as they drove along, she began to wonder if it had all been another of her wild imaginings. Perhaps she'd finally lost her grip and could no longer tell fantasy from reality.

Looking in the rearview mirror, she caught him gazing back at her, the blue eyes crinkled, a little smile playing at the corner of his mouth. His beautiful, hungry mouth. Lily felt the heat rise up from her bosom and returned her gaze to the road just in time to save them from going off in a ditch.

"Mother, want me to drive? One of us banged up is enough," said her son.

"Sorry. Lost my concentration there for a minute." Glancing in the mirror again, she saw that Brett was grinning from ear to ear now. Concentrate on driving! she admonished herself.

Brett was put into a walking cast by the doctor, though he had to use a crutch to help him get about at first. Mary had tea waiting for them when they got back to Innismere.

"It must be a grand feeling to be in action again," said Tristan as they sampled the scones and savories set out in the drawing room.

"Aye, it is. I'm not meant to be a pasha. Fancy my independence too much. I'm damned grateful for your putting up with me the past couple of weeks, though."

"Looked a cushy setup to me, getting all that attention from every female in the house. Rotten way to go about getting it, however," said Tristan.

"Evileen won't know what to do with herself without you to distract her from her regular chores, Brett. But don't overdo it. Don't think you can jump back into your old routine after being flat on your back for two weeks."

"Mother, give a chap a break. Don't nag him like you do me."

"That's all right, Tris. I appreciate her motherly concern for me." His blue eyes were wicked.

"I am his stepmother, so I may legally nag him."

Brett put down his teacup. "I've a favor to ask of you, Tris. Would you give me a lift down to the stable. I need to check on some things."

"You're not going near that animal!" said Lily in alarm.

He stood up clumsily and reached for his crutch. "It's about time we faced up to each other, but I will be careful, I promise."

"He's a big boy, Mum. Besides, Charlie's meek as a mouse when you're not around. Must have heard what a hard time you were giving Brett before, and tried to get even."

"Only he got even with me," said Brett. "I'll tell Charlie that the two of us are mates now." Lily looked down at her cup, hoping no one noticed how pink her cheeks had become.

Ian's phone call came at ten that night. "I'm wasting this suite, this lovely bed without you, Lily," he said.

"I'm sure you won't be lonely for long," she heard herself answer. Instantly she regretted the remark.

"That's a bit below the belt."

"I'm sorry. I wish I were there with you," she said, feeling ashamed of herself.

"Are you suggesting I should go find myself some company, Lily?"

"No. I shouldn't have said that; it was awful."

"I can easily arrange it, you know."

"I'm sure you can. I'm sure you were planning to anyway, Ian," she flared back. There was silence on the line. "Please, let's don't fight long-distance—I hate that," she pleaded.

"You started it, Lily."

"You started it by going to those women in the first place."

"My mistake was in telling you about it. Would you have been happier if I had lied?"

"I would have been happier if you'd never needed anyone but me, as I never did anyone but you. What does it matter now? Do what you have to, Ian."

"I intend to."

"Good. Just be sure to have yourself tested before you come home to my bed!" She hung up on him and sat there, her heart pounding.

She *had* started that. Why? To make it easier to return to Brett's bed?

Lily waited until she heard Tristan and Bella come up to their bedroom, then ran barefoot down the long halls to the Mandarin room. She rapped softly on the door. "Yeah?" came Brett's voice.

She slipped inside, locking the door behind her. He was sitting on the side of the bed in a dressing gown.

"Expecting me, were you, Mr. Fallon?" she said as she walked over to him.

"Actually, I was just about to go off to sleep, hoping to have a repeat of the incredible dream I had last night."

"Odd—I had a lovely dream last night myself," she

said. He grinned up at her like a tomcat, and she bent over to kiss him. He ran his strong hands over her bottom.

"You knew I'd come, just as you weren't surprised last night," she said, combing her hands through his hair. The sutures were gone, leaving a thin, red scar on his brow. He undid her robe and stared at her breasts. She felt a moment's self-consciousness which fled the second he touched her.

"The odds were pretty good since you were pissed at me in the morning, that you'd have changed your mind by evening, Lil." He pushed her breasts together and ran his mouth wetly from nipple to nipple. She shivered and closed her eyes.

He tugged her dressing gown off, then stood up and opened his. "I want to feel you against me, your skin on mine. Feel that, Lil! There's nothing better than that first, full touch."

She pulled his mouth down to hers, and in the passion of the kiss, he lost his balance. They fell back on the bed, laughing. She kissed the sweet little hollow above his collarbone and wriggled her fingers through the blond curls on his chest—so unlike Ian. Don't think of him, she warned herself. Let him have his French whores; she had beautiful Brett.

"Let's not rush it this time," he said. "I apologize for last night. I was out of practice, and you've been driving me crazy for months. I'm usually not that quick on the trigger."

"Did I complain?"

"I think I heard some mention of false promises."

"I don't care, really. I could lie here all night like this and be happy."

"Oh, no! I promised you a good night's fucking, and you're going to get one." He smiled his dangerous, sweet,

Brando smile. Last night had been mysterious and exciting in the half-light, like Eros and Psyche, but she was glad she could see him fully now with the lamp on. She wanted to turn a spotlight on him, examine him in minute detail from perfect head to irresistible toe.

"If you insist, my darling," she said, running her hands down his back, feeling silky skin over hard muscles, to the dip of his waist and over the twin marble hills of his buttocks.

"I damn well do insist," he said, slipping his hand between her legs. She gasped and caught his arm.

"Don't you like that?"

"Yes, but. . ."

"You're used to doing it for yourself? My treat this time." Lily clutched the bedclothes and moaned. "Just let yourself go," he coaxed. "We've no secrets from each other now, you and I." He mouthed her breast and bit down on the nipple, just to the edge of pain.

Lily cried out as her body convulsed with pleasure.

He paused and gripped himself, eyes closed.

"Don't stop!" she cried.

"Just puttin' on the brake a bit." He lay back on the bed, chest heaving, erection waning.

"Damn!" she cried in frustration.

"I'll be back, just give me a minute." Lily ran her hand down his muscular arm and waited.

When he was at full attention again, she moved to straddle him as before, but he stopped her.

"I know you like it on top, but I'm the director this time." He stood beside the bed and maneuvered her to the edge. "This should just work on this bloody great bed, and I can look at you. Yes, it's perfect." He leaned over to kiss her, pinning her arms to the mattress.

"Don't hurt your leg."

"Stop mothering me."

"I want to be your mother, your everything." He kissed and nipped at her skin as they made love, reminding Lily of a stallion she'd once seen mated. It hadn't looked very loving to her, the way the stallion bit the mare's neck; now she was more appreciative. To her intense disappointment, he withdrew and clutched himself again.

"Sorry. Want to make it last," he apologized through gritted teeth.

"Did the Aborigines teach you that little trick?"

"No. An educated lady who liked sex to last more than five minutes. Hang on, I shall return."

Lily stroked the rippling muscles of his abdomen. "Your body is so beautiful, Brett. When I saw you smithing that time, I wanted you so damn badly! And you knew it, didn't you, you cocky thing? I've wanted you from that first moment I saw you on the terrace."

" 'What a sexy bitch,' I thought the time we met. And you lookin' at me like I was something nasty on the carpet.

"Come here, Lil. Let's have another go at what we've both been wantin' for too long now. I think we could just manage the old missionary if I hang my friggin' plaster over the edge of the bed. Yes, that works nicely. Hang on girl, we're goin' all the way this time."

The alarm went off; Lily struggled to silence its insistent clamor.

"Five thirty!" Brett groaned.

She stretched sensuously against him. "Yes, my love. I have to get back to my room before anyone's awake."

He brushed her shoulder with his lips. "That's inhuman. We've had maybe an hour's sleep."

"An hour wasted."

"True. You know what I'd like better than anything, Lil?"

"Please, no! For once, I'm totally sated thanks to me Aussie stud."

"You'll want this, too. A bath! I've not had a proper bath in weeks. Be a good girl and draw me one. That and some whoppin' good tucker, and I will have had every sensual experience I care to in the past six hours."

"You *are* greedy."

"Right." He pressed against her back. "It's either a bath or another drillin' for you, my lady."

She sat up. "I suppose we could both use a bathe. We reek of sex." He whistled as she walked naked to the bathroom.

Lily winced as she sat on the cool enamel to draw the bath. If he was that good a lover as a cripple, it didn't bear thinking about what he'd be like in full form. Brett Fallon was not at all the animal of her fevered imagination. He was gentle and tender, infinitely sensual, and quite obviously practiced. A number of women must have cried when he left Australia.

"Penny for your thoughts," he said from the doorway.

"I was thinking what a wonderful lover you are. I don't believe you've spent all your time with the horses." He limped over, pulled her to her feet, and kissed her.

"Think about me every minute of the day, Lil, because I'll be thinking of you." She embraced him tightly, feeling saddened to be so besotted by him, yet forced to hide it from the world.

"Lil?" he murmured into her hair.

"What, my darling?" she said smiling up at him through misty eyes.

He tenderly touched her face. "This may ruin my romantic image, but damn, I have to use the dunny. Would you mind?" She looked blank. "Need to point Percy. . .Splash me boots. I have to take a piss, my Lady," he explained.

"By all means," she said, stepping away from him and turning her back as he headed for the toilet. Should she leave—what was the etiquette of this situation? In all their years of marriage, Ian had never once mentioned any bodily functions, much less performed one right in front of her.

He peed long and loudly. Lily began laughing. It was like a horse! He finished at last and stumped back over to her. "Sorry, Lil, but this is real life, not a romance novel."

Still laughing, she helped him in the bath without wetting his plastered limbs. "Your turn, now," he said, his leg cast balancing on the edge of the tub. She arranged herself facing him.

"You've a beautiful body, Lil," he said sluicing water over her breasts.

"Oh, please! After two children, nothing's as it was," she protested. "I wish I'd known you when I did have one."

"You're beautiful now. This is a real woman's body, not a girl's. I'd rather know you now."

She ran the soap over his broad shoulders and chest. "Now, this is what I call beautiful," she said. He leaned back and let her wash him.

"This is great. Couldn't stand not really gettin' clean with those friggin' sponge baths."

"Evileen will be delighted to give you a proper bath everyday," she teased.

"You're the only one lays hands on me, Lil. Only you." She had to kiss him.

"Daphne better not try."

"Forgot all about her."

"Good. Tell her to get lost. You no longer need her," she said, rinsing the soap off him.

"Why don't I need her? You have him."

"That's totally different!" she exclaimed. He pulled her closer and lathered her breasts. Tucking her legs around him, she said, "Promise me you won't sleep with her, Brett."

"I won't—if you don't with him. Look, let's just enjoy the moment, Lil. It's going to be a difficult road ahead for us."

"I wish he'd stay in Paris!"

He kissed her. "Put him out of your mind. You belong to me now." He rinsed her carefully.

"Now for the best part. On your knees." Gently he soaped between her legs.

She held his face to her breasts. "I love you, Brett." Noting his frown, she added, "I know you can't say that to me, and it doesn't matter—I still love you."

"Look, do me a favor. Don't love me, okay?"

"I have to. I can't separate it—it's not just sex for me."

"It will be easier if we just keep it fucking, Lil." She shook her head in disagreement. He put a soapy hand around her throat.

"I can't love you, Lily. The minute it gets to that, I'm gone. Understand? This has got no future to it. Neither of us wants to hurt him."

"I've made up my mind I won't feel guilty about Ian. He uses whores when he's away."

His brows furrowed. "You're not using me to get even, are you? I promise you'll be very sorry if you are."

"No! Maybe I was a bit at first, but not now. You know better than that."

"I don't know. You're a hard one to figure. Just don't ever try it." His fingers tightened slightly on her neck.

"Did she do that to you, that Josie?"

"That's ancient history—private history. I don't want to know what goes on between you and Ian, and don't ask me about her."

"I thought we were to have no secrets?"

"As concerns each other, our bodies, but that's all. The less I know about you two, the less I'll go mad thinking of you sleeping with him. Let's just keep it sex, pure and simple, between us. We have great sex, and that's enough. As hot as it is, it should burn out fast, and maybe we'll just get away without hurting anyone."

Lily rinsed herself and got out of the bath. Wrapping a towel about her torso, she left him. She was tying her dressing gown when he limped out of the bathroom.

"I know that sounds hard, Lil, but it will be better in the long run."

"The voice of experience speaks."

"Yeah. My stepbrother tried to kill himself when he found out about Josie and me. It's going against all reason getting involved with you in the first place. I don't want another great drama on my conscience."

"If those are the rules, we'll play it like that then. I shall try to think of you as my gigolo and hope it only lasts a week or two." Holding her head high, she left him.

Brett did not join the family for lunch, so Lily, who managed a long afternoon nap, didn't see him again until dinner. Over the leg of lamb, Tristan announced that Brett would be going out with Bella and him to celebrate his new mobility.

"Are you sure you're ready for that?" Lily asked him.

"I'm not ready to go ravin', but I'm up to liftin' a few pints with my good hand, yes. Unless you insist I stay home."

"I would never presume to tell you what to do, Brett. If you feel up to it, then by all means go."

"Right. I will then," he said, leaning back in his chair and regarding her with a defiant air.

"Where are you going?" she asked Tristan.

"Thought we'd do some pub crawling in the city. The Brazen Head, Mulligan's, Nesbitt's, whatever. You're welcome to come along, Mum, a great pub mavin such as yourself."

"No, thank you. You young people run along and have fun. I'll dig in with a good read."

"Just as well. Tonight, we're going to find a sexy girl for Brett, and I'm sure you wouldn't approve."

"I'm a bit out of commission for wooing the ladies," said Brett.

"Nonsense. Your prick's not in a sling, is it? Sorry, Mother. The plaster's a great gimmick for seducing the ladies, Brett, as if you needed any help with that."

The night passed slowly for Lily after they left. Ian, obviously still angry with her, didn't call. Stifling an unworthy impulse to go through Brett's things again, she undressed for bed. She had just fallen asleep, when she was awakened by the sound of voices arguing in the hall. Slipping on her dressing gown, she went to investigate and found a very wobbly-legged Tristan, blood down the front of his shirt, being supported by Bella and Brett.

"He was looking at her arse. Had a perfect right to toss my drink at him," Tristan grumbled. He looked up and saw his mother's anxious face.

"Mum, top o' the evenin', or is it bottom o' the mornin'? Don't look so worried. Ran into a bit of trouble at the Bad Ass, but nothing we couldn't handle, eh, bro?"

"How could you let him get in this condition?" she asked of Brett.

"Give him a bloody break, Mum. He's not my keeper. If I want to be an ass, I will, and no one can stop me." Bella looked beside herself with worry; Brett, bemused and apologetic.

"Get him on to bed," said Lily shaking her head. The two of them helped Tristan off to his bedroom.

When Brett limped back down the hall, Lily was waiting for him. "What got into Tristan? No one is more peaceable than he normally."

"About ten pints of Guinness got into him," said Brett. "I tried to get him to ease up, but he was determined. Don't be too hard on the lad, Lily. He's just blowing off steam. Even a saint has to do that now and again."

"He didn't break his nose, I hope?"

"Just bloodied it. The lad held his own rather well. I was impressed."

"Fighting is infantile! Surely you didn't join in, in your condition?"

He held up his unplastered hand—which sported grazed knuckles. "Couldn't leave a mate to go it alone, could I? I agree, fighting is stupid, but there are times it's impossible to avoid. Women never understand that."

"Did this start over Bella?"

"Don't blame her. It's not her fault that every man who looks at her wants to bed her."

"Including you?"

Brett held up his hands in surrender. "I'm going to bed. Had enough donnybrooks for one night." He limped down the hall. She called out to him. He paused. She motioned for him to return, but he stood there stubbornly.

"Do you want me to beg you?" she asked. Slowly he made his way back to her.

"I really am tired, Lil. Didn't have a chance to catch a nap." She pulled him in her bedroom, then locked the door.

"It doesn't matter. As long as you're with me," she whispered. She took his bruised hand and kissed it. He put his arms around her.

"Sorry about Tris. He was determined to get pissed. I swear I tried to stop him."

"I don't blame you," she said.

✪ ✪ ✪

Lily studied him from her vantage point, lying with her head on his chest. There was something about the squared off point of Brett Fallon's chin that said, "I will get the job done." There really wasn't any angle from which he wasn't miraculous. The blue vein in the hollow of his throat and the mole on his jaw were ravishing. Brett had several moles on his face and body—accent points to emphasize the fineness of his skin, and the muscles and bone beneath. He was, in one word, perfection.

Lily twined a golden chest curl about her finger, and longing to hear his voice, asked, "Are you asleep?"

"Only resting—saving my strength," he murmured, the corners of his mouth turning up slightly.

"Good boy," she purred, running a nail down his biceps. Why was she such a fool for muscles—it was very shallow of her. His hand played in her hair.

"Are you happy, Brett? Right this minute?"

"I feel very peaceful."

"But, happy?"

He propped his head up on his arm and looked down at her. "I suppose so. When I'm with you, Lil, I'm as happy as I ever am." It wasn't the ecstatic answer she wanted, but she knew it was the truth. She slid up and kissed his mouth.

"How 'bout you, Lil?"

"There can't be a happier, more satisfied woman on the planet than me," she answered without even having to consider it.

"That makes me very happy, then," he said, brushing her cheek with the back of his hand.

"I feel I was never truly alive 'til now, Brett. My whole

life has changed. Everything feels. . .enhanced, clearer, more intense!"

"Come on now, don't talk like a romantic fool."

"It's true. I was just sleepwalking through my life until you," she said, tracing a finger down that line on his cheek that deepened so attractively when he smiled.

"Let's don't get. . ."

"Sloppy? Gooey? Sorry, but it's the way I feel. Of course it has nothing to do with that nasty *L* word; it's only because I've been properly fucked at long last."

He checked his watch. "I'd better clear outta here. It's getting late."

"No!" She clung to him. "Tristan will have a terrible hangover, poor child, and it's Sunday so the servants are off. Stay with me just a bit longer. I like this part almost better than the sex. I feel so close to you now, Brett. Like there's nothing we couldn't say to each other."

"It is nice. Is this what it's like to be married?"

"Sometimes, when things are good. Do you think you'll ever marry, Brett?"

"No," he said flatly.

"Have you ever even considered it?"

"Never. I fancy my freedom. I've yet to meet the woman I could face every morning across the breakfast table for the rest of my life. I'd have to be damned sure I'd never want another more than her, because I'm one for fidelity, believe it or not."

"Your elusiveness is part of your attractiveness," Lily mused.

They were startled by a knock on the door to the adjoining bedroom. "Lily, are you up?" called Ian's voice.

"Oh, my God!" she whispered, climbing over Brett and scrambling for her dressing gown. She threw him his clothes and gestured toward the bathroom door.

"Just a minute, darling," she called in a shaking voice.

As soon as Brett had disappeared into the bathroom, she let her husband in.

"You're home early," she said breathlessly, her heart doing double time.

"Yes, the picture I was interested in looked like a possible forgery. I was afraid to chance it. Why was the door locked?"

"I was alone last night. It makes me feel more secure to lock the bedroom doors. Silly, I suppose."

"Brett wasn't here?"

"He's in a walking cast now, and Tristan and Bella took him out last night to celebrate his new freedom."

"I see. You were sleeping very late."

"Yes. Had an awful bout of insomnia night before last. Think I caught up on my sleep last night." Ian walked toward the bed, and she thought she'd faint from nerves. Surely he could tell what had been going on there minutes before. The bedclothes looked as if World War II had been fought on them.

Ian turned to face her, his face anxious. "Lily, I want you to know that I did not have a woman in Paris. That's not a thing I've done as frequently as you seem to think. I see how much the idea of that disturbs you, so I make a promise to you that I shan't do it again." He looked at her for response.

She had only been half listening, her eyes fixed in horror on the toe of Brett's shoe peeking out from under the lace dust ruffle of her bed.

"Lily?"

She crossed to her husband and stood between him and the incriminating shoe. "You're so right—it does bother me terribly, Ian."

"They never meant anything to me at all. I only resorted to such alliances out of loneliness for you, Lily." His dark eyes were pleading and soft.

She stepped back, shoving the shoe out of sight with her foot as she did so.

"Can you forgive me my weakness? Will you be able to trust me again, Lily?"

She took his hands. "Of course I can." He leaned down to kiss her, but she turned her head. "Sorry, darling. I need to bathe and wash my teeth."

He smiled. "As soon as you've freshened up, I have a 'forgive me' present for you."

"You give me too many things. You spoil me, Ian."

"I want to spoil you. How many men have a beautiful, faithful, forgiving wife? When you're ready, I'll be waiting." He smiled seductively at her and returned to his bedroom.

Lily sank down on the bed and felt she would be sick. How horrible! She fished Brett's shoe out from under the bed and hurried to her bathroom. Apparently, he had made his escape through Damien's room. She hoped he had not overheard Ian's pathetic apology.

✚ ✚ ✚

Tristan had a secret ambition that summer. Bella was in on it, and in fact, it was her idea for him to have an exhibition of his best photographs. He already had a large number of excellent color photos of Bella, the countryside, and race scenes. All he needed now were some good black and white studies. To this end, he prowled the city, camera in hand, with Bella as his assistant. Dublin was a very picturesque city, the streets filled with great Irish faces, from the genteel denizens of fashionable areas, to the often more intriguing characters north of the Liffey.

One of Tristan's favorite hunting grounds was the area between St. Patrick's Cathedral and the river known as The Liberties. This was a warren of Dickensian bleak tenements that dated from the eighteenth century when a doubling of the population and high land rents had sent droves of poor people into the city looking for work and creating some of the worst slums in Europe. As many as fifteen would live in one small room with no plumbing; waste was thrown out the window. The ordure in the courts behind sometimes reached up as high as the first floor windows. It was a witticism of the period that the beggars of London gave their cast-off clothes to their Dublin counterparts. Typhoid wiped out thousands of people living in conditions not fit for animals.

The Liberties made a sharp contrast to the nearby exclusive squares of St. Stephen's Green and Merrion. Here, elegant Georgian townhouses trimmed with cast-iron lacework sported brightly painted front doors with leaded glass fanlights above.

Tris and Bella found the children playing on the narrow, cobbled streets of the slum areas seemed just as happy as those in finer neighborhoods and particularly amenable to having their pictures taken. The Catholic city was full of winsome young, some sweet and shy, others cheeky or abusive. Tristan would give them a few coins for ice cream—"no posing, please."

Bella never forgot the little girl holding out a cigar box on the O'Connell Street Bridge. She was a beautiful, blond child, despite the ratty hair, torn clothes, and snotty nose. After Tris had photographed her, Bella talked with the child and couldn't resist taking a tissue to her nose. She slipped off her watch and put it in her box along with the few coins the child had collected. "That's for you and no one else," she told her. The girl darted off to show the prize to an older boy begging down the bridge. The boy, whose pants were held up with twine, jabbered with the girl in some foreign-sounding language.

Tristan explained that the two were probably tinker

children talking Shelta, their own language based on Gaelic. The gypsy-like tinkers, or Travelers as they call themselves, were not proper Romany Gypsies, but descendants of Irish peasants set adrift by Cromwell and the Famine.

"Why did you give her your watch, Bella?"

"She's never had anything good."

"I adore you for it, but they'll sell it for a few pounds," he said, putting his arm about her.

"I don't care, I wanted her to have it. She's so sweet. It's not right for her to have to live like that."

"They choose to live that way, my love. Who knows, perhaps it's better to be free to go where you want, than to be slave to some stupid job and your possessions."

They finally got into trouble on a foray into a tough neighborhood off O'Connell Street. Tris was photographing a gang of teens lounging outside a pub, when one of the boys accosted them.

"Hey, you with the camera, what the hell would you be doin'?" a stocky, black-haired boy yelled.

"Only taking a few shots of the pub," said Tristan pleasantly.

The youth sauntered over, cigarette dangling from mouth. "You had yer friggin' camera pointed at us. We're not bloody chimps in the Phoenix Park Zoo, man."

"I'm a professional photographer taking shots for a Guinness ad campaign," replied Tris calmly. Bella slipped her hand in his.

"An advert, eh? You make the big money on that sort of thing. You should be after payin' us for our part, right?" He had a narrow, mean face, his front tooth missing.

"Give me your name and address, and I'll see that the company compensates you if they use the shot."

The boy laughed and flicked his cigarette into the gutter. "I'd be a fuckin' eejit to believe that one, mate. You pay up now on the front."

"I don't have any money on me," said Tristan, squaring his shoulders.

"No money—shit! A posh lookin' gent like you? I believe you've strayed on the wrong side of town with your fine lookin' lady there. Ain't you the brave one!" he sneered, looking Bella up and down. He called back to his friends leaning against the wall and smirking appreciatively. "Didn't know the Grafton Street swells were movin' in on our territory, did you lads? Another balless wonder from Ballsbridge!" This witty remark was greeted with a chorus of encouragement from his gang.

"I don't want any trouble," said Tristan, taking Bella's arm and heading down the street.

"Wait, boyo, I'm not through with you," yelled the punk, following behind them. He grabbed the strap of Tris's camera and swung him around.

"Don't run away from me when I'm talking to you, yer poufter!" They struggled over the camera, and it smashed against a lamppost.

"Damn you!" said Tristan, plowing his fist into the bully's stomach. "Run!" he gasped, dragging Bella along with him.

They rounded a corner, the gang of toughs on their heels, and ran straight into an officer of the Garda.

"What's going on, then?" the Garda barked.

"Nothing, sir," panted Tristan, smiling back at the red-faced boy and his friends.

"Go on, get outta here, ya holligans!" the officer yelled, shaking his fist at them. The boys slunk back round the corner.

"I'd advise you not to stray off O'Connell, lad, unless you know what you're about. You're likely to get in a brouhaha in some of these neighborhoods."

"Absolutely, sir," said Tristan.

"Did they smash your camera, then, son?"

"No sir. Just a stupid accident." The Garda insisted on escorting them back to the main thoroughfare.

"Is anything wrong with Tris and Bella?" Ian asked after he'd been home a few days. "He seems very subdued, has hardly spoken a word to me since I've been back. Doesn't he seem off to you, Lily?"

"I hadn't really noticed." she replied. She'd not been thinking about her son or anything else but Brett, and what they would do with Ian home, she realized guiltily.

"I don't think it's my imagination. Talk to him, Lily, and find out if they've had a spat or something."

"Darling, I'm always interfering in his life. Why don't you talk to him? It would be good for both of you."

"I will then. Brett out with Daphne again?"

"I've no idea. I wish you'd stop promoting that."

"The boy deserves to get out and enjoy himself after all he's been through. I told Hubert the truth about Brett by the way. I wanted him to know he's not merely a horse trainer."

"Lord, Ian! Do you want such a private, family thing to get about? Now the entire county will know. They'll be gossiping about the D'Arcys again."

"Let them; I told you I was going to acknowledge Brett. Back to Daphne—I don't understand your continued objection to the girl."

"I just don't fancy being responsible for her broken heart."

"I'll take the blame. Who knows? It might just as easily end up with wedding bells, and then we'd feel marvelous about playing Cupid. At the very least, Brett should be able to get rid of some of the frustrations he must have, since he does not strike me as a celibate.

"Speaking of which, there's time before tea. Care to come up to my room and see my etchings, little girl?" He leaned over her chair to kiss her, sliding his hand down into her blouse.

"Ian, someone might walk in on us!" she protested.

"All the more reason to adjourn to the privacy of the bedroom. Come on, where's my wild girl of last night?"

"You're a maniac about sex since you came back from Paris, Ian."

He kissed her ear. "It's you, my darling. Suddenly it seems you're just blooming. I don't think I've ever found you more desirable than you are just now."

"All right! Let's go up before we get caught by Kelly and give him a heart attack." Actually she was feeling rather aroused herself, she realized, as she followed him upstairs.

Later, lying in his arms, Lily marveled guiltily at her ability to go from one man's bed to another. What sort of slut was she becoming? If she were so in love with Brett Fallon, it followed that Ian's touch would leave her cold; she'd found the contrary to be true. One lust seemed to feed the other. "Just call yourself lucky," said a voice in her ear. This way, she didn't have to fake it.

"I love you, Lily," Ian murmured. She patted his thigh. "You haven't told me you love me in a while," he added plaintively.

"I thought you knew I did by now." She turned to him. "I do love you, Ian. You must always know that."

He held her tightly to him. "I need to hear you say that as often as possible."

Her heart went out to this man she'd spent her life with. It was true, she did love him and desire him. Lily tried her best to shut out the insidiously traitorous thought of Brett.

Due to her total obsession with Brett Fallon to the exclusion of all else, Lily had also neglected her garden. On a warm summer day, a week after Ian's return, she dressed in a cotton skirt and sleeveless blouse, donned her straw hat, and set about clearing the flower beds of uninvited guests.

A shadow fell over her shoulder. "What the hell is going on, Lily? I'm beginning to think last week was a fever dream." There was a definite edge of emotion to his voice. She bit back a smile. He did care, after all.

She continued cultivating about the phlox. "What do you expect me to do now that he's home?"

"Give me a word, a sign—something!"

"I don't like sneaking behind his back. It makes me feel funny."

"So, we totally ignore each other 'til he goes off again. Is that the program?"

"I'm not an accomplished adultress, Brett. You probably know more about the logistics of this."

"Lily, this stinks! I don't fancy bein' in this limbo. One moment you tell me I've made you come alive for the first time, then the next I'm part of the woodwork."

"Please, Brett, don't get so excited. They can see us talking from the house." Taking her basket of refuse, she led him to the lower part of the garden where a compost pile was kept behind a Victorian gingerbread dovecote.

She tossed the weeds on the pile. "Did you have a lovely time with Daphne yesterday?"

"Yeah, I did. Aren't I entitled since you have a lovely time with him?"

"I realize I can't stop you from going out with her, but promise me you won't sleep with Daphne, Brett."

He laughed. "That takes cheek! He's given it to you every night—or is he still not interested?"

"We weren't going to discuss him, remember?"

"Yeah, well I'm lyin' in my bed every night, feelin' he's screwin' you, and it's makin' me crazy."

She felt a little tug of triumph. "Do you see how I'd feel if you slept with Daphne? My husband has his rights, but please don't start anything with her. I couldn't bear it."

"If I can't have you, Lil, old Daph's looking better by the minute."

"That's blackmail! Ian will be going to London in a few days. Can't you wait, for God's sake?"

"No, I can't. Waiting's not my style, anymore than it's yours." He caught her about the waist and kissed her roughly.

"Promise me about Daphne."

"I don't even want the girl. It's you who's got me coming and going and laying awake nights, Lil."

"Good. You deserve to suffer like I have." She kissed him and stroked his face. "Just be patient. It's only a matter of four days, and we can be together."

"Bugger patience! You've put me in this state of rut I'm in, damn you. I'm not waitin' any four friggin' days!" Taking her arm, he pulled her over to the dovecote. "Take off your panties," he said as he undid his belt.

"Brett—we can't possibly!"

He unzipped his jeans. "The gardener's out front mowing the grass, and no one comes back here but you. Come on—off!" He lifted her skirt and tugged impatiently at her underpants.

Trembling, she obeyed him. Brett pressed her against the wall of the dovecote and ran his hand between her legs. "Wet as a river, you nasty girl," he laughed. "You like the edge as well as I do, don't you?" He lifted her blouse and groped her breasts, tugging them out of her brassiere. She sighed and slid her leg up his thigh, bracing her back against the wall. He kissed her and thrust wildly between her legs. Her nails dug into his shoulders. The lewdness, the risk, the sheer exciting awfulness of what they were doing swept over her in a flashfire of passion.

"Fuck me! Fuck me, Brett!" she cried in his ear. He threw his head back and groaned. They almost lost their balance.

Brett sighed and kissed her face softly. "Wait, my arse!"

She brushed her lips across his cheek, her body still throbbing with the pleasure they'd just shared. At that moment, she didn't care if Ian himself had walked up on them. "It's so good with you."

He held her face in his hand. "Yeah, it's good. Don't go forgettin' that and treatin' me like the woodwork, Lil—if you want any more of that." He kissed her again, then pulled away and began tucking himself back in his pants.

Lily straightened her clothes and picked her panties up off the ground.

"I feel much better. How 'bout you, Lil?" he asked with a grin.

"I feel like a cheap hooker," she said, sobering now that the passion was spent.

"Never cheap, Lil," he said, limping off, whistling cheerfully.

She rescued her hat from the compost where he'd tossed it. *I am a whore,* she thought.

✚ ✚ ✚

Ian pulled up his gelding in the center of the green sward stretching for over a mile to the house. With its frame of great trees in full summer leaf, this view of Innismere was one of his favorites. Tristan posted up beside him on his gray hunter, Maeve and Fionn loping at his heels.

"Now, there's a photo for you, Tris."

"It's beautiful, almost too perfect," he said. "Nature's unplanned artistry is more to my liking, Dad."

"Well, I like this. There's nothing I would add or subtract from this picture."

Ian studied his son's handsome, young face. How best to approach this delicate subject? The boy looked at him as if he knew what was coming. Might as well just do it. "I realize you've been going through a period of rejection of your heritage, son. I had my rebellious years as well."

"With Brett's mother?"

"Later on. There was a time when I thought I wanted to be rid of all the D'Arcy responsibility, to just be a musician. Screw the title, the house, and all the other baggage. My father was not the sort of man with whom I felt comfortable broaching such doubts, so I more or less went through my crisis on my own. And I came to the conclusion that this was my true lot in life. Preserving this estate for you and your children. You'll come round, too, son. I know you love Innismere every bit as much as I ever have. Now that you're married, you'll begin to really appreciate what this means. With all the impermanence about today, it's incredible to think that generations of D'Arcys have lived in that house—have trod this very ground. God willing, generations to come will do the same. It rather puts one in tune with the flow of history, the rhythm of life to think of that. It puts one's little daily worries in perspective." Tristan looked glum at this prospect.

"You'll understand more what I'm talking about when your first child comes. Though of course, there's no rush, as young as you are."

"Bella and I are rather thinking of not having children, Dad, the world going to hell in a handbasket as it is. If the bomb doesn't get them, the depletion of the ozone will."

"Don't be foolish. People have feared the end of the world since Biblical times for various reasons, yet we go on. Producing the next generation is the whole point, Tris. I don't consider anything else I've done to equal the importance of my children."

"That's a bleak philosophy. The object of being born is to breed more people? Surely there's more to it than that, or what's the point of going through all the torture?"

"The point is to do as good a job with your children as you're capable. I think your mother and I have done admirably by you and Violet." Fionn sighted a hare and sped off after it, Maeve limping arthritically behind.

"By the way, son, is everything all right between you and Bella?"

"Of course. Why do you ask?"

"Your mother and I have noticed you don't seem your usual self of late, and . . ."

"Ah, I see. You've brought me out here to see if I'm having marital problems? I wondered about the sudden surge of fatherly interest."

Ian frowned. "There's nothing on earth I'm more interested in than you, Tristan. If there's been a lack of communication between us, it's because of that—well, terrible memory we share. I've been reluctant to force myself on you because you seemed to want it that way. But surely you must know how much I care about your welfare."

"Yes, I know you do, Dad. I'm sorry. I'd no call to say that."

"It pains me a great deal that we're not as close as we were, Tris. That Tony stands between us and may always do so."

"Please, Dad, I don't ever want to speak of that!" said Tristan, looking away.

"I know you don't, neither do I, but it's not going to go away. It happened, and I have to go the rest of my life knowing there's nothing I can ever do to erase that ugly image from your mind. That all the pain you've been through the past year, are still going through, was inflicted by me on the person I most wanted to protect from hurt."

"I can't talk about it, Dad. Just know that I don't hold it against you. I don't understand it, but you're my father and I love you."

"You're very generous, son," said Ian. "I'd give years off my life to take that moment back." He cleared his throat. "I've been so worried that I caused you irreparable harm, but I think you'll soon get your life on a forward track again.

"Do you remember my bringing you out here on the front of my saddle when you were three, son?"

"I have a vague recollection of it. I think I remember the saddle hurting my bottom."

"I told you then, 'This is all yours, as far as the eye can see. Make sure your son has the same vista.' I doubt you recall that. My father did the same to me." Tristan closed his eyes.

"Son, you have a lovely wife and a marvelous future ahead of you if you'll but reach out for it. As for the future of this planet, I expect the D'Arcys will be around for another century or two to enjoy it. You young people always carry optimism and pessimism to the extreme. I've not a doubt that one day, you'll rid your son out here and give him the same speech."

Tristan stared off at the mountains, his face unreadable.

"And please, if you have any problems, no matter what they are, bring them to me. I will do anything within my power to help you."

"Sure, Dad. Wave your magic wand and fix it all up for me, please."

"I will if I can, son."

"Thanks, but you can't help me, Dad," he said, giving him his heartbreakingly beautiful smile.

"There's always a way out, Tris, no matter what the problem."

Fionn came galloping back and flopped down at their feet, panting and slavering, his long, pink tongue lolling out of his mouth. Another victory for the hares. His mother came slowly running on three legs in the distance.

Tristan gathered up the reins and urged the gray forward, signaling a finish to their talk. "It's getting late. Bella will be missing me, Dad."

Ian thought his heart would burst with love and concern as he watched his son canter away from him towards Innismere.

✠ ✠ ✠

Kelly brought the mail to Lily on a silver tray. "The morning's correspondence, my Lady," he said with a stiff little bow.

"Thank you, Seamus," she said loudly. He had his hairpiece on crooked, and it was difficult to look at him with a straight face. She took the mail and he shuffled off.

Swiftly she sorted it into piles. An aerogram envelope with small, cramped writing caught her eye. Addressed to Brett, it had first gone to a Wexford address. The return address was Sydney, and the sender, J. Fallon. Josie—Brett's former lover. Lily's pulse quickened. She'd give anything to know the contents. Could one really steam a letter open? No, she had vowed never to lower herself to such depths again. She put the letter on the bottom of the pile and flipped through the rest of the mail, filing it to be paid or answered. Back to the Josie letter. She slipped it in her pocket.

Upstairs in her bathroom, Lily turned on the hot water tap in the sink until steam was visible. She held the gummed edge of the envelope as near as possible. A splash of water wet it. No good. Getting out a nail file, she tried to lossen it, but the paper tore. She slit it open— to hell with it. It was dated three weeks prior and read:

Dear Brett,

I hope this letter finds you well. Don't be angry that I'm writing to you, please! Jim gave me your address. I think you probably hoped to never hear from me again, but I just had to. I left Harry and am working in Sydney as an office temp. Thank God I haven't forgotten how to type! I want to take computer courses at night. Sally still asks about Uncle Brett. Harry got so hot every time she mentioned you—one more reason I had to move on.

Brett, I will never forgive myself for what I did to you! I was insane, I think, looking back. When you stopped coming round, I really lost it. I told him about us because I wanted to get even with you for hurting me. As terrible as it turned out, I thank God he never hurt you, Brett. I had to warn you he had a gun, because I'd have died if he killed you! I should have known poor Harry would only hurt himself.

I stayed with him 'til he recovered, but neither of us could pretend anything was left. I suppose I ought to feel guilty about him, but I don't. Harry never really wanted me 'til he thought someone else did.

Jim says you're training for some rich man near Dublin. I hope it's all going great for you. Why did you have to go so far away? Are you that much afraid of me, Brett?

I think of you every day. I love you and want you back! I'd do anything to get you back, Brett. I mean it—anything! If I sell everything, I have enough money for airfare for me and Sal to Dublin. What would you do if I showed up? I wouldn't come unless you tell me I'm forgiven, and you want to see me. I don't expect marriage or anything like that. I'll cook and clean for you. I feel so alone now. Please write me—it would mean everything! What kind of future do I have, if I can never hold you in my arms again? I'm begging you. I have no shame at all! Just say the word and I'll come to you—

> Love forever,
> Josie

Included was another photo of the dark-haired girl and the tow-headed child looking older. Sally. Was she Brett's child? Lily stared at the picture. Brett simply could not get this letter. She struck a match, lit it, and dropped it in the sink. When it was ashes, she washed out the basin and scrubbed at the scorch stain.

She looked at her flushed, guilty face in the mirror. Yes, she had done an awful, even an illegal thing, but if he still kept this woman's picture, he might care for her yet. If the child was his, how could she ever compete with such a claim on his heart? Should Brett ever find out the letter had been sent, he would have to assume it was lost in the mail.

Lily sent a mental apology to poor Josie and hoped that she would never be as desperate and pathetic over Brett Fallon herself.

Galway

❖ ❖ ❖

IN JULY, CHARLIE won again at Down Royal in Ulster. Ian decided to run the colt next at Galway, then Phoenix Park, to get him in shape for the Group I Memorial Stakes at Leopardstown in September. If he did well there, they would enter him in the October St. Leger on the Curragh course where he would be competing against some of the best three-year-olds in the world.

Brett Fallon moved back to the stable apartment, saying he would be closer to his work there, and the "Fu Manchu" room was too much for him anyway. Ian, innocently playing into their hands, suggested Lily fix his room up so it wouldn't be so bleak.

Armed with color swatches and measuring tape, Lily at once set about the job. Letting herself in the stable apartment, legally this time, she found it in the same disorder as before. "I will cook and clean for you," Josie had said in the letter. She would certainly have had her job cut out for her, Lily reflected. Brett was a pig compared to fastidious Ian. All the maid ever had to do in his room was dust and make the bed.

Lily was taking the measurements of the room when Brett walked in.

"Thought I'd better get up here fast, before you find

those porno pictures of mine," he said, tossing his hat on the table.

"You don't have any dirty pictures."

"Already looked, have you?" He limped over to her.

"Porn is for those who haven't any satisfactory sex life of their own. I've a feeling you've never needed it."

"You may be right." He pulled her to him and kissed her neck. "Any fancy ideas for my room?"

"Not yet. I think I shall have to spend a great deal of time over here working on the problem."

He shook his head and grinned. "You're a sneaky bitch. I say we start by decorating my bed over there." He picked her up and stumped over to it.

"You'll hurt yourself." She laughed.

"A little git like you won't strain me—unless you put on a few more pounds in that nice, ripe arse a yours."

"I do not have a big ass!"

"Not at this moment, but it has the potential. If you should ever quit dancing, I hate to think what could happen." He jerked off his shirt as she watched breathlessly.

He leaned down to kiss her. "What are you waiting for, Lil? Get it off!"

"We could have nice conversation first, or a bit of romantic foreplay, Brett."

"Fuck that! We both know what we're here for, and I have to get back to work. Get it off, or I'll take it off for you."

She smiled up at him.

Lily worked on the stable flat the next two weeks, even painting it with Brett's help. They were in his new double bed taking a "smoke-oh", when there was a knock at the door. Lily grabbed her clothes and scurried to the bathroom.

It was Bella. "Brett, I have to show you something,"

said the girl excitedly. Brett, having just managed to get on his jeans, invited her in.

She pulled a brown ball of fur out of her jacket. "It's a baby lop-ear—isn't it adorable! Timothy has a hutch, and the doe had babies. Just feel it!"

He took the tiny rabbit and held it up in the palm of his hand. "Cute. Amazing little ears." He gave it back to her.

"Isn't it the softest thing you've ever felt? I wanted to show Tris, but I can't find him. Have you seen him?"

"No, he's not been down here today, dolly."

Bella frowned. "I wonder where he could be? Well, I'd better get the baby back to its mother. See you later, Brett."

As soon as she heard her daughter-in-law leave, Lily came out of the bathroom, dressed.

"Close," said Brett. "Want a beer, Lil?"

"No." It irritated her that he could be so casual after such a narrow escape. "She's really just a little girl, Bella. Isn't she?"

"But big in all the right places," said Brett, opening a bottle of Foster's.

"Don't—I hate that!"

"Because you're jealous of the girl."

"That's not it at all. I don't like you to tease about Bella. Tristan and she are so young, just children really. I wonder how they'll ever make it."

Brett chugged half the beer, then belched loudly. "Ah, I needed that. Good sex and a good brew. I'm in Aussie heaven!"

"Why do I delude myself that you're a sensitive person!" she cried heading for the door.

He barred her path with his plastered arm. "Don't go away cross now, Lil."

She shoved him out of the way. "I must be mad to risk everything to be with you. Ian is twice the man you are."

"So, quit comin' here then. I'm wastin' my work time up here keepin' you serviced every day. I'm sure Paddy and the boys know we're not up here hanging curtains."

"You can be the sweetest, tenderest. . .and then you turn into an arrogant, crude jerk!"

"But, I keep you smilin', don't I, Lil?"

"There's more than sex to a relationship, but you wouldn't know about that, Brett Fallon. There's love, and closeness, and honesty. You don't have the guts for anything but the fucking, do you?"

"You get all that rubbish from him. If you got all you needed, you wouldn't be down here with me, now would you?"

"Ian's every bit as good a lover as you are, and the difference is, he means it!"

"So get the hell outta here and go to him, then," Brett snarled.

"I intend to!" Lily slammed out the door.

That very evening, Tristan took Brett into the village of Kilcullen for a "lad's night out" at a pub called The Hideout. He ordered them two pints of stout at the bar. The two brothers took a long drink.

"Ah, the best stout to be had outside Dublin," said Tristan wiping his mouth. "Though it used to taste better before I became legal."

"Aussie beer's still better," said Brett.

"Sod that. You can't be a proper Paddy if you don't prefer stout."

"Sorry, maybe I'll learn."

They emptied their glasses, and Tristan ordered two shots of Redbreast. "A gentleman of the finest taste," said the beaming publican.

"What's this then?" asked Brett, giving the dark amber contents of his glass a sniff.

"A whiskey liqueur, aged to perfection in a wooden keg for twelve years." They each knocked back the glass.

"A shortcut to knee walkin', I'd say," Brett gasped.

"Never want to drink more than four or five of these," said Tristan, signaling for a refill.

"Come on, lad, you're not going to pull another night on me, are you? My arm's still not out of the plaster, and I'm not up to fighting form. We don't have Bella to drive us home either."

"I can drive home from here with my eyes closed. Come, I want to show you something, Brett." He led him through the dark, crowded pub, its log walls hung with a motley collection of fish and animal trophies, moth-eaten tiger skins, and a crocodile badly in need of dental work. Tristan paused before a long box hung over the stone fireplace.

"Sir Dan Donelly, the first and only pugilist to be knighted," Tristan read. "His arms were so long he could button his knee britches without stooping. He was a great fighter the early part of the century. Leave it to the Irish to display his mummified arm."

"Beaut! A strange race, the Irish."

"Don't forget you're one of us." They settled in an alcove at a table under a springbok head with cowboy hats dangling from its antlers.

"This country drives me mad at times," said Tristan. "The politics, the Church in bed with the state, the hypocrisy, and the cursed IRA and Orange men. All that moronic, fanatical nationalism. But every time I'm away, I can't wait to get back. I'm an Irishman through and through, even if I'm not always proud of it. Dublin may be a little, backwater town, but it's my town, you know?"

"That's good. I like what I see of this country, the people especially. They're fair dinkum, friendly and down to earth like the Aussies."

"Do you think you'll go back, Brett?"

"Absolutely. Always intended to. It was just a good time to get out of town for a while."

Tristan caught the eye of a blond barmaid, and she hurried over. He ordered another Redbreast.

"A pint of lager, Foster's if you have it," said Brett.

"You're Australian. I just love Aussies," cooed the girl.

"Guilty as charged."

"So what would an Aussie be doin' in Kildare, then?" the barmaid asked.

"I've come half way round the planet to Kilcullen because I heard they have the fastest horses and the most beautiful women in the world."

"Go on with ye."

"See if you can dig me up a Foster's, darlin'," said Brett with a wink. She sashayed off.

Tristan grinned and shook his head. "So, what's happened to Daphne Pynchon? Haven't seen her about lately."

"I like her. She's a nice girl, but that's all there is to it."

"Too nice? Is that the problem?"

Brett shrugged. "I just didn't want to get involved."

"Damn, women throw themselves all over you, Brett, yet you're never interested. I don't get it."

"I thought it had been established that I don't like women, Tris." The boy look startled. "You were supposed to laugh at that, lad. I'm not flattered that you didn't."

"Sorry, you gave me a turn there. I'm paranoid about that."

"I'm just choosy when it comes to women. Can do without the grief, unless they're damn well worth it." The barmaid returned with their drinks. She sat the Foster's down in front of Brett with a sultry smile, and he blew her a kiss.

"Am I invisible?" said Tristan with a laugh.

"She can tell a satisfied man when she sees one, little bro."

"I guess. I say, Brett, have you ever got a girl pregnant back in Fallon's Station?"

"That's an off the wall question. As a matter of fact, I have a kid back home, Tris."

"Really? How old?"

"Tomi must be about fourteen now."

"Christ, that means you were. . ."

"Fifteen. His mother was a fourteen-year-old Aborigine girl, name of Keri. You remember that Abo stockman we had I told you about? He took me home to meet his family camping outside Woolongong. She was his little sis."

"And you got her pregnant when you were fifteen?"

"Right. I tend to get in jams with the ladies. That's why I'm skittish."

"Was the child raised Aborigine?"

"Yeah. What was I to do? I was a kid myself. He and his mum live with a white bloke now in Brisbane. I send them money through Jim, and he keeps me informed."

"How sad. You must worry about him?"

"It's a bit of unfinished business I've got to take care of soon. Don't like the sound of the situation Tomi's in now, his bein' a half-caste which is no picnic. I'd like to get him with me when I go back."

"You're amazing, Brett. What a life you've had!"

"In yer boot. I'm thirty, and I have nothing to show for it."

"Except a life full of passion and adventure and a son

as well. I've been so cosseted, it's as if I'd been wrapped in cotton wool."

Just then a thin little man drinking by himself stood up and began singing "Rose of Tralee" in a reedy but not unpleasant, impassioned tenor.

" 'For the Great Gaels of Ireland are the men that made God mad, For all their wars are merry, And all their songs are sad,' " Tristan quoted solemnly.

"Shall we shout him a drink? Might cheer him up. Shout ourselves another round as well," said Tristan, signaling the blond barmaid their desires. "Luckily she's hot for you, Brett. Makes for great service."

"Just one last one for me," said Brett. "I'm feeling low myself tonight."

The girl returned quickly, and paused just long enough to give Brett a shot of her impressive cleavage as she bent down to put the Foster's in front of him, "Anyone ever tell you you look like Mel Gibson?"

"Never. Are you tellin' me that, darlin'?"

"No, I'm not. I'd tell you you look better than Mel." She carefully put a napkin in front of him before leaving.

"Damn!" said Tristan. Brett examined the name and phone number written on the napkin and put it in his pocket.

"Are you going to ring her then? She might be worth the grief." Tristan laughed.

"No, I'm not going to ring her. Just didn't want to hurt the girl's feelings."

"I like you, Brett. Even if you weren't my brother. I like you enough to ask an incredible favor of you."

"Just ask it, little bro."

"It's more a gift than a favor, really. Brett, I can't have children. My balls are fucked from a social disease I picked up from a girl I knew before Bella."

"Damn, Tris, are you sure?"

"I've been to two specialists. It's irreversible. I'll never father a child."

"I don't know what to say. That's damn crook! I'm sorry, lad."

"I know you're sorry. So am I. So is Bella. We planned on a big family. Now, she says it doesn't matter. I know that it matters more than anything. Can you imagine anyone better suited to be a mother than Bella?"

"She'd make a fine mother. You can adopt."

"No!" Tristan slammed his fist down on the table, and the glasses jumped. "Maybe it's from Father preaching to me about the family all these years, but I want a child with D'Arcy blood."

"But, if that isn't possible?"

"There is one way it would be possible," replied Tristan, staring at him intently.

"You can't mean?. . ."

"I do mean. That's the favor, or the gift I want to give you, brother."

"You can't be serious? Do you mean donate sperm, or something like that?"

"I want you to sleep with Bella—just once of course."

"Shit! You're mad!"

"Maybe I am, but do you know what it feels like to be eighteen and know you will never have a son? It will be the end of the family line. Uncle Damien's not going to procreate, Mother's forty, and Violet is not the motherly type. This is it for the D'Arcys. I might not have cared about that once, but there is something rather grand about a family continuing in a direct line for seven hundred years.

"More than any of that, Bella needs a baby, and so do I. At first it was only to humor her, but now that I know it's impossible.. . ."

"I feel for you, Tris, but I couldn't sleep with Bella. You adore each other. How could you even think of such?"

"You are the only person on earth who can help me, Brett. The only one. I trust you not to take advantage of the situation. The true beauty of it is that your child would get all that was denied you. It's justice, Brett. As the eldest son, you should have Innismere, in all fairness."

"Hell, I don't want it!"

"Your son might. Think about it, Brett. It's just so right. Your son will carry on the line, a true D'Arcy. It's beautiful!"

"It's nonsense, and I won't do it. I might be persuaded to be a sperm donor if you're that desperate, but it would be a great wrong for me to sleep with your wife."

"I don't want to bring a doctor or any fourth party into this. No one should ever know but the three of us."

"No, and that's final. If this is what you brought me here to talk about, let's go home." He drained his beer.

"I can't believe I have to beg you to sleep with Bella. Mother and I have both noticed how much you admire her, but that's never bothered me, because I trust both of you. Is it so hard for you to go to bed with her just once? You can pinpoint ovulation to the moment these days. Just one night, Brett. Do I need to tell you how beautiful she is?"

"That's beside the point. Let's call it a night. You've had too much to drink and aren't thinking clearly."

"Brett, if you won't help me, I don't know what I'll do," said Tristan emotionally.

"You'll adopt a child or learn to live without, but I'm not getting in it. Come on, lad," said Brett getting to his feet.

"No, fuck you! I'm getting totally squiffed!" Brett sat down again. "Go on, get out of here," cried Tristan.

"I suppose I'll hang about with you and get drunk as well, bro. This hasn't exactly been my day either." Brett hooked his arm about the boy's neck affectionately.

"Where's that sexy sheila? We need another round here."

Lily avoided Brett Fallon for the next week. It was so true that Ian, in spite of his weaknesses, was the better man. She'd loved him all her life, and only temporary insanity over her marital problems had driven her to Brett in the first place. He was right—it wasn't love. How could she love someone so unworthy? Worst of all, how could she so cruelly betray someone she did love?

Feeling burdened with guilt, Lily resumed church attendance, explaining to the vicar that she had been ill the past few weeks. A small white lie, comparatively—her lust for Brett was an illness. She prayed fervently for strength and forgiveness.

Monday morning, feeling refreshed and shriven, Lily took a walk in the garden. Everything was in peak bloom now; Monet would have been pleased. She sat on the teak Lutyens bench at the bottom of the garden and looked at what she had learned to call the garden front of Innismere House. What a contrast to the plain old back of her childhood frame home in Boston! Closing her eyes, she could picture the lines of embarrassing wash her mother would hang out to dry in their tiny backyard. It came to her afresh how incredibly lucky she'd been in her life. Aside from the stellar dance career, she had more than she'd ever been sophisticated enough to even dream about. She led a wonderful, privileged life with a man she loved; what greedy woman could want more? How could she ever have been stupid enough to jeopardize it all for an unworthy man like Brett who just happened to be beautiful and amazing in bed?

Just then a jarring figure limped into her blissful, impressionist landscape. *Speak of the devil*, she thought.

"Mind if I intrude?"

"Yes, I do mind," she said coldly, belying her racing pulse.

"Too damn bad. I have a doctor's appointment. Have you forgotten? Supposed to have the plaster off my arm today. I need you to drive me, but we don't have to do anything so familiar as talk to each other on the way."

"Tristan can take you."

"He's gone. No one about but you, Lily, so I guess you're stuck with me. Though perhaps I could drive myself without a crash."

Later in the Mercedes, Brett said, "About this frostbite you've been giving me lately, Lil?"

"Just that natural cooling down you referred to before, I expect." She looked ahead at the road, though she could feel his eyes burning into her.

"I get your drift. It's over, whatever we had there?"

"Exactly." She was not going to look into those damned, hypnotic, blue eyes of his, or she'd go weak and forget all her resolutions.

"Just bam like that, it's over? You're full of shit, Lady D. But if that's the way you want it, fine. I don't fancy being' a low-down cheat myself."

"I rather thought that was your natural inclination."

"Probably too right about that. Does seem to be a trend for me." They didn't speak again until they reached the doctor's office.

In the waiting room, Lily pretended to read a racing magazine. There was a picture of Charlie in it for the win at Down Royal. How happy and excited they'd all been that day, and how she had longed for Brett that night, lying next to Ian. She tossed the magazine aside and looked up to see Brett. He showed her his arm which was pale and noticeably thinner than his other.

It was raining on the drive back, the sound of the wind screen wipers the only noise in the car. Glancing down at Brett's weak-looking arm, Lily thought about how much pain and suffering she'd put him through. She felt a softening of her resolve to be cold to him.

"Tristan was drunk again the other night when you two went out together, wasn't he?"

"We both had a few."

"You don't need to cover for him. I heard you putting him to bed. I've an awful feeling he and Bella are having problems. I interrupted a bit of a row between them this morning. Bella looked as if she'd been crying. Did Tristan mention anything to you?"

"No. The honeymoon is over, I imagine, but they'll make it. You'd be pleased if they didn't, if the truth be known, Lily."

"Once I hoped it would end in annullment, but now I think it would destroy Tristan. He does love her."

"And she loves him, so don't waste your time worrying about them."

Lily turned the wipers on high as it was really coming down. "I do worry about them. Something is wrong, I know it. Tristan was always such a sunny child, but now he goes about looking like a funeral. He never takes pictures anymore. He says he smashed his camera, but why doesn't he have it fixed or buy a new one? Ian spoke to him but got nowhere."

"Just let them work it out on their own. Every couple has to deal with problems, Lil." She looked across at him and he smiled sadly.

"I've never known anyone like you, Brett. I'm never sure who you really are, or even if I like you."

"I feel a bit the same way about you. Maybe it's because

we're cut out of the same cloth, you and I. We both try to be good, try to belong, but neither of us can quite pull off the stunt. There's a lot of rogue dingo in both of us, Lil."

"Speak for yourself," she said, leaning forward to better see the road in the downpour. Brett suggested she stop 'til the storm was over, so she turned off on a side road and parked the car on the shoulder.

"Reminds me of the time up at the castle," said Brett as the rain drummed on the car roof. "I really wanted you then, Lil. Thought about making a move, the temptation was so strong having you in my arms, but my conscience won out. I'm not sure I'd have ever made a move, if I hadn't been injured and at your mercy."

She had to smile. "Please! You almost raped me."

"The way I recall it, you lured me into Charlie's stall after you'd worked him into a killing rage, then you came round to my sick bed everyday looking beautiful and half-dressed, while I lay there helpless, doped to the gills, and desperate for any sort of entertainment. I damn well think you planned the whole thing."

She laughed. "You are incorrigible!"

He touched her hair. "I was an insensitive ass the other day, Lil. I get like an echidna when my vital organs are threatened. That's this spiny, little ant eater we have at home. It protects itself with barbs when someone's getting too close."

"Exactly which of your vital organs was I threatening, Brett?"

"My heart." Instantly something went soft inside her. From the look in his eyes, he wasn't merely being glib. "It was starting to feel too damn nice with you, Lil, so I had to go and ruin it." His hand moved from the back of her seat, along her neck to her shoulder.

"The problem is I miss you, and I think you miss me,

too." He grasped her hair and pulled her to him. She turned her face away.

"Please, Brett," she protested without much conviction. He kissed her ear, then moved his lips down her neck; she felt herself weakening.

"There's no way this is anywhere near finished, Lil," he whispered in her ear, his hand seeking her breast. "You know it, and I know it."

She pulled his hand away from her blouse.

"Come on, Lil. My right hand's never touched you. He deserves a little reward for all he's been through."

Lily ran her fingers up his newly healed arm. "I am sorry I did that to you, Brett."

He caught her face and kissed her mouth.

"Lily, Lily, I want you. Haven't you punished me enough?" She tried to push him away. "Come on, I know you want it. It's been so long." He pulled her hand into his lap and rubbed it over the hard bulge there.

"We can't, Brett."

"Sure, we can. No one will be along this road for a while, and the windows are steamed." He kissed her hungrily.

She hit him on the side of the head with the flat of her fist. "I mean it—I can't!" He let her go, and she straightened her clothes.

"I want you, too, Brett, but it's just too wrong. I can't live with myself anymore. We've almost been caught twice, and if we don't put a stop to it now, we will be. Think what it would do to Ian—to Tristan! I know that somehow he's already found out about his father, and it's disillusioned him terribly. It would knock all the props out from under him if he found out about us. I would never forgive myself."

"You're right," said Brett, running a hand through his hair and moving away from her.

"Do you understand, Brett? I just can't go on with a sin like this on my conscience, as much as I do care for you. It's horrid feeling ashamed of yourself all the time. I've never done anything really awful before, and I just don't have the stomach for it."

"Yeah, I know what you're sayin'. Maybe it'll be easier to look myself in the eye when I shave in the morning. Let's get on home, Lil—the storm has passed."

✪ ✪ ✪

The end of July, the D'Arcys traveled to Galway to run Charlie in the prestigious Galway Purse. This old Norman city was just over a hundred miles due west of Innismere on Ireland's Atlantic coast. To everyone's surprise, Tristan had announced that he would not be coming on the trip because he had an appointment at Trinity to see about entering the college for the fall term. Of course no one had argued with that. He insisted that Bella not miss the race, however, as he would be tied up with interviews and tests.

The five-day Galway race week was one of the most popular August attractions for natives of Connaught as well as tourists from all over, and the city and surrounding towns were swamped with visitors for the event. Ian and Brett went to the track every day leaving Lily to entertain a rather mopish, listless Bella. She tried to interest the girl in shopping forays about Eyre Square and exploring the very interesting city of Galway, which in medieval times had been such a Norman-English enclave that an actual law had stated that "Neither O nor Mac should strutte ne swagger through the streets." Cromwell made them pay dearly for their royalist sympathies when he sacked the city in 1652, tearing down the walls built to keep out the "mere Irish." Bella seemed uninterested in all Lily's efforts at playing tour guide.

Over lunch in the Oyster at the Great Southern hotel, Lily tried to draw out her daughter-in-law. Bella grew teary-eyed and nervous when Lily asked if there'd been a row with Tristan. She could not, however, be persuaded to talk about whatever the problem might be. Afraid that the girl might break down and cry in the restaurant, Lily did not press it, but suggested that if she ever needed advice or someone to listen, she wanted very much to help.

"The first year is so difficult, darling," said Lily. "You and Tristan get on twice as well as Ian and I did. I thought we would end in divorce court for sure." Bella made a dismal pass at a smile, and that was as far as the inquiry got.

The races were such a big event for Galway that the city closed down every afternoon, and the roads were jammed out to the course at Ballybrit four miles away. A carnival atmosphere prevailed, and many a race patron spent afternoons in the beer tents, or watching the musicians, fortune tellers, and other colorful sideshows, without ever setting their eyes on a horse.

To Lily's disgust, Daphne Pynchon was there, her horse entered in the Galway Plate steeplechase, the most important chase of the Irish summer season. Everytime Lily saw Brett Fallon, the silly girl was on his arm, and Brett was looking very pleased about it. Even if she weren't going to have anything more to do with him herself, it did gall her to see him go straight after Daphne without missing a beat.

The day before Charlie's race, Ian was called back to Dublin by a break-in at D'Arcy's. Watching him leave, Lily realized her willpower was about to be given the acid test.

She had her first opportunity to speak to Brett when she saw him standing alone at the track, gazing off the bluff at Galway Bay.

She walked up behind him. "Inishmore, Inishmaan, and Innisheer," she said. He looked startled. "The Aran Islands you were looking at," she explained. "Too bad we haven't planned an excursion out there for you and Bella. Dun Aengus on Inishmore goes back to 4000 B.C. Very mystical. The islanders have to build up any soil out of seaweed, it's so stony."

"Do they? That's amazing, Lil," he said, mocking her. The sea wind ruffled his hair and his eyes made the sky pale in comparison. Lily looked away, her heart pounding.

"So how's Charlie?" she asked.

"Fit and ready to run. How have you been? Feeling better about yourself now that you're an honest woman again?"

"I feel. . .bored."

He laughed. "Could have told you that. Goodness can be very boring—so I've heard. Give me a call when you can't take it anymore. I've been feeling a mite bored myself lately."

"With darling Daphne around, how could you?" she retorted.

"This was all your idea, Lil, so don't complain. If you'll excuse me, I have things to do." He walked off, leaving her feeling angry and humiliated.

Ian called around eight to say they were still taking inventory to see what had been stolen, and he would be in Dublin another day.

After an early dinner by herself, Lily sat alone in her cramped hotel room near the track and looked at the telephone. "Call me when you can't take it any longer," Brett had said. She made a stiff drink from Ian's flask, and made up her mind to stick to her guns and not think about him. She hadn't even thought to bring a book, it was too early to go to bed, and Bella was not very good company. Her glance flicked back to the telephone. "Call me!" God, she missed him so! Drinking, praying, nothing helped. Tossing back the rest of the whiskey, Lily picked up the phone, and asked for his room.

"Yeah?" said his voice on the line, going through her like a knife.

"It's me," she whispered.

"Lily, speak up girl—can barely hear you."

"Ian won't be back 'til tomorrow."

"So?" He wanted her to beg, damn him!

"So, I can't bear to be good a moment longer, and don't you dare gloat."

"Now would I do a thing like that, Lil?" She could hear the grin in his voice. "What can I do for you, Lil?"

"You can get your smart ass over to room 115."

"Whoa now. I don't take well to being ordered about by women, no matter how bored they are."

"Prick! Please come to my room—I miss you desperately!"

"Much nicer. I did promise I'd have a drink with the lads first, you understand."

"Don't keep me waiting too long, Brett. My conscience may flair up again." She hung up on him. Damn him! He would have his revenge for her turning him down in the car.

She bathed and perfumed herself, and put on her most beautiful gown. For all the good that would do. She smiled to herself thinking how exciting it would be after not being together for so long. She climbed in bed and began reading a magazine to pass the time until Brett's arrival.

✪ ✪ ✪

Clad in a towel, Brett Fallon was shaving for the second time that day when he heard a knock at the door.

He smiled at his reflection in the glass and wiped off the last bits of soap. So, she couldn't take the nice long wait he'd given her!

It was Bella, a raincoat over her nightgown, and a distraught look on her face. She said she needed to talk, so he invited her in, put on his dressing gown, and fixed them both a drink. The girl looked as if she needed one badly.

"I came by earlier, but you were out," she said.

"Right, I took Daphne out for a bite to eat. So, why the sad face, dolly?" he asked as they sat on the bed, the only seat in the very basic room.

"It's about Tristan," she said. Her eyes looked swollen as if she'd been crying.

"Yeah?" He took her hand to encourage her.

Bella took a deep breath. "He told you his idea about the baby?" she asked tremulously.

"I hope he told you that I heartily vetoed that plan."

"Yes, but it didn't do any good. He won't take 'no', Brett."

"He'll damn well have to! I hope you've tried to discourage him about this?"

"Yes! We've been arguing for weeks, but he won't listen to me. I never want to sleep with anyone but Tris, but he insists I have to do it."

"Or what?"

A tear trickled down her flushed cheek. "I don't know. He's been so weird lately, not like my Tristan at all. He won't take pictures or do anything but drink and talk about a baby. If only I'd never thought of it! This not being able to have children, on top of whatever is wrong between him and his father. . .It's as if he thinks everything is against him, and the only hope is a child."

"What's wrong between Ian and Tris?"

"I don't know. He never says. Don't you notice how

stiff they are with each other? My family may have been working class, but at least we hugged each other. Tris and his Dad never touch, and Ian is so kind and wonderful. I just don't understand it. Whatever it is, Tris is frightened to death to even speak of it. I would think he'd tell me anything, but not that."

"I have noticed what you're speakin' of, now that you mention it. I suppose it has to do with him not going to school like he was supposed to.

"About the way Tris's acting lately. Finding out he's sterile was one hell of a blow to his ego. A woman might not understand that. Just stand by him, and he'll calm down, love. He's not had time to adjust to the shock yet."

"I don't know how much time there is, Brett," she whispered. She pulled a small bag out of her coat pocket. "It's cocaine. I found it in his jacket at home."

Brett whistled softly. "That's rum! Has he been into drugs before?"

"He was in London, before I met him. I flushed it down the toilet and told him I'd leave if he ever took anything again. He swore he wouldn't, that he didn't need it anymore. That I was the only drug he needed." Her lower lip quivered and tears hung on her dark, auburn lashes. "Now he's starting again, and I love him too much to ever leave."

Brett put his arms around her comfortingly. She kissed him on the lips.

He held her away from him. "What the hell do you think you're doin?"

"What I must do if I'm to help him," she pleaded.

"Did he put you up to this? Is that why he didn't come?"

She shook her head. "I take my temperature every morning, and it was up today. That means the time is right. We've got to do this for Tris, if we love him, Brett."

He stood up. "No way! I could horsewhip him for putting you. . .us through this. I couldn't have sex with you, Bella. It would be physically impossible—disgusting like incest or something!"

"I know you don't want me, Brett, but you could pretend I was someone else—I could pretend. Please!" she looked up at him with pitiful, brimming turquoise eyes.

"That's not it—any man would want you. It's that it would be wrong and plain stupid." Bella curled up in a ball on the bed and sobbed as if her heart were broken.

It dawned a "grand, soft day"—gray and drizzling—for the Galway Purse race in which Charlie was entered. Lily woke early to find with a shock that Brett had stood her up. She was having tea in her room in a very foul mood when he called.

"Don't hang up," he said. "I was out late with the lads and got so pissed, I knew I wouldn't be any good, so I went on to bed."

"I don't find it very complimentary that you'd rather get drunk with the boys than make love to me," she snapped.

"Sorry, Lil, but I couldn't get away—there was only one car. Why didn't you come to my room after me?"

"I'm not that desperate! Besides, I fell asleep reading."

"Not very complimentary. I've an incredible headache this morning, if it makes you feel any better. Don't suppose you'd care to drop by my room and give me a quickie head rub before I go to the track?"

"I hope your head cracks in two!" She slammed down the receiver. What a bastard he was—in every sense of the word!

Lily was having a cigarette to calm her nerves when there was a knock at her door. So, he thought he could charm his way out of this one, did he? She flung open the door, and there stood Bella, looking pale and waif-like.

"Have you a thermometer, Lily? I think I have a fever."

Bella had a temperature of over a hundred, so Lily put the girl in her bed and the two of them spent the morning talking. Or rather Lily talked while Bella lay listlessly and listened to her. She expounded on how wonderful it was that Tris was going to Trinity in the fall, and how Bella must support and encourage him.

That topic exhausted, Lily turned to another subject of prime interest—Brett and Daphne.

"Ian seems to think they're a perfect match, absolutely altar-bound. You see more of them than I do. Do you think he's serious about her?"

"I don't know about serious," said Bella. "They get on well. He took Daphne out the past two nights, so I suppose that means he likes her a lot."

"He took her out last night? He told me he was going drinking with the lads last night."

"He told me that he'd taken Daphne to dinner," said Bella, who was longing for her mother-in-law to quit talking so she could sleep.

"You saw Brett last night? How late?" asked Lily as if she were a prosecutor scenting blood.

"Pretty late. Maybe around ten. When I went out for a walk because I couldn't sleep. Lily, do you mind if I take a nap? I'm so tired."

"Of course, darling," said Lily distractedly, her mind awhirl with suspicions. Why had Brett told her he was out with the boys? Obviously a cover story for the real way he'd spent the night—in that slut Daphne's arms.

Ian made it back just in time for the Galway Purse. Charlie was boxed in for half the race until Rafferty slipped him through an opening. The Innismere colt won by two lengths.

A smiling but subdued Brett Fallon was waiting when they all arrived at the winner's enclosure. Ian embraced him in a rare moment of effusiveness. Lily kept a cool distance. Tommy Rafferty dismounted from Charlie grinning widely. The photographers crowded in as the winner's rug emblazoned with Galway Purse was draped over the lathered, black colt.

Ian had Paddy and Connors join the group. "Sir Willie must be pleased up in heaven, or wherever," said the old groom.

"This would be a perfect moment if Tris were here," said Ian, putting his arm about Bella.

Lily kissed her husband, and he returned it wholeheartedly, his excitement overcoming his natural reticence. She saw Brett look away from them and felt a moment of hollow satisfaction.

Tristan had already returned from Dublin by the time they reached Innismere. Bella raced upstairs and found him lying on their bed, his eyes closed.

"How are you?" she asked, sitting beside him.

"I've a four-day hangover," he whispered hoarsely. Bella stretched out alongside him.

"Are you going to tell me, Bella?"

"He didn't want to," she whispered.

"But you convinced him?"

"It was terrible for both of us."

"What martyrs you both are," he sneered.

Bella sat up. "Don't you dare act like that. It was the worst thing I've ever had to do in my life, and you'd damn well better appreciate it."

Tristan pulled her back down into his arms. "I do. Only forgive me if I can't be thrilled about it. You can't

have had any more torturous a time than I've had thinking about the two of you. Let's just pray it worked so we
can get on with our lives and forget we ever had to do
this." Bella held his face to her breast.

✠ ✠ ✠

On their return from Galway, Kelly announced that
Damien had called and would be arriving the following
day with a guest. Ian had to leave for London early in
the morning, so Lily would have to entertain his brother.

"I wonder if the guest is male or female?" Lily mused.
Silly question, she answered herself.

"Might be his new talent—some rocker from Ulster,"
said Ian as he undressed for bed.

"Whom you've no doubt bankrolled?"

"Damien has to hit someday, by the law of averages."

She put her arms around him. "You are a very nice
man."

"And you are one of the few ladies in the horse world
who doesn't resemble one."

"Is that a compliment?"

He kissed her. "Of the highest. I've said it many
times—I am a lucky man."

"I'm the lucky one if the truth be told. So, what did
you and Brett talk about on the drive home?"

"I've offered him head trainer's position next season.
I'll mollify Frank by making him stud manager. Next year,
we'll have Charlie at stud with tax-exempt fees coming
in. He should be in demand with his pedigree and winning record, especially if he does well this fall. I also plan
on investing in two or three good yearling fillies with an
eye to breeding. It's time Innismere Racing Stable and
Stud became more than just an expensive hobby. With
someone of Brett's skill and intelligence, I think we can
become a profit-making concern."

"Exciting! Was Brett very pleased?"

"Actually, he said he needed time to consider it. I was surprised."

"Surely he'll accept. He'd be a fool not to."

"I hope so. Daphne should be an added enticement. In the meantime, Lady D'Arcy, would you stay with me since we were cheated out of last night?"

Lily ran her fingers through his hair; so much silver in the black now. "If you want me to."

"I do. It always saddens me to wake and find you're not beside me. You aren't having as much difficulty sleeping as you were, are you?" He sat on the bed looking handsome in his red paisley dressing gown. She sat beside him.

"I've been thinking how wonderful you've been not to take a lover through the separation and my problem, Lily. I'm afraid many wives would have."

"Too much talk," she said, pulling his robe open and running her hand over his lean belly, so white against the scarlet.

Damien D'Arcy and Rory McCalla arrived in time for lunch the following day. Rory was to be Damien's "Next Big Thing"—he'd been sure of it since he'd heard the young rock singer in a Belfast pub. Thanks to his direction and a demo tape made with Ian's money, Rory had been signed to Island Records; they were to begin soon on his first album.

"Oh, oh," thought Lily when first introduced to the singer who was twenty and looked seventeen. Rory was thin to the point of wasted, spotty-faced, and barely taller than she—not exactly ugly, but certainly no teenaged girl's dream fantasy. With his frail body, shoulder-length, lank, black hair, and orthodontist's dream of jumbled teeth, Rory McCalla resembled some feral street urchin, rather than a potential superstar.

"Don't judge 'til you've heard the tape," Damien whispered, sensing her skepticism.

Rory ate with the elegance of a stray dog expecting his dinner to be snatched away at any moment. Damien kept them entertained with amusing banter about the contract and the glittering future of his protegé as the boy wolfishly packed it away.

Bella, the only rock fan in the group, asked the singer who he sounded like.

"I dunno. A bit a Stevie Winwood, and a touch a Robert Plant, but mainly meself," he replied modestly, his thick, Ulster accent garbled even more by a mouth full of food.

"Rory, my dear, is the greatest blues singer to come out of Ireland since Van Morrison. You'd swear he was black just listening to his voice," said Damien.

"You're not metal or punk are you?" Lily asked.

"Mother, punk died about ten years ago. Haven't you heard?" said Tristan.

"I'm just rock n' roll, mum," said McCalla. "Pass the butter over here."

Bella handed the butter dish to him. "I can't wait to hear your tape." Rory stopped icing a slice of bread with the butter long enough to fling her a smile. In spite of the teeth, his smile was cute, Lily reflected. Maybe that would be enough to make him a sex symbol.

After lunch, Damien played the demo tape while Rory stared in open awe at the rich furnishings about him. There was no describing the contrast between the unprepossessing singer's looks and his powerful, rich voice. Closing your eyes, you could imagine a great, bull-chested black man rather than the slight, Irish boy. Damien smiled sweetly through the tape, like the cat who ate the canary.

"So what so you think?" he asked at the end of the six-song tape.

"I think you're fabulous," said Bella. Rory beamed at her.

"Sounds as good as anyone I hear on the radio," said Tristan.

"Don't look at me," said Lily. The last record I bought was 'Abbey Road.' You do have quite a voice, though. Even a tone-deaf person like myself can tell that."

"Very disappointing to have missed Ian," said Damien. "I really wanted him to hear Rory. This time he's going to get his money back ten times over."

"I do hope so," said Lily. "I've fixed the Mandarin bedroom for Rory, Damien, in anticipation of his being such a big star." She'd really put him there because it was as far away as possible from Damien's room. If the two were sleeping together, she wanted to discourage it while they were at Innismere. Rory did not look gay, but she was suspicious of everyone lately.

"If you will excuse me," she added, "it's a lovely day, and I'm going for a ride."

"Go ahead, my dear," said Damien. "Continue about your business as usual and pay us no mind. We're here for a bit of peace and quiet. If all goes as planned, it may be the last Rory gets for years to come."

Brett was not in his flat, so Lily went looking for him in the stable. Billy Rafferty told her he was in the feed room. She found him moving heavy bags about in the dusty, airless area where the grain was stored.

"What?" he said, pausing to wipe the sweat out of his eyes.

"Are you really up to working so hard with your arm just out of the cast?"

"I need to build it back. What do you want with me, Lil?"

"I hear Ian's offered you head trainer. You are going to take it?"

"No. I'm leaving at the end of this race season." Lifting a bag of oats on his shoulder, he stacked it across the room.

"Leaving? You can't possibly!"

"It's gotten too complicated around here, and I miss home."

Lily was so stricken that she forgot she'd come to berate him for lying about how he'd spent the night before the race. "Do you mean you could actually leave me like that, Brett?" she cried.

He went to the door and shut it. "What do you want me to do, Lily? Stay on for the next twenty years and be your back door man, when you're not pissed at me or having an attack of conscience?"

"The season is over in three months!"

"So, we'll be finished or will have killed each other by then, one or the other."

She threw herself on him. "You can't leave me—I won't let you."

"I have to go, Lil. I feel like a shit everytime he's good to me. I can't take much more of this."

"I'll be good to you, Brett, I swear. I know I haven't always been, but I will if you'll just give me another chance. I'll do anything you want—anything." She kissed him frantically.

He pushed her gently away. "I am going, Lil. I've made up my mind. There's nothing you can do to prevent me."

Lily backed away from him, then pulled her cotton

polo shirt up over her head. Taking the ribbon holding her hair back, she shook it out.

"What are you doing? Someone will walk in here!"

"Let them. I don't care anymore." She unfastened the front hook of her bra. "I *will* make you stay, Brett." He stood there, hesitant.

Lily turned her back to him, unzipped her riding breeches, and lowered them to the top of her boots. Leaning over to brace her hands on a pile of feed bags, she looked over her shoulder at him. "I'm ready, palamino."

Damien knocked on the door to the Chinese bedroom. "It's me. May I speak to you, Rory?" He entered and found the boy propped up like a shaggy-headed, spindly doll in the huge opium bed.

"How are you getting on in these amazing digs, lad? Great bed, eh?"

"Chink shit, is it? Never seen the like in me life. Think I'll have a room like this when I'm rich."

"By all means—you have excellent taste!" Damien sniffed. "Is something burning?" He opened the smoking drawer of the bedside table and discovered a lighted cigarette.

"Let's not burn down my brother's house, Rory."

"Just having a toke to calm meself. The way that posh sister-in-law a yours looked down her nose at me."

"Your imagination. She quite liked you, Rory, as they all did. The demo blew everyone away."

Taking a drag on the cigarette, Rory said, "She liked me all right. She's so fuckin' beautiful!"

"Bella?"

"The eyes on her, and the body! She's nice, too, not like Lady hoity-toity."

"Bella's a lovely girl and very much in love with her husband."

"Why not? He's bloody rich, with a pretty face and pommy manners. I wonder if that Bella's ever had a real man?"

"Lest you forget, Rory, Tristan is my nephew, a very decent lad of whom I'm terribly fond. Bella is a very big no-no. . .like drugs."

"It's only a friggin' joint. I told you I ain't into drugs, and I ain't. A toke just relaxes me now and again."

"I've nothing against marijuana in great moderation, and I'm sure you're too clever a lad to get into anything heavier."

"Damn right! I'm not goin' to end up on the needle like half the blokes I grew up on the streets with, because I'm makin' somethin' of my life," said the boy fiercely.

"Good lad. Just a few ground rules. No dope of any kind when you're performing. Nothing roughs a singer's throat worse than that stuff, and never bring it through customs."

"Jaysus, mother—I'm not an eejit!"

"And, no moving in on Bella. You'll have plenty of girls as soon as your record's out. Have to beat them off with sticks."

Rory grinned at that prospect. "Aye, bring 'em on! Sex is my vice, not drugs."

"Your habit will be sated, I promise you. No underage girls, please."

"It's full-grown women I fancy with bloody great tits and ginger hair. I do fancy that. And blonds!"

"One of every flavor, I promise, Rory." Damien sat on the edge of the bed. "Give me a drag, love, for old times' sake."

"Didn't know you smoked, Damien."

"Had a few tokes in my day. Prefer the smooth taste of a good whiskey, actually. One can gauge one's level of inebriation more easily." Damien inhaled a puff and handed it back to Rory who finished it and snubbed it out in the ashtray. Damien smiled down at him. There was something touching about the thinness of the boy's arm.

"Ya waitin' for a fuckin' goodnight kiss, Damien?" Rory asked, at once all wariness.

"If you want."

"You keep yer bloody queen's lips off me, D'Arcy," he growled.

"Only ragging you, my boy," said Damien, getting to his feet.

"Yeah, well don't you ever try anythin' like you did in Belfast. I like women, damn ya!"

"I know that. I was in me cups the other time, or I'd never have tried to mix business and pleasure. You are quite safe from these bloody queen's lips. Goodnight, sweet Rory."

"No hard feelin's. I ain't a pouf, but if you are, that's yer business, see?" He crossed his slender arms across his childlike chest, and cocked his head to the side. "You ever made it with a woman, Damien?"

"Never appealed to me."

"Jaysus, that's sad," said Rory in disbelief.

Damien crossed to the door.

"Hey, Damien? You're an all right gent even though." Damien bowed and smiled at him.

In the hallway, Damien thought to himself, *I somehow doubt that you spent three years in reform school, Rory, without making it with another lad, but I will leave you your illusions. I have lots of patience and something else you've never had that you need more than a rainbow of big-breasted girls. Love.* Damien smiled to himself as he went along the darkened corridor to his room. Such an irresistible child, Rory, with his underfed body and waif face—the silver religious medal gleaming on his pale, hairless chest. Those thin, blue-veined arms with just a blip of biceps, barely hinting of the strength that had kept an orphaned boy alive on the streets of Derry's worst slums. Sweet and sad boy, his whole twenty years a blighted wasteland, from which his one glorious possession, his voice, was about to deliver him.

Damien rounded the corner, almost walking into Lily.

"Heavens, you frightened me," she gasped.

"Ah, Lily," said Damien, taking in the fact that she was fully dressed though she'd retired hours earlier. "Where are you off to in the dead of night? To visit the gamekeeper?"

She blushed suspiciously. "I was just going down to the kitchen to heat some milk. My insomnia. Where are you coming from, Damien? Been tucking in the superstar?"

"I was. He was a bit anxious about the impression he'd made on the family. Feels out of his element, much as you did once upon a time, Lily. You should sympathize."

"I had been to knife and fork school, however."

"The manners are a tad rustic. He's a proud lad, and it's delicate working on that sort of thing without hurting his feelings."

"Table manners would probably be a minus in his line of work," said Lily with a smile.

"Indeed. I'm off to bed now, dear. *Bonne chance* with your insomnia."

"Won't you join me, Damien? I'll even put some rum in yours."

"No thanks. As much as I'd like to catch up on what you've really been up to out here in the dull, old country, Morpheus calls. See you in the morning, love."

Brett Fallon and Damien met each other for the first time over breakfast the next morning.

"I've been hearing great things about you from Ian," said Damien. "He says you're Svengali with the horses."

"Charlie gets the credit, not me. Also the jockey, Paddy, Connors—we're a team."

"Ah, Paddy. Does he still dose the horses with poteen for what ails them?"

"I hope not," said Brett with a laugh.

"It works on him. Why not the animals?"

"Paddy's a character. Been around forever, I guess. Always talking about Sir Willie."

"An unpleasant topic, though no one can deny that my father was a great horseman. He knew horseflesh and how to screw you in a deal as well as any man in Eire, I think."

"So I hear. I imagine the old bugger's twirlin' in his grave at my turnin' up like the bad penny."

"I think he'd like what you're doing with Innismere Stables, lad."

Lily joined them. "So, you two have met?"

"Yes. We're discussing Father and what a prick he was," said Damien.

Brett threw down his napkin. "If you all will excuse me, I'll be off to work. Nice to meet you, Damien."

"Indeed. I'll be down for a ride later, if it doesn't rain."

"Right on," said Brett. He nodded at Lily and left them.

She helped herself to one sausage and a small serving of scrambled eggs from the covered silver dishes on the sideboard, then sat down across from her brother-in-law.

"Well!" he said, wiping his mouth. "Someone forgot to tell me that our Brett is a quite stunningly sexy young man."

"Wasn't your governess terribly attractive?"

"I was too young to notice, or more likely, didn't care

even then. But Brett! The blue eyes make one quite weak in the knees."

"That's a rather unbecoming statement from his uncle, Damien."

"Please, Lily. I'm not that much of a reprobate."

"Sorry. I'm still cross about your comparing me with your brutish singer. So, where is Van Morrison II?"

"Sleeping in. A habit acquired from a lifetime on the dole or working nights."

"About the governess, Damien—did you have any idea Ian and Miss Culhane were having an affair?"

"Not really, until she disappeared off into the night, and Father and Ian were glowering at each other over dinner for weeks after. I tumbled then, though perhaps I did sense something earlier. I recall Ian coming home from school a foot taller with his spots cleared up and hanging about Miss Culhane rather more than seemed necessary. He was quite charming to me in her presence, instead of bashing me about the ears as usual."

"Ian never did that."

"My brother was not always a saint, a stance he only assumed later in life."

"From having to put up with me, eh?" Lily laughed. "Could you tell if she was attracted to him?"

"She was very discreet. I did catch her once staring out the window during my maths lesson. I looked out and saw that it was Ian walking in the garden that had her so fascinated."

"A tragic story, really, their loving each other, but the timing being so utterly wrong. Ten years wouldn't have made such a difference later. I feel for Miss Culhane," said Lily thoughtfully.

"My, you must be mellowing in your old age, Lily. I'd expect you to hate her guts in your usual jealous fashion."

"Is that a snide way of alluding that my fortieth is coming up, Damien? I've told Ian and Tristan that I want my birthday ignored this year. Never forget that you'll always be a year older."

"Forty is the prime of one's life I've found, and I'm sure you shall to. We've only just begun to peak."

"I hope you're right. I don't feel any more decrepit than when I turned thirty. You're right about my mellowing though. I've even overcome my maternal jealousy of Bella."

"Good. Such an angel, Bella. One of the few women I've met who seems actually as good as she looks."

"She's a darling. I noticed your Rory certainly thought so. Bella has no idea of her effect on men; she's so innocently flirtatious. Someone like Rory might get the wrong idea, and believe me, Bella and Tristan don't need any more problems right now."

"Don't worry. I've warned Rory off. Are the lovebirds having troubles then?"

"We're afraid they may be. Tristan is acting peculiar, and Bella cries a lot. The good news is he's been accepted at Trinity this fall."

"My old almost alma mater. I hope he has a longer and more distinguished career there than I did."

"So do I." Finished with breakfast, Lily excused herself to go play lady of the manor, as she put it.

Damien stood and bowed to her. "A role you were born to play, Lily."

Daphne Pynchon turned up that afternoon and whisked Brett away, plunging Lily into a black mood. He had still not returned by that evening when Tristan, Bella, Damien, and Rory went off to explore the Dublin rock clubs.

At eleven, having grown more desperate with every tick of the clock, Lily went to Brett's stable flat to wait for him. She was sitting on the bed having her third glass of Bushmill's and water when they returned. It was difficult to say who looked more startled to see her there, Brett or Daphne.

"Lily, is something wrong?" said Brett, deciding to play it as if only an emergency could have brought her to his room.

"You're damn right something's wrong!" Lily glared at Daphne.

"We, uh, were going to have a nightcap," Brett stuttered.

"Oh dear, and I've finished off your whiskey. Did you two have a lovely time? Brett's going back to Woolly Bully in October, Daphne, did he tell you? So in case you envisioned raising little horsies with him, you'll have to revise your plans."

Daphne turned to Brett. "I'll go. Thanks anyway." To Lily she said, "I apologize for being so thick, Lady D'Arcy. I should have understood." She smiled sadly at Brett, then left them.

Brett's face was so furious it frightened her. She closed her eyes. "Proud of yourself?" he said, his voice flat and hard. He picked up the empty bottle of Bushmill's from the table and threw it in the dustbin.

"You were going to make love to her, weren't you?"

"I don't have to make explanations to you, Lily."

"You slept with her in Galway—probably have been all along. I'm such an idiot!"

Brett crossed to the bed and jerked her to her feet. "This is none of your damn business, but I have never been to bed with Daphne. I'm a one-woman man, and you're it—you bitch!"

"You're lying! You were bringing her up here to bed, and I know you were with her that night in Galway when you said you were out with the boys drinking. Bella told me you were. You're a liar and a cheat, Brett Fallon!" She thought he would hit her then, but he only shoved her down on the bed.

"What do you want from me, Lily?"

"I want to be free of the power you have over me. I want not to give a damn who you screw."

"Keep this up, and you won't have to deal with me at all. I just may not stay 'til October. I'll say this one more time, and you'd better listen. I did not make love with Daphne in Galway or anywhere. I went out with the lads after I saw Bella that night. Yes, I had taken Daphne to dinner earlier, then we parted company. As for tonight, I told Daph that I was leaving, and we were comin' up here for a farewell drink as friends, all we've ever been. I also told her I was involved with someone else—I felt I owed her that. Now, thanks to your little performance, she knows exactly who I'm involved with."

"Are you telling me the truth, Brett?" she pleaded.

"What does it matter? I'm so tired of all this bullshit," he said hollowly.

She put her arms about his hips. "I'm sorry, my darling. If you say it, I believe you. It's only because I love you so that I get paranoid. Promise me you won't leave, Brett."

"I can't stand this constant hot and cold, Lil. The minute the ropes and chains come out, I want to be gone."

"I know. I'll trust you from now on, I swear!" She pressed her mouth against the cold metal of his zipper and his hands were in her hair.

Everyone was late rising the next morning, so Lily was able to get back to her bedroom without being caught. Later, washed and dressed, she was passing Tristan's room when she heard raised voices within. She paused long enough to hear her son shout something about Rory

McCalla. She hurried to get out of earshot, having already had quite enough of eros gone wrong. Her own problems were all she could handle at the moment.

"I can't believe you thought I was flirting with him," said Bella.

"He thought so, and why not with the way you were dancing with him!"

"That's the way I always dance, as you well know. Should I have refused when he asked me and said, 'Sorry, my husband is too jealous'?"

"He had his filthy little hands all over you. I thought the two of you would get it on right there on the dance floor!"

"God! That is ridiculous, Tris, and you know it!"

"The little shit was drooling over you all evening, and all you did was encourage him. You're one of those stupid girls who'd go to bed with a mangy dog if it could play a guitar and sing!"

Bella slapped him. He wrestled her down on the bed. "Teasing little bitch—always playing so innocent. Getting men worked up, then saying, 'Who me? I never did a thing.'" He forced his knee between her legs.

"Stop it, Tris!"

"So innocent. You do it on purpose, don't you?" He roughly shoved up her nightgown. She struggled to push him away, but he was much stronger.

"Not like this, please, Tris," she pleaded.

"Shut up!" he hissed and pushed inside her. He gripped her face as he moved. "Got every male in counties Kildare and Dublin wanting to do this to you, you little prick tease." He climaxed quickly and lay a dead weight on top of her. Bella was perfectly still, her eyes closed.

Tristan began shaking, and her arms went around him. "It's all right, Tris," she whispered in his ear.

He rolled off her and lay on the bed, chest heaving. "All right? I just raped you, and it's fucking all right?"

"You're just upset over. . .everything. I understand, really I do."

Tristan covered his face with his hands. "I'm losing it, I really am."

Bella touched him, and he jumped as if scalded.

"Don't you have human feelings, Bella? I do that to you, and you just lie there and say it's all right? Yell at me, call the police, my father, anything but say you understand!" He stood up and zipped his trousers.

"I'm getting out of here before I go mad." Throwing on a sweater, he rushed out of their room, slamming the door in his wake.

Brett was lying in bed thinking of Lily and the tempestuous night they'd spent when Bella came to his flat.

"What's the matter?" he asked at once.

"It's Tristan. We've had this horrid row, and he's gone off in the car."

Brett put his arms around her and held her awkwardly. "This isn't about us, I hope?"

"No—well, maybe. We went out last night with that singer Rory. I danced with him, just to be nice, and Tristan was furious about it. This morning, he said awful things—that I tease men on purpose, but I promise I never. It was so terrible, Brett."

"Calm down now. Tris will get over it and be very sorry later."

"He was sorry already, and he cried. I told him that it was all right—that I understood what made him act that way. He got furious all over again, Brett. I don't know what to do. He was never really jealous before. I mean, he would tease about it but not be an ass like he was this morning. He has no reason to ever be jealous. He knew I didn't give a damn about that stupid Rory. He knew!"

"Men will be assholes when their pride is wounded, dolly. Come have a seat, and I'll make you a cuppa to calm you down. Okay?" She nodded tearfully.

Bella sat on the bed while Brett rinsed out a mug in the bathroom sink, and poured her some tea from the pot he'd just made.

Bella wiped her eyes with a tissue. "It *is* because of us, isn't it, Brett?"

"Probably. I told you it would only make things worse. Have you found out yet?"

"I go to the doctor tomorrow. Does Tris act odd around you?"

"It's not the same. How could it ever be?" He handed her the mug of tea. "This will make you feel better, dolly. Best tonic in the world."

"You're so sweet to me, Brett. Thank God I have you to talk to when Tris is. . .gone." Tears welled up in her eyes again.

"No more waterworks, please. You've already got me into trouble once with those tears of yours."

Bella smiled. "I wonder if I am?" she said, putting her hand on her stomach. "I don't feel any differently. Wouldn't I?"

"Perhaps it's better if you're not. I was a damn weakling to go along with it."

"Why did you, Brett?"

"Don't ask me! I'm saying no, no, a thousand times no, and the next thing I know. . .I'm a sucker for female tears, I guess. And you're very persuasive, Bella. I'm not made of stone."

"So now Tris can't look at either of us without thinking what went on."

"Right, poor bugger."

"I told him it wasn't great. I mean it was okay, but not. . ."

"I get your drift, dolly." He sat beside her on the bed. "Poor little gal. Looked like you'd been to a funeral after. Lucky I have a big ego."

"It was awful. I mean, it's not your fault, Brett. I'm sure you're the best, but it makes such a difference when you love someone."

"You're right about that one," he said, putting his arm about her shoulders.

"Have you ever been in love, Brett?"

"I dunno. Maybe once."

"It's so much the best thing there is," said Bella fervently.

"And the worst, eh?" He kissed her on the temple.

Lily came in the door and almost dropped the tray she was carrying.

Bella jumped up, scalding herself with the tea. "Lily!"

"I brought Brett his lunch."

"Bella and Tris had a row. I was giving her a shoulder to cry on," said Brett.

"Yes, he was. Thanks so, Brett. I'll run now." Bella hurried out.

Brett held his hands up. "Don't give me hell over this, Lily. That was the truth."

"I believe you. I heard them arguing earlier. You'd have to be an unimaginable cad to fool with her, wouldn't you?" She put the tray on the table. "Was the row serious?"

"Who knows? Anything could be to a teenage love affair." He got up and moved behind her, putting his hands on her waist.

"I'm so worried about them, Brett."

"They'll make it. Worry about us, Lil."

"I do—God, how I do!" she sighed leaning into him.

Damien and Rory McCalla left that afternoon, earlier than planned. "He can't take the peace and quiet," Damien explained.

"Keep your fingers crossed on the album, Lily. And be careful," he added, before climbing in their hired limousine.

"What?"

"Just keep your head. You've been damned fortunate to have Ian, never forget that."

"How did you know?" she gasped.

"Didn't, 'til now. Just projecting myself into your shoes. He's a very attractive boy, but no one will ever love you as my brother does." He kissed her cheek.

"Take care. The next time I see you, I intend to be a rich man."

Lily stood in the drive and stared at the car until it was out of sight.

✛ ✛ ✛

When Ian returned from London, he surprised everyone by announcing he'd entered Charlie in a race at Deauville the last week of August. "I assume no one is averse to a week of racing, the beach, French cuisine, a little roulette, and couture boutiques, eh, Lily? I'm really looking forward to racing Charlie on his home turf— show them what a champ they lost."

Before Brett left with Charlie a week prior to the race, Lily took him back to the doctor to have his leg cast off at last. They took the Jaguar he'd only been in a few times, so that he could drive it home.

After seeing the doctor, Brett got behind the wheel and

sighed. "The little things you never appreciate, like driving and bein' able to bend your knee."

He drove fast, with the top down as it was a warm August day. Looking at him smiling to himself as he skillfully maneuvered the Jag along the winding roads, Lily thought how he was born to have the wind in his hair. His injured right arm looked strong as ever now; he'd been doing push-ups and lifting weights to build it back. She closed her eyes and let the wind rip her hairdo to shreds. In spite of everything that had happened and the uncertain future ahead of them, she felt perfectly happy at the moment.

"Yeah, I'm going to miss this baby," said Brett. Lily felt that like a blow to the stomach. He hadn't mentioned leaving lately, though he still hadn't given Ian an answer about the trainer's position. She had been hoping that she'd persuaded him to change his mind.

A few miles from Innismere, Brett slowed down and turned off onto a narrow dirt lane. He flung her a smile. "Har, har, me beauty. I'm stealin' ye away to do God know's what with ye." He turned into a gated farm lane and stopped.

"Where in the world are we going, Brett?" she asked, examining her wind-battered reflection in the visor mirror.

He climbed out to open the gate. "Paddy's secret fishing place. That's how much the old bugger trusts me. I don't give a damn about the fish, but when he showed it to me, I filed it away for future use." He drove the Jag across a bumpy field and parked it under a tree.

"Aren't we trespassing?"

"Belongs to Paddy's thirty-fifth cousin by marriage, or some such. No one comes out here but the old Pad, and he's workin' today." He got a blanket out of the boot and led her down a path through the trees to a small, pebbly beach on the river.

Brett spread out the blanket and doffed his sweater. "Haven't been nude swimming since I was a kid. How 'bout you, Lil?"

"Never, unless you count when I was a baby at the beach."

"Time for some adult-rated naked swimming, Lil. Get your things off now." He finished undressing and walked to the edge of the pebble strand to dip his foot in the water. "Warm as a baby's bath." The scar on his shin was horrible. How my foolishness has marred his perfect body, she thought with intense regret.

"Get on with it—this isn't our first date, girl," he called in high spirits. Lily removed her bra and panties wishing the sun weren't so mercilessly bright.

He looked her up and down as if he were appraising a horse. "Turn about," he directed. She did so, feeling foolish and desperately sucking in her stomach.

He came up behind her and slid his hand down her flank. "Not bad for an old crone of forty."

"Who told you!" she exclaimed in dismay.

He laughed and cradled her breasts. "Tried to sneak it past me, didn't you?" She struggled in his arms, but he held her and forced her to kiss him.

"You bastard."

"Stop callin' me that. It's a mite offensive when you really are one, Lil." He scooped her up and limped out into the water, then dove under, taking her with him.

She came up sputtering. "It's f-freezing, you lying bastard!"

Laughing, he slipped his arm about her waist, and they floated together, his familiar body feeling strange and exciting in the cold, brown water. "I love you, Brett Fallon," she said through chattering teeth. He held her face in his hands, and she knew he would say it at last. He kissed her sweetly, and she clung to him, willing him to say the words.

"Let's get out before we get a cramp. My balls have shrunk to marbles."

They got out of the water and flung themselves on the blanket, wrapped up in it, and huddled together.

"Fucking country is never warm!" he shouted.

When they'd got the chill off, Brett spread the blanket in the sun. They let it warm their bare skins. Lily raised up on her elbows and looked at him. The sun shone full on his face revealing lines about his eyes, and gilding the tips of his thick lashes.

He smiled lazily up at her. "You are so incomparably beautiful, Brett," she said with a catch in her voice.

"Sure I am. Then why are you crying?"

"Because you've become so necessary to me—like the air, food. How shall I live without you?" He ran his rough hand along the curve of her body and kissed her. They made love for a long, slow, sweet time. Afterward they felt quite warm, the leaves overhead casting shifting, dappled patterns over their bodies.

"If only," Lily sighed.

"If only these rocks weren't so friggin' uncomfortable?" he murmured, eyes closed.

"If only we could be as free as this always." She tested her teeth on the warm, salty skin of his shoulder.

Brett sat up and flung a stone into the water. "We could be. We could go nude swimming, make love when we want, spend all night together in the same bed, and look people in the eye in the mornin'."

She saw from his expression that he was perfectly serious. "Oh, Brett."

"We can be free to do anything, Lily. All we have to do is leave this place where everything is impossible for us. As soon as Charlie's finished for the season, I'm gone. I'm askin' you to come with me, Lil."

She stared at him in stunned shock.

"I know I'm insane to ask you, but I have to get out of here, and I don't want to leave you behind. You say you love me, and I guess what I'm askin' you to do is prove that. I see that damn well floors you, so don't give me your answer now. Think about it. Because, with or without you, Lil, I'm goin' home."

She stroked his arm. "Why do you want me to come, Brett?"

"I told you—I'd miss you."

"Like you will the Jag? That's not good enough."

He gestured clumsily. "Whatever we have here just isn't ready to finish, and I don't see that it will be by October," he said gruffly. "I've gotten used to having you drive me mad, Lil," he added, trying to smile.

"Damn you, Brett Fallon. Can't you just say it?"

He looked away. "You want my blood, eh?"

"I want everything you have."

He looked back at her. "I love you, Lil. Are you happy now?"

"Don't whisper it!"

"I love you," he said firmly.

"Bloody scream it!"

"I love Lily!" he bellowed. A startled wagtail flew up above them.

She embraced him. "And I love you, you dear, stubborn, beautiful man!"

They didn't get home until teatime. Lily explained her wild hair saying they'd been caught in a shower with the top down. She ran upstairs to repair herself leaving Brett with Bella and Tristan.

"So, you're out from under wraps now?" said Tristan as Bella handed Brett a teacup.

"Right. Feels damn naked, too." Pulling up his pants' leg, he showed them his pale, scarred shin.

"Terrible!" said Bella.

"None too pretty. I'll have to avoid the beach at Deauville for fear of scaring the children."

"She's not pregnant," announced Tristan who was having a whiskey instead of tea.

Brett almost choked. This was the first mention Tris had made to him about what had happened in Galway. He glanced quickly at Bella. She looked frightened.

"I imagine she was mistaken about ovulation because of the temp brought on by a virus, or stage fright—according to Bella." He gave her a sardonic look.

Brett put down his cup. "I'd take that as a sign it wasn't meant to be, Tris. Damn good thing, too. I hope you've given up on this harebrained scheme, because I'm not getting sucked in again, that's certain."

Tristan shrugged nonchalantly. "Probably right. It's just not in the cards. Wouldn't be too pleasant studying with a squalling brat around anyway. Now Bella can get into modeling if she wishes."

"I don't care about that, but I do want to help you study. Maybe I can educate myself so you won't be stuck with a stupid wife who's only ever waited tables."

"You could enroll at University College, Bella. Get your own degree," suggested Brett.

"And you could mind your own business," said Tristan.

"Sorry. Thought just popped into my brain. If you two will excuse me, I'll be heading on back to the stable."

As soon as Brett had left, Bella said, "That was so rude, Tris!"

"Just because he's fucked you, it doesn't give him the right to plan your life."

"You made him fuck me!" cried Bella, running from the room.

Deauville

✪ ✪ ✪

DEAUVILLE AND ITS sister resort Trouville were in high gear in August as usual, the streets jammed with Rolls and Ferraris belonging to the European jet set in town for the races, gambling, and social life. At this time of year it was customary for the Parisian rich to desert the heat and bustle of the city and retire to their emerald-lawned villas on Normandy's Côte Fleurie. In a short few months, the resort area originally established as a retreat for Napoleon's court would be all but empty, battened against icy blasts off the English Channel as the rich moved on to St. Moritz and Gstaad for winter pleasures.

The D'Arcys usually traveled to Deauville in August or to Paris in September for the L'Arc de Triomphe race at Longchamp. This was the first time, however, that one of Ian's horses had been entered in the races. As always at Deauville, they stayed at the luxe hotel, the Normandy, situated on the seafront park next to the Casino. Their spacious, adjoining rooms on the top floor looked out to sea—Lily and Ian's suite, Tris and Bella's room, then Brett's, all interconnected by doors which could be left open if desired.

After checking in, Ian went out to the track to check on Brett and Charlie; Tristan and Bella donned bathing suits and headed for the beach.

Lily rang for the valet to press their clothes, then sat down and wrote a note to Brett on hotel stationary.

My darling Palamino,
    I've been counting every hour 'til I see you again. How time has crept like a snail the past six days! I do hope you haven't met any pretty jockeyettes, and that you're feeling quite rested and fit. I can't figure out how we'll do this, but we must be together as soon as possible. *J'ai faim et soif pour tu!*
    "The one who loves you."

Going through Tristan's room to Brett's, she slid the letter under his pillowcase.

Full of excited anticipation, Lily went down to explore the boutiques for sexy resort clothes, narrowly missing Brett who was getting his key from the concierge. Carrying his own small bag, he went up to his room, which was twice as big as his stable flat, and three times larger than the room he'd shared with Paddy at the track stable the past week. He would have been fine staying at the track, but Lily had insisted he come to the hotel. He sighed heavily, thinking how Ian was paying a bundle just so he could sleep with his wife.

All Brett's clothes were dirty—he supposed a place as posh as this would clean them, though. He opened the doors to the balcony and looked out over Les Planches, the mile-long boardwalk fronting the umbrella-dotted beach beyond. Deauville was hardly a sun worshippers' paradise; the skies were often gray and the Channel water chilly, but no one seemed to mind. Brett felt an intense wave of longing for the brilliant beaches of his homeland—for real sun, real sand, and above all, warmth.

He took a shower and lay down on the bed. Something scrunched beneath his head; he fished out Lily's note.

Damn, she shouldn't have taken a chance like that—it might have fallen into the wrong hands. Cheeky bitch! He smiled, thinking he was hungry and thirsty for her as well. He'd had about all he could take of the smell of manure, and male and horse sweat. Sniffing the note, he thought he detected her scent, a subtle yet stirring flower fragrance he'd dubbed "Eau de Lady." Only a beautiful, rich woman could smell like that.

It would be very tricky getting together here. It occurred to him, not for the first time, how adept she'd become at deceiving Ian. Was he a complete fool to love a woman who could flit between two men like that? But then, how could he fault her when he was just as guilty of deception as she? He should have known better, too.

What had become of Josie and little Sal? Of Harry? A family destroyed by him. That had been no marriage to begin with, though. Harry was always either working or out drinking with his mates, leaving poor, young Josie home alone with the baby. It had started with his feeling sorry for her and had ended up a desperate, constricting affair. "Sal called you 'dad' the other day," Josie had casually said to him. That had brought him to his senses. It just wasn't right to confuse the little girl like that. It had gotten too heavy anyway, with no place to go. He knew he didn't love Josie. It was just sex and compassion for him, but it obviously meant a damn lot more to her. He hoped she was all right now. Harry, too, even if the bugger had gone out of his way to be a prick to him since childhood.

Lily was the first woman he had been forced to admit he was truly in love with. Lily with her temper, her deceit, and the airs she could put on, all mixed with her warmth, her sensuality—the grace and class of her. That night at the Arab's party he remembered seeing Lily standing alone in a black dress, dripping with jewels. Never had he known true beauty and elegance 'til that moment. Brett tore up her note and flushed it down the toilet. *She also has bigger balls than I do, that was sure,* he thought.

He had drifted off to sleep when he was awakened by a call from her. Ian was in the shower, and she just had to hear his voice. How was his leg? Had he missed her? She wanted to come to him right then, but there wasn't time. They were dressing to go to Les Ambassadeurs in the Casino for dinner. Ian had told her to call him to say he was expected as well. "I have to go. The water's stopped," she whispered. "I adore you. Tell me you love me, Brett?" He hesitated. "Please!"

"I love you, Lily," he said, feeling like a performing dog. The line went suddenly dead, and he lay back on the bed, totally miserable.

Brett adjusted the tie Ian had loaned him and looked about at the vaulted ceiling, chandeliers, and gilt of the Casino's formal dining room. He felt like an intruder amidst such opulence and privilege.

Ian gravely studied the menu through his glasses. "Seafood is the best choice, of course. The sole's been caught only hours ago in the Channel. The langostines are always superb, also the piccaata de veau Normande—with cream and Calvados, their wonderful cider brandy. Super if you care for veal."

"Just order something you'd like for me, Ian," said Brett. "I'm ignorant when it comes to fancy food. I'm not really that hungry." Lily gave him a knowing look from across the table. She'd had her hair done in a sleek chignon and was wearing a simple black dress gussied up with a king's ransom in D'Arcy jewelry. She looked stunning, a fact she seemed quite well aware of. Brett wished she'd stop throwing him those sultry looks; they were making him hot under the collar.

After a memorable meal, they were having coffee laced with Calvados, when a small, plump man approached their table. Ian introduced the Comte de Lazarre to Brett.

"So this is the man who turns my lion of a colt into a lamb. What a mistake I make to let him go! I see him at the exercise this morning, and he looks *incroyable*. I congratulate you, Monsieur Fallon." Before leaving, the Comte invited them all to attend the polo matches the following day.

An orchestra began playing, and the diners started to file out on the dance floor. Ian stood up and held his arm out to Lily. "Shall we show them how to do an Irish jig, me love?"

"My, you are in a good mood tonight," she said, rising to join him.

Tristan looked across the table at Brett. "Shall we take turns jigging with Bella?"

"You two go ahead," said Brett.

Tristan shrugged. "I dunno, it is old fart music."

Bella caught his hand. "Come on. We can practice for when we're old farts."

Ian and Lily made a very handsome couple, thought Brett as he watched them on the dance floor. There was no way she was ever going to leave all this; he was a damn fool! He tossed back the last of his brandy.

Ian and Lily returned to the table; she held her hand out to Brett. "Your turn now," she said gaily.

"I'm not that good at walking yet."

"Be a sport and give me a breather," said Ian, patting him on the shoulder. Brett acquiesced, hating himself and Lily for this blatant charade. She led him out to the center of the crowded dance floor and floated into his arms like the graceful dancer she was.

"Well, are you having a good time?" she asked, smiling up at him.

"I'm in hell, I think."

"A very plush hell—don't be such a poop!"

He looked down into her eyes, and her gay smile fled. "How do you juggle the both of us, Lily? You're damned amazing."

"Somehow, I don't feel that's a compliment."

"It isn't. You can't have any heart to do this to him. . .to me. Playing us off while you bask in the desires of two men. You really enjoy this hell we're in, don't you, Lil?"

"What have I done to make you suddenly so angry with me, Brett?"

"Lily, you may be havin' a wonderful time, but I can't take it."

"I know this is difficult for you, darling. You feel shamed by your position, and so do I, but what other choice do we have? If the choice is shame or giving you up, I pick shame every time. If that makes me a terrible person, I don't care. I'd suffer any humiliation to be with you."

Her gray-blue eyes were so full of emotion, that he had to have her close to him. "Lily, there is another choice. When are you going to give me your decision?"

"Just a bit longer, my darling, please! I don't want to destroy him."

"You're destroying me."

Her little hand at the back of his neck—"I'll make it up to you tonight, my lover, I swear." Brett closed his eyes and felt tears. "Don't you want me to come to you?"

"Yes, I want you." He sighed, her perfume filling his brain. Over her shoulder he caught sight of Bella staring at him as she danced past with Tristan. He moved away from Lily's embrace.

"We'd best get back to the table," he said.

Ian had paid the bill and suggested they all have a

round of gaming before retiring. He gave everyone francs to play with; Brett politely refused him.

Brett quickly lost ten pounds at the crap table—the only game he was familiar with. He wandered over to the roulette wheel and placed chips on thirty and thirteen. He lost again. Deciding to observe a while and see if he could figure the thing out, he noticed a young woman at the end of the table, a large pile of chips in front of her. She was extremely attractive, her dead-straight, shoulder-length, black hair cut in a fringe. Round her neck she wore a long chain hung with a large, multifaceted, blue stone that spun with hypnotic brilliance when she leaned forward to place her bets; one of those blue stones that Lily wore all the time. The woman caught him studying her, and a flicker of interest lit her pale, blue, cat eyes—then back to business with the chips.

"Rien ne va plus," said the croupier, signaling the end of bet placing. He spun the ball on the wheel and the girl won.

Brett moved beside her. She smiled at him, totally aware of his interest. "I think I need lessons," he said.

"I'm a good teacher," she said with a French accent.

"I imagine you are. You know how to win, I see. Could you give me a few pointers?"

"Never bet *de single nombres. Très stupide. Regardez.*" She placed her chips on several intersections of four numbers, and on the word "impasse" and the color black.

"Rien ne va plus." The ball fell on black twenty, and the French girl collected more than she lost. Following her example on the next round, Brett won for the first time that evening. He turned to offer her a thank-you drink, but she was deep in conversation with a small, gray-haired fellow. She gathered her chips, tipped the croupier, and flung him a *"Bonne chance,"* before going

off arm in arm with the little man. Her father? Not likely, thought Brett.

Ian and Lily left for the hotel after a bit, but Brett hung around to watch Tristan lose his stash at baccarat. He returned to his hotel room after midnight, and was just climbing into bed when he heard a light rap at the door. It was Lily in her dressing gown.

She threw her arms about his neck. "Don't be angry with me. Ian's asleep and I can't bear it!" she pleaded, covering him with kisses. He lifted her off the floor in an embrace.

"Oh! I believe you are glad to see me." She laughed. He peeled off her robe—she was naked beneath. Without saying a word, he picked her up and carried her over to the bed. Moving over her, he kissed her so fiercely, he cut his lip. Lily gasped and arched under him, her nails raking his back.

Brett wiped the blood off his mouth and looked down at her. "You like it rough, don't you, Lil?"

"Just a little."

He sucked at her breast, then bit down. She groaned aloud with pleasure.

"Brett tie me!" she murmured in his ear.

"Do what?"

"Tie my hands to the bed rail. I've always fancied trying that."

"You're kidding."

"No. It's just a fantasy of mine. Use the sash to your dressing gown—something soft."

"Does he do shit like that to you?"

"No, I've never done it before, but I know it will be very exciting. Please!"

"It's already exciting."

"I know, darling, but can't we be a bit creative?" Her

eyes glinted with an excitement he'd never seen in them before.

Getting up, Brett jerked the sash off his dressing gown and found the silk tie Ian had loaned him. He trussed her wrists securely to the headboard. "Want your legs bound as well?" he asked, half sarcastically.

"Not for starters. That makes me a bit nervous." She tested her bonds and smiled up at him. "Come on, doesn't it excite you just a tiny bit?"

"Maybe if you were gagged," he said, stretching out over her, his weight supported by his arms. He teased her nipple with the tip of his tongue, and she moaned and twisted under him. Forcing her thighs open, he kissed and probed her, waiting 'til she reached orgasm to enter her. Lily cried out and fought her bonds as he stroked slowly. She grew so vocal, he worried that Tris and Bella next door might hear them.

"Where's that gag," he whispered, putting his hand over her mouth.

"It feels so heavenly, but I need to hold you. Untie me now," she gasped.

He withdrew and reached up to free one wrist.

"Yes! I can't stand not being able to touch you."

Brett flipped her over on her stomach and retied her hand.

"Darling?"

"Let's stick to the creative plan, Lil. I think I like bondage." He ran his tongue up her spine, lifted her hips and re-entered her. Keeping up a relentless, slow, steady rhythm, he brought her to climax again and again, 'til their bodies were slippery with sweat. Lily buried her face in the bedclothes to stifle her cries.

"Stop," she pleaded at last in a shaking voice. "Please, Brett."

He'd held it off so long that it seemed he couldn't now,

then suddenly it hit him with a rush so great he thought his brain would explode.

They lay joined together for some time until she asked in a small voice to be released. Undoing the slipknots, he rubbed the red stripes pressed into the flesh of her wrists. They held each other in silence 'til he had almost fallen asleep. He felt her move away from him, and a short time later heard the door close.

After spending the morning watching Charlie work out, Brett returned to the hotel to eat and clean up for the afternoon's polo matches. Wandering out to the terrace restaurant, he spied Tris and Bella lunching at a table under a gnarled apple tree. He wanted to avoid them, but Tristan waved, so he went over.

"Join us, old man," said Tris, pulling out a chair. Brett sat down reluctantly.

"You two look like natives already," he commented. Tris was a pinky tan, and Bella was covered with sunburn and freckles. Without makeup, her hair up in a flurry of red curls held by a tortoise barrette, she was breathtakingly lovely.

"Wouldn't mind dropping out and going to Tahiti," said Tristan, sipping a gin and tonic.

"Think what beautiful pictures you could take," said Bella.

"And you could learn to do that dance, the one that puts men into a state of paralytic rut. Bella'd be great at that—don't you think so, Brett?"

Brett just smiled noncommittally. He wasn't about to step in that trap.

"Tell Brett the exciting news," said Bella, eyes sparkling.

"You tell him. It's your idea."

"I took Tris's best photos by this gallery on Nassau

Street near Trinity, and they want to have a showing of them later this fall. Isn't it brilliant!"

"Good on ya, Tris. You take the best snaps I've ever seen, that's certain."

Tristan shrugged. "I'm not sure I want to do it."

"Tristan! That's what you were working toward all summer," Bella protested.

"I've lost interest, really. It will be a lot of effort, and to what point?"

"So that everyone will see how talented you are. All the trouble we went to walking all over Dublin, nearly getting mugged."

Tristan frowned at her. "I'm going to university in the fall. What's the point of an exhibit?"

"None, I guess," said Bella, looking away.

"Can't you keep your hand in with the camera while you're in school?" Brett couldn't resist asking.

"If you're going to be an artist, you have to pursue it full time. Everyone's been on my back to go to school, and I am, damn it!"

"Right you are," said Brett. Deciding he'd rather eat alone in the room, he excused himself. It was a shame he and Tris couldn't even have a chat anymore without getting into it.

Later in the shower, Brett considered calling Lily to see if she were in the room. He had a funny feeling about the night before, and needed to connect with her on a more normal basis. He decided against calling because if she were alone, she would only want to go to bed, and he had a strong mind to avoid that the rest of the trip. Somehow the sneaking around seemed even worse here than at Innismere. He'd spent the morning with Ian watching Charlie's exercise, his mind picturing Lily writhing in bound passion. If Ian had only known what a weird scene his necktie had been part of! A man could only get so low, and Brett reckoned he'd bottomed out.

He strolled out of the bath toweling his hair and found Bella sitting on the bed. "Damn, you could knock," he said, wrapping the towel about his waist.

"I did, but you were in the shower," she said with a nervous giggle.

"What do you want? Where's Tris?" he asked suspiciously.

"He's having a drink at the bar. I, uh, wanted to apologize for how rude he's been to you lately."

"I understand where he's coming from. It was the crazy notion to father your baby I couldn't follow. I'm glad he's come to his senses about that."

Bella stretched out her sunburnt legs and studied her painted toenails. "He hasn't, Brett."

"Hasn't what?"

"That's why I'm here. He thought it would be a good time to persuade you again." She looked at him apologetically.

"You're kiddin'."

"If only I were. It's that time, and he wants us to try again."

"I don't believe him! He lets you do the dirty work, because he hasn't the nerve to tell me himself. You can turn right around and tell him I think he's a coward as well as a madman. That there is absolutely no way I'm fallin' for that again."

"I told him that already, but he made me come. He's obsessed, Brett! I agreed because I knew there was no point in arguing with him, and I didn't know what else to do." Bella stood up and walked over to the open balcony door.

"I'm going down there then and set him straight once and for all," said Brett.

"No, please! He's tight, and he'll do something awful. He's drinking all the time now." Her chin quivered.

"Tears won't work this time, Bella. You know how odd he's been with me lately. I'm not getting further into the mire with him. Go on and get out of here before I get angry at you, too."

"Can't I just stay a bit? Just long enough to make him think we did it," she pleaded. "Then when I don't get pregnant this time, he'll have to give up on it."

"This family is too fucked to be believed! Go on now, Bella. I have to get dressed."

"I won't look," she said and ducked out on the balcony before he could object. She leaned out over the rail revealing too much of her curvy bottom in the shorts. Her legs were beyond perfect.

"Shit!" Brett sighed. He dressed quickly and got himself a beer. She looked grateful when he called her inside and offered her a drink, too.

"Have a seat," he said more kindly. It wasn't the poor kid's fault. Perched on the edge of a stuffed chair, pretending to drink the beer, Bella looked all of fourteen.

"Look, dolly, I don't mean to be rough on you. This isn't your fault, but I'm getting very pissed at Tris for the way he's using both of us. I intend to tell him so, too."

"Brett, he told me he saw some men doing coke in the Casino loo—that he could really feel it pulling him."

"He's using that to manipulate you, Bella. Tris is going to have to face it that you will just have to adopt a baby. Who cares if it has D'Arcy blood? A baby is a baby."

"I think he wants it to be D'Arcy for his dad. Even if they aren't close, I know Tris loves him very much."

"Ian would be the last man to go along with this, as straitlaced as he is."

"Brett, this is none of my business, but are you and Lily. . .you know?"

"What! How'd you get such an idea?"

"I saw the two of you dancing together last night. There was so much heat between you, I was afraid Tristan would notice. The way Lily is so curious about you, and she just hates Daphne. Are you?"

Brett took a long swig out of the beer bottle. "Now do you see why it's particularly wrong for me to go to bed with you, dolly? I'm in enough trouble as it is."

"Do you love her?"

"At times I do, then again I despise her at times. I can't stay away from her, though. That's why I'm leavin' come fall."

"How sad—how awful for all of you! Tris worships her. It would kill him if he knew."

"He dead sure wouldn't have sent you here had he known. Do you see how twisted it's all become?"

"Heavens yes! And here I am throwing myself at you every two minutes. I'm not very good at it, am I?"

Brett had to smile at that. "Come on, dolly. It's time you got back to your husband and told him nothing has or will ever happen between us. I suspect he'll only be relieved." He walked her to the door.

"I'll miss you, Brett, I really will," she said.

"I'll miss you, too, dolly. Now get out of here and no more of this bullshit, please."

Brett had just ordered himself a sandwich when the phone rang. It was Bella again, calling from the hotel bar. Tristan was dead drunk, and she needed his help.

Hurrying down, Brett found Tristan being assisted by two very polite security men, while Bella stood by wringing her hands.

"There he is gentlemen, my brother come to rescue me and save the family escutcheon from stain," said Tristan, barely able to stand.

"I'll take over, mates," said Brett, slipping an arm round Tristan to support him.

"Ah, yes, the real man of the family," babbled Tris. Bella looked close to tears.

They got him to the lift without making a scene. As the lift door closed on them, Tristan said, "Why the hell didn't anything happen? I've made a total ass of myself, and she tells me you won't touch her. You did it once—why not again? What could it matter now?"

"It matters. We'll talk about it when you're sober."

"Look at her. She's so friggin' sexy every man in England, Ireland, and France wants her but you, Brett. It's insulting. Don't you feel deeply insulted, my dove?" He leaned sloppily on Bella.

"Not in the slightest," she said, struggling to hold his weight.

They got him to the room and on the bed at last. He lay there while Bella removed his shoes. With difficulty he focused his eyes on Brett. "I dunno. It's not normal for a man to have sex only once in five months, and that at gunpoint I gather. You teased about this before, but I'm thinking maybe you do have the D'Arcy secret vice, Brett. Well, in Uncle Damien's case, not so secret."

"Tristan!" said Bella.

"Oops, didn't mean to let family skeletons out of the closet. It all started with the one who painted his eyes with kohl, favored lavender silks, and carried a muff—the old taint. Are you one of the tainted gang, Brett? Like Damien and Dad?"

"Tris, don't talk about your father like that," said Bella indignantly. "That's disgusting even if you are pissed."

Tristan laughed. "Ask Uncle Tony. He knows the truth about Dad. Only he wrapped himself about a tree and can't speak just now."

"Go on, Tris," said Brett gently. "You're letting your

imagination carry you away and saying things you'll regret later."

"Regret? I'll regret seeing them 'til the day I die. That was the end of Tristan the believing, the gullible idiot. That was when I woke to the truth that you can't trust anyone, not even your own father." He began crying. Brett and Bella exchanged helpless looks.

"Take care of him, dolly," said Brett, turning to leave.

On his way out, he heard Tristan pleading, "Lie down with me please, Bella. I didn't mean to embarrass you. Do you still love me?" He shut the door between the two rooms not wanting to hear anymore.

Brett was considerably disturbed by what Tristan had let slip in his drunkenness. It sounded as if the poor lad had stumbled in on Ian and a male lover. How unbelievably rum a scene! No wonder the boy was so fucked! Who was this Uncle Tony? Did Lily suspect that Ian might have other vices besides a weakness for prostitutes?

Unsurprisingly, Tris and Bella bowed out of the late afternoon polo matches, with the excuse they'd had too much sun. That left Brett, feeling very uncomfortable, sitting with Ian and Lily, and their hosts, the Comte and Comtesse de Lazarre. At the halftime intermission of the match, Ian and the Comte went off together to get a closer look at the ponies. Helene de Lazarre was talking with a friend, leaving Brett and Lily ostensibly alone together for the first time since the night before.

"So, how are you today, Lil?" asked Brett who felt oddly nervous at being with her.

"I feel divine, and you?"

"I've felt better."

"That was quite incredible last night," she whispered. "I don't know if I'd ever want a repeat, but it was. . .memorable!"

"Not getting into whips and chains for our next creative encounter then?"

She laughed. "Maybe very soft, velvet whips."

He grinned. "Like the Marquis de Sade scene, do you?"

"Only with you, Brett, never anyone else."

"Oh, thanks."

She leaned against him. "I feel that open with you. I've never felt that safe with anyone else."

Looking abruptly away from her hot gaze, he asked, "Is there an Uncle Tony in the family I don't know about?"

"Why do you ask?" He noted the sudden wariness in her voice.

"Tris mentioned him."

"He's not a relative. It's Tony Neville, Ian's great friend from school and Tris's godfather. Tony was tragically killed in a car crash this past fall. Perhaps you've noticed the photo in Ian's study of him and Tris with Tony and his son Julian at Eton graduation?"

Brett did recall that particular picture because it had reminded him of what a gulf lay between the world he knew and the one Tris had grown up in. Tony was the handsome, blond man in the photo then. Was he Ian's lover as well? The marital problems and Lily's sexual frustration—that all made sense now. Did she know about Tony? Damn, he wished that Tris had never let that bomb slip!

"Thinking about last night?" Lily whispered in his ear. He took her hand and pushed back her bracelet. No visible marks. "I thought they'd never go away," she murmured.

"I never want to do that again. That's not my idea of making love," he said gruffly.

"I agree. Last night was only play, and my feelings for you are much more serious than that. You move me like no one ever could," she said, stroking his hand under her program.

"Prove that then, Lily," he said, pulling his hand away.

Ian and the Frenchman returned to their seats, and they watched the rest of the match in which a French team defeated a British one, while most of the goals were scored by South American players. Afterward, the Comte invited them all to his daughter's birthday party later that night at the Casino.

Le Brummel Disco beneath the Casino D'été was decked festively with balloons and streamers in the de Lazarre's racing colors of blue and silver. "I feel a tad ancient," said Ian, looking about the room thronging with tanned, handsome French youths.

"I feel quite young myself tonight," said Lily who was looking nowhere near her real age in a short, navy dress which plunged down the back to a polka-dot bow above her derrière.

"I'll give it the old school try but don't plan on staying late," said Ian under his breath as they headed over to speak to their hosts and the plump birthday girl, Sophie.

Brett was standing by himself with a drink in hand when Lily joined him. They watched Bella dancing with Tristan who showed no sign of the hideous hangover he should by all rights be feeling—an amazing tribute to the recuperative powers of the young.

"I can't believe Bella wore that dress," said Lily. "So inappropriate. It was Ian's dead mother's."

"I'd say she brings a lot of life to it," said Brett.

"She's not wearing a bra. One can't in that type gown."

"I know. That's the best part of it."

Lily gave him a look.

"I don't suppose we'd better dance, but why don't you ask Helene? She finds you terribly attractive."

"Thanks, Lily, but I don't need you pimping for me," he replied, taking a big gulp of his strong whiskey and soda. *The sooner I get pissed, the better,* he thought.

"Come on—Philippe is a huge client of Ian's. You'd be helping him to be nice to her."

"Should I screw Helene, Lily? Would that really score points for Ian?"

"Please don't be churlish tonight, Brett. It was just a thought. Ian's told them who you really are, and you appear to fascinate her. See, she can't keep her eyes off you."

"Maybe I ought to take up being a professional ladies' man. Hang about places like this looking for rich, bored women. Think there's a future in that for me, Lil?"

"I imagine you'd be a great success. Now do behave yourself and please try to keep Tristan from drinking too much. He gets even more determined if I say anything."

"I'm not my friggin' half brother's keeper."

"God, you are surly tonight! I can see you've got the old quills out, but I'm not going to let you get to me. I'm in Deauville and in love, so fuck you." Her gaze traveled down his body. "See you later, handsome."

Bitch, he thought. Couldn't she see he wasn't in the mood? He felt a wave of sympathy for Ian as Lily dragged him out on the dance floor with the reveling young people. Tris and Bella were dancing erotically together. Damn if she had on any panties either in that siren of a dress, he thought. Her swinging breasts began to stir an answering call in his groin. Had he ever in his life imagined he'd be turning down a piece of work like that?

"Don't you dance, Monsieur Fallon?" asked a sultry voice behind him. Brett turned and gazed into the artfully madeup dark eyes of the Comtesse de Lazarre.

"No, ma'am. Not this fast anyway. I'm just a workin' class bloke who hasn't spent much time on the social circuit."

She laughed appreciatively. "*Compris.* This appears very frivolous to you, I think. You are a man of more serious pursuits, *n'est ce pas?*"

"I'm a man who doesn't belong here," he said, finishing off his drink.

"I believe you are a man more for the sports—the outdoor and the indoor. Am I correct?" Helene fitted a Gauloise into a holder and waited. Brett fumbled with his matches. She steadied his hand with hers as he lit the cigarette for her. Her nails were long and scarlet, her diamonds, eye-boggling.

The crowd began to clap as the Comte took the floor alone with his daughter and put on a game if inept show of disco dancing.

"Poor darling," said Helene in Brett's ear. "He looks the fool, but he is a good papa. I think Monsieur Fallon is *jamais,* never a fool."

"You'd be dead wrong. It's been my specialty all summer, Countess—is that what I call you?"

"Helene, *chéri.* Would you be so kind as to fetch me another champagne." It was not a question. Brett pushed through to the bar and got both of them a refill, his mind working on how to extricate himself.

"*Merci,*" she purred, batting her once no-doubt-very-lovely eyes at him. She was in her late forties he judged, but very well preserved and expensive looking. A diamond as big as a car lamp hung above an inviting bosom.

"Philippe is so angry that you have made something magnifique out of his bad horse he gave away. What is your secret for taming such a wild creature?"

"A lot of time and patience."

"*D'accord!* A man needs these with *les femmes sauvages* also, does he not? Time, patience, and gentle hands."

"If you say so, ma'am."

"Helene, if you please. And you are Brett? So short and curt—as you are. I like very much this name."

The singer was wailing a pop ballad now, and the gyrating on the floor had slowed to a more sensuous level. Helene put down her champagne and stubbed out the Gauloise. "It is not so frisky now, Brett. We dance, and you will show me this patience and good hands of yours." Brooking no refusal, she took his arm and led him out on the dance floor.

Brett saw Lily watching them, so he caught Helene about the waist and pulled her against him.

"Ah, so you do know how," she said with a suggestive laugh. She swayed voluptuously against him, sending up wafts of heady scent from her bosom.

Running her hand up his arm, she asked, "Do you like the sun and sea bathing, Brett?"

"Every Aussie does, unless he lives in Alice Springs— the desert."

"We have our yacht in the marina. Would you like to come sailing some afternoon when your work with the horses is finished?"

"All the D'Arcys you mean?"

"I mean you. I send my chauffeur to get you, and we spend a lovely afternoon in the sun. We have music, champagne or whiskey as you prefer, some wonderful food. Would you like?"

"And would the Comte be coming along with us, Helene?"

"Philippe would never miss the races or the polo." Her fingers toyed with the hair at the nape of his neck. "I am curious to see if you will look as beautiful in a bathing suit as my imagination expects."

"Usually swim naked, Helene."

Her eyes lit up, and she laughed. "Splendid! I do as well."

The song ended. "Thanks anyway for the invite, Countess, but there are several other ladies that need me, and first come, first served, you know." He took her arm and steered her over to her husband.

He was heading for the door when he ran into Ian and Lily. "Brett, just whom I was looking for. This music is making me jumpy as a cat, but Lily wants to stay on. Would you mind squiring her about and seeing that she gets back to the hotel safely?"

"Of course he doesn't mind," said Lily. She kissed Ian on the cheek, and he made his escape.

Smiling brilliantly at Brett, Lily slipped her arm through his. "I believe they call this a gift from the gods. At times I almost think Ian wants us to get together. Wipe that scowl off your face, my darling, because we are going to have a good time. Would you mind getting me another glass of wine?"

"Certainly, my precious—Gigolo Brett here at your service," he said, clicking his heels together. "Your every whim is my command." He found a bottle of wine, and the two of them sat down at an empty table.

"So, Gigolo Brett, did Helene manage to rape you on the dance floor?"

"Did her best. I should write home to my mates and tell them they're missing a great scam servicing the sex-starved, riches bitches. I'm nothin' but an ordinary bloke, and they act like I'm Mel Gibson. What the hell is it?"

"Perhaps they've never seen a real man before. I hope you're not lumping me in with Helene, Brett. That's not very flattering. Sex isn't all I want from you, and you know it."

"The hell I do! All I am is a young, hard cock to all of you. A friggin' stud like Charlie."

"How can you say that of me? It was you who wanted to keep it just fucking, remember?"

He shook his head and tossed back the wine.

"Brett, please don't be a bad boy, don't play the porcupine, not tonight, because we have the whole evening handed to us on a platter."

"I'm not going to touch you, Lil. Not while we're all in each other's pockets in this place."

"Don't be silly!" Under the table she slid her hand up his thigh. "You know what I really fancy doing tonight, darling? Making love out on the beach under the stars. I've never done that. I imagine the sand is a bother, but it sounds so exciting."

He grabbed her hand and squeezed hard. "Damn it, Lily, aren't you listening to me? This is real, not fantasy here. I'm talkin' you and I facin' life together to try and build something good. No more footsy behind Ian's back and rough sex for kicks—I'm talkin' real, damn it! I've had it with the bullshit and having to spend mornings with him, and me thinking I just fucked holy hell out of your wife, you poor, dumb bastard. And that dumb bastard is my friggin' *father!* I can't take this any longer." He stood up, knocking over her wine.

"Where are you going, Brett?"

"To tell Ian what's been going on. I won't live this nasty charade a moment longer."

She clutched at his arm. "Are you mad! It would destroy him if you did that."

"Well, it's destroying me living like this. We either break it to him now, or we forget the whole thing, Lily."

"Get hold of yourself, Brett! Now is not the time or the place. He's having a wonderful time and is so excited about Charlie. It would be too cruel. I don't know what he'd do."

"Lily, it's either him or me. We tell him and stop living a lie, or the two of us are finished." Brett knew he was tight and behaving irrationally, but it felt good to act the man for a change.

"Don't do this. Don't ruin everything, please. Brett," she pleaded.

"So it's him you choose? I always knew it would be. Good-bye then, Lily. You were a helluva great fuck!"

As Brett shouldered his way out of the disco in a blind rage, Tristan and Bella approached Lily. "Mother, where's Dad and Brett?"

"I appear to have been deserted. Not to worry—the night is still young. Excuse me." Tristan watched in surprise as his mother approached a handsome French boy and went out with him on the dance floor.

"Has Mum flipped out? Who the hell is he?"

"She wants to stay and dance, I guess," said Bella, leaning against him. "I can think of more fun things to do, can't you?"

He shook his head impatiently. "We can't leave Mother here alone. She's obviously had too much to drink." They watched as Lily and the French boy danced with wild abandon.

✚ ✚ ✚

Every morning at six, the strings of horses left the stable for the beach for their daily exercise gallops. That was the most enjoyable part of the Deauville trip for Brett, those beach gallops with the gulls keening overhead. Charlie seemed to thrive on running on the damp, packed sand, and he positively relished the alternate workouts up to his hocks in the surf, the water making an ideal conditioning resistance. The big, black colt had really come alive since he'd been on French soil; perhaps the sea winds reminded him of his early days on a Normandy stud farm.

Brett inhaled deeply. Get all the smoke, booze and smell of perfumed bitches out of my system, he thought. The sea air was just what the doctor ordered for his hangover this morning, though it did little to relieve the ball of nausea in his stomach that threatened every time he thought of the scene at the disco with Lily.

His malaise was so obvious that Ian clapped him on the shoulder and told him to take the rest of the day off at the beach. There must be a special rung in inferno where adulterers were tortured endlessly by the kindness of the men they had cuckolded, Brett reflected as he walked back to the hotel.

Deciding that the beach would be a good place to avoid Lily, Brett changed into his bathing togs and headed for the sand in front of the Normandy. He'd just relaxed and almost dozed off, when someone plopped down beside him. It was Tristan.

"Didn't mean to startle you, old man. What's this hanging about the beach like idle riffraff?"

"What d'ya want?"

"Want? Don't be paranoid. Thought I'd just try and make up for being an ass lately. Bella insists I have been, and I'm sure she's right. Bella has an infallible sense of rightness."

"Yeah?"

"So, I'm sorry I've been beastly to you. Want to thank you for helping me out of the bar yesterday. Might have been an international incident, but for you."

"Keep your head out of the bottle—I'm tired of babysitting you."

"My, you are in a mood. What's bothering you?"

"Bit of a head this morning. I'll be glad when this friggin' race is over."

"Don't tell me you're not having fun, Brett? At this moment we are in the center of the *riche* universe. It's something to remember when you're back counting kangaroos. Bella tells me you're leaving at the end of the season."

"Maybe sooner, the way I'm feelin' now."

"I'm sorry—truly. Things have got rather skewed between us lately, and I regret that. You're someone I admire as a real man, you know?"

"Thought I was a fairy?"

Tristan laughed. "I was totally out of it. Bella told me I said rot about Dad, too. Just having you on. We drunks have a warped sense of humor."

"You're an acknowledged drunk now, are you?"

"I seem to qualify. I've alienated my wife, my brother—have generally repulsed everyone. The title seems to fit."

"Then stop drinking so much, you damn fool! I've no sympathy with you. You've got the greatest little girl in the world, and every other damn thing, except you can't have kids. That's bloody crook, but you still have it better than any other bloke I ever met. Keep it up, and maybe, if you try very hard, you can blow it all."

"I suppose I seem a whiny, little brat to you, eh? Throwing a tantrum because there's one thing on earth I can't have."

"Something like that. Look, I know you've had some bitter blows, Tris. Setbacks anyone might have a problem dealin' with, but Jesus, why let it muck you about? Just cut your losses and count the good. Here you are one of the privileged few on the planet, and you don't even appreciate it. You have a family that cares about you, and a girl who'd do anything for you. That's fuckin' rare! You should be kissin' the ground Bella walks on. If you've got a girl like that, what does the rest matter? Not a damn whit."

"You're really rather a romantic, aren't you, Brett? The last chap I'd ever expect to be one. Must be that Celtic blood in your veins."

"It's just knowin' a good thing when you've got it."

Tristan clapped him on the back. "I know you're absolutely right, bro. Now that we're friends again, come have lunch and a drink with us to seal it." He motioned to Bella sunning herself down the beach, and she came running over, turning heads in her old, blue, one-piece suit despite the abundance of bikini clad and topless women about them.

After insisting that she cover up with a T-shirt and a scarf about her hips Tahitian style, Tristan led the way down the boardwalk to Ciro's, Deauville's most popular lunch spot.

They were early enough to beat the crowd and get a table on the terrace. Tristan ordered shrimp, crab cocktail, and salad with a bottle of muscadet from neighboring Brittany to wash it down.

At a nearby table was the black-haired girl from the Casino, again with the old man. She smiled at Brett, and he lifted his wineglass to her.

"Who is that?" asked Tristan.

"My roulette teacher."

"She looks as if she might instruct one in more than roulette."

"She's gorgeous," said Bella, popping a shrimp into her mouth.

"Oh, hell," said Tristan. They followed his gaze—it was Lily with the dark French boy on her arm.

She paused dramatically at their table. "Darlings!" she said, giving Tristan a peck on the cheek. "Don't get up, Brett. I'd like you all to meet my friend Jean Paul."

The boy smiled and nodded. "My English, it sucks."

Lily patted his tanned arm. "See you later. We have a table reserved." With open mouths, they watched her leave.

"His Eengleesh, eet sucks! Has Mother lost her senses—he's barely older than I am! Had to drag her away from him last night by the hair before she made a fool of herself in front of Dad's friends," said Tristan irritably.

"They're just having lunch," said Bella, carefully avoiding Brett's eyes.

"It's in damn poor taste," Tristan went on. "You don't suppose she's decided to have a mid-life crisis fling right here under Dad's nose, do you?"

Bella looked at Brett, then quickly away. "It's just lunch, not a fling, Tris."

"Look the way she's laughing and flirting with him. You'd think she'd be a bit more discreet. Mother's French vocabulary is limited to *jete*, *battement* and *pot au feu*. How do they communicate? Don't answer that."

Brett pushed his chair back. "I'm going back to the room to clean up. Should be some good races this afternoon. See you two there." He got out his money to pay, but Tristan insisted that it was on him. He walked past Lily's table without looking at her. *Fuck her*, he thought. Don't let her get to you like she's aiming to do with that kid.

That afternoon at the races at the Hippodrome de la Touques, Lily was conspicuously absent.

"Where the hell is she?" said Ian, checking his watch. "Did anyone see her earlier?"

Neither Brett, Bella, nor Tristan spoke up.

"Probably running up the charges at the boutiques," said Ian, looking across for him.

Everyone lost money on the races but Brett who abstained from betting. He told them he was saving his money to put it on the one race where he was sure of the outcome.

"I wish I had your faith," said Ian.

Charlie was entered in the most important race of the Deauville meet, the Prix Jacques le Marois. In the mile race he would be running against the stiffest competition of his life with three-year-olds owned by Rothschild, the Aga Khan, and Niarchos. Brett based his confidence in Charlie on the fact that he had started late in the season and was now at his peak, while other horses racing since March were now beginning to show the strain. His brilliant response to training on the beach had increased Brett's hopes even more so.

After the races, they returned to the Normandy to change for dinner. Brett thought of canceling, but he didn't want to give Lily the satisfaction of knowing she'd hurt him.

He was ready too early as usual, so he went down to the bar for a drink. The minute he walked in, he saw the black-haired girl sitting alone at the end of the bar. He ordered a beer. The girl smiled at him and took out a Paris Opal, an invitation if he'd ever seen one.

Moving down next to her, he lit the cigar. She inhaled deeply. "Allo," she said, looking him over with her Siamese cat eyes. She was wearing a very short, black dress and very long, black gloves that set off her pale, translucent skin to perfection.

She exhaled a long stream of blue smoke through cherry lips. "How is the big gambler from underneath?"

He laughed. "I broke even the other night, thanks to you. I'm hardly a high roller. So where is your father tonight?"

"*Henri est malade.* He had a bad *moule, pauvre cher.* He's in the room now, *trés nauseux.*" She smiled as if this were good news.

"*Quel domage.*" He smiled back at her. "Is he your husband?"

"*Non.* 'E is just Henri—*mon ami.*"

"Would your *ami* care if I bought you a drink?"

"*Mais oui!* But I do not care," she said with a swing of her black-silk hair. Brett ordered her another Bellini.

"I think you must have a horse, *non?*"

"I did shower. How could you tell?"

"Henri take me many times to the races. I have become a student of horsemen. Most are not so pretty as you. What is you horse name?"

"Charlemagne. He's in the Jacques le Marois. He's going to win it. I'd bet on him if I were you, because he's an unknown here—only raced in Ireland, and the odds should be very good."

"*Merci bien* for this tip."

"I owe it to you for the roulette tips. What is your name?"

"Angelique Barré, *et vous?*"

"Brett Fallon. You staying here at the hotel, Angie?" She made a face. "Henri take his wife to Normandy. 'E take me to Royal. *Degouté, non?* Normandy is much more good."

"So why are you here tonight?"

"I think I may see you. I think you need more *leçons dans les jeux.*"

"Very kind of you. I can use all the lessons I can get." They were joined by Ian. Brett introduced him.

"Do you follow the horses, then, Angelique?" asked Ian.

"*Oui.* I love the excitement. I am lucky *aussi.* You must be the owner of the famous horse Charlemagne, *non?*"

"She's a student of horsemen," Brett explained.

"I have a feeling Mademoiselle Barré is a student of men, period," said Ian with a smile. "I do own Charlemagne, but Brett is the man who's worked the magic on him. He's the secret of my success. Talks French to the horses, puts them in the mood to run."

"Why you make me talk my bad English then?" she asked with a pretty pout.

"Charlie's more polite about pretending to understand me than most of the French I've tried to *parlez* with," said Brett. They smiled at each other.

"Here's Lily at last," said Ian, spotting her at the bar entrance. "I need a word with you in private before I go, Brett. *Enchanté*, Angelique."

He took Brett out of earshot and said, "The girl's a professional, you know."

"No way. She's no virgin, but I've never seen a hooker look that good," said Brett.

"She is one, believe me. Very high class, of course. They hang about the luxe hotels when the race crowd's in town." He stuffed some bills in Brett's pocket. "Here, the treat's on me. You should be about due. Be sure and protect yourself." He was off to take Lily in to dinner before Brett could refuse.

Returning to the girl, he said, "So, Angie, what are your plans for this evening? Will you be nursing poor Henri?"

She shook her head vigorously. "I am terrible nurse."

"Good. *Voulez-vous diner avec moi ce soir?*"

"*Pardon?*"

"Must be the Aussie spin I put on it. Would you like to have a bit of tucker—dinner with me?"

"The two of us. . .alone, *mais oui.*"

"Excellent idea. It's privacy you're after. We could go to my room and order up something, eh? What are you in the mood for?"

She blew a wisp of fringe out of her eyes. *"Des huitres et du champagne."*

"A well-balanced diet. I hear the oysters are very expensive here. Any idea how much they'd cost, Angie?"

"A hundred pounds should cover it," she said crisply.

"Those are some oysters!"

"Ze best in Deauville." She ran her gloved fingers over his hand on the bar. "You get you money's worth, Brett, I promise."

"I wouldn't doubt that for a minute. Shall we go then. I'm very hungry."

As soon as the lift door closed on them, she ran her hand up his arm. *"Dur, comme le roc. J'aime les hommes forts."* When he kissed her, she rubbed her thigh between his legs.

"Comme le roc!" She laughed. "I think I enjoy this *diner."*

He kissed her throat, and cupped her behind in his hands to pull her against him. *"Mon Dieu."* She sighed. Pressing her against the wall of the lift, he palmed her breasts.

She grabbed him hard. *"Maintenant!* Lock ze door."

"Keep your skirt on. Is it cheaper in the lift?"

She smoothed her dress down. *"Tu es juif."*

Once inside his room, Angie kicked off her high heels and looked about curiously. "Much better than le Royal," she pronounced. "You order the meal, and I go do my face." She headed for the bathroom.

Brett removed his jacket and Ian's overworked tie and pushed the button for the waiter. He arrived almost at once and took the order.

Angie reappeared wearing the terry robe provided by the hotel, the long black gloves still in place. Standing in front of him, she doffed the robe and stood there in black bra, stockings and garter belt—no panties. She held her arms out and turned like a model for his inspection. "You like?"

"I like," said Brett, eyeing the blue bruise on her white rump.

Smiling, she walked out on the balcony. He followed and brushed her gleaming hair aside to kiss her neck. "Do you like the sea, Angie?"

"J'aime la mer, les étoiles." She held her thin arms up to the stars. He cupped her breasts which were as small as an adolescent girl's. She turned to kiss him, then began unbuttoning his shirt.

"You make me enjoy myself, *vraiment,* and I do it for seventy-five, Brett."

"I get the picture. If I make you truly enjoy yourself, say more than once, would it decrease accordingly?"

"Chiche!" Her eyes lit up as she ran her hands through his chest hair. Removing her bra, she rubbed her small breasts against him sensuously.

"I think there's time before the champagne arrives," said Brett, leading her back inside and over to the neatly turned-down bed. They fell across it.

"Chocolat!" exclaimed Angelique, pointing to the candy left on the pillow by the maid. Brett put one in her mouth.

"Give me some." He kissed her. She laughed as he licked the chocolate off her lips.

He sucked her mauve nipples, and her laughter turned to moans. "Tell me Angie, have you got any uh—French letters on you? Safes? Les rubbers? Mum never taught me the word for that."

"Attendez!" Hopping out of bed, she found her purse and held up a handful in various colors and textures.

"I'll let you choose. As long as it does the job." She opened a packet and expertly placed an ordinary, flesh-colored one on him. The woman obviously knew her men.

"Don't you take off the gloves then?"

"You no like?" She stroked his testicles with her black satin fingers.

"You've got a point there, Angie. Come here." He rolled her over on the bed.

There was a knock on the door leading to Tristan's room—they froze. "Who is this?" said Angie.

"They'll go away," said Brett hopefully.

The door opened. "Oh gosh, I'm sorry!" said Bella, standing there in her dressing gown.

Brett pulled the covers over them. "What is it—something wrong?"

"I saw your light was on, and I needed to talk. I didn't realize. . ." sputtered Bella.

"Who is this?" demanded Angelique.

"Just a friend," said Brett, sitting up. "Is there a problem with Tris, Bella?"

"He's asleep," she said, backing away.

"What did you need to talk about?"

"I'll tell you tomorrow, Brett. Please excuse me."

"Can it wait?"

"Sure—it's okay."

"Something's up, I can tell by the way you're acting."

"*Merde!*" said Angelique, sitting up in the bed.

"Don't go, dolly," said Brett, getting up and retrieving the robe from the floor.

"*A trois is plus cher,*" said Angelique, flipping her hair back.

"Look, Angie, could we take a raincheck? This is family."

She got up, flounced into the bathroom, and slammed the door.

"Brett, I'm so embarrassed. Wasn't that the pretty girl from the restaurant?" said Bella.

"It's all right, dolly. You're more important," he said, putting the money Ian had given him in the girl's purse.

Angelique charged out of the bathroom dressed; he handed her the purse and her bra. "Another time, eh, Angie?"

"*Quel* disappointment!" she said and hurried out the door, almost knocking over the waiter.

"Care for some oysters and champagne, Bella?" said Brett, getting out some francs for the waiter who averted his eyes discreetly as if this sort of ménage was commonplace—which it probably was.

When he had left, Brett poured them both a glass and downed an oyster off the half shell. "She was a prostitute. I've never paid for it in my life, so why start now?"

"I thought she was a model or an actress, she was so glamorous," said Bella who was looking like quite the nymphet in bare feet and scrubbed face.

"The gloves are a tony touch," said Brett with a grin. He tossed back the champagne. "So, tell me what's wrong now, dolly."

"I wanted to warn you that Tris still hasn't given up."

"What? It doesn't matter, because I won't do it, and that puts an end to the matter." He poured himself another glass of champagne. "Mmm. The frogs know how to make this stuff. Cheers, Bella. Have some oysters."

"No thanks. When I first came in here, I thought it was Lily you were with. Scared me to death!"

"She and I have ended it, so you don't have to worry about that happening." He sat heavily on the bed and finished his champagne.

"I'm sorry. . .I suppose. Maybe it's best though. It would hurt Tris and Ian so badly if they ever found out."

"Yeah, and I'm sick and tired of feelin' the bastard in every sense of the word."

"She was making you jealous with that French boy, wasn't she?"

"I imagine that was her aim. Pretty ridiculous at our age, eh? Ian gave me the money for that girl. He thought I was in desperate need. Some ugly irony, right?" Brett put his empty glass on the table and leaned his head wearily in his hand.

"Do you still love her?"

"Yeah, I do. No matter what a bitch she can be. Lily forced me to love her, and now I have to learn how not to."

Bella reached out to stroke his hair sympathetically. "I'm sorry you were hurt, Brett. We're both in a rotten mess, aren't we?"

"I'll say. I'm no saint, but bein' in this family has got me stooping lower than I ever thought I would. Look what you have to deal with, kid, just because you fell in love with Tris."

Bella leaned down and kissed his forehead. "It's not fair, is it?"

"I like the hell outta you, Bella. That's one thing clear to me in the midst of this muddle." She stroked him soothingly, her hands feeling cool on his skin. "She'll be right, Bella. You're a great girl, and he loves you like crazy. You'll make it."

"I hope so. If only it would hurry and get better," she said wistfully. He could feel the heat and softness of her breast against his cheek as her fingers stroked through his hair.

"I wish you didn't have to leave, Brett."

"I can't wait to get on the other side of the world from the friggin' D'Arcys. I only wish I didn't have to stay 'til

October." The nearness to her unfettered, lush breasts was beginning to affect him, Brett realized.

He frowned and grabbed her wrist. "What the hell are you doin'? You're working' on me again, aren't you?"

"He's never going to give up, Brett. I know him. Please just once. . ."

"Bloody, fuckin' hell, I give up then. Come on, let's do it!" He pulled her roughly down in the bed with him and jerked up her nightgown. Pushing forcefully inside her, he moved until he climaxed.

"There, are you satisfied? Is Tris happy?" he snarled in her frightened face. She turned her head away, and a tear trickled down her cheek. "Shit!" groaned Brett, rolling away. He lay there breathing heavily while she sobbed softly.

He pulled down her nightgown. "Bella, I'm sorry. Did I hurt you? Don't cry, please!" She shook silently. He cradled his body around hers. "That's been building up in me, and I took it out on you, little girl. It seems like nobody gives a damn about anything but what I can do for them in bed. Doesn't anybody give a shit about me?"

"I do—I care about you, Brett." Bella sniffed. He held her tightly, burying his face in her hair.

✛ ✛ ✛

Ian and Lily were breakfasting when Brett entered the hotel dining room. Ian waved him over. "You look in a fine mood today," he said with a twinkle.

"Feel bonzer," said Brett as he studied the menu and ignored Lily. In honor of their guests from across the Channel, the hotel featured a big, English breakfast. Brett ordered the works.

"Never got around to dinner last night," he explained. Lily gave him a lethal look over her teacup.

"Think I'll come watch the exercise gallops today," she

said. "I've done all the shopping I care to. Everything is so overpriced here. It gets tiresome spending so much time by oneself."

"You looked very entertained at Ciro's yesterday," said Brett.

"Who were you dining with?" asked Ian over the French racing papers.

"A new friend. Speaking of new friends, you could get a disease from the sort of girl you were with last night, Brett."

"I know, but some things are worth the risk," he replied with a smile.

"Lily, please let Brett lead his own life," said Ian peering over his glasses at her.

"Just a bit of stepmotherly concern," she said, smiling back at Brett.

"Try minding your own stepmotherly business," he retorted.

Lily flushed. "I find it incredible in this day and age with AIDS out there, that men would be so desperate as to pay for sex."

"Aren't we the wowser, Lily. Would you feel better if I told you she paid me?"

"Enough!" said Ian, tossing down his paper. "I thought you two had called off the hostilities. Lily, what Brett does is absolutely none of your business."

"Of course you approve of what he did. You probably paid the girl for him," she fumed.

Breakfast was finished in a tense silence.

She was too angry to accompany them to the exercise after all, and Brett did not see her for the rest of the day. He watched the afternoon's races from the lads' stands with the jockeys and stablehands, then went out with Paddy and the Rafferty brothers to an inexpensive bistro in Trouville for dinner before retiring early to his room.

He was awakened in the night by Bella crawling into bed with him. "We have to make dead sure this time," she said, doffing her gown with an air of returning to the salt mines. Brett didn't argue. He was tired of turning down a gift like that. This time, though, he didn't let her shut him out when they made love. She wept afterward, as he kissed her face.

"It's not betraying him to take a little pleasure out of it, dolly. You owe it to me so I don't feel like I'm murderin' you. If we have to do this crazed thing, we might as well enjoy it, right?" She turned her tear-stained face away. Bella was not a demure, actressy crier tuned to the effect she was having, as was Lily. Bella wept with her whole body, her mouth distorted into a mask of Greek tragedy, her nose running, like a twelve-year-old whose puppy had been run over by a bus. It was demoralizing, and made Brett feel guilty and miserable.

Awkwardly, he tried to soothe her. "Does he know you're here with me?"

She shook her head. "I promised him I'd do it, but he doesn't know when. I wait 'til he's asleep so he doesn't have to get pissed worrying about it." Sitting up, she wiped her eyes and fished about for her nightgown.

"I'd best be getting back before he wakes up and misses me."

Brett caught her hand and kissed it. "You're a good girl, Bella." She smiled sadly at him and left the way she'd come. He stared at the ceiling and felt like a child abuser.

The day of the Prix Jacques le Marois, skies were threatening all morning, and by post time, it was starting to rain. Rafferty had difficulty getting Charlie in the starting gate—a crack of thunder caused the colt to rear and plunge. The gates flew open, and Charlie came out last— off to a poor start in the mile race.

It was pouring rain now. Ian watched anxiously through his glasses as Rafferty caught the colt up to the field. The track was level, which experience said favored a good galloper who could come from behind—a position they were definitely in now. At the half-mile mark, Ian said, "Move, damn you!" As if he had heard, Charlie began to reel in the distance between himself and the two lead horses. As they galloped down the finishing straight, he passed the second horse on the rail, and began to pull even with the lead. It was raining so furiously now that it was difficult to see what was happening. There was another loud lightning strike, and Ian saw Charlie fling up his head, then falter. He crossed the finish a half length behind the winner.

Ian sighed and lowered his glasses. Lily who'd been clutching his arm throughout the race said, "So close— I can't bear it!"

"Second in a field like this is a victory," Ian forced himself to say. Had the thunder caused the colt to lose it at the last minute like that? He was not normally a jittery animal, thought Ian.

"Fuck second—I wanted to win!" said Lily. She looked at him, and they both laughed. He put his arm about her and kissed her brow. "I believe you've been hanging about with the stable crowd, Lily." He excused himself to go talk to the jockey and see what had happened.

Ian found Rafferty and the rider of the winner in a loud altercation, the latter with blood mixed in with the mud on his face.

"What's going on here?" said Ian, grabbing Tommy by the arm.

"Bloody little prick hit Charlie in the face with his whip! We were robbed—Charlie won that race!" sputtered the Irish boy.

The French rider shouted a stream of Gallic oaths, gesturing hysterically at his bloodied nose. Stewards were approaching, drawn by the tumult.

"You're saying he deliberately belted Charlie—coming down to the wire, was it?" said Ian to Rafferty.

"Yes, sir. Charlie had him at the end. He still had plenty to go, and his nag was fadin'. We was just about to pass him when he reaches over and whacks Charlie across the head. It was terrible vicious! You should see his eye, Sir Ian, if you canna believe me. If Charlie's not blinded, I'll be that surprised!"

"Where's Brett?"

"Him and Paddy took Charlie off to the track vet, sir."

Ian signaled to a steward, told him of the accusation, and they all headed for the stable to check on the colt's condition. They found that indeed Charlie had a swollen, weeping, left eye, treated by the vet with an antibiotic dressing. The doctor voiced his opinion that it was inflicted by a direct, not a glancing blow, and was likely to have been intentional; that it would cause scarring and possible blindness.

"Damn French jockeys are notoriously dirty, but we're not going to let them get away with this," said Ian grimly.

"According to Rafferty, he was bumping him, and when that didn't scare them, he laid for Charlie with his stick," said Brett.

"I knew something was amiss when he threw his head up and stumbled, but the visibility was so poor. I want the tape of the race reviewed," Ian said to the French steward.

✦ ✦ ✦

That night there was a celebration dinner after all for the D'Arcys; everyone but Brett gathered at Le Grill du Casino to toast Charlie's being declared the winner after the inquiry had been mounted. Despite the deluge, the tape clearly revealed the French jockey raising his whip, then Charlie flinging his head up in pain and falling back. The jockey had tried to say it had been an accidental slip, when he'd been whipping his own mount, but the German rider who came in third supported Rafferty's contention that it was intentional. A vote of the stewards had disqualified the French horse, and Charlie was in. To appease the French race goers, Rafferty was suspended from racing in France for the remainder of the season for fighting.

Around ten, Lily excused herself pleading exhaustion. Changing into her dressing gown, she went through her son's room and knocked on Brett's door.

"Yeah?" he said, seeming surprised to see her.

"I was worried about you. I couldn't go to sleep without telling you how sorry I am about Charlie. How was he when you left the stable?"

"How would you be if someone slashed you across the cornea?" He looked dead tired and in no mood for socializing; he made no move to invite her in.

"Everyone missed you at dinner. You should have been the guest of honor after all."

"I didn't feel like celebrating."

"I know. Everyone was subdued. Look, could I come in? Tristan may be back any minute." He stepped aside to let her in, then returned to packing his bag.

"Will Charlie be able to race again?" she asked timidly, feeling as if he were an unfriendly stranger.

"No way. He may well be blind—I'm feelin' pretty rum about it." He threw a shirt in his case and closed it.

"At least you won some money, didn't you? Ten to one odds—how much did you bet?" she asked, aching to break through the wall he'd erected between them.

"Everything. All my salary I've saved, and the money

I've won on him through the season. Not a bad little stash."

"Wonderful! What a risk to bet everything."

"I did hold back enough for a one-way ticket to Sydney." He almost smiled. "Just called Quantas as a matter of fact and made a reservation on a flight out of Manchester next Saturday."

Lily stared at him in dismay. "Saturday? Brett, you can't! I can't bear for it to end like this between us."

"Now that Charlie's career is finished, there's no point in my staying on. I told you I was leavin'."

"You're tearing my heart!"

"You made your choice, Lil. I don't blame you, really. What woman in her right mind would leave all that you have for a loser like me?"

"You're not a loser. You don't understand that it's not the things I can't leave—it's Ian and Tristan. How could I do that to them?"

"Right. I understand you." He lifted his bag off the bed and put it on the floor. "I appreciate that you were worried about me, but I'm tired, so if you'll excuse me. . . ."

She put her hand on his arm; he flinched. "Brett, I won't let it end like this."

"Don't. Let's don't prolong the agony, okay, Lil? I've had enough. Enough of wanting what I have no right to and never had a chance at in the first place. Where is Ian, by the way? Did you sneak off from him while he was asleep?"

"He stayed at the Casino. I imagine that about now he's struck up an intimate chat with your pretty prostitute. She was there by herself, and I could feel him wanting her. I expect you gave her an excellent recommendation."

"I'm sure she's damn good, but I wouldn't know about it. Whores just aren't my thing, Lil."

"You didn't?. . ." He shook his head. "I never went to bed with Jean Paul either—I just wanted you to think so. Heavens, he was Tristan's age. I felt like his mother. Casual affairs with young boys aren't my thing."

He smiled sadly. "So, we were just torturin' each other, eh? Love is a stupid condition. That's why I've avoided it for so long."

"I'm sorry for what I've put you through, Brett. All I ever wanted was to love you, and have you love me. It seemed so pure and simple a desire," she said emotionally. His expression softened, and she moved into his arms.

"I wish to hell I didn't love you, Lil," he said. She lifted her mouth to his; the flash of desire was instantaneous between them. Later, lying in each other's arms, neither could even remember undressing or moving to the bed.

Looking down into her eyes, Brett said, "He can't make you feel like this. I know he can't." She tearfully nodded her agreement.

"Come with me then, Lil. I can't give you riches, but I can give you this every night. That's not nothin'!"

She brushed her lips across his cheek. "It's the most precious thing, my love."

"I won't have much to offer you at first. I'll have to hire on somewhere, but I aim to have my own operation in time. It's a fair go I'll be a success, because I'm a hard worker, and I know what I'm doing. I'll never be able to give you Innismere, darlin', but we could have a decent life. . .and great nights! What d'ya say, Lil?"

She ran her hands through his springy hair. "Brett, I've never told you this, but I could never give you children. There were complications with Tristan's birth."

"No matter. I have a kid. Tomi's his name, and I want him to be with me. You'd be a lot better mother to him than his own, I wager."

"A boy? Tomi? I thought. . .Well, I just picture you having a little girl, somehow."

"So will you do it—come with me, Lil?"

She closed her eyes. "I'd come in an instant, if it weren't for Ian. He does love me, even if I don't deserve it. Once I thought I knew him as well as I knew myself, but lately, I don't know if I do at all. Such hidden, dark corners in him. I'm afraid of what he might do it. . .And poor Tristan is already so confused and more fragile than I ever supposed. You are asking me to wound, to give up these people I love, Brett, not just things."

Brett turned on his back and stared at the ceiling. "I know I'm askin' everything of you, Lil. It won't be an easy choice, but it's a choice you're going to have to make. I am leavin' Saturday come hell or high water. By the way, I made the reservations for two—I'm a gambler to the end."

Lily put her arms around him and nestled close, feeling as though her heart would break. How could anyone make such a terrible choice? She couldn't even think of that now. She knew she should get back to her room on the chance Ian had not connected with the French girl, but she couldn't bear to leave Brett. Just a few moments longer—time with him was too precious.

It had been an exhausting day. They both drifted off to sleep.

Brett felt something warm and perfumed slide beside him. "Mmm," he sighed, half awake. His hand closed around a generous mound of breast—his eyes flicked open.

Wiggling her bottom against him, Bella said, "Hurry, Brett. I drank champagne, and I'm so sleepy."

On the other side of him, Lily sat bolt upright. "What is going on?" she asked in a quavering voice.

Bella jumped out of bed with a little shriek, grabbed her nightgown off the floor, and held it in front of herself.

"Bella? What in God's name is she doing here in your bed?" gasped Lily.

Brett sat on the edge of the bed scratching his head, trying to get his sleep-benumbed brain to function. "She's made a mistake. Had too much to drink, and got in the wrong room. Right, dolly?" Bella, seeming to have lost her powers of speech, nodded furiously and backed toward the door, trying to cover her nakedness with the skimpy nightie.

"Bullshit!" exclaimed Lily. "I clearly heard her say your name. She knew exactly where she was, didn't you, Bella?"

The girl looked piteously at Brett for help. "Go on, dolly. I'll handle this," said Brett, showing a calm he did not feel. Bella backed her way to the door and made her escape.

Lily jumped out of bed and grabbed her dressing gown off the floor. "Come on—handle it! I'm dying to see what lies you'll come up with for this one, Brett Fallon!"

"Now, Lily, I know this looks rum, but believe it or not, it's not quite as rotten a kettle of fish as you think. Just don't go out of control over this."

"I have just found myself in the same bed with you and my daughter-in-law, and it's obviously not the first time she's made this little social blunder of hopping in with you. I have every right to go totally bonkers. How long has this been going on?"

"There is no 'this.'"

"Excuse me. How long have you been screwing her then?"

"Belt up, will you, and let me explain!" he flared.

Lily crossed her arms and glared at him, waiting.

"Well. . .you really have to ask Tris to explain it," said Brett lamely.

"Tristan? You monster! You fiend! You sleep with his tawdry little slut of a wife, whom he adores, and dare to insinuate that he approves? You are a lying son of a bitch, and what's more, you're hopeless at it. To think that I was ready to give up everything for you. What a middle-aged fool I've been! My first instinct was to mistrust you, Brett Fallon—why didn't I listen to my feelings!" Brett stood there helplessly as Lily stormed out of the room. He sat heavily on the bed wondering what had hit him.

Bella opened the door and peeked cautiously inside. Seeing Lily was gone, she came over to him. "Brett, I'm so incredibly sorry. What in the world are we going to do?"

"Your timing's fabulous, Bella. I thought we were through with the breeding season."

"I wanted to make absolutely sure. You said you and Lily were off."

"You need a daily bulletin as to whether it's on or off with us. As of now, I'd say it's definitely off. Where the hell is Tris?"

"He's still down at the bar—pissed I imagine. Will she tell Ian?"

"How can she without incriminating herself?"

"I can't tell Tris to explain, because I'd have to explain about you and Lily."

"It's a stalemate all the way round. I can't tell Lily it was only to get a D'Arcy heir since I promised Tris to keep it secret," said Brett gloomily.

"I'm such a dunce! Do you think Lily would forgive you even if she knew the reason why, Brett?"

"Probably not. Don't blame yourself, dolly. I should have had the brains to lock the door. Let's chalk it up to that little black cloud of bad luck I carry about with me." He lay back on the bed.

"Go get that husband of yours before he turns into a screamer again, Bella. I've had enough trauma for one night."

❂ ❂ ❂

The day after their return to Ireland, Brett came to Ian's study to tell him his decision about the trainer's position. Ian was visibly distressed when he turned the job down.

"I don't understand—this is a terrific opportunity for you, Brett. I intend to buy some fine yearlings at Goff's or Tattersall's, and I wanted you to gentle them for me. You would be in charge of their training from the beginning. Is it the money, or haven't we made you feel welcome? I know Lily has been cool at times."

"The money's fine, and everyone has been great to me, but I miss my home. I may be one hundred percent Irish, but at heart, I'm an Aussie. Also, I've got unfinished business back home—a lot of people I ran out on," said Brett, nervously twirling his hat in his hands.

"I wish you'd reconsider. This isn't just a job you're turning down. I wanted you to be a part of Innismere, as you deserve. I wanted to offer you the legal surname of D'Arcy as well—if you would accept it?"

Brett shook his head and smiled. "Bit of a silk shirt on a pig, that. I don't really feel a D'Arcy. I'm an ordinary bloke, so I'll stay Fallon."

"You'd come to feel it, Brett. I think you've a bit of a chip on your shoulder, no doubt because of the shameful way your mother was treated. I wouldn't blame you. You talk about taking care of unfinished business—that's what I wanted to do with you. To somehow make up to your mother through you."

"I'm afraid that's something you never can do—it's too late. Maybe you owed her something, but I don't expect or feel that I'm owed anything from you. I'm afraid my decision to leave stands firm."

Ian stood up slowly. "This is a great disappointment to me, Brett. I had such plans for you—for the racing stable. You see, I need you, even if you don't need me."

"Frank's a good man who's put in his dues here. I had no right butting in on his job for my own personal reasons."

Ian smiled and held out his hand. Brett clasped it.

"I'm sorry to lose you for more reason than one, Brett."

"Thank you, sir. I could use a note of reference."

"Of course—my highest praise." They walked to the door together. "Everyone will be very sorry to see you go, Tristan especially. He thinks of you as a brother."

"I'll keep in touch."

"Please do that. If you need money, a stake to get you restarted, just ask."

"I've made a bit on old Charlie. Pretty flush really, thanks to him. I would like to follow his record at stud."

"I'll keep you posted. We're going to breed him to Violet's Season in February. Should make for an exceptional foal."

"Charlie will be relieved, I'm sure," said Brett with a grin.

"No doubt." Ian looked at him and sighed. "Brett, I'm not good at emotional words, though I feel them, but I must say—you do both your mother and myself proud."

"Thank you, sir," said Fallon, looking intently at the band about his hat.

She found him lying on his bed in the stable flat.

"What do you want, Lil?" he asked wearily. For the

first time in his acquaintance with her, Lily D'Arcy looked like hell. Her hair was dirty, her face devoid of makeup, her clothes merely thrown on with no thought as to color coordination or attractiveness. She looked every bit of forty. Somehow that only deepened his love for her.

"I want a better story about you and Bella," she said, looking fierce and determined to get to the bottom of it.

"There is no story, Lil," he said, closing his eyes. There was a dull ache in the back of his skull that no opiate could ease.

"You don't deny that you've been sleeping with her, do you?" He was silent. "It happened at the Galway race, too, didn't it? The penny finally dropped. Tris not being there, your not showing up that night and lying to cover up. Bella's being so peculiar the whole trip. It wasn't Daphne you spent the night with, was it?"

"You figured it all out, Lil. You've got me."

She covered her mouth. "Can't you even lie or act ashamed? I loved you, Brett. How could you be so callous? I could have sworn you were sincere with me."

He sat up and stared at her. "I never, ever lied to you about my feelings, Lil."

"If you did love me, what is Bella then? Sex? Revenge? Please tell me the truth, because I don't understand this." There were smudges under her beautiful eyes—sleep was just as evasive for her as it was for him these nights.

For a split second, he thought, *I must tell her the truth, screw Tristan.* He dismissed that idea. The truth would be just as offensive to her. He had brought this on himself through his own weakness and stupidity; now he would simply have to suffer the consequences. "Bella is nothing. A friend. My little sis. Sex had little or nothing to do with it. She draws every breath for Tris, as you know."

"Then why? How could the two of you do such a thing

to Tristan and to me? No, how could *you* do it? Bella is only a child."

"I cannot answer you, Lily. It's not my right to. There is an honorable if misguided explanation. Bella and I did what we did because we care about Tristan and are concerned about him. It had nothing at all to do with affairs or desire. If that's too hard for you to swallow, if you simply can't take my word for it, then perhaps you don't love me quite as much as you thought you did."

"You are actually saying you had sex with Bella, over a period of months, for honorable reasons, Brett?"

"Tris is the only one who can explain it, but since you don't want him to know about us, I guess it will just have to stay unexplained."

"It would kill Tristan if he were to find out about you two. And to think, he loves you like a brother."

"I did it because I *am* his brother, damn it!"

Tears streamed down her face. No pretty crying for Lily now. "Brett, this makes no sense. I'm not a half-wit!"

There were tears in his eyes as well, now. "I'm sorry, but that's the best I can do, Lily. You either trust me or not. The choice is yours."

She stood there wavering between what she had seen with her own eyes, and what she wanted to believe. "Brett, how can I trust you? You're making me crazy," she said pitifully.

"That makes two of us, Lil." He sighed.

She backed away from him, her face ugly with her pain. "I just can't! I won't be made a fool of!" She turned blindly for the door. He heard her stumble on the stairs. Could he ever have doubted that her pride would win over her love?

Lily took to her bed for the next two days feigning illness. Indeed, she was ill from spending her nights weep-

ing. The fourth day after their return from Deauville,
desperate to get out of the house, she took her mare Lady
Jane out for a ride up to the old castle.

The fresh air lifted her spirits as usual, but the sight
of the ruin only brought back bittersweet memories of
her ride in the storm with Brett. Everything had been
ahead of them then; now it was all ashes.

Walking under the stone gateway, she recalled their
taking shelter from the rain. She closed her eyes and con-
jured up the feel, the smell of Brett as she stole those few
exciting, illegal moments in his strong arms while the
lightning crashed about them. God, how she had wanted
him then, and he'd confessed his own temptation. Their
consciences had won that day; they might have gone on,
each burning and wanting, but neither willing to make
the first move—until fate had finally stepped in in the
shape of an angry black colt. Now the grand passion of
her life was to end on this pathetic, humiliating note. In
the real world, one didn't go off to reign for eternity on
Mt. Olympus with one's lover. Bitter gall was her reward,
not ambrosia.

If only Brett had just confessed his sins with Bella, done
a mea culpa, and begged her forgiveness, instead of taking
the preposterous stance that it was all for love of Tristan.
What incredible balls that took! Tears of anger filled her
eyes again for the millionth time.

Forcing her emotions back, Lily mounted her gray
mare and began the descent down the hill. It had been
a poor idea to ride up here. The contrast between the
pre-affair excitement of the castle in the storm with the
bleak, post-affair vista that stretched before her was too
heartbreaking.

Reaching the wood, Lily urged Lady Jane into a canter.
All the while she'd been judging Brett Fallon guilty, another little voice had been saying in her ear: he's leaving

Saturday and you'll never see him again. Did it really matter so much that his flesh had been weak in this one instance? Bella was one of those unconscious temptresses whom few men could resist. The truth of the matter was that she loved him no matter what he'd done. It was unthinkable that he could just vanish out of her life forever. She had to stop him!

She rode the mare into the stable, dismounted, and tossed the reins to the stableboy.

"He's down at the office," Rafferty called after her. Normally she might have been embarrassed that he knew it was Brett she was after, but she was way past that now. Rounding the corner of the stable alley, she caught sight of Brett and Bella embracing each other outside the office. Brett looked up and saw her standing there.

"Did you want me, Lil?" he called as Bella moved guiltily away from him.

"You're the last thing on this earth I want!" Lily cried before turning to run from them.

Ian looked up from the Goff's fall yearling catalogue he was perusing. "What is it?" he asked at the sight of her face.

"It's Brett," she gasped.

"Not another accident?"

"I just caught him kissing Bella in the stable."

Ian's air of alarm dissipated at once. "So? They're good chums."

"It was a sexual kiss. I hadn't wanted to tell you this, but in Deauville, I caught Bella coming out of Brett's room in a skimpy nightie. I'd gone to ask if she'd brought any nail polish remover."

"You're suggesting that Brett and Bella?. . ."

"Telling, not suggesting. Brett doesn't even deny it. That's why I've been so out of sorts since we got back.

I thought that once they knew I was on to them, they'd put an end to it, but if they're going to carry on brazenly. . . You've got to stop them, Ian, before Tristan finds out about it!"

"Lily, there has to be another explanation. Bella is very much in love with Tristan, and is not that sort of girl anyway. Your antipathy to Brett has caused you to misconstrue something that is in all probability very innocent."

"Aren't you listening? Brett admitted his guilt to me. He's slept with her in Galway and Deauville. I always felt he was somehow out to steal Tristan's birthright. It seems he's settled for his wife."

"I cannot believe that either of them would do this," Ian insisted.

"You are so naive—people simply are not as honorable as you are. You mustn't let Brett get away with hurting Tristan like this."

"Assuming it's true, which I doubt, what do you want me to do, Lily? Brett leaves soon. Isn't Tris better off ignorant?"

"You've got to punish him! How could you let him get away with this—this rape of the family? You talk constantly of the honor of the D'Arcys, yet when it's really at stake, you want to hide your head and hope the trouble disappears. I give up on you, Ian D'Arcy. I truly do!"

As soon as Kelly had ladled the vichyssoise and left the dining room, Tristan cleared his throat. "I have an announcement to make. . .we are pregnant." A stunned silence followed. Lily looked from Bella to Brett, both of whom were staring at their soup bowls.

"I say, isn't anyone pleased?" said Tristan.

"Just a bit of a surprise, son," said Ian, recovering his wits. "I thought you wanted to postpone having children."

"Well, we've changed our minds—might as well get on with it. Bella's only just found out this afternoon at the doctor's." Bella smiled weakly, still avoiding Lily's glance.

"How far along are you, Bella?" Lily asked in a strained voice.

"Not very far, actually," she said, her sunburn deepening.

"You can expect a grandchild just a wee bit short of nine months, Mother," said Tristan heartily. Lily jumped up from the table and ran from the room, her napkin over her mouth.

"Is Mum that afraid of becoming a grandmother?" asked a bemused Tristan.

"She's still not feeling well, I expect," said Ian. "Well. . .this is exciting news. What do you think, Brett?"

"Great. Looks like I'm going to be an uncle."

"Right you are. Should have a bit of bubbly to celebrate, don't you think?" He rang for Kelly.

✪ ✪ ✪

"I love you, I love you!" she cried, leaning down to kiss his face. "Swear to me you'll never deceive me again!"

His blue eyes opened and looked straight into hers— he laughed; a harsh, ugly sound.

"Don't be a *cochon*, Lily. I have him next," said Helene de Lazarre. Gesturing languidly with a jeweled hand, she added, "Save some for the rest of us, *chérie*." Lily looked about the opium bed where Daphne Pynchon, Bella with a baby at her breast, and the French *putain* from the Casino lolled nakedly about Brett Fallon.

Daphne smiled at her with a mouth full of braces. "We all must share him equally."

The black-haired French girl tapped her alabaster thigh with a studded whip. "I am paying him six thousand francs, so I get ze most!"

Brett laughed lazily and waved his hand. "Belt up, you wenches. There's plenty for everyone. You'll all be in foal come spring."

A thin-faced, dark-haired girl pointed an accusing finger at Lily. "She can't have babies!" sneered Josie Fallon.

"No tucker for you then, mate." Brett laughed, giving her a kick that sent her sailing off the bed. It was a very long way to the floor.

"Please, I'll do anything, anything," she screamed as she fell through space.

Ian was shaking her. "Lily! Lily!" Her eyelids refused to open. "How many have you taken, Lily?" His voice sounded desperate. He slapped her cheek, and with the greatest effort, she returned to consciousness.

"How many what?" she mumbled.

"Pills! You had a full bottle of sleeping tablets, and it's empty." His face was frantic as she tried to focus on the meaning of his words.

"Two. Took two. The bottle spilled," she whispered. It was only a dream—thank God!

Ian searched about on the floor and under the bed and found the tablets. "Damn, you had me worried. I don't suppose two will hurt you though." He stroked her face.

"Lily, I've had the truth out of them. It's rather shocking, but it's not nearly as sordid as you think."

"Brett's baby?" she murmured.

"Yes, I'm afraid it is, but there are extenuating circumstances." She hadn't the strength left to cry. Ian kissed her brow.

"You sleep, my love. I'll explain it all to you in the morning. You're in no condition to follow it now. Just rest assured that Bella and Brett did not betray Tristan." He kissed her again, turned off the light, and quietly left the room.

*   *   *

Tristan brought in his mother's breakfast tray the next morning at 9:30. She was awake, though still in bed. "Are you feeling any better today, Mother?" he asked, looking concerned.

She sat up on the pillows and managed a feeble smile for him. "A bit, darling."

"Good. Look what Mary's sent you—fresh orange juice and quark with strawberries to tempt your palate." He fixed the tray across her lap.

The sight of the sour cream and berries almost made her ill. "Tristan, I don't think I really want any food. Tea is all I need, thanks."

He sat on the bed beside her, his brow furrowed with worry. "I think you should see a doctor, Mum. You haven't felt well since France. Perhaps you ate some bad seafood."

"No, I was just exhausted. I really feel much better. Don't worry," she said, patting his hand.

"I do worry. Father says you got yourself all in a dither because you thought Bella was slipping out on me with Brett. I wanted to explain it to you—you see I engineered the thing myself."

"Please don't tell me something awful. I just can't deal with it now," she pleaded.

"I have to tell you because I don't want you making yourself ill imagining what never happened. It's not some kinky ménage thing, so don't look so horrified, Mum. You see, I found out a few months ago that I can't father children."

"Oh, Tristan!"

He took her hand. "Please don't cry, Mother. I've come to accept it. One thing that made it easier to take somehow was my idea for Brett to father Bella's baby. Just let me finish, and then you can tell me how insane that was. I asked Brett to do it, forced them both to be together so our baby will be a true D'Arcy. It seemed logical to me to ask my brother to do what I couldn't. I realize a normal person would just adopt—that was what Bella and Brett both thought we should do, but it seemed so fitting to me for Brett to be the one. It isn't fair that I get everything, and he gets nothing. This way we will have an heir with D'Arcy blood, for Father, Brett will be compensated for his accident of birth, and Bella and I will have the beautiful baby we longed for. I know it sounds mad when you first hear it, but it makes wonderful sense to me. Can't you understand, Mother?"

She held his hand to her lips. "I'm so very sorry my darling."

"I know you are. It doesn't depress me now nearly as it did at first. Having the baby in May is going to help tremendously."

Lily stroked his hand and cried. "If only you'd told me."

"I had this misguided notion you and Dad never need know. I certainly couldn't tell you all before the deed was done—you'd have freaked, and I was dead set on it. I especially wanted to save Dad the pain of knowing it was the end of the straight line for the D'Arcys. Now it isn't." He tried to smile and looked so young and vulnerable with his blond hair falling over into his eyes. Lily still had a box of white-blond ringlets from his first haircut.

He leaned over and kissed her. "I'm sorry I've caused you distress, Mum. I know I've been a thorn in your side for the last year and a half, but I'm going to straighten up now, I promise. Get off the booze and go back to school, and try to be the best dad around."

She couldn't hold back her sobs any longer. He put his arms round her and patted her back as if he were the parent and she the child.

"I hope you won't hold this against either Bella or

Brett. I forced them to do it at gunpoint, I swear. He tried everything to get out of it. Too bad he's gone now thinking everyone is upset with him."

"Gone?"

"Yes, he left last night. Bella went down to talk to him, and he'd already left. Took nothing but what he came here with."

"What day of the week is it?"

"Friday. He left a letter for Dad, that's all. I guess I don't really blame him for getting out. I say, do you feel all right, Mother?"

"Not really. I feel sick to my stomach. Please leave me, darling. I'd rather be alone." He left her room, and Lily ran for the bathroom.

She remained ill in bed the remainder of the day, refusing any food or company. The next morning, Bella brought up her breakfast tray and found her dressed.

"Thank goodness you're better, Lily. Ian was going to call the doctor."

"Yes, I've had a bath, washed my hair, put on my face, and feel quite human again and ready to get on with life," said Lily with false chipperness.

"I'm so glad. I was really getting worried. Are you hungry? Timothy's sent you some grapes and melon from the garden."

"Thanks, that sounds lovely," she lied. Actually, she wasn't hungry though she hadn't eaten in a day and a half. She was past food somehow, might never need it again—except perhaps a little tea with honey now and then.

Lily lifted the bud vase off the tray and sniffed the single red rose. A faint, far-off scent emanated from the gold crown at its center. Poor, passionate Siobhan who'd preferred putting a bullet in her heart to life without her lover. Now Lily could understand her. In the intercepted letter to Brett, Josie had said, "What will my life be if I can never hold you in my arms again?" The thought went through Lily like a physical pain.

She returned the vase to the tray, and for the first time noticed the envelope propped against the teapot. She picked it up and examined her name scrawled across it in bold, angular writing.

"Brett left that for you," said Bella. "I hid it from the others because I was afraid they might think it odd."

"You're thoughtful as always, Bella. I want to apologize to you for the hideous things I've said and thought."

"I understood. Brett and I were in such a spot not being able to explain since we'd promised Tris to keep it a secret. I felt so sorry for Brett. The other day when you saw us in the stable, I'd just told him that my test was positive. I'll leave you alone now, Lily."

She was too mesmerized by the letter to notice Bella's departure. Running her finger over her name on the envelope, she thought that though she'd never seen Brett's handwriting before, she had known it at once. She ripped it open. The words, too few of them, swam before her eyes.

"I loved you, Lily. Why couldn't you have believed in me? Brett."

✠ ✠ ✠

Lily ran into the drawing room, a purse and raincoat in her hands. Ian, Bella, and Tristan took in her agitated manner and untidy hair.

"Lily, are you all right?" asked Ian, getting to his feet.

"I've got to get to the Dublin airport at once, and I can't find the keys to the Mercedes. Has anyone seen them?"

"What on earth do you need to go to the airport for?" asked Ian. Bella and Tristan exchanged worried looks.

"I must get a flight to Manchester. Have you seen the keys?"

"Manchester, England?" asked Tristan in astonishment.

Kelly came in bearing the morning's mail. "Have you seen the Mercedes' keys, Seamus?" said Lily, hysteria mounting in her voice. "I distinctly remember leaving them on the Venetian table in the hall as usual."

"Pardon, your ladyship?"

"Have you seen my goddamn car keys?" Lily screamed. The old man nearly dropped his silver tray.

"Calm down, Mother," said Tristan, getting up. "I'll go have a look for them."

"Lily, I think perhaps I should call the doctor," said Ian.

"I am not mad! I simply must get to Manchester in time for the Quantas flight that leaves at five forty-five."

"This is most extraordinary," said Ian, looking at her as if she might foam at the mouth any moment.

"It's Saturday, and Brett will be on that flight. I must catch him! Please someone, help me!"

Tristan returned from the hall. "Here they are, Mother. Fell on the floor."

"Thank heavens!" said Lily, clutching the car keys to her breast.

"Give them to me, Lily," said Ian. "I'll take you. You're in no condition to drive." She handed them over to him, and he left to bring the car around.

Lily turned to Tristan and put her arms about him. "I love you so much, my darling boy. Please don't hate me."

"Mother, what is this about?"

Lily turned to Bella. "Tell him for me, will you love? I haven't the courage." The two embraced. "I hope you have a beautiful child, Bella."

She went to Kelly, still standing by with the mail, and

impulsively kissed him so vigorously that his toupée went askew. "Thanks for putting up with me, Seamus. I shall miss you and Mary." She hurried out as the butler speechlessly tried to right his wig.

"Mother has completely flipped out," said Tristan. "Tell me what, Bella?"

Ian was quiet as he drove along the Cork-Dublin Road into Dublin. She waited apprehensively for the questions to come.

"I realize you must feel somewhat guilty about Brett," he said at last. "It's admirable that you feel you must go all the way to Manchester to persuade him to stay, but do you really think it will do any good? As much as I regret seeing him leave, I think he was right to go. How could he remain at Innismere with things as. . .confused as they are now? He couldn't live under the same roof with Tris and Bella under these extraordinary circumstances."

"I'm not going to persuade him to stay, Ian. Of course he can't—for more than one reason." She looked askance at him. How in the world to tell him?

"Ian, you must know what's been going on? You have to, as smart as you are. Or else you've not learned a thing about reading me in all the years we've been together?" He stared ahead at the road, but his knuckles were white on the steering wheel.

"Are you going to force me to say it?"

He looked over at her then, and the hurt in his black eyes struck her more to the heart than any words could have. "I was hoping that it was just my paranoia—my feeling that you ought to take a lover, considering the provocation. My knowing that Brett would be an irresistible choice. I've quelled such thoughts by telling myself

you would never do something so scandalous, or so hurt-
ful to all of us. I assume I was wrong about that."

"If you knew how I've dreaded this moment, Ian. Your
finally knowing how shameless I am, but there it is. I
didn't want to love him, but I couldn't stop myself. That
sounds very adolescent and silly, I'm sure, but it's God's
truth. I suppose you think I'm having a mid-life crisis or
something, and maybe I am. All I know is I'd rather be
dead than be without Brett. I did think of taking that
whole bottle of pills—I truly did!"

He was quiet, digesting this for several miles while she
wondered what to say next. "I assume this began while
he was convalescing?" he said at last.

"Yes. While you were away. We both fought it tooth
and nail, because neither of us wanted to ever hurt you,
Ian. The whole thing has been very difficult and guilt-
ridden."

"But very powerful, I gather." They exchanged glances
and she looked away. "Brett's letter he left for me said,
'I'm not worthy to be your son. You've always been honest and fair to me, while I've been deceitful in return.'
I assumed he was referring to Bella. Now I see why you
were so upset when you thought they were having an affair."

"I wanted to kill him!"

Ian sighed heavily. "I thought you'd outgrown all your
impetuosity, Lily. You've always been more emotional
than I, but this does surprise me. Perhaps I haven't
learned that much about you in all this time."

It began raining, and Ian turned on the wipers.

"Ian, I can't believe that you're taking this so calmly.
I've been so afraid it would destroy you—thank heaven
it doesn't seem to be doing that. We are so different. If
our roles were reversed here, I'd be out of my head. As
I was over Tony's letters. Did you really love Tony, Ian?"

"I think you've gotten quite enough blood out of me for one day," he replied.

"Sorry—I had no right to ask. It's that now I could understand and forgive if you did. For all the good that does."

Ian turned the car onto Swords Road for the airport. "What are your plans? What do you intend to do once you hopefully intercept Brett at Manchester?"

"I'm going with him to Sydney. You see, he made a reservation for me as well. I'm counting on him being enough of a gambler that he won't cancel it until the last minute. He knows very well how changeable I am."

"That's beside the point now. You haven't any clothes, any money—he can't have that much. How will you get on?"

"Somehow—I don't know, and I don't care right now."

"You may grow to care, Lily. You've become rather used to a luxurious lifestyle, you know."

"I came from a modest background, and I can return to it. Money isn't the important thing."

"Tell me, if you had known from the outset who Brett was, would it have made any difference?"

She thought a minute. "No. I was a goner from the first moment I saw him, I think. That's why I fought against him so hard. I'd have wanted Brett if he'd been my own son."

"*Coup de foudre*, eh? I felt that the first time I saw you at that concert, Lily."

"I've loved you, Ian. I still do."

"Only I don't stir the unholy passion in your breast that he does. I'm sorry I've let you down in that respect."

"You've never let me down in that or any other way, Ian. You've always been everything any woman could want in a lover or a husband."

"We both know that's not entirely true, Lily."

They were silent as he turned the Mercedes onto the airport entry road.

"Which airline?" he asked gruffly.

"I don't know. . .which do you think?"

"May I suggest Aer Lingus. They fly that route constantly." He pulled over at the Irish airline terminal and stopped at the curb.

"So. . .this seems to be the rather unromantic ending to our fairy tale, Lily," he said quietly.

She put her hand on his arm. "Thank you for being so incredible about this, Ian. For staying your calm, reasonable self, as always. For helping me."

His eyes were soft when he looked at her. "After twenty-two years, you are at least my closest friend, Lily. I want you to be happy."

She leaned across the seat and embraced him, too emotional to speak, but words were superfluous now anyway. He held her tightly for a moment.

"Go on, then, damn you!" he whispered. She kissed him once more, then got out of the car, and ran into the terminal.

✪ ✪ ✪

Lily checked her watch for the tenth time in the past half hour. It was five o'clock. The plane lurched sickeningly as it continued circling above Manchester. They'd told her a transit time on the ground of forty minutes was necessary to get from the Aer Lingus terminal to Quantas; Brett's plane was due to depart in forty-five minutes, and her plane from Dublin hadn't even landed yet. She buried her face in her hands and groaned aloud in frustration.

"We'll make it, dearie," said the woman in the seat next to her. She sounded as if she were trying to convince herself of this. It had been a very rough flight, and the woman had spent most of the trip with her eyes closed, white knuckles clutching the armrests. She was going to visit her daughter who'd just had her first child, she'd volunteered before Lily had feigned a nap to curtail the friendly chitchat.

The plane shuddered free of a storm cloud, and Lily saw out the window that they were quite low now and surely about to make their landing approach. There should have been an hour-and-fifteen-minute layover in Manchester, plenty of time to catch the Sydney flight, but God was obviously trying to punish her for her sins by throwing up obstacles. First, all the early flights had been sold out, and she'd had to hang around and wait standby for the 3:45 flight. Luckily she'd got a seat, though it was thirty minutes late taking off due to a gale blowing off the Irish Sea. They'd continued to lose time stacked up over Manchester.

What would she do if she missed Brett's flight? Once he took off without her, she had lost him forever. She had no idea where he was going after Sydney. He obviously wasn't headed for Fallon's Station and the stepbrother who hated him. Josie Fallon? Lily strained to recall the address on the letter she'd burned. Would Brett make contact with his old lover? Ironically Josie was the only possible contact Lily had for finding Brett should everything fall through now.

She ran her thumb over her naked finger. Her left hand felt too light, not right at all since she'd slipped off her wedding band and the beautiful, old sapphire and diamond ring that had belonged to Ian's mother. She'd left all her other jewelry behind, but hadn't thought about her wedding rings which felt like part of her body after all these years. They were now in a zippered pocket of her purse. Should she send the ring back? It was a family piece and especially sentimental to Ian.

Ian! God, how she'd hurt him. He could always hide his feelings, but she knew he had to be deeply wounded— if he really loved her as he'd always said he did. All her bridges were burned now. After her dramatic exit, she just couldn't go home with her tail between her legs. Her entire future depended on catching Quantas's Flight 10 to Sydney—now entirely up to God's mercy. Lily had the sick feeling that she didn't warrant any of that.

The plane came down smooth as silk on the runway after its bucking bronc of a flight. The woman next to her kissed her rosary and said, "Praise Jesus for terra firma!" Lily smiled at her in agreement.

It was 5:30 when she reached the Quantas terminal. She was stopped from entering by a thin weasel of a security guard when she couldn't produce her ticket. Impatiently she explained that someone on the plane had her ticket.

"I'm sorry, madam. No one enters the international area without a ticket," said the guard officiously, looking quite pleased to be able to disappoint her.

Lily glared at him. She was not getting this close to her goal only to be turned away by some power-mad peon. "I demand to speak to your superior," she said in her haughtiest voice.

"Madam, those are the rules. No one gets in here unticketed."

"I *have* a ticket, only my husband has it, and he is on the plane already by now. If you don't phone your superior or the head of Quantas right this minute, I'll see that you lose your job! What is your name?" She scrabbled in her crammed purse and found a scrap of paper. "Mr. Pipkin, you're a very stupid man." The weasel glared at her menacingly. They were joined by another guard.

"What's the problem, Charlie?"

"She's got no ticket. Says her husband is on a Quantas plane with her ticket."

"Please, please help me. It's a matter of life and death that I be on that plane. It's five forty and the plane is due to leave in five minutes!" Lily implored of this guard who was gray-haired and looked slightly more sympathetic than the first one. "Look, I'll give you money. I have fifty Irish pounds on me. Please just call the gate and have them hold the plane until you can confirm that I do have a ticket," she pleaded frantically. People were staring at her as they hurried in and out of the terminal. She was making a public scene, something she normally had a real abhorrence of, but was prepared to scream and cry and roll on the floor if that's what it took to get through to these petty little men who got off on wielding their pitiful bit of power in life, particularly over someone they viewed as upper class.

"Put your money away, madam," said the gray-haired guard. He took a radio from his belt, and made a call. Above them the hands on the wall clock moved inexorably toward five forty-five.

The guard kept up his muffled conversation on the radio as she paced nervously. She needed to come up with some fabulous story as to why she had to be on that plane. "I'm running off with my lover," just wouldn't cut it with these two. Perhaps she should say their baby was undergoing a heart transplant in Sydney, and she had to be there. No, that was too awful. For once her clever talent for lying seemed to have deserted her. All she could think of was the truth: The man I love is on that plane, and I have got to be with him! Mr. Pipkin looked like a man incapable of love and passion, and the older one had probably forgotten what it was like.

As the long hand of the clock jumped to the nine, Lily

cried out in anguish. Too late—the plane would be pulling away from the gate, taking Brett from her forever. She bowed her head and sobbed in defeat.

"I've called the Quantas station manager, madam. He'll be round shortly to check this out," said the older security guard.

"It's leaving now, it's too damn late," she cried.

"Flights have been delayed all afternoon because of the weather. It may well still be at the gate," he said kindly.

Brett Fallon looked out the window beside him; the skies were clearing at last. Hopefully they'd soon get this buggy off the ground. The good-looking, blond stewardess who'd given him the eye when they were boarding was demonstrating the oxygen masks with a decided dramatic flair. He closed his eyes. The sooner he left this part of the world, the better, as far as he was concerned.

He again thought of Lily—something he couldn't seem to prevent no matter how he tried. The pain on her face when she'd misunderstood about Bella. "You're the last thing on this earth I want," she'd said. She never would have gone with him anyway, even if the Bella fiasco hadn't happened. A woman like Lily was born to the high life, something she'd never have seen again with the likes of him. His brain had been muddled by love or desire or whatever to think for a second that she would walk away from it all. Well, he'd learned a few things from the experience. Most importantly to never let love delude him as to the realities of life. *Fuck love!* he thought fiercely. Once was enough for a lifetime. Looking on the bright side, Ian would never know the extent of his betrayal now. That was something. Ian was a hell of a good man, though he would never feel to him like his father. Thinking about Lily was like picking at an open wound, but he'd lived without her for thirty years, and he'd damn well learn to live the rest of his life without her, he told himself.

The pressure inside the cabin altered noticeably. They must have reopened the door to take on a late passenger. Brett's eyes flicked open and fastened on the two aisles disappearing into the Business Class section. Fool! Didn't he ever give up? The answer to that one was Lily's ticket still in his breast pocket, beneath which his heart was accelerating.

Then there she was, hurrying down the aisle nearest him, eyes flicking left and right, a uniformed Quantas official behind her. Brett was so stunned to see her materialize like that before him, just as he'd fantasized her doing, that he sat frozen in his seat.

Her eyes fastened on him the instant he stood up. He stumbled over the man on the aisle seat, and they stood facing each other. Lily clutched an enormous purse to her breast, hair straggling, eyes rimmed with mascara puddles, and the most beatific expression of relief and love transforming her face. He shook his head and smiled at her, and she ran into his arms.

"I knew it was you. The second they opened the door, I knew it had to be my crazy Lil," he said, as she clung to him crying and laughing.

"I can't believe I've got you! I thought the plane had left," she said, sobbing, leaning into his chest.

"You've got me all right, lady," he whispered into her hair. The airline official stood by patiently, a bemused smile on his lips. Every neck in the cabin was craned to stare at them, the stews even gathered at the bulkhead to watch the show.

"Have you got my fucking ticket?" Lily laughed through her tears. Brett disengaged himself and fished in his jacket for the ticket. The man standing behind Lily tore out the necessary sections and returned it to him.

"A bit of better planning in future, please," he said with a wink.

"Thank you so much for believing me, Mr. Bartholemew," said Lily, wiping her eyes. "I shall write the airlines and tell them what a gentleman you were."

"Delighted to be of assistance, Mrs. D'Arcy." Brett held out his hand and thanked him as well.

"I'm pleased it had a happy ending, Mr. D'Arcy. Enjoy your trip now."

The man on the aisle stood up to let them in to their seats.

Lily held Brett's brown hand in her lap and stroked it. So like Ian's in spite of the roughness. "I was so afraid I'd never see you again," she whispered tremulously. "Thank God you didn't cancel my ticket."

"I know you better than that, don't I? You're worth an eight-hundred-pound gamble, Lil."

She leaned against his strong shoulder and said a silent prayer of thanks to God who'd had mercy for even a sinner such as she. The plane began to taxi out of the terminal area.

Brett pushed up the armrest and put his arm about her. She ran her hand inside his jacket and over his beautiful chest. It would be over twenty-four hours before they'd be able to express their feelings properly, the way words never could, but this would do wonderfully for now. She was sure she looked awful after all the histrionics she'd been through during this incredible, life-changing day, but he didn't seem to mind.

"What made you do it, Lil? What made you chuck it all and come with me?"

"Your letter. I may have doubted you there for a bit, Brett, but I do believe in you, like nothing I've ever believed in in my life." He crushed her small hand in his and brought it to his mouth. The blue of his eyes shimmered. "And I couldn't face the rest of my life without you to call me 'Lil'."

He turned her face up to his and kissed her tenderly on the mouth. "I'll make it good for you, Lil, you'll see. You won't regret it, I swear to you," he said gruffly.

As the plane took off into the rain-washed skies above Manchester to take her to the next stage of her life, Lily thought that of all the rash, impetuous decisions she'd made, this was one she could never imagine regretting.

Damien

❂ ❂ ❂

DAMIEN STOOD ON the pavement in front of No. Eleven Kookaburra Lane, Manly, N.S.W. It was a nice house to be sure—a neat, white bungalow shaded by some tropical Australian fantasy of a tree bearing long, fuzzy, red blooms. Set in a densely packed but pleasant, working class neighborhood of the town across the harbour from Sydney, No. Eleven might have easily fitted into the ballroom of Innismere. He opened the gate and was at once charged noisily by a small black and white unidentifiable bit of dog. Damien offered a few soothing blandishments which were ignored and was considering a well placed kick to the chops, when Lily opened the door to the screened porch.

"Shut up, Dink!" she yelled. The dog grew even more vociferous, so Damien made a dash for the house with the mongrel yapping at his heels. Lily slammed the door in its face. "Ridiculous animal. You can't imagine how many postmen he's nipped!"

Damien smiled. "You look different, Lily, but damn, you sound the same!" She laughed and embraced him.

"Damien! It's been so long since I've seen anyone!"

"Well, you ran away to the ends of the earth, my dear. It's not every day that one drops by Sydney."

"I look ghastly, go ahead and say it. I've gained weight,

and this dress is so frumpy. But thanks for warning me you were coming. I'm usually in shorts or jeans. I'm afraid I've let myself get a mess, I'm so busy all the time."

"You look ravishing. The few pounds, the color in your cheeks—I don't think I've ever seen you look better, Lily."

"I always adore your little lies, Damien." She laughed.

But he wasn't lying. She'd got a bit thin and brittle-looking the summer before she had left Ian. Now she had a more rounded, relaxed look about her that was very attractive. His brother had asked him to look in on her and make sure things were all right. If first impressions proved accurate, Damien thought that he would have to report that Lily was doing very well indeed—not really the news Ian was looking forward to hearing.

Lily took his hand and led him into the cool interior of the house. "It's so damn hot today. What about a beer or a glass of lemonade?"

"It is warm, and I've come with the wrong clothes since I thought March was the start of the Aussie fall," he commented. "Lemonade is perfect. I've given up alcohol, can you imagine?"

"I'm very impressed. I'm trying to reform Brett, but I can't seem to wean him off beer."

"It's more a matter of vanity than morality for me, love. It was all going straight to my paunch. It was either booze or sex appeal, and the latter won out."

"I think you'd be terribly sexy, paunch and all, but I'm glad you've quit. Sit down, darling, and I'll go fetch our drinks." Lily left him in the front parlor, a tiny room which she'd made quite warm and attractive, and had obviously done so with a minimum of expense. He was examining the framed photos on a table, when she returned with a tray.

"Something familiar at last," said Damien, indicating the pictures of Tristan and Violet as children.

"I couldn't leave without those. Every time I went through the airport x-ray machine, the silver frames set the gongs off, and I'd have to empty my purse." She handed him a lemonade, and they sat down.

"I always expected the unexpected from you, Lily, but your taking off after Brett with nothing but pictures of your children truly stunned me. I was that sure you'd never give up Innismere and all the things you loved so dearly."

"I never thought I would either. I suppose I surprised myself as much as I did you, really. All the things suddenly didn't seem to matter to me anymore.

"Do have something to eat, Damien. It's all terribly unfattening," she said, offering him a plate of luscious-looking hors d'oevres.

"They look quite irresistible," he said, taking a cheese puff. "I'm flattered you've gone to such trouble on my account."

"Actually I made them for a party tonight, but it won't matter if we nip a few."

"A party? Is it an occasion?"

"My job. I've been catering for the families Brett trains for."

Damien looked startled at that revelation. "Bit of a comedown for Lady D'Arcy, eh?" she said with a smile at his embarrassment. "It helps pay the rent. I'm also teaching ballet at a school in Sydney several times a week. We're trying to save enough money to buy our own training facilities and stable. Thank God I have some marketable skills to contribute."

"You're amazing, Lily. I always knew that, but I never realized how resourceful you were."

"I've had it so easy for so long, Damien. It actually feels good being able to pull my own weight for a change."

The door slammed, and a boy sprinted past them with an armload of books.

"Tomi, come here please," Lily called.

The child stuck his head round the corner. "We've a visitor from Ireland, Tomi. Come meet your father's uncle, Damien D'Arcy."

" 'Lo," said the boy, reluctantly edging into the room. He regarded Damien with bright, blue eyes from under dark, brown brows. It was apparent at once from his dark complexion and very curly, though blondish hair that he was half-caste. Damien held out his hand with a friendly smile hoping he'd hidden his surprise better than he thought.

"This is Tomi Fallon, Brett's son," said Lily brightly.

"A pleasure indeed, Tomi," said Damien as the boy withdrew his hand quickly. "How's school going then?" Damien asked rather lamely, having been bereft of his usual social poise by the shock of discovering he had yet another relative he'd known nothing about. The boy shrugged, every pore in his lanky young body longing to be away from this interview. "Stupid question," said Damien. "I imagine it's as much a bore as it ever was."

Tomi didn't return his smile; like a wild creature, he regarded every stranger a foe to be highly wary of—guilty until proven innocent.

"There's lemonade in the fridge," said Lily, jumping into the social breach. "Have a couple of cakes but the rest is for the party tonight," she added. Tomi departed their company gratefully.

Lily sighed. "Sorry about his lack of manners, but we've only had him for three months. Before that, he'd been let run wild for the last fifteen years."

"He's charming looking. So exotic with the dark and the blue eyes."

"His mother was an Aborigine girl Brett got involved with when he was very young. She was only too happy to give him up to us. It's rather a difficult situation really, but Brett's determined to make a go of this."

"Very admirable, but a tad trying for you, I imagine," said Damien.

"More lemonade?" Lily asked, avoiding comment.

Tomi reappeared clad in a T-shirt and bathing costume. "Going to the baych with m'mites. Be back by evo," he said, mouth full of chocolate.

"I've a party tonight, Tomi, so dinner will be at six. Don't be late," said Lily. "Your father will help with your lessons after since I'll be busy."

"Got no lessons," the boy replied with a frown.

"I imagine you have something," Lily insisted. Tomi mumbled a remark and headed for the door. "Tomi!" Lily said sharply.

"Shit!" he swore under his breath though quite audibly.

"Would you say good-by to Damien then?" Lily directed, a faint pink on her cheeks.

"G'bye Damien, sir," said the boy, parrot-like.

"Tomi, do you like rock music?" Damien asked.

"Yeah," he said suspiciously.

"Then how would you and a mate like tickets to the sold-out Rory McCalla show tomorrow night at the Entertainment Centre?"

"Fray tickets ya mane?"

"Absolutely. Backstage passes as well. I'll introduce you to Rory." Tomi smiled for the first time, showing startlingly white teeth against the dusky skin. When the sullen mask of wariness was lifted, he was a very striking boy.

"How lovely!" Lily exclaimed. "Do thank Damien, Tomi." The child shot her a furious look, and Damien could only be sympathetic. Tomi stared at the floor, stubbornly refusing to do as ordered this time round.

"Grand then! I'll have the tickets at the box office for you an hour before show time, all right?" said Damien.

"Ripper," said Tomi, with a hint of that appealing smile. "Bye nah," he said on his way out the door. They could hear him calling Dink.

Lily shook her head. "The two of us have been butting heads a bit, as you can see. He's been living with his mother and this lowlife she took up with in Coolangatta and has had almost no schooling. Has to take special classes. Tomi's bright but so undisciplined. All he wants to do is go surfing with his friends. Brett thinks he can make up for all the missing years, but I wonder if it isn't too late."

Lily busied herself rearranging the canapés on the plate, then broached the subject nearest to her heart. "So what news of Tristan, Damien? When Bella wrote me that he'd entered a clinic for substance abuse, I was so terribly shocked. I knew he was drinking way too much, but drugs never entered my mind. I suppose Brett and I were the final straw?"

"That threw him, of course. He'd always put you on a pedestal, and you fell off with a rather resounding clunk, I must say. But from what I've gleaned from Bella, his problems started long before that, so don't heap yourself with blame. Anyway, he's come to grips with the problem, had professional counseling, and he's got that girl behind him, so it looks good, Lily."

"Bella's such a darling. She's the only one who's written me, you know. I'd have gone mad if it weren't for her telling me what's been going on with Tristan. He sent my letters back unopened, marked 'addressee deceased'. And to think what a horrid bitch I was to that girl."

"She's a rare one, that's a fact. You should see her now, a perfect Titian madonna."

"And the baby due in three months," said Lily wistfully. "My life is so totally changed now, it seems so long ago that we left." She looked at Damien. "Do you know about Brett's connection?"

"Yes. Ian was in a very low frame of mind there for a while, needed a brother to listen. I must congratulate you all. This may go down in D'Arcy annals as one of their more amazing intrigues. But what of Violet? Has she kept in touch?"

"I wrote her a letter trying to explain and apologize, which of course was impossible. She answered me, the gist being that I'd hurt her father too deeply for her to ever forgive me. I did appreciate that she at least answered." She got tearful at this point. "I know I deserve this, but it's so hard having them hate me, Damien."

The two struggled to control themselves, Damien who had a sympathetic soul coming out the loser. He had wanted his pound of flesh from his sister-in-law for destroying what had seemed to him the only reasonably happy household he'd ever been part of, but now he had to forgive her. Lily had paid for the brass ring she'd been bold enough to grasp and would go on doing so.

"I really feel guiltier about Violet than I do about Tristan because I was never as good a mother to her as I wanted to be." Lily sniffed. "We were almost rivals over Ian, and were both so naturally headstrong we had to cross paths. Then there was her attraction to Brett before she knew who he really was. But I do love her and find her so remarkable. Have you seen Violet at all, Damien?"

"Yes, I have. After you left, she quit her job and came home to look after Daddy. Don't feel responsible, she tells me she was fed up with working all hours for little pay. Recently she's become involved in a film project, doing the costumes for a movie as a favor for a friend, Eamon O'Hara, the fine director. The time frame is the thirties; Vi is very keen on clothes of that period. For the first time she's doing her own design. Terribly talented, your daughter."

"Oh yes! This O'Hara—tell me about him."

"He's quite brilliant, about forty-five and yes, Violet is involved with him. The bad news is he's married and has a dozen children or some such. Our Vi does like to take impossible lovers. She's quite passionate and impulsive. Can't imagine where that comes from."

"Don't look at me. Please tell me she's at least happy, Damien."

"Deliriously so. For the first time she's being challenged artistically, and she revels in it. As for the gentleman, he makes her happier than she's ever been in her life, so she says. Don't count on any more grandchildren, legitimate anyway."

"Damien, don't make me laugh. This isn't in the least funny. Violet may be hurt by this middle-aged lecher."

"Then again, the lecher may be the loser. Don't underestimate our Vi. She's the toughest one in the family, Lily."

"I hope you're right, only I think she's much more vulnerable than anyone realizes."

Lily took Damien's hand. "So how is Ian?" The heart of the matter at last.

"He's doing very well. . .now. He had a sinking spell at first, but he's showing signs of rallying."

"I was amazed how easily he let me go. I was so afraid he'd hurt himself, or me, and I did it so bluntly, yet he just took it. I should have known."

"The calm acceptance act was just show, I'm afraid. As

I said, he was really undone there for a while, but he's come through with the help of the family. . .and Daphne Pynchon."

"Daphne! You're teasing, Damien. You heard what a thing I had about that girl."

"It's no jest, Lily. As soon as Daphne heard along with the rest of Eire that you'd decamped, she hopped over with condolences. She and my brother have a lot in common, I gather."

"That's too funny. But fitting, actually. Ian was always going on about what a jolly, decent, attractive girl Daphne was. Good for them! If she can't have Brett, who better than Ian?"

"Life is strange, eh? The wheel of fate turns, and where she stops nobody knows. Ian's spirits have decidedly improved since Daphne began coming round, even if she can't hold a candle to you."

"Thanks for that, Damien." Lily kissed his cheek. The front screen door creaked open. "Brett!" she said, with the same light in her eye as a child might have for the impending arrival of Father Christmas. Excusing herself, she ran to greet him.

Though they were out of sight from the parlor, Damien couldn't help but overhear their meeting.

"Darling!"

"Mmm. I smell of horseshit."

"I adore horseshit—I'd better by now."

"Why don't you come wash it off me?"

"Shh, Damien is here." This was whispered, but carried clearly into Damien. The acoustics in the house were good enough for Rory to perform there, he reflected with a smile. After a moment, the two appeared, Brett with a not terribly eager expression on his tanned face.

Damien stood. "Well, Brett, we meet again," he said, offering a hand. Brett took it and smiled with noticeable relief as he realized that Damien was not going to be a hostile witness.

"Good to have you here, Damien," he said. "Did you come just to see if I've been treating her right?"

"I'm in town for the first leg of my lad Rory's world tour, actually. And it gave me the excuse to look up Lily. From her radiant glow, it's quite obvious that you have been treating our Lily very well indeed," said Damien, who was a bit dazed from the the impact of Brett's blue-eyed, athletic charisma.

"I see. I know Lil's happy to see a familiar face. You're stayin' for dinner, I hope?"

"Darling, the Douglas party is tonight. I'm so disappointed that we can't have Damien over."

"I do want to have you two and Tomi as my guests for dinner at my hotel before I leave. Though of course that can't compare to a meal cooked by Lily's own expert hand."

"Right. She's too good," said Brett, patting his lean belly. "I need to go wash up, but don't leave before we can have a drink together, Damien." He excused himself.

"I should love to stay, but Rory has some press interviews in an hour, and I must be there to make sure he doesn't put foot in mouth as he's wont to do."

"Is he as great a success as you expected?" Lily asked as she walked him to the door.

"Beyond even *my* dreams. His album is in the top ten round the world. His single, 'Belfast Girl,' is number one in the U.K. and Australia, and climbing in the States. The past six months have been a madhouse. Rory's had sold-out tours in England, Ireland, and Europe, so we're going for larger venues on the world tour."

Lily hugged him. "I'm so pleased for you, Damien. If anyone deserves success, it's you. But is it all you hoped it would be?"

"It is, but success comes with its own set of problems. Such as protecting Rory from the hordes of underage girls who want to rip his clothes off, and conversely protecting the little girls from Rory who'd like to do the same thing to them. Then there was the story in the yellow press, accurate for once, that Rory had been in the boys' home for theft and assault when he was sixteen. I managed to neutralize the damage, and he came out of that an underclass hero, overcoming his environment, etc. It's been a challenge, believe me. The lad's got a temper, so I have to hover about making sure he doesn't slug some rude journalist. But he's a good boy on the whole, and God knows he's a talent."

"So you have your superstar after all. I'm so pleased, and I know Ian is, too." They had reached the gate by now.

Damien took her hand. "Ian wanted me to tell you something, and I promised him, though I know it's pointless. He wanted you to know you can always come home to Innismere if the honeymoon with Brett should end. Which I can see it hasn't."

Lily shook her head. "I've never been as happy as this in my life. I'm sorry."

"Don't be sorry. Ian will survive."

"I pray so! I'll always care for him, but we were truly never suited. Not like Brett and me. Brett never lets me get away with anything, whereas I could always buffalo poor, sweet Ian."

"Women have always loved my brother, so don't fret about him. There'll always be a Daphne to console him. By the way, he wants to know if you want all the things you left? He's willing to ship you all your clothes, furs, and jewels he gave you, excluding the family pieces."

"Where would I wear those things now? Tell him to give them to Daphne. I'm sure she'd adore having my rejects," said Lily with a ghost of the old spirit Damien was so fond of.

"Actually, there are two things I do want from Ian. A divorce for one. I'm sure it would be no trouble for him to get a British divorce with the grounds I've given him. Brett wants to marry me so we'll be a nice tidy family with Tomi. I ran off with a renegade, but he's turned law-abiding on me. The other thing is, could Ian see his way toward giving us, or selling very cheaply, one of Charlemagne's foals? I'm truly shameless to ask, and Brett will be furious to learn that I have, but he put so much into that horse, it only seems fair to me. It would help us so much in the horse business."

"Yes, you are shameless, Lily, but since my brother is a saint, he'll probably give it to you."

"I wouldn't be surprised. Ian really is too good. Perhaps that was part of the problem since I'm not good in the least. I've lived my life so selfishly."

"If the truth be told, Lily, Ian is the most guilt-ridden person I know. In talking to him after you left, it was clear to me that he felt it was deserved punishment for his sins, God knows what they might be." A look of compassion filled her eyes at this.

"Let me repeat, my dear, if you ever want to come home, Ian will be waiting with open arms. You are, and always will be, the love of his life."

"Tell him for me that I shan't change my mind. I don't want him waiting around for me. I just want Ian to be happy, and I know he will be, as soon as he lets go of me and all his other ghosts." She embraced Damien and added, "If he really wanted me back so desperately, he'd be here instead of you, anyway."

After one last embrace, Damien was off. Lily watched him until he reached the corner, then waved.

He walked along perspiring in his wool suit on that

arm Australian afternoon and reflected on the vagaries of love. Though most condemned her for putting her own happiness above that of her loved ones, he had to admire Lily's courage in giving up everything for Eros's fleeting embrace. The unsympathetic had no doubt simply never experienced a true, killing passion themselves, Damien thought. Would the love Lily had sacrificed all for really last, or would its consuming fires be dampened by the cold, gray reality of grubbing for a living, raising a sullen stepchild, and guilt over the hurt she'd brought to those dearest to her? Time would reveal the answer to that one. Damien at least preferred Lily's solution to the one his mother had chosen when she'd learned of the death of her lover.

As he headed down to the quay to catch the hydrofoil back to Sydney, he caught a glimpse of the blue expanse of the harbour and the city in the distance bathed in that marvelously clear light that reminded him of Ireland. Exotic birds called to each other in the branches overhead, and Damien whistled along with them, suddenly feeling rather optimistic about all their futures. Surely happy endings weren't only for storybooks, he thought.

Suzannah O'Neill lives outside Nashville with her trial lawyer husband, two children, three dogs, a cat, two horses and a parrot. This is her first novel.